Deadly Dawn

The world basked in the dawn of a new era of peace and friendship. Gorbachev had ushered democracy into Russia. The American President was speeding disarmament. Global war was supposed to be history.

But behind the scenes in both Russia and America something else was happening that could turn the dream of peace into nightmare confrontation and conflict. And suddenly the fate of the world hung on a Russian military genius's fanatical patriotism . . . an American scientist's daring brain . . . a beautiful ballerina's uncertain loyalty . . . and a super-computer's secret chip. . . .

SOFT WARS

SOFT WARS

by

Selmer Bringsjord

A SIGNET BOOK

SIGNET
Published by the Penguin Group
Penguin Books USA Inc., 375 Hudson Street,
New York, New York 10014, U.S.A.
Penguin Books Ltd, 27 Wrights Lane,
London W8 5TZ, England
Penguin Books Australia Ltd, Ringwood,
Victoria, Australia
Penguin Books Canada Ltd, 10 Alcorn Avenue,
Toronto, Ontario, Canada M4V 3B2
Penguin Books (N.Z.) Ltd, 182-190 Wairau Road,
Auckland 10, New Zealand

Penguin Books Ltd, Registered Offices:
Harmondsworth, Middlesex, England

First published by Signet, an imprint of New American Library,
a division of Penguin Books USA Inc.

First Printing, September, 1991
10 9 8 7 6 5 4 3 2 1

PUBLISHER'S NOTE
This is a work of fiction. Names, characters, places, and incidents either are the product of the author's imagination or are used fictitiously, and any resemblance to actual persons, living or dead, events, or locales is entirely coincidental.

For Elizabeth, my closest colleague

PROLOGUE

Triangles

September 13, 1992—The Himalayas

Hanging. In gale-force wind. Twenty-six thousand feet above sea level. Unroped. No axe. No crampons. Hanging by the smooth-soled toe of a boot and two numb, wedged-in fingers.

"Alex!" shouted Matt from below. "Lock on!"

Hanging on a near-vertical ice-wall of Gasherbrum, a Himalayan peak half again as high as the highest summit in Colorado or California.

Blinding glare.

Searing pain in his calf and forearm.

"Alex! For God's sake! Come on. Lock on."

Dr. Alexander Nelsen refused. Too weak at this point to speak, too weak to look down toward Matt, he moved his head slightly but unmistakably in a sign of refusal while staring straight ahead, and then continued his hunt for a new hold on the wall of ice.

"Getting killed won't prove shit. There's nothing there. Lock on and we'll think about it calmly, take our time. Come on, Alex."

Matthew Nelsen had a comfortable perch, locked on by a string of carabiners, which were in turn attached to a string of ice screws his brother had hammered into the ice.

Alex, on the other hand, was soloing.

Going for it unroped.

And now he was stuck. Nothing. Only solid ice and rock, smooth, not even the hint of a crack.

Hanging. Lactic acid choking his muscles; the pain crucifying. A fall now would spell a fatal descent the equivalent of two World Trade Centers.

"Alex, your toe's slipping! Jesus! *Lock on*!"

Alexander's toe-hold gave out, ice crystals fell into Matthew's face, his arms shot out to catch his falling brother.

A snap, like the sound of a branch snapping in two: Alexander's arm had stretched beyond the limit set by the length of his tendons.

But he held on.

Two fingers. That was it. Two frozen fingers, lodged into a tiny ice-encrusted hole. Two fingers open to the elements: the leather glove that earlier shielded them had been shredded to bits by the stress of the climb.

Matt opened his eyes and saw that his brother was still alive, dangling. He kept his arms outstretched.

"Alex! Lock on with your free hand! You still have a chance!"

Alex shook his head.

Then, slowly, ignoring the pain, focusing all his remaining strength into the muscles of this one straining, life-sustaining arm, Alex gradually managed a two-fingered pull-up. And rebraced himself against the vitreous wall by setting the sole of one boot on a slippery knob no bigger than a grape.

"Good," Matt said, breathing for the first time in fifteen seconds. "Now. Lock on."

Another negative shake of the head. Alex continued searching in the glare, the wind, the ice.

"What! What are you doing? This is fucking insane. Lock on before you kill the both of us."

A gust kicked up and drove ice crystals into the faces of the two climbers. It was like getting hit by a swarm of knives.

But with the flood of airborne ice came an evanescent break in the glare.

And there it was.

Alex lunged for a protuberance of ice further up—and simultaneously threw his leg over to the right, aiming his toes at a rather distant icy notch.

"What the . . . !" Matt yelled.

But his brother made it, and the new position afforded a crack into which Alex breathlessly hammered a piton-like "Wart Hog" screw. He clicked the carabiner on, not for himself, but for his brother, and yelled hoarsely down:

"Another."

"You too, bro," Matt commanded.

"No, not yet."

"*Yet*? What the hell's it gonna take?"

"I think I can do it solo."

"You *think*?"

"I can."

"You said you think."

"Yeah, but I'm sure now."

"What changed?" Matt asked. "You haven't even looked up yet."

"This is hardly the time for a debate, Matt."

"Right. Stop arguing and lock on."

"No."

Matt gave in. He'd fallen three times; though roped, and thus saved by the nylon cord, he'd been slammed each time with g forces powerful enough to rattle the brain of a fighter pilot. Argument now was as taxing as the climbing itself.

Operating solely on desperate remnants of adrenaline, Matt inched painfully on, falling three more bone-jarring times, but each time saved by a screw that was a bit closer to the peak.

Alex slipped into a rhythm: wind, ice, drop in glare, focused search, crevice found, reached, pull-up, screw driven in.

Again.
And again.
And again.
And so . . .
They made it.

Both their oxygen tanks were depleted; the masks flapped helplessly in the breeze like dead, tethered birds. The two brothers desperately sucked down what oxygen their lungs could find at over four miles of altitude, and after two minutes of wheezing their respiration evened out. And then they reclined, gazing out across the ethereal view a Himalayan peak provides.

"There's something I've been meaning to ask you," Matt said.

"Shoot."

"Why do you *do* this?"

Alex smiled. "A little late, wouldn't you say?"

"Not at all. If you answer as I fear you will, I'm gonna radio for a fucking copter to take me down."

"I see. Well, you're going to have to yell awfully loud."

Matt bolted upright, rifled through his pack, and, not finding the unit, hissed, "Shit."

"Back at camp, Matt. Fifteen thousand."

Matt nodded a just-par-for-the-course nod and said, "Still, why *do* you do this?"

"Guilt," Alex said, taking a swig of water, something his body desperately needed.

"Oh, boy, here we go. Just what I feared. It *is* pathological. You've got a death wish."

"Right, and I suppose it's normal to hang at twenty-five thousand feet on the side of an icy wall just to put Wall Street in perspective."

"Look, it depends on the climb, brother of mine. You told me this wasn't going to be any worse than Yosemite."

"Yeah, and I've got some Himalayan land I want

to sell you for condos. Why *do* they pay you so much, anyway?"

Matt frowned, and returned to his original line: "Guilt, huh? For what?"

"Birth."

"You cryptic bastard. I should never have asked."

"No, listen, Matt. I'm serious."

Matt put his pack behind his head for a pillow and went completely horizontal, took a deep breath, and prepared for the usual profundity.

"Suppose," continued Alex, "that there is a God, a Creator. To some he gives, and to some he doesn't, and that's that. You don't deserve it; you don't earn it. He gave you a knack for deals. And he gave me the ability to make computers dance. What did *we* do? Went to school to refine the innate talent—but big deal. If anything, that was fun. These climbs are expiation, Matt. My penance. Here I *earn* everything. There's no luck whatsoever."

Matt had done his best to tune out his brother's philosophizing, but reflecting on the soreness that suffused his body, he grunted assent to the proposition that up here you earned—every bloody inch. And then a thought struck the investment banker. Matt, sporting a five-day beard, sat up, looked over at his brother, removed his glasses, looked some more, and said, "I hope for my sake that someday you'll be *lucky* enough to have someone bring the mountain to you."

Alexander Nelsen took another swig of mountain water and smiled at the paradox, as relaxed as could be. But Fate took it very seriously.

September 14—Moscow

"China," she volunteered.

"Anarchic," replied Colonel Peter Andreevich Kasakov, taking a sip of vodka. He had two pillows behind his head, his muscular chest was exposed, and a sheet was drawn up to just below his navel. Annastasia Ivanova Marianov was on her side, huddled up beside him, thigh against thigh. She was naked.

"All right, let's see . . ."

"Give up," he said. "There simply isn't a single communist nation left on the face of God's green earth. When Castro was thrown out on his ass, that was, as they say in America, all she wrote." Peter took another sip.

Silence. Anna reflected. He thought he sensed her dutifully Marxist brain lumbering in vain search of a vestige. She was searching, all right, but inside, deep down, there wasn't much regret.

"Face it," he said. "Even my father's starting to. And if *he* can, you can."

She sighed.

"But with everything that's happened," Anna said, "with everything Gorby's done, are you . . . are you . . . ?"

"Out of business?"

"Well, yes," she said, lifting her head from his chest and looking at him. It pained her considerably to do so: today in practice she had performed two *fouettés*, each consisting of thirty-two consecutive spins on toe, and her neck had rebelled halfway through the second one.

"Is *Space* out of business, my dear?"

"That's different. The Directorate of Space Operations has become simply an arm of Glavcosmos, which is and always has been a fanatical champion of *perestroika*."

"Shit, you sound like *Pravda*."

"Maybe. But I believe it."

"You're sure?"

"About Glavcosmos being a champ—?"

"No," Peter laughed. "Are you sure about Space working for the civilians?"

"Not completely. I'm a dancer, not a spy."

"You're on our payroll."

"For services that don't go beyond these walls," Anna said.

"Maybe you'll branch out one day. You have the training."

"Maybe." Following the ritual, she ran a fingertip across his lower abdomen, suggestively lifting, just slightly, the edge of the sheet that covered his genitals. "But then again, maybe not."

Peter was still thinking business. And now he thought out loud: "The old tanker's been dropping hints that Space is up to some nasty shit. You know, he's still at it. His last fucking breaths, and it's still Marx and Lenin. There was a time when he was an evangelist, and he's never been able to get that out of his hardline head. Come work for the worker. For the common man. The American Communist Party, in the sixties, had more than its share of Christians who saw Marxism going hand in hand with the early, communal Christian Church. He didn't spend a dime on recruitment during those days. He threw a party in the Village, spouted some pseudointellectual horseshit, and pimply kids'd come out of the woodwork, creaming to sign up for the Hammer and Sickle."

Peter laughed. Anna felt him shake with amusement beside her. And it was amazing what the drive for survival could do: rather than die, she felt herself deeply thrilled by the power hinted at in the slight movement of his frame. If she didn't act the part, she would be killed. It was as simple as that. Eight years ago, midway through a rape which she just managed to stave off, he had initiated their master-slave arrangement with a neat incision on the back of her neck. In the commotion she didn't feel the razor's cut. She continued to kick, then saw a strange smile upon his face, and then felt the warmth of her own blood rolling down her shoulder. Failure to acquiesce, he announced, would mean another, fatal slash. Since then her dreams of liberty had been dashed violently a thousand times, and her subconscious had finally taken over, instilling in her the elemental desire that kept him happy and kept her alive and relatively free of bruises. No one knew. Hers was secret torture. Anna wore her hair up while she danced, she was by all outward signs chaste and clean of line and pure. But here—here she lived the life of a prisoner in a sordid cell. She was gripped by an ambivalence beyond her conscious will: there was the deep self-protective craving to please. And then there was the constant prayer, a mantra, for his permanent, even violent departure. There was considerable irony in the fact that the ballet story lines through which Anna moved more often than not turned on the fact that the shortest distance in the world is between passion and hate.

Five minutes ago her face had been streaked with tears, pain shooting throughout her womb. And now she was serenely stoking the fire that led him to seize her.

"What's so funny?" Annastasia asked, smiling along with him, running a finger across his cheek.

"Well, to think that the stagnant, corrupt piece of shit that passes for the Soviet economy was at one time identified with a Christian utopia—perhaps you will agree that that is *some*what amusing."

She traced one of his prominent cheekbones.

"My father would see it differently," Peter said, "but in my mind we were always stealing for our country, not for the feeble ideas of some long-dead thinker who can't hold a candle to even the most dim-witted of American Presidents. Truman was a fucking haberdasher who backed into the Oval Office, but he wrote some essays that run circles around the shit Lenin coughed up."

"And now?" Anna said absently, running a finger through Peter's long dark hair.

"Now?"

"Whom or what do you steal for now?"

He looked directly into her eyes for the first time in quite a few hours. "Thievery is the most secure profession in the world, my dear. The need to take never dies. It is eternal. I take what I want, no matter what; my directorate follows suit. And Gorbachev's *Russia* needs to take if ever a nation did. The convertible ruble is making our republic look more and more like the fucking Weimar. Every now and then you see an old lady wheeling around a pile of worthless cash, a sickening look of determination on her face. Much of the middle class lives in disused railway cars; the lower classes make Hindu untouchables look like pampered royalty. The other day I went to buy some fresh fish and found only cans of boiled seaweed."

"One can steal prosperity?"

"One can steal anything."

She kissed him. First on the chest, and then, sliding up, on the ear. "I don't want to talk," she purred.

Peter grabbed her suddenly around the neck and said serenely, "Good. Because if you tell anyone any of this, I'll kill you."

Anna's neck was like the soft fluttering neck of a bird; he could feel her pulse, a quickening pulse, and he found the rhythmic palpitation upon his skin rather pleasant. He held her by the throat with one hand, put down his tumbler on the night table with the other. It was minimal pressure by his standards, but enough to impair breathing. He had taken her so many times through the night, in so many ways, and with such abandon, that her nerves had reached a state of utter quiet. She had been floating, as in a sensory-deprivation tank; reduced to a thin, even flame of pure disembodied consciousness—but a flame that, now, with the advent of his grasp, sputtered. As he tightened his hold around her neck, Anna had a brief fearful vision of the flame—dying.

She rasped: "But you have told me nothing . . . nothing . . ."

"Compromising?"

Anna moved her chin up and down on the back of his hand.

"I'll be the judge of what's compromising."

Another near-imperceptible nod.

"Please."

"By all means, my dear," he said.

Under the sheet, he slid a hand up her thigh, brushed her crotch.

"No, I mean please, please release me."

On a whim, he depressed her Adam's apple. She coughed. Managed a whispered protest: "Peter."

He caressed a nipple. Kissed her neck. And returned his hand to find her wet. Then, swollen again, he rolled over and entered her. And released his hold upon her neck. Anna breathed deeply, breathed normally for the first time in half a minute. And the first sound to leave her lips was not a reprimand, not a complaint, not a protest, and certainly not a scream. It was a sigh. Of fresh, self-protective desire.

PART I

1

The Man

December 23—Cobleskill, New York

Searching. For the rock.

"Where the hell *is* the bastard?" he said to himself out loud, but in a whisper, lest he wake some of the slumbering farm animals past which he was stealing.

A clear, cool, starlit night in the Schoharie Valley. Skintight black lycra climbing clothes, minerlike headlamp on a speed-skater-type hood, sufficient rope for the descent around his neck, gloves to protect against the friction of the sliding drop, and a pack with all the essentials: beer to be river-cooled, cheese and bread, lantern, and his laptop machine.

Alexander Nelsen searched for the landmark, a large glacier-deposited rock—twenty-five paces due north of which, surrounded by mountain laurel, was one of his secret portals, discovered years ago from underneath, after he had quietly slipped away from his group and the tour guide, hiding till Howe Caverns was shut down for the night. At two hundred feet down, light is nonexistent. He had explored for hours, squeezing through ink-black bat-infested tunnels no other human had seen—and then there it was overhead: light. A fissure the size of a pinhole, the tiny shaft as thin as a laser beam. A vertical climb on a sheer face of limestone. Ramming the pipe upward until he could suck air down into his lungs. Up in the elevator with the first group of the day in suspiciously grubby attire. Returning at night and digging down at his marker. Penetration. And then, with the help of plywood and two-by-fours, a cover; and then the cover covered with soil and sod.

Now: sleeping cows, fields of corn, motionless tractors and tillers, and, in the distance, a dark-windowed clapboard-covered colonial—the landscape looking not much different than it did when Lester Howe made his discovery in 1842.

What'd they do, move *the thing?*

IBM International Headquarters, Armonk, New York

As clear in Westchester as in the Catskills. A full moon. The constellations so bright as to be detectable by first-time astronomers.

Donald Rizzi, IBM CEO—hirsute bear of a man, chest and stomach that would have been at home on the professional wrestling circuit, suit jacket long discarded, shirt collar unbuttoned, tie loosened, circles under his eyes—emerged onto the roof of IBM's international headquarters for a breather. It was indeed a glorious night. He took in Manhattan's skyline in the distance. As well as, further east, the gray, flat expanse of the Sound. Given the size and power of International Business Machines, and Rizzi's position within it, looking out thus was like looking out upon his demesne. He stretched, lifting his hands up toward the stars. Rubbed the black stubble on his face. Ran his fingers through his hair. Sucked air in through his nose, released it evenly through his mouth. And, looking up at the heavens, he saw a glittering scorpion, his sign. Rizzi, standing on the roof of his kingdom's brain, savored the power of his position coursing through him.

Palm Springs, California

The man was old, and wore tattered clothes, but he lived in a Spanish-style mansion and his wife played bridge with a former First Lady, and Thunderbird, of which, on a lark, he had become a member, was down the road, and he now and then drank priceless wine, and surrounding him in his home office was a floor-to-ceiling, dizzying, blinking, humming array of state-of-the-art computer equipment that made the cockpit of a 747 look like a dash of a Chevy. He looked at his watch. One-thirty-five. He nodded and smiled.

Not long now, the old man said to himself.

Cobleskill

Ah.

Nelsen dug, revealed the portal, felt a blast of cool fifty-two-degree air against his face, secured the rope, and disappeared from the surface of the earth.

Armonk

Rizzi, coffee in hand, reentered in the lumbering gait of a grizzly and rubbed his craggy face as if trying to wipe off his weariness.

There was a man at his machine!

"Hey! What the hell do you think you're doing?" Rizzi barked.

The stranger had supergreasy, shiny jet-black hair and a handlebar mustache, waxed to perfection. He was holding Rizzi's keyboard upside down and was spraying something at the keys from what seemed an aerosol can. The man was the epitome of nonchalance.

"I *think* I'm fixing your keyboard. Little pressurized

air often frees up the dust that soils the connections. Low-tech, but usually effective."

"There's nothing wrong with my keyboard."

"Really? Got a call this afternoon from a . . . a Joyce Mathers. She said the J was out of commission."

"Christ. Joyce is my secretary. Her machine's in the outer office."

"Gee, I'm sorry." The repairman put the keyboard down. "Shoulda gone with my intuition: Joyce didn't seem like the kinda dame who'd be using a HAL 8000. And you know, I *thought* the office was kinda big. You the head honcho?"

"Yes. Now, if you'll ex—"

"Listen, I'm gonna clue you in on something, Chief. The security around here suck . . . stinks. I mean, I'm here at off hours, wouldn't you say? But hell, I just waltzed past your guards downstairs. Should they be playin' gin when they're on duty?"

"I'll make a note of your concerns."

"Well, you know, I'm way down on the totem pole and all. But I do take the max on my stock option. I figure Big Blue is partly mine, and I ought to keep my eyes open, hold up my end."

"Just the right attitude, Mr. . . . ?"

"Vander."

"Just the right attitude, Mr. Vander. Now, I'm afraid I'm going to have to—"

"I'm going, I'm going. Maybe next time we won't have such a backlog, and I can come during normal hours. Unfortunately, you're not even last on my list for the night. There's a guy down in three-twelve who—"

"Mr. Van—"

The repairman put his fingers to an exaggeratedly closed mouth, nodded, and walked out, carrying nothing but the can of air. The absence of a briefcase should have been a dead giveaway. But you see what you want to see, and Rizzi wanted to see his screen.

The CEO shook his head and sank his bulk back down in front of his machine; blinking to force his eyes into focus, he looked again at the projections. Digital, Apple, Cray, UniSys, Hewlett Packard, Compaq—the whole gang. Versus IBM. With the help of a monstrous program and a massively parallel prototype fresh from Fishkill, Rizzi had simulated the performance of each corporation over the next five years. And the results weren't bad. Not bad at all. Mainframes were gone. Obsolete. Ditto minis. Both machines replaced by desktop wonders. But IBM looked solid as a rock. Rizzi took a sip of hypercaffeinated coffee from his NY GIANTS-inscribed mug, which looked tiny in his enormous paw. Then he took another deep breath.

A solitary figure in the only lit office in the entire Armonk complex. One-thirty-seven in the morning.

Work—at least, work of sufficient intensity and duration—can solve any and all problems. That was Donald Rizzi's motto. And as the recently appointed CEO of IBM, Rizzi practiced what he preached: eighteen-hour days, no vacations, no weekend getaways; golf, his only recreation, once a week, but only at four-forty-five in the morning, the first fairway shrouded in darkness, and only for nine holes; lunch in his office, dinner too, breakfast gobbled down in the limo coming in. A diligent man. Perhaps *too* diligent, if you believed the testimony of two ex-wives who were now swimming not only in the Caribbean but also in money.

But Rizzi was also innovative, an entrepreneur in the sea of molasses-paced white-shirted, wing-tip-shoed wallflowers that had allowed IBM to get beat too many times by smaller, hungrier companies. Rizzi had stormed into the workstation market, a perennial thorn in IBM's side, by sequestering a young team of sleep-averse engineers, pumping the atmosphere of a start-up company into the room, giving them unlimited funds and letting them go. They delivered, and Sun and Apollo, perennial workstation powerhouses, as well as newcomer Sony, took beatings.

And then there was the idea of putting cutting-edge machines to work *within* the company. Which was why Rizzi himself had upon his desk, at this moment, IBM's fastest machine: thirty thousand gates per very-high-density logic chip, sixty-four processors, a clock-speed of .75 nanoseconds—enough speed to complete more than one instruction in one-billionth of a second. Enough power for Donald Rizzi to simulate a five-year period of intricate global corporate competition in five seconds.

He decided to change a few variables.

Punched in the modifications.

And that's when it happened.

The keyboard froze. The screen went black. And then, shimmering up on the color monitor, there materialized a big, bold, bright, blindingly red letter Z.

"What the . . . ?"

Cobleskill

Having descended to the subterranean world, Alexander Nelsen was having a beer two hundred feet below the surface of the earth, in a tour boat, beside a hundred-foot waterfall on the River Styx, in the dead of night. Dante himself would have found it inspiring. It was a fitting purgatory: Bats. Stalactites and stalagmites. Rushing water. No light, save that emanating weakly from his headlamp.

Purgatory. But was it enough to achieve the metamorphosis he sought? He would emerge without her; things would be no different that way. But could he forget her now that it was over? *Was* it over?

We have to decide, Alexander.

Decide what?

Where we'll live. The JAL stewardesses know us a bit too well, I think. Whirlwind weekends in Tokyo and Manhattan have lost their glitter. For me anyway.

What do you suggest?

This is my home.

True enough. And I live in America.

Yes, but you don't feel the same as I.

I wouldn't say that. America is my *home.*

What conviction.

Maybe I don't wear it on my sleeve, Aki.

Well, I guess I do. My grandparents lived in Hiroshima.

And that determines where we'll live? Quite a jump, isn't it?

In a sense we're still rebuilding.

You speak like you're on some kind of mission.

Perhaps I am.

Look, isn't this premature? Doesn't this, uh, doesn't this presuppose marriage?

That's another problem.

It is?

What will our children call home? Better yet, regardless of where we live, what nationality will they be?

Aki.

Will their eyes be like mine or yours? Blond Norwegian hair or black Japanese hair?

It doesn't matter.

It matters to me.

Yes, I see that.

Maybe we both need some time to think these things through.

You make it sound as if we're pondering the origin of the universe.

You see? Things I take seriously, you don't. You drag me to Namibia to look for a winged serpent thought to be a pterodactyl. Through caves, just out of the reach of leopards. But when I ask you to think about whether marriage is such a good idea, you freak out.

You told me that trip was pure magic for you.

That's what I told you.

Ah, I see.

I'm a computer scientist, Alexander. First and foremost.

I just dabble, is that it?

Well, admit it. You'd rather be . . . skiing. Getting you to talk about your research is like pulling teeth.

Mmm. Well, maybe we should *spend some time apart, thinking.*

Yes, I think so.

If I run I can catch the seven-thirty-five.

I'm not stopping you.

Okay. Well, so long.

Good-bye, Alexander.

Three weeks of thinking. It seemed like an eternity.

He saw her without clothes, full of desire; felt her perfect silky skin, saw her smile, heard her sigh as he entered her.

Nelsen decided to log on to the mail server at Brown University, his intentions unclear. Talk to her if she was on line in Japan? See if she had left a message? Maybe send her one?

His laptop unfolded, hummed to life, its screen brightening; 64 meg RAM, 800 meg optical laser disk, 128 megahertz, a paper-thin screen as clear and dazzling as a graphics-quality monitor of four years back. He activated the internal cellular modem, which sent signals directly up the elevator shaft used during the day.

Connect.

Password in.

He had a message. But not from Akiko.

Dr. Nelsen, we have an emergency. An infection in the new HAL 8000. Maybe viral, maybe bacteriological, maybe a parasite—can't tell. Can't tell anything, in fact. And it's on the Chief's machine. Restarting does zip. We need you yesterday. Get back ASAP on Bitnet. ELLERY@YORKTWN. Better yet, if you've got an Ether board with you, nab me at the familiar Ethernet address. EQ.

Palm Springs

The moment having passed, the old man, in triumph, left his office and returned to his recently acquired heavily carved Honduras mahogony bed. He thought, as he took off his robe: All the *Macka* had to do was add the file to the internal disk and restart. Child's play. I hope.

"What is it, honey?" his wife asked, stirring, but half-asleep.

"Odds and ends," he said, slipping under the covers.

She murmured indecipherably and returned to sleep. She'd been living with "odds and ends," resolved in the dead of night, for over forty years. Her husband's night-owl habits hadn't changed a whit, despite their move to a mansion.

Armonk

Rizzi's office had been transformed into something resembling Grand Central Station at rush hour. The Disease Control Team, headed by Ellery Quinton, had invaded en masse, and had quickly relegated the CEO of the corporation for which they worked to second-class citizen.

"It's a virus?" Rizzi asked, unable to get anyone's attention.

Nothing. Lab-coated computer epidemiologists raced to and fro like ants. The nautical flavor of Rizzi's office had been swallowed up by shouting, dashing men, humming machines, and phones and modems that blinked and chirped.

"Do you think it's a virus?" Rizzi boomed.

Ellery Quinton turned toward the Bear and frowned. Twenty minutes ago he had been sound asleep beside his wife in Yorktown Heights, near the IBM research center in which he worked. Now he was looking at a nightmare, the Bear pawing at his back.

"What's going on, Ellery? Talk to me."

Quinton, after turning back to the screen, said only, "You look awful, Chief." Then, loudly, to no one in particular: "Has anybody called Fishkill?"

A chorus of nos sounded. "I'll message them," one of the technicians said above the din.

"Nothing from him yet," Quinton said, still facing the monitor, now and then punching at the keyboard. "Where the hell is he?"

"This Nelsen can help?" Rizzi asked. He had noticed that "Nelsen" seemed to be rolling off everyone's tongue.

"He's the Man," Quinton said. "If he can't, nobody can. He *wrote* all this code. And he makes a living not only writing it but also protecting it."

"Where is he?"

"Dunno."

"How can you be sure he's available?"

"We have him on retainer. Twenty-four hours around the clock."

"But what if he's sunning in Hawaii, for God's sake?"

"Irrelevant."

Rizzi began, "Irr . . . ," dropped the line of inquiry, and asked, "What can *you* tell me?"

"Only that we need Nelsen. In a hurry. How the hell am I supposed to make sense of decompiled code in hardware I don't understand? The HAL series is parallel; brain-based neural-net shit. I'm a linear LISP jock, for God's sake. Nothing distributed. The same goes for most of my men. Anyway, I'll tell you this: the off-the-shelf antiviral stuff has failed: this is something completely new. It's nothing like nVIR, or Polynesian Brain, or Dropping Tears, or Ramblast—nothing standard. But then again, nothing's ever hit any of our high-end machines."

The Zorroish Z began to grow. Then it began to move, to wave and ripple, as if fluttering in wind.

"What the hell is this Z shit?" Quinton said to himself.

A number of nearby technicians, looking on, shook their heads.

"The graphics are more than respectable," Quinton said. "We're talking animation. Achieved apparently without the help of a package designed for the purpose. Someone's descended into the rarefied depths of the HAL 8000 and brought back animation. That takes some muscle.

"Somebody get me some 'scuzzi' cable," Quinton shouted. "I'll try starting up off different media, and a fresh copy of the operating system."

Within seconds Rizzi's machine was being reconfigured by three men whose hands moved like those of a magician.

"What about my data?" Rizzi asked.

Quinton shrugged.

"Will the data survive?" Rizzi repeated, not without some rancor.

"I just got through telling you this is an anomaly. An unknown. I don't *know* about the data."

Someone shouted: "Got him!"

"Run it down to me here," Quinton instructed.

A stream of characters flashed on the new machine now parked beside the infected one.

"Let's see. He's in . . . Cobleskill? Where the hell is Cobleskill?"

"Get a copter in Albany," Rizzi barked to no one. "Determine his exact location, fetch him and jet him into Westchester, then copter him here. Move."

Rizzi might just as well have been invisible.

"Donald, no offense, but stay out of this, okay?" Quinton then opened a small briefcase, removed a smallish black box, and hooked it up to the machine now receiving Nelsen's transmissions. And then he said out loud, "What the hell's in Cobleskill, Alexander?"

With the help of a stored voice-segmentation pattern for Nelsen's voice, the reply came back—clear as a bell: "Caves."

"Ah."

"What do you have, Ellery?" Nelsen asked.

"Nothing. Not a clue."

"New strain?"

"Who said virus?"

"True," Nelsen granted. "Sum it up."

"Now's the time to talk, Don," Quinton said to the CEO. Rizzi, talking into thin air, summed up his use of ECONO-SIM, and then the advent of the Z.

"Hmm. Sounds like a trojan. In the executable code. Do we have a contagion?"

"None of the HALs are netted. They're all protos. They don't even have hookups for simple comm. Hell, we can't even print off the bastards."

"You changed start-up?" Nelsen asked.

"Yep. I've tried starting up off a slew of other external media," Quinton said, "but for some reason the normal chain is broken. It wants to hear from the internal disk first, even when the drive is loaded. How 'bout Cannibal? Can I release it?"

Nelsen had made a small fortune by creating and selling antiviral programs. Cannibal was a thousand times more vicious than any virus: once released into a system, it sought out and destroyed viruses with the foaming fervor of a rabid Doberman.

"No," Nelsen said. "This is like an alien life form. You shoot it to hell and then there's nothing left to satisfy your curiosity. Let's find out what this little prank is all about."

"Okay," said Quinton. "You're the boss."

"All right. Listen, Ell. We'll override the call to the internal disk."

"How would I—?"

"Send me the code for the operating system that's on the external disk."

"But I just got through telling you that the HAL can only go solo. There's no way I—"

"You have a scanner? Hand-held? With OCR capability?"

"Stand by." The entire antiviral team, save the guy still trying to raise the Yorktown Research Center, had gathered around Quinton. Somebody dashed off for a scanner, and was back in seconds.

Quinton dragged the hand-held scanner over the screen, reading in the characters upon it; he hooked the scanner up to the machine being used for comm, opened a new window which held the scanned-in text, and then clicked this text off to Cobleskill. A second later Nelsen's "Thanks" bounced back through the voice synthesizer.

Nelsen changed the code for the operating system in the external laser disk, telling it to ignore the disk inside the infected machine. Then he mailed back the emended code.

"I marked the changes with a series of five consecutive asterisks, fellas."

Quinton's fingers flew over the keyboards. He automated a search for the marker, found it, punched Nelsen's changes into the corresponding spot in the code up on the HAL's screen, and overwrote the old code with the new. Then he restarted off the external disk. After two seconds they had a normal greeting to HAL's UNIX-like operating system. The prompt blinked reassuringly. Everyone cheered.

"Okay," Quinton said.

"I heard. Now. Send me the code for ECONO-SIM."

"Roger."

The financial-forecasting package was sent and received.

"All right, hold on," Nelsen said. "I need my tools."

Nelsen accessed an account at his home in Providence, brought up a mass of code onto the screen in Howe Caverns, uploaded, and began to use it to analyze the code on the infected disk.

The team in Armonk heard the *Snow White* tune "Whistle While You Work" coming through from Cobleskill. Then: "Connectionist shit gone. Firing second-order logic with hyperresolution. Infected agent now translated into cellular automaton. Running. . . . I have superimposition with healthy program. Difference isolated. Firing recompilation. Stand by."

A dazzling representation of Nelsen's tools at work appeared for the crowd to see. A mass of 3-D cubes came to life, died, were reborn, died again—the process giving rise to a hypnotic, throbbing display. The images continued to dance. Silence punctuated only by the clicking of Nelsen's fingers on his keyboard.

"Got it! Uh-oh, what have we here? Ell, what did Yorktown say?"

Quinton, as well as all the technicians in the semicircle, and Rizzi too—they all looked four machines away to the guy who had been waiting to hear from Yorktown. He turned and looked at them, and said. "I'll read it to you verbatim, gentlemen." Then he turned back to his screen and said, " 'HALs? What are you talking about? Fishkill took them all away. They were in yesterday. Said there was a defect in the circuitry or something. Hell, no one here understands these analog machines.' "

"Fishkill! Fishkill didn't make them!" Rizzi boomed.

"Somebody *stole* them?" Quinton said.

"That's what I was afraid of," Nelsen said. "I found a little comment here. It says, 'Don't bother selling us your only HAL. It's fucked up. And besides, we have all the others.' "

"Jesus," Quinton said.

"Did Yorktown get a description of this guy?" Rizzi asked.

"Yes," the guy corresponding with Yorktown said.

Rizzi asked, "Greasy hair? A handlebar mustache?"

"No," the technician replied. "It says here beard and a thick unruly mop."

But within ten seconds Rizzi had verified that no Mr. Vander worked for Big Blue as a repairman. Five seconds later he was talking to the FBI. And they opened the case with two suspects. Who were really one and the same.

2

The Macka

**December 26—Twenty Miles Outside Ithaca,
New York**

"Comrade, look, we don't need it," Colonel Nickolai Vasilyevich Vanderyenko said.

Malachev didn't heed the tacit order.

"We do *not* need it," Vanderyenko repeated. "Please . . . put . . . it . . . away."

Vanderyenko's partner, Captain Lazery Petrovich Malachev, continued to disobey. Indeed, with a taunting flourish, he raised the weapon, eased its extended nose through the open window, and deftly placed a nearby oak tree within its sights.

"Comrade, wait, you—"

And fired a whisper-quiet bullet deep into the trunk of the tree.

"Why?" Vanderyenko asked, sighing.

Malachev responded with an indifferent, thoroughly uninformative shrug. Then, apparently satisfied with the gun's performance, he drew the silencer-elongated barrel back into the car and returned to his patient and fastidious examination of the weapon.

They were in a gray Avis-rented '91 Ford LTD. Waiting. Parked on the shoulder of a smooth two-lane highway which, under overhanging branches of maple and locust, snaked up and down brown, dormant corn fields, past silos, through tiny sagging hamlets, over gorges, eventually reaching Cornell University, twenty miles to the north. A clear, cool, moonlit winter evening in New York State's Finger Lakes region. A variegated dusk had come and gone. Twilight. Perfect sleeping weather. The two waiting Russians had the windows of their Ford down; now and then a gentle breeze, hissing through the leaves beside them, passed through their vehicle and touched two ungentle men.

Vanderyenko, half the size of his partner, persisted: "This isn't Afghanistan, Comrade Malachev. Put the fucking gun away."

Captain Malachev, *spetsnaz* officer, quite enamored of guns from birth, still disobeyed: he waved the large steel barrel defiantly, examined it from a number of different angles, buffed the shimmering weapon a few more times with a handkerchief, looked at the gun approvingly, and then pointed the hand-held cannon vaguely in the direction of his partner—and smiled.

"Hey!"

"Don't worry," Malachev said. In a tone about as concerned and comforting as that of a gladiator.

"It's not loaded?"

"No, it is," Malachev responded softly, nonchalantly. "I'm just not going to fire it, comrade."

But Malachev now directed the barrel unambiguously in the direction of Vanderyenko's head.

"What the *fuck* is your problem?"

Malachev merely shrugged—again. It was complete, incorrigible, ominous indifference. Vanderyenko suddenly wondered if the new peacetime link between his GRU directorate, Directorate Z, and *spetsnaz* had been wise. They were all, it seemed to him, certifiable maniacs. And Malachev was the worst. A former Olympic boxer; a tenacious, utterly physical, single-minded communist; a man whose deep animus for America was founded, firmly but unreflectively, on simple historical facts, such as that the White armies of the Civil War, which had sought to raze Lenin's new Red government, had been assisted by the United

States. Malachev had won a gold medal by relentlessly punching the head of his American opponent as if it were America.

"Listen," Vanderyenko said, "this isn't a fucking commando raid; this is surgical theft. Put that monstrous . . . that . . . that . . . What the hell *is* that, anyway? A ground-to-air missile launcher or something?"

This time Malachev deigned to speak. "This tiny thing? Aah, this is just a silenced SSK .44 magnum redhalk with Leupold's 2X LER scope. I've got hand-held SAMs in the trunk, though."

"What?" Vanderyenko exclaimed.

"You heard me."

Vanderyenko rolled his eyes. "You know, this operation—"

"Save it," Malachev interrupted. "You can never have enough firepower."

"You should have worked for Castro, you know that? Down in some Central American jungle, trying to export the kind of shit Gorbachev got rid of."

Malachev looked profoundly unperturbed. "*Tried* to get rid of. Anyway, we'll see," he said calmly.

"*You'll* see. That we don't *need* guns. You're a novice here. Whether you can swallow it or not, on this turf you're a novice. Appearance is everything in America. You wear the right clothes, sport the right expressions, and there isn't *any*thing you can't steal. I haven't fired a shot yet, and there are a lot of wizards back in Russia with perpetual hard-ons because of the equipment I've sent over."

Malachev looked decidedly unimpressed. "We'll see."

Vanderyenko took a deep cleansing breath and dropped the debate; he'd had enough—especially in light of the fact that his recalcitrant accomplice was a rookie. And besides, thought Vanderyenko, it's almost showtime. The GRU thief reached for his briefcase, popped it open, and pulled out the last element in his disguise: a wig. Malachev laughed as Vanderyenko, looking in the rearview mirror with the intensity of a starlet, stretched the black-haired wig down over his own sandy-brown hair, and, comb in hand, began to create a perfect part—one befitting a clean-cut state trooper. He was already clad in the appropriate uniform, which he'd stolen from Troop D Headquarters on the Northway, by posing as a hunched-over, one-foot-in-the-grave janitor. And he had the tool of the trade: a radar gun. Posing as a local baseball coach wanting to clock the pitches of his local fastballing phenom, he had *borrowed* it from the Ithaca police force.

Everything seemed in order. And this was hard for Malachev to swallow.

"What about the car?" the *spetsnaz* officer asked as his partner began to craft an increasingly convincing hairstyle.

"What *about* the car?"

"Markings. Sirens. You know."

"We're unmarked, Comrade Malachev. I've wired lights behind the grille; that's all we need."

Malachev nodded. "But what if *real* cops come along during the op?"

"Then we're feds," Vanderyenko replied. "Looking for drugs. Everybody expects everyone to be looking for drugs everywhere, over here. Some local-yokel cop wouldn't bat an eyelash."

Malachev nodded again. Grudgingly. "What about publicity? Won't we have every cop in the Northeast on our ass within an hour?"

Vanderyenko frowned superciliously. "No, Uncle Sam wouldn't want *anyone* to know that a supercomputer was missing. After all, then it might possibly be in the hands of the Sovs. And that would be too embarrassing. We're supposed to be Neanderthals, you know. Everything in the Soviet Union is supposed to clunk, creak, fuck up; the symbol of our economy is the bloody Dalselmash tractor, a true piece of shit. We're supposed to be after personal computers—machines more our speed. Supercomputers? For Ivan? No way; too slick for a former communist. They'll keep the whole thing under wraps. Just like with all the uranium that's unaccounted for. Hell, I know some pinhead terrorists who have enough uranium to throw the earth off its axis."

Malachev nodded once again. And began to digest the fact that his American-born boss, though nonviolent, was sharp.

"Admirably planned, Nickolai Vasilyevich," Malachev said, "but to play the part right, you *will* need this." Malachev waved his .44 again. Then he slid the weapon into Vanderyenko's holster.

Vanderyenko grinned—for the first time. And nodded good-naturedly. They *were* on the same side, after all.

"How long, *Macka*?" asked Malachev, using Vanderyenko's code name, Russian for "mask." Actually, given how well known it was in the Soviet espionage community, it would be more accurate to regard it a *nick*name. And so in the present context *Macka* was a term of endearment: Malachev wanted reconciliation.

Vanderyenko looked at his watch. " 'Bout ten minutes," he said, all animosity gone from his voice.

Now and then a car drove by. But no trucks. Not yet, anyway.

"How'd you know?" asked Malachev.

"Oh, simple. Something like this is common knowledge over here. I knew ages ago that Cornell was going to be a supercomputer center. Hell, it was in the New York *Times*. Couple of phone calls to the university posing as a reporter wanting to do a story on Cornell's push into supercomputing—that got me a rough timetable. Universities over here are like businesses: they're always looking for a little publicity. And I was working for *Time* magazine."

Vanderyenko smirked, glanced at his partner in search of a complimentary nod, but found in Malachev's visage only a blank, uncomprehending stare.

"*Time* is a very widely read magazine here," Vanderyenko explained. He had quite forgotten that his partner's reading material didn't exceed *Pravda*.

Malachev nodded, said, "Okay. And then?"

"Well," Vanderyenko resumed, "after I had a rough idea of when, the rest was easy. I started sending E-mail messages on Bitnet to various users of Cornell's mainframe. Everybody—"

Captain Malachev raised his hand, frowning; then said, "E-mail? Bitnet?"

"Oh, sorry. Electronic mail. Goes over computer networks with the help of phone lines. Bitnet is just one such network. It's a slow one, but ideal for conversation and correspondence." Malachev looked a bit skeptical; Vanderyenko noticed, and said, "You look like you've seen a ghost, Comrade Malachev. E-mail is something you should understand now that you're on the GRU's payroll. I use it to stay in touch with home." Vanderyenko pulled from under his seat a five-pound Compaq 686 16 meg RAM laptop computer complete with built-in cellular modem, and flipped the machine open and on. A color VGA screen lit up. "Here, look, I can send a message direct to Moscow, in seconds." Vanderyenko proceeded to do just that: he typed in the message: "IN POSITION TO RECEIVE ANOTHER DELICACY," and sent his communiqué by selecting POST from the appropriate menu. The note took an initial wireless leap into New York Bell, then bounced around various Bitnet nodes in the Northeast, hopped out to the west coast, and was transmitted by satellite into Moscow's phone system, from which it pulsed instantaneously into the GRU's own system. Ten seconds after Vanderyenko's passing of the note, it was on file in the GRU's Command Post Directorate. Ten seconds after that a technician brought the mysterious message to his superior, who in turn brought it immediately to Vanderyenko's lifelong friend, Colonel Peter Kasakov, who was Chief of Directorate Z. Kasakov, upon reading the message, smiled.

Malachev said, "But surely security is comprom—"

"Nope," Vanderyenko interrupted. "It's perfectly secure. I'm afraid, my friend, that the classic ways are rather outdated now. The Vienna Procedure is something still used by the troglodytes in the KGB, but for us, brushing contacts in the street, face-to-face meetings in parks—this is nonsense, something you'll find us doing only in American novels. Someone, one of these days, ought to wake up Le Carré."

"Le who?"

Vanderyenko looked at his partner and said, "Forget it."

"But your transmission, *Macka*. Surely it will be archived and scrutinized."

Vanderyenko shook his head. "Needle in a haystack, comrade."

Malachev looked considerably off-balance. He was, in fact, wondering a bit—*quite* a bit—about his role. The *spetsnaz* captain was a highly trained killing machine; that was the bottom line. Someone who could go toe to toe with a Green Beret or a Seal. And here he was teamed up with an Americanized technothief who was as light as a feather, and who had an aversion to guns. *Shit*, said Malachev internally.

"So anyway, Lazery," Vanderyenko resumed, "I bounced a few electronic notes off Cornell users, asking when the Crays were going to arrive. People talked. They always do over these networks. Accordingly, I narrowed it down to within a week."

"Yeah? And then?"

"Well, then I phoned Cray."

"You *phoned* them?"

"Sure. After identifying myself as the Provost for Computing, I said: *Where* the *hell* are my supercomputers?"

"And they told you?"

"Yup."

Malachev wore a look of incredulity.

"It's a free society," Vanderyenko explained. "An open one. Very good atmosphere for thieves, you know." He grinned at the *spetsnaz* officer, who was still shaking his head.

The absence of substantial caution on the part of the transport company wasn't irrational. They were not, after all, hauling uranium. What the hell would a terrorist group do with a Cray 4S? A number of such groups *had* uranium, but they didn't have, and were unable to recruit, the brains needed to build a thermonuclear device—despite the fact that the procedure for doing so was explicitly described in various technical journals and books. And a supercomputer, for terrorists, was of infinitely less value than uranium: it was superuseless. After all, it took a veritable army of technicians, operators, and programmers to keep a meaningful application running on the Cray for one measly minute. And the Russians . . . well, according to the orthodox view held by the American intelligence community, the Russians found it easier to get their hands on the design features and then build a clone for themselves—which was, in fact, something that they did do, continuously.

But they didn't do it well. Sure, the KGB had illegals in Cray, had illegals, indeed, inside NEC, IBM, and so on. But it took Ivan forever to build a clone, plans or no plans, and by the time he finished, the product of his considerable labor was wholly obsolete.

When it came to advanced hardware, stealing the real thing was a helluva lot more effective than filching the blueprints. Which was something Andreev Ivanovich Kasakov, now General of the Army, current GRU chief, had, thirty years before, grasped. Andreev had founded Directorate Z, the GRU directorate devoted exclusively to theft of high-tech items. Blueprints for bombs were fine, but bombs were better. Wiring and circuit diagrams were nice, but computers, intact and ready to work right out of the box, were preferable. Getting the specs on a missile was dandy, but getting the missile itself was superior. It was a three-decade-old pipeline. Not from military bases to Moscow, not from the Pentagon to the Kremlin, not from corporate labs to Russia, but from American *universities* to Moscow. Universities—where the latest military technology, under no security to speak of, was developed. Directorate Z was forever in college—at MIT, at Harvard, at Cal Tech, at RPI. Forever wandering around labs in professorial attire, bearded, a bit disheveled. Introducing themselves to researchers as curious colleagues from other departments, other schools. Asking questions about nascent weapon systems with sly grins in a commie-bashing demeanor. Calling campus security with stories of lost keys and deadlines approaching. Posing as nerdy grad students in search of some skutwork on classified grants, as people from campus PR, toting cameras and microphones, as insurance investigators investigating the theft of what they themselves, Z, had stolen.

And so on and so on.

Peter Andreevich, Andreev's son, was now in charge of Z. And Peter had the *Macka* in the field. Target, today: Cornell.

Toward which Rudy Randall steered his supercomputer-carrying truck.

Of course, there was *some* security, but it was all perfunctory. Cosmetic. And so the target rolled on, vulnerable as could be, like a large deer walking in a wide-open meadow, within the sights of a high-powered rifle.

Rudy Randall knew just where he was: no more than thirty-five minutes from Cornell, his destination. He had dreaded leaving the interstates, and now that he was off them, snaking his climate-controlled, padded truck toward the university, he saw that his dread had been quite justified. It was slow. Too many turns. Too many hills. But still—Rudy glanced at his digital dashboard clock—only thirty minutes to go. Good, he thought. I've got to take a leak.

"But it's big, isn't it? And heavy?"

Vanderyenko nodded.

"Well?"

"Well what?" Vanderyenko said.

"Well, how the hell are you going to move the thing? How are you going to transport it? You going to steal the truck?"

Vanderyenko had his eyes on his side-view mirror. It was time. He expected, at any moment, to see headlights of a larger size than those that had hitherto passed. But there was nothing yet.

"Well?" Captain Malachev persisted.

"We're going to put the machine in our trun . . . No, you've got the fucking SAMs in there, don't you, John Wayne?"

Thirty-three years ago, with KGB help, Vanderyenko had been given the name of a Michigan-born child who had died thirty-*four* years ago at the tender age of two. Willy Krakow. The Russian techno-thief had been born in White Plains, New York, to ostensibly Polish parents, one ostensibly a housewife, one ostensibly a locksmith, both ostensibly Krakows. Nickolai Vanderyenko had played Babe Ruth baseball and sandlot football, had flown kites in the park with American playmates, had taken field trips to the

Museum of Natural History. He learned about the legends—Washington, Lincoln, Jefferson, Revere, and so on. He brought schoolmates home, sometimes to sleep over under banners of American college football powers—Notre Dame, USC, Michigan. He strolled Mamaroneck Avenue, watched the stores on it come and go; he and his friends would wander through Saks and Altman's, chewing bubble gum, trading baseball cards. When he was seven he hopped a ride into Grand Central, and hopped a ride back, undiscovered both ways. Normal stuff.

Along the way, a number of trips to Poland, which always ended up being trips to Russia, where his parents were suddenly and unaccountably elevated to royalty.

Then, one day, the explanation. Of why Willy had been taught Russian. Of why Willy couldn't *tell* anyone he knew Russian. Of why Russia was actually Willy's home. Of why shadowy men were forever coming and going through his parents' humble White Plains house. Of why his father would disappear on business for weeks at a time, taking a small set of his locksmith tools with him. And indeed of why his father's face was protean: sometimes a banker, sometimes a vagrant, sometimes a plumber, an electrician, a phone repairman—and on and on.

And, ultimately, Willy was told of Directorate Z, which was the family business.

It was a jolt, of course.

But.

No hesitation whatsoever: Willy didn't rebel. Not in the least.

First in his class at White Plains High. Member of the Drama Club. Large roles in a number of theatrical productions.

College: Yale, on full support. Major: Drama.

* * *

So Vanderyenko knew John Wayne.

But Malachev didn't. Malachev hadn't been to the States before his new job—a job involving special peacetime ops for Directorate Z. And then returns to the Motherland. The *spetsnaz* officer didn't know John Wayne from Adam.

"John W—"

"Okay, listen, no problem," Vanderyenko broke in. "We'll split it, some in the trunk, some in the backseat."

"Spli . . . Ah, you're going to dismantle the thing."

"Lazery Petrovich, you're one quick son of a bitch."

Malachev ignored the insult, and turned to look at the backseat, upon which slept the supine corpulent body of Viet Markov—bearded, ill-kempt, wrinkled clothes, swathed in a good many empty Cape Cod potato-chip bags and Hires' root-beer soda cans.

"The bastard's sleeping," Malachev said.

Vanderyenko turned around and looked for himself. "You're right," he said serenely. Then he turned back, admired his newest face in the rearview mirror, sighed contentedly, and resumed his vigil for the truck.

Rudy Randall's first reaction, when he saw the blinking lights of Vanderyenko's LTD in his right side-view mirror, was to punch his radar detector very hard—so hard he ripped a cut on two knuckles.

Damn these back roads! Nobody around to let me know when some piss-ass Smokey's waitin' to nail my ass.

Then, though there was now a significant amount of blood on his hand, he grabbed the detector and flung the device violently across the cab. The "Passport" thudded against the passenger-side door.

You're a piece of shit, you know that?

Rudy pulled over. Vanderyenko and company pulled up behind the truck. And then Vanderyenko stepped out, walked up to the cab, and, standing beneath and alongside Randall's open window, addressed the driver:

"Sir, do you have any idea why I stopped you?"

"No, Officer, I don't," Randall replied.

"I'm afraid you were speeding, sir."

Randall wasn't *sure* he'd been clocked, and he knew that if he hadn't been, he'd wriggle out of the ticket. Consequently he said: "Gee, Officer, I was only doing forty-five. Ain't that well below the limit?"

Vanderyenko raised his radar gun; Rudy Randall read, in glowing LED: 65.

Shit, thought Randall.

"Step out of your vehicle, sir."

Randall hesitated. He'd expected the norm: copper goes back to his cruiser, writes it up, comes back, passes it through the window, and it's back on the road again. Vanderyenko's request was a curve.

"Please step out of your vehicle, sir." Vanderyenko placed his hand over his holster. "Sir, I will ask you now for the last time. Step out of your vehicle."

Randall obeyed: hopped down to the pavement. Rudy had sideburns, long, bushy; sported a Milwaukee Brewers baseball hat, a potbelly, and swollen tattooed biceps. He was a large man.

"Close the door, please. Then stand facing the cab, your hands on the door."

"What's goin' on here? Okay, so I was a little over. That ain't no capital offense, fella. Hell's your problem?"

Vanderyenko put his hand on his holster again and said, "Do as you are asked, sir."

This time Rudy Randall didn't bend.

"What ya gonna do, chief, fuckin' shoot me? You tell me what gives here and I'll cooperate. Otherwise I've about had enough."

It was a snag—out of the blue, unanticipated: Rudy Randall was one tough bastard, not about to be intimidated by some small college-studentish trooper who looked about as mean as a mouse.

But then Malachev stepped out of the shadows. He was holding one of the SAMs, and he had it aimed directly at Rudy Randall's chest. He wore a tight-fitting hooded olive-green stretch outfit—the characteristic attire of *spetsnaz*. Dark eyebrows. Dark eyes. Shoulders as wide as a table. Muscles everywhere.

"What seems to be the problem, Sergeant? This perp giving you any trouble?" Malachev walked toward Randall, nudged the end of the five-foot-long, six-inch-diameter SAM against Randall's solar plexus. The truck driver's eyes were open as wide as possible; his lungs were suddenly ineffective. Rudy Randall, wheezing a bit, had a vivid vision of his upper torso disintegrating. He turned and, as Vanderyenko had directed earlier, placed his hands on the door of this cab.

Malachev nodded to Vanderyenko, who approached the driver. Rudy Randall prepared for a search. He was not prepared, however, for the prick he felt on his neck; nor was he prepared for the fact that, within seconds, his legs gave out. As if from a great distance through a telescope, Rudy Randall saw his ankles being grasped by the big dark motherfucker. Then he felt his back sliding across the blacktop. Then he sensed that he was airborne. And then, after impact, before losing consciousness, he smelled grass and weeds.

"It's locked," Malachev said.

"No kidding," Vanderyenko said. "Keyless entry pad; see?"

Vanderyenko aimed his flashlight at the correct spot at the bottom of the paneled door, illuminating the pad.

"Four digits," Vanderyenko said. "Each from zero to nine. That's 6,561 possibilities. It'll take a minute or two for this baby to run through them." Vanderyenko held out a small device for Malachev to see. "Primitive, but effective. It simply tries each permutation, one by one."

Vanderyenko, wielding a screwdriver, uncovered a web of wires, and configured the device. Each set of numbers flickered on a small LED display as it was being tried. A *click* sounded after about two minutes.

"That's it?" Malachev said.

"That's it," Vanderyenko said. "Be my guest, Captain." The GRU thief motioned to the door.

As if lifting a single sheet of paper, Malachev, in one motion, threw up the sliding overhead door. And what happened next happened in a flash, but registered in Vanderyenko's brain as if it transpired in slow motion.

The first thing the beam from Vanderyenko's flashlight picked up was the bed toward the front of the interior. The bed, the books, the little nightstand—Nickolai took it all in within two seconds. And, having seen the cramped abode, he thought, in an instant, before he even saw the figure: The driver was switching off. He's got a friend.

And then Vanderyenko saw the figure, standing above him in the truck, lit up by the beam. He saw the face, filled with purpose, and he saw the hand, which was holding what appeared to be a tire iron. And then he saw that the iron was heading for his own head. Rapidly.

Vanderyenko's brain sent a message to his legs: leap backward. But before the legs began to obey. Vanderyenko saw the threatening hand, still illuminated by his flashlight, severed from the arm to which it had been attached. And then, after what seemed minutes, he saw the blood splattering, in flashlight-lit drops, and felt the warmth of a stream upon his own face.

Vanderyenko reached instinctively for his holster:

empty. He looked over at Malachev, who was holding the smoking .44.

"You can never have enough firepower, Nickolai Vasilyevich," the *spetsnaz* officer said with a smile.

Vanderyenko was suddenly gripped by nausea, but he fought it back, and the operation continued.

They threw the body of the second driver next to the first. Both were still breathing, but the second was laboring, blood still spurting from his stump.

The *Macka* then woke Markov. Without missing a beat, the rumpled hacker entered the body of the truck without commenting on the blood, waited for the other two men to remove the protective casing around the Cray, and then set to work, pulling from a black "doctor's" bag the requisite tools. Now and then he laughed to himself, and hummed, thoroughly absorbed with the task. Occasionally he paused for some Cape Cod cheddar-flavored popcorn, or a Snickers bar, or a Dr. Pepper—food that he pulled out of his toolbox. Sometimes, pondering his next move, he stroked his crumb-infested beard.

Within one hour the three men had the Cray stored in the LTD.

Within two hours, under a still-bright moon, Rudy Randall woke to the sight of his partner's handless limb, and screamed, deep, long, from his very soul.

3

Inheritance

December 28—Zagorsk, Outside Moscow

He planned to die in his Russian teahouse, in the heart of the forest that had, forty years earlier, supplied the chestnut, pine, and birch which now, still fragrant and as strong as granite, gave the retreat its rustic beauty.

He was on his back, in bed—emaciated, shrunken, chalk-white, his remaining flesh pendulous on fragile bones. But his eyes were still as spirited as when he was a young colonel in the Red Army, fighting Hitler's forces. His mind had not been touched by the cancer: there was an inner core of smooth, shining, fearless, indestructible militarism. A core not the least bit frightened by death's grip.

She—she did not want him to die. At least not without the standard palliatives. A morphine-filled syringe was in her right hand, a sterilizing alcohol wipe was in her left hand, and tears were in her eyes. Katrina Mikhailovna Vokryshkin looked down upon him, empathy overflowing, and saw the pain, felt it herself, it was so severe.

"Please . . ." She beckoned. "Allow me to help you, Comrade General."

"Never," whispered Andreev Ivanovich Kasakov hoarsely, a ring of iron in his voice. "Never."

Katrina retracted the syringe. She had once before attempted to give the shot over his protests, at which time she had accidentally implanted the needle directly into the bone of his forearm, eliciting a smile from him and a scream of horror from herself.

Andreev's son, Peter, looked on, and understood his father's refusal. Katrina burst into fresh tears; she found the refusal a painful enigma, something that ran violently against her Hippocratic nature. But Peter understood—he looked at his father and understood.

They had been close, more like brothers than father and son: two soldiers, two soldiers sharing vodka and stories and spying and laughter, even, not long ago, a fair number of unwilling, struggling Western women. But now it was nearly over—the old bear was finally and irrevocably old, his flesh hanging on his bones, his body racked with metastatic cancer. An indomitable spirit remained, however, burning in the old man's eyes. Spirit that his son understood, spirit that caused Andreev Ivanovich, former General of the Army, former Chief of GRU, to reject the morphine Nurse Katrina offered. Painkillers are beneath a Hero of the Soviet Union. It's as simple as that, Peter thought. Andreev had scars from wounds inflicted by the Nazis, wounds more painful than the cancer, wounds he'd endured with a smile, knowing the Germans were simply fucked—fucked because they couldn't take the fierce cold of a Russian winter. Andreev had lain there wounded in the snow at Stalingrad—lacerated, bleeding, tourniquet tied around a leg of pulp. He had lain there taking the pain, because he knew the Russian warrior was at his best in the cold, while the Germans, as a matter of tradition, simply froze. He had in fact seen the future: the Nazis soon surrendered.

And now he's reliving it, Peter thought. The cancer is his final wound, the pain his final foe, something to be conquered without the aid of drugs.

Katrina, her face glistening, turned and departed, leaving father and son alone. The two had business.

Cancer or no cancer, there was business. The Great Game goes on, unhindered even by the deaths of mighty players.

Andreev raised a thin, pallid, bony arm and pointed at the black-and-white picture of his own father hanging on a memento- and trophy-covered wall. The strength of the first-generation socialist was palpable up there in the photograph, a strength indicated not only by the breadth of his shoulders but also by ancestral eyes that glinted like sun-ignited ice on the Moskva River.

"Is his death to be in vain, my son?" Andreev began, his voice, of necessity, a whisper. "He was one of the first true communists, a sailor from Odessa who took part in the storming of the Winter Palace, a man who fought valiantly in the Civil War. He died before I was born, fighting near the Caspian. And she," Andreev Kasakov continued in a rasping whisper, raising again his thin chalk-white arm to point at a picture of his mother, "she was a communist at the beginning of the war—a lieutenant in the Guards who died in the battle for the liberation of Donbass. Is her death to be in vain also?" Andreev asked, his voice now barely audible.

The Hero of the Soviet Union motioned with a trembling hand for what was now his nectar—the vodka. And then, buoyed by the mere fact that the soothing liquid was on the way, hoarsely continued, "Gorbachev is back. Resurrected like Christ himself. Rumor has it he was cowering in Australia. Maybe he was. But now the bastard is back, once again hurling vile insults at our saints, once again taking aim against the precepts at the core of that for which many a martyr has died."

The cheeks were hollow, the eyes sunken deep into their sockets, but it was still an expressive face—a face that now was creased with an utter, burning hatred. A hatred that was not present in his son's visage.

"Let me tell you, son," the old tanker continued, "that after Lenin and Stalin had their way, very few turned. If you turned, you died; it was as simple as that. In one night, after the Poland debacle, Lenin took from our GRU ten heads, very literally. And of course in thirty-six and thirty-seven everyone was shot, Berzin himself included. But after these purges, loyalty was absolute."

The father paused and looked into his young son's eyes.

"You think Stalin was a butcher," Andreev commented, "but I would point out, my son, that during his so-called period of 'terror and lawlessness,' political trials were held in the market square, and blood was spilled in the open, and yet during *glasnost* we punished, drugged, and murdered in secret sanatoriums."

This was something Peter had had pointed out to him countless times.

Sustained talk for Andreev, given his physical condition, demanded the equivalent of a marathon in a young, healthy man; the old tanker's soliloquy had just taken him a full twenty-six miles. But Peter had pulled out the vodka and glasses they kept hidden from Nurse Katrina, and had poured generously. And now he passed a healthy dose of Stolichnaya to the former General of the Army, keeping a glass for himself. The old spymaster, veteran of Smersh, the brutal counterespionage unit that had cleansed the Motherland of traitors, overseer of Operation Daria itself, in which blueprints for the first atomic bomb were stolen from the United States—the old tanker, upon throwing back the contents of his glass in one gulp, grimaced and smiled at the same time. Death and life, pain and pleasure—they were all mixed together now for Andreev Kasakov.

Peter threw down his own drink, refilled their glasses, the senior Kasakov threw down another of his own, and the two allowed a soothing silence to form—a father-and-son silence undisturbed by differences in loyalty to Marx and Lenin. They were positioned before a bay window of Andreev's design. Outside, it was sunny. A breeze rippled through what leaves remained on the boughs of chestnut and birch. Evergreens shimmered. The golden cross atop the shining onion dome of Zagorsk's Cathedral of the Dormitoin could be glimpsed on the horizon, on fire from the sun. The hubbub of Moscow, from this tranquil spot in the wilderness, seemed thousands of miles away, but in reality was within a half-hour's drive.

The two GRU spies, father and son, reflected upon their quandary. *Their* quandary. They didn't share a political orientation, but they shared a concern for the Motherland. They threw down more of the clear, smooth alcohol, looked out at the sun-dappled forest. Defeat and death, on this bright sunny day, seemed to be enveloping them.

Presently Peter said, "I'm a patriot too, Father. We have our martyrs, and they should be venerated. But the people want what the people *always* want: food, and roofs under which to *eat* their food. And ideology will leave their bellies empty. We need realism. Action. Violence, if need be. Aren't you the man who told me that the Soviet soldier is a master of improvisation? You fixed your own tanks and motorized vehicles while the faggot Nazis sent back like weeping women for mechanics. Didn't the brave citizens of Leningrad live on a bean a day during the siege? There is always an opening to be found. Always a way of surviving, even in the dead of winter, without food. Aren't those your words?"

Andreev nodded, smiled. But he had, at bottom, little faith.

How many times had he thought of ending the agony? The General of the Army raised a thin arm and, with near-skeletal fingers, touched his scalp near the implant all GRU agents carry, a tablet sewn just under their skin to avoid detection. He ran his middle finger over the tiny rise in his scalp and thought about situations he had been prepared for throughout his career: face a bloody spit-covered mess from a violent interrogation; boots to the ribs, the head, the testicles; unwilling to cooperate with the imperialists, wealth in the West if he does. Then, with a look of proud defiance, Andreev gouges out the tablet and swallows the cyanide with a smile. Victory. The death is sweet, pleasant, painless. He has taken the correct option, his decision the product of levelheaded calculation. No big deal. No great honor due. *Whatever is necessary.*

"All right, my son," Andreev said, his voice like gravel, brought back by the liquor. "You want me to fuck ideology, I'll fuck it." Andreev looked away from the window directly at his son. "As always, we must conduct a systematic search for the unexpected. And then, having found it, we pounce."

The inebriation and camaraderie had begun to temporarily mask the propinquity of death; Andreev had regained some of the strength he had possessed not long ago, before the cancer had gripped his body. The old tanker—the old bear who had flicked Nazis off the face of the earth like fleas, the GRU spymaster—began to smile.

"What?" Peter said.

"I have been working on a foundation for you. And the cornerstone is decentralization. I expect Gorbachev to put an effeminate dove in charge of the GRU, now that I am gone. So we must find a way to put power and self-determination into one or more of the directorates themselves. There will never be another Berzin, I'm afraid; Penkovskiy alone dealt the military-intelligence arm a fatal blow. And now we have the openness of *glasnost* on top of this. No, I have come to see that attempts to return the GRU, as a whole, to its full former glory are bound to fail."

Andreev paused, sipped, and added, "But sometimes, Peter, the parts are greater than the whole. I have been working on building such parts for you."

"What are the specifics?"

"First things first," Andreev said, raising his hand, causing flaccid flesh on his arm to swing. It was amazing how, near death, the body could be so frail, the mind so nimble.

Peter nodded.

"When I begin to think like you, when I force myself to drop our old ideals, I see elements outside the GRU that might prove helpful, Peter Andreevich."

"I can think of none, Father."

"Think Council."

"The Council?" Peter exclaimed.

"That's right. Suppose I too piss on Marx and Lenin and Stalin. Do I not then have a good many friends, my son?"

"Vasputin," Peter said after some thought.

Andreev smiled, said, "The people love him. And he's a mile left of Gorbachev, his cardinal enemy."

"And he's just power-hungry enough to be used," Peter said.

"And then there's Yankolov," Andreev said.

"Yankolov? The new KGB chief? You are jesting, surely. Yankolov is a fucking eunuch. His idea of propaganda is a film in which KGB officers proudly display their favorite kitchen recipes, and martial-arts instructors look like fucking ballerinas. Yankolov? Yankolov is Mikhail Sergeevich's ultimate puppet."

"In his soul, Yankolov yearns to be Hamlet. Set the stage so that this seems to him possible, and you will have a man who is willing to cut Gorby's balls off with a razor blade."

Peter laughed. The mental image of such castration he found quite appealing.

"Can anything change the fact that the GRU and the KGB are mortal enemies?"

"You give Yankolov a glimpse of paradise, and even if it's paradise GRU style, he'll bite. The KGB is eviscerated. They answer like children to the newly elected Soviet legislature, which is filled with liberals not yet weaned from their mother's breasts. The KGB has their hands tied, just like the CIA, which is of course bound and gagged by the American Congress. Yankolov, in his heart of hearts, wants freedom. Freedom like the old days."

The two men threw down another dose of vodka and recharged their glasses.

Peter was struck again by the fact that his father's illness and utter solitude had done nothing to diminish the old bear's powers of analysis. And it *was* an utter solitude: the women, in the end, quite predictably, hadn't a shred of loyalty; there was nothing beyond their desire for the virility, the charm, the sense of adventure, the physique and rather famous Russian cock. In the end, Peter was his father's only comfort. Andreev, a hard-liner unwilling to genuflect before the reformations that had taken place, had only a few friends, all of them in the covert and military world that sneered at *glasnost* and *perestroika*, but all of them busy. They would make time for the funeral, of course, but visits before then were considered wasteful. And she—they both simply called her "she," something they'd always done—she had died bringing Peter into the world. Andreev had never remarried. There had been countless women on four continents, including, in stolen passionate moments at great capitalist estates, a good many wives of Western men of power, but he never remarried. Russia was his wife, as much as she was Peter's mother. The man who, like a light attracting moths, had drawn beautiful women well into his sixties; the man who had regaled dignitaries and intellectuals—this man, save for his son, was alone. It was a claustrophobic solitude that would have destroyed most minds. But Andreev's brain was clear. He understood the battle being waged. A battle without a foreign enemy. A battle within the Motherland.

"Gorbachev," Andreev said. "As you know, I fought beside his father," the former General of the Army continued philosophically, his voice now miraculously strong. Peter looked up at the picture of his father's 1st Armoured Army, snapped just after this group of true Russians had repelled the German Zitadelle in the Great Patriotic War. Frozen therein was a mix of blood and dirt and bandages, and smiles. In the background rose the black, oily flames of a doomed Porsche Ferdinand, the German tank whose death warrant Andreev Kasakov had personally signed. He had discovered that these tanks, though heavily plated, could be boarded on the move, allowing flame throwers to be lethally squirted over the engine ventilation slats. The sight again sent a shiver down Peter's spine. "I had no better comrade," Andreev continued. "He would have died for me, and I for him. I thought his son was cut from the same cloth. But we've lost him. And so we must move on. To your own Directorate Z."

Peter, drawing his eyes down from the picture, and feeling by comparison his own impotence, snickered. "My men are devoted solely to the theft of high technology. We are thieves."

Andreev nodded. "Thieves, but damn good men. I have seen to that. Never underestimate Nickolai Vanderyenko, the *Macka*. And do not underestimate your newest recruit from the States."

"Markov."

"Markov, yes. But *Macka* is the boss. He now heads up a formidable international team of young, enterprising illegals. And he has excellent ties to *spets-*

naz. They do what he says. He has Malachev on his payroll."

"Malachev? Are you sure?"

Andreev nodded, smiled. "Not only Malachev but also a number of other young and ruthless lions that in turn work *under* Malachev."

Peter raised his eyebrows.

"Youth. That is the key, my son. Young men and women who realize ours is now a world in which wars will be won by the ingenious use of technology. The grimy, the nitty-gritty, the nuts-and-bolts—all of it is shit now, my son. You can take the kind of bravery we showed against the Nazis and piss on it. Look at Iraq. The 76-mm L30, the *Katyusha* rocket and their modern counterparts, are all toys. Worthless," Andreev said with a deprecatory wave of his hand. "We are entering a new era. One in which software sabotage is as powerful as a thermonuclear device. One in which computer chips are infinitely more valuable than uranium. One in which only youth schooled in the new ways will thrive."

"And one in which ideology matters not a whit," Peter added.

"Agreed." Andreev smiled. For a Hero of the Great Patriotic War it was a momentous concession.

"I have managed to put together another directorate just as young as yours, Peter."

"I know."

"You know?"

"Space."

"You have been spying on me, my son," Andreev said.

"A bit. And on them. I have their Moscow office wired well enough to hear their eyes move. Internal spying is nothing new. Beria did it. Even Berzin."

Andreev nodded to concede the point. "What have you learned?"

"Nothing yet."

"Well, here's a little preview. I have made two young scientists the heart of this directorate: Captain Dimitry Ignatov and Dr. Galya Matra."

"A woman?"

"A *brilliant* woman. A bit of a maverick, but brilliant."

"And what is Space up to?" Peter inquired.

The Hero of the Soviet Union smiled—broadly enough to reveal his deteriorating teeth and gums. But mischievously enough to spark in his son's mind a film of past seduction. Even with the cancer everywhere, there was in the old tanker's face a hint of the fearless elegance that women, not very long ago, had found irresistible. "I have managed to give Space one main project, Peter. A primitive version of what the Americans call Star Wars."

Peter smiled. How many times had he underestimated his father?

Andreev held out his glass for more vodka; Peter poured; and the dying master spy took a number of unhurried gulps, content with silence.

"Space is run by another youth. Someone GRU has been grooming for over two decades. Bazakin."

"Bazakin? The name is not familiar. What's the patronymic?"

"That is it; that is all he has ever gone by: Bazakin."

"Who is he?"

"A scientist. Perhaps the best the Motherland has to offer. He is Chief of the Directorate of Space Operations, overseeing Comrades Ignatov and Matra."

"And this Bazakin's expertise?"

"Technology."

"Technology? That is far too general, Father. What is his specialty?"

"Technology," the old bear said again, teasing, but still, Peter saw, serious.

Peter shook his head with a grin.

"And *that*, my son, is your raw material. It is the best I can do. The rest is up to you. Should you ever reach a position of leverage, I am confident that you will know how to find the jugular."

Peter nodded, indicating acceptance of the challenge.

The two spies toasted, poured down another full glass of vodka. They looked out again, in silence, at the forest, and at Zagorsk's cathedral shining still in the distance above the trees. The ritual was complete, the bottle empty. Nurse Katrina returned shortly thereafter to find the two men asleep, asleep beneath pictures the profundity of which she understood. She disposed of the empty bottle, washed the glasses, and placed them in the cabinet next to a fresh full bottle of vodka she hadn't the heart to remove.

4

Who You Gonna Call?

January 5—San Mateo, California

Twenty-year-old Senior Engineer Fred Pattison—his glass wobbling precariously, a smirk upon his champagne-moistened lips, eyes glazed over, giggling—asked, "When are they due, Jeffie boy?"

Jeff Renear, Fred's boss and president of Neuron Data Corporation, ignored his employee's taunting tone, looked at his watch, and replied evenly, "Fifteen minutes."

"Shit!" the engineer responded in mock terror. Then Pattison burst into laughter, slapped Renear raucously on the back, took another formidable gulp of champagne, and spilled some of the bubbly on his white lab coat. Dr. Fred Pattison was clearly drunk, noted Renear. As were the other two engineers on the team. Renear, though he'd had only two glasses, was himself slightly inebriated: the Korbel had caught him by surprise, and had given him an almost immediate brain-slowing buzz. And the odd thing was, nobody on the team drank. None of the four engineers on the Neurocube project, in fact, did drugs of *any* sort. Not because they weren't of the *type* that did drugs, but rather because in their work with the fastest computer on earth they reached highs as great as any chemically produced ones. And when they left the lab they headed for less sedentary thrills. While doing drugs you generally sit still; and it was while sitting still that Renear's team meditated on gigaflops, and felt the intoxicating hum of a neural net machine that blasted away every manner of Cray. When out of the lab the last thing they wanted was lack of motion: they surfed, skateboarded, swam, jet- and water-skied, biked, ran, lifted weights—all in the California sun. Wholesome thrills; no drugs. But today was different: today was a celebration.

After one essentially sleepless year of feverish work, the four-member team was finished. Their prototype gleamed on a table at the center of their party. The Neurocube. A neural-network computer which, on paper, was simply the fastest and most powerful computing device the world had ever seen. A polished black magnesium cube only ten inches on a side, small enough to be tucked under a desk. A massively parallel machine modeled on the human brain itself; a machine that represented a rejection of the serial Von Neuman architecture that had dominated Artificial Intelligence, or AI, since its inception in 1958. Renear and his engineers hadn't exactly built a digital brain, but they'd looked seriously at neurobiology for inspiration, and had, to a significant degree, approximated the human nervous system by putting together, in novel fashion, an interconnected spiderweb of half a million team-playing processors. The result was a quantum leap in raw computing power. A leap so large the team itself found it incomprehensible. Now and then they all pinched themselves, half-expecting to wake from a dream.

But today the dream promised to end, or at least Renear saw it that way.

They were brilliant engineers. And the Neurocube was wondrous. But today the venture capitalist who had financed the project was on the way in for an update. Harold Reitman. And Reitman, Lear-jetting in from the East Coast in his sharp hand-tailored suit, spoke a different language, and asked different questions, such as: It may be fast, but who's gonna buy it? How much they gonna pay?—questions for which Renear had no easy answers. After all, he was a hardware man through and through. An engineer.

"How long now, Jeffie boy?" Fred Pattison asked again, smiling broadly, his lips wet with champagne.

Renear frowned.

"Lighten up, man. How long?"

Renear looked again at his rather bulky computer-with-built-in-cellular-modem watch. "Ten minutes."

"Nervous, are ya?"

Renear didn't answer.

"Aww, come on, Chief. We *did* it. We *made* the fucking deadline. With an hour to spare. These guys are gonna be ecstastic, uh, esstacic, uh, ecstatic—yeah, that's it. You've got nothing to worry about. Here, have an . . . another . . . goblet." Fred found "goblet" enormously funny; he burst out laughing, spilling a bit more of the bubbly, this time on his Reeboks and the floor.

It was a clash of two cultures. The venture-capital firm of Reitman and Shuster on the one hand, and the team of young computer engineers on the other. The financiers in suits, the computer engineers in T-shirts and jeans. The backers in their fifties and sixties; the hackers in their twenties and early thirties. One group lived in conference rooms, limousines, with phones everywhere; the other worked with microscopes in clean rooms.

A secretary—tan, blond, shapely, gum-chewing—stuck her head in and excitedly said, "They're here!"

"Give us a minute," Renear said.

"Okay," she said with a dental hygienist's smile.

His three engineers grabbed what champagne remained, wished Renear good luck with more slaps to his back, and, laughing, left the room. Not knowing what else to do, Renear pinched his cheeks quite violently, rubbed his hands over his face, and, without the benefit of a mirror, tried to comb his hair with his fingers.

They strode in. Two men. Harold Reitman was turned out in a perfectly cut London-made suit framing a button-down shirt of gentle blue, on which was flawlessly knotted a subdued antique silk tie. His silver-gray and glistening hair was combed straight back, his cufflinks glimmered. His was a fresh, closely shaved, suntanned face that would have been quite at home in a fashion magazine. Renear detected the subtle aroma of no-doubt-priceless cologne. Reitman radiated deals. Big and breathless deals. The Neurocube was just one of many ventures he currently had in the frying pan: he had a team of AI scientists off Boston's Route 128 designing a multimillion-dollar computer program that was supposed to replace air-traffic controllers. He had another group of Silicon Valley engineers working on building a portable battery-powered notebook-size computer as powerful as an IBM mainframe. And so on. Accompanying Reitman, Jeff was pleased to see, was an old friend, a familiar academician: Josiah Rosenkrantz, professor emeritus from Cal Tech, one of the grandfathers of computing, at Penn for the building of the monstrous vacuum-tubed ENIAC, the first computer, and, at seventy years of age, still a seminal figure in the move toward neural computing. Except Rosenkrantz was out of uniform. Where had the fraying leisure suit gone? Where was the cheap polyester oxford shirt? The stained tie of a paisley pattern that would have been an unspeakable eyesore on Wall Street? Rosenkrantz was dressed sharply; he looked ready for hunting in the English countryside. Renear had never seen Rosenkrantz looking like this before. Not in ten years. Not once.

Well, when you work for somebody like Reitman, I guess . . .

"Welcome gentlemen. Here, have a seat." Renear,

fighting the disarray left behind by the party, arranged three chairs around the table upon which the Neurocube gleamed, and the three men sat. The two visitors took in the machine, and Reitman, turning back to face Renear, looked pleased: he pressed the tips of his fingers together, brought his joined hands toward his chin, nodded slowly, smiled, and said, "You're finished."

"Yes," Renear responded.

"Excellent. The bottom line on power?"

"Are you prepared to assimilate the num—"

"Am I prepared?" Reitman said, smiling broadly. "Well, let's see. Suppose we go back first, just a bit, to the Cray Y-MP/832, with eight parallel processors. It was king in 1989, correct? At 2,144 megaflops, I believe. The NEC SX-2, at 885, was in second place. Then Seymour left Cray, of course, and within one year built the Cray-3: gallium arsenide logic chips, clockspeed of two nanoseconds. Nice enough," Reitman said. "But then came Chen, supported by Big Blue, and armed with a cadre of disenchanted Cray people: in 1992 they reached a hundredfold increase in power. Chen's group was blown away by Thinking Machines later in the same year: they brought out a parallel machine with thirty-gigaflop performance, with the help of 256,000 processors, under the same hood. And that brings us here, Mr. Renear. To your Neurocube."

"Impressive," Renear said.

Reitman shrugged regally, in the manner of a man quite beyond deriving pleasure from the compliments of mere mortals.

"Of course, Harold," Renear said nonchalantly, "the sort of numbers you've just given are inapplicable here."

Reitman's eyebrows raised, a few wrinkles appeared on his smooth, sun-bronzed forehead. Renear did nothing to alleviate the tycoon's perplexity; he merely shrugged a shrug of his own. So Reitman looked to his companion, the elderly professor. Who, receiving the glance, addressed Renear:

"You mean you've achieved a genuine net?"

"Yup. As you well know, Professor Rosenkrantz, in the past every so-called neural-net machine has in reality been a general-purpose parallel machine fooled into doing the right sort of emulation. The hype's been there, but the machine hasn't."

Rosenkrantz reddened, and swallowed. It was the first time Reitman had seen his placid, slow-moving consultant shift into a higher, less coherent gear. "You can't be . . . How did you . . . ? I've been trying to . . . For years I've been, we've *all* been . . ."

"Josiah," Reitman said, as he put his hand on the shoulder of his guru.

Rosenkrantz ignored the gesture, and, still looking straight at Renear, said simply, "How?"

"Simple," the president of Neuron Data said, glowing, looking rather more like a surfer than a computer builder. "Minsky can swallow his single-layer perceptrons and kiss my California ass, Professor. I did just what you told me to do when I was at Tech: I looked at the brain. I looked at it from the standpoint of neurophysiology, instead of the standpoint of computer engineering. So the Neurocube has a counterpart to 'granny cells'—single nodes that represent chunks of multifaceted information. So the Neurocube's net carries info in the form of the *probability* of firing, rather than average rate. So my machine enjoys a degree of plasticity that rivals the cortex: you can rip out a mess of nodes and, just like the human cortex after even severe ligation, the remaining web reconnects, and you're back in business."

"And the medium itself?" Rosenkrantz asked. "Is it . . . is it optical?"

"We have a fully analog machine, with the help of . . . chips, Professor."

"Chips? But—"

"Extraordinary chips," Renear added.

"*How* extraor—"

"My team has achieved GSI."

"What?" the elderly professor exclaimed.

Renear nodded. Reitman, looking on, found himself mired in a swamp of utter uncomprehension. His face looked strikingly like that of an American's upon seeing the game of cricket for the first time.

"A billion transistors per chip? How?" Rosenkrantz asked again. "MOSFETs?"

"Nope."

"MESFETs?"

"Nope."

"Then I don't—"

"*MOD*FETs, professor. No dopant. No impurity. And that means an increase in mean free path."

"Jesus H. Christ," Rosenkrantz said. "You're talking 2010 here."

"We *were* talking 2010." Renear smiled. "This is 1992."

"How about a translation, gentlemen," a newly humbled Harold Reitman said.

Rosenkrantz looked at his employer for the first time in minutes, then back to his former student. "What can you give Harry in terms of the old numbers, Jeff?"

"Well, the translation to standard machines, even to the machines projected into 2005, is problematic. But let's see, if our calculations are correct, I believe the Neurocube, configured as a cellular array of ten million by ten million, is capable of five hundred gigaflops."

Reitman squinted. "That's uh, uh, that, holy shit, that's five hundred billion floating point operations per second. In terms of clockspeed, you're talking—"

Rosenkrantz waved his hand preemptively. "You haven't heard the bad news, Harry."

"Bad news?"

Renear and Rosenkrantz exchanged knowing glances.

"What is it?" the venture capitalist prodded.

"A neural network, Harry, isn't programmed in the traditional sense of the word. It's trained. You're supposed to give it experience, much as the human brain comes to acquire information through life experience. Unfortunately, while Jeff here has a Ferrari, we don't have any drivers. Neural computing is currently one big bottleneck: we don't quite know how to train our nets—what to expose them to, *how* to expose them to things, for that matter."

"What are you telling me? I spent fifty million dollars on this place to get back a clump of wet silicon slop?"

"Not silicon, Mr. Reitman," Renear corrected. "Aluminum gallium arsenide mated to a substrate of—"

"All right," Reitman broke in. "Listen, I don't give a fuck what it costs; just get this Neurocube to *do* something."

"I'm afraid," the professor responded, "that you will want not just *something*. You want to take this machine to its limits, you want to show the world what a Neurocube can do. You don't want garden-variety neural-net behavior. The neural-net community is one that has grown accustomed to flashy programs. Not long ago I trained a net to read and speak a significant bit of English, by feeding in phonetic transcriptions of the informal and continuous speed of a child. After sixty thousand presentations the net had learned to read and speak with an accuracy of about ninety-five percent. My results, presented at IJCAI 1990, were somnolent. This program of mine is par for the course, and I can assure you that it isn't trivial. You want something even flashier. You want history, Mr. Reitman."

"Fine," Reitman said. "Then get somebody who can make these fucking Neurocubes dance. What's the mystery here? Surely you two know of someone appropriate. Don't you?"

"Well," Renear said, "there's a guy who claims you can treat our nets as ordinary probabilistic automata, and that you can then start programming in the ordinary sense. He's worked out the mathematics, and he says—"

"Who is this guy?" Reitman demanded.

Renear looked at Professor Rosenkrantz. The gray-haired academic was thinking of another gifted Cal student of but a few years back, a young man who had become nearly a son. The professor looked at Renear. The engineer was thinking of his arguably insane but brilliant friend. They thought for an additional two seconds, and then, in unison, the two men said, "Alexander Nelsen."

One Hundred Miles West of Lake Louise, Canadian Rockies

At about the same time Jeff Renear and Dr. Josiah Rosenkrantz were thinking about *him*, Professor Alexander Nelsen was thinking about *them*. As he fell, he thought, wistfully, that it was a shame his mentor, Rosenkrantz, wouldn't see the culmination of the work Alex had initiated in the conversion of neural to digital computing; and he thought, in mildly melancholic manner, that Renear would never see his Neurocubes taken to the limit.

They wouldn't see because Nelsen was about to die. In the deepest grave ever to hold a corpse—1,567 feet below the ground, to be exact, in Louise's Shaft, the deepest cave on earth, one no spelunker had ever managed to conquer.

Nelsen had always thought, in the back of his mind,

that it would be the caving that would finally end it. Everything else, when it came right down to it, was easy by comparison. If you verified that the run was clutter-free, and checked the holding power of your bindings before pushing off down the sixty-degree slope, then high-speed skiing, even when approaching the human limit of 155 miles per hour, was straightforward. If you pack your own main chute with painstaking care, and stay cool enough to pull your reserve should the main, for some reason, fail, then even base jumping from mile-high Norwegian cliffs is far from suicidal. And rock- and mountain-climbing, even when free soloing without ropes, are not nearly as tough—as tough as inching down into a black icy pit that could swallow a skyscraper, alone, with ice-cold mountain water roaring down into the bottomless shaft over your lactic-acid-plagued body, your waterproof neoprene suit not keeping out the numbingly frigid water, the rock wall over which you inch more often than not crumbling in your hands as you grab for a hold or seek to drive steel anchor bolts into . . . dust!—and your headlamp invariably fails from the impact of rocks smashing upon it, and then there is no light, not a speck of it, and consequently it matters not whether you work with your eyes open or closed, and indeed it's better to do the whole descent and ascent with them closed so as to heighten your sense of touch, which is threatened by the water, which comes and comes, and numbs; and sometimes, when you take a rest, hanging by an O-ring you have prayed will hold, you sleep, and you wake to the utter terror of forgetting which way is up, which is down; and when you do clear the downrushing water and listen, all you hear are "whistlers" dropping past your head, rocks which, when they do hit your helmet, sometimes leave you in a daze for minutes; and sometimes the endorphins cause a high as intense as that caused by crack, and you're not sure whether to scream from agony or ecstasy.

But unfortunately there is little ecstasy in unplanned free-fall. In Alexander Nelsen's case, there was the ultimate in compressed cogitation: his brother, Matt, when just a kid, promising then that the day would come when he'd take Alex, his big brother, one-on-one in hoop. And jumps and climbs—all over the world. And the beautiful but untamable Akiko, with whom he still intended, deep down, to reconcile. And Josiah Rosenkrantz, who became a second father, and introduced him to parallel computing. And Jeff Renear, whose Neurocubes . . . whose Neurocubes he would never, never see.

Impact.

Death? As swift as that which comes upon an insect smashed by a human hand?

No.

Water. *Ice* water. A river. A subterranean river. He was alive!

The current overwhelmed him, smashed him against the side of the shaft's vertical walls. He grabbed, slipped, grabbed again, too sharp a rock, released, grabbed yet again—and held. He trudged back against the torrent, gradually, and after an hour of steady progress on legs he could no longer feel, his face brushed against his rope, one of whose bolts had failed. But he still wore his harness, still had a supply of bolts and carabiners. He had to get back up to the first bolt, from which the ordinary rebelays would resume. And, with Renear's Neurocubes dancing in his head, Nelsen *made* it to the first bolt, after which the rest of the ascent was a piece of cake.

Louise's Shaft had been conquered. By a man who saw no point in telling this to anyone but himself.

5

Men and Machines

January 10—Virginia,
Suburbs of Washington, D.C.

Lillian looked up from her knitting, said, "James, do you know who called me yesterday?"

James Buchanan was lost in the sports pages of the Sunday *Post*, and, though just across the table from his wife, hadn't heard her voice.

"James?"

No response.

She said again, louder, "James!"

"Uh, yes, dear. What is it?"

"Do you know who called me yesterday? Out of the blue?"

"No I don't, dear. Who?"

"Sharon Ann Bates."

"Sharon Ann who?"

"Bates. Bates. You don't remember? Well, I guess that's understandable. After all, it's been fifteen years since we knew Sharon and her husband, in Virginia Beach, when you were stationed there. Cape Henry Shores. Remember?"

Buchanan remembered. Not the area, not their house, but her. She was suddenly vivid: Southern belle. Busty. Blindingly white smile. Beautiful, some would say.

"And?" said James Buchanan.

"And what, dear?" Lillian Buchanan said, teasing,

her nose now buried mockingly in the little wool sweater she was knitting for her grandson.

"What did Sharon Ann want after fifteen years?"

Lillian looked up, smiled. As usual, she'd made her point. "It was strange. She just wanted to tell me that some people had called her about you."

"Me?"

"That's what she said, dear. You."

"What did they want?"

"They asked for her opinions. 'How she felt about you'—that's how Sharon phrased their inquiry."

A light lit, and began to gradually brighten, in James Buchanan's brain. "I see," he said.

"She's not the only one, dear."

"There have been others?"

"Yes. Jane."

"Jane? *That* Jane?" Buchanan said, motioning toward Jane Conlon's house, a Georgian mansion across the street.

"That's right, dear."

"What did *she* say?" he asked.

"Same thing: she had been solicited for opinions on your character."

It was obvious. Buchanan grasped it. And it showed on his face.

"What is it?" Lillian asked. "What's going on?"

No response.

"Is the phone business related?" Lillian asked.

"Phone?"

"Oh, I didn't tell you?"

"No, you didn't."

"Sorry. Well, some men were by the other day, dear, to install a new phone. I don't think it's an over-the-counter piece of equipment. It's strange."

He nodded. Grinned.

"What is going on here, James?"

"Well, dear, I may be coming out of retirement soon."

Silence. Lillian squinted a bit. Then it clicked for her too: "Background checks? A secure line?"

He nodded.

"I thought running the NSA was going to be it."

"So did I."

"And now what?"

James Buchanan smiled.

"And *now* what?" Lillian repeated.

"We'll see," he said slyly.

This was her cue, but for once she didn't take it. They had separate worlds: he the cloak-and-dagger; she, from old and incalculable money, philanthropy, decorating, knitting, gardening. They were sitting in her world: her "outside room," a Machin conservatory supported by four pillars which, come spring, would be clematis-covered. Today shafts of sunlight filtered warmly through—a beautiful day, a beautiful setting. But, for once, though they were here at home, she began to force herself into his world. Her husband was polite and unobtrusive when she was with him. He mowed his lawn with a John Deere tractor, and couldn't for the life of him break ninety on the golf course, and didn't let it bother him. But in his own world Buchanan was regarded to be a lion.

"You'll accept?" she asked.

"Perhaps."

"I don't know why you'd even *consider* it," she said emphatically.

"I'm not sure I follow."

"Well, in this day and age, what is there to *do*? Democracy doesn't seem to need your help."

He shook his head.

"What?" she said.

"I don't buy it. Not for a second. The Soviet Union, from where I stood at Fort Meade, looked the same as she's *always* looked—ruthless and hungry."

"That was eleven years ago, James. Now you play golf."

"Now I'm old enough to appreciate the classics, one of which is that when democratic reform fails, demagogues and dictators thrive. Hitler and Mussolini took power in floundering democracies, and some would say Gorbachev's reforms have failed."

"You know, dear," Lillian Buchanan said. "I think you're out of step. The cold war is dead. *Dead.*"

"Perhaps."

January 10—Troy, New York,
Police Headquarters

"I should never have gotten involved in this research project," Detective Lou McNulty said. *"Never."*

"Ah, but we're Trojans," Chief of Police Harry Benoit said. "We can't resist technology. Never could. RPI was here before MIT was even a dingy shit hole on the Charles. The engineers up on that hill"—Harry gestured toward RPI, Rensselaer Polytechnic Institute—"won the fucking Civil War—with what was then high technology. Troy, you know, was the friggin' armpit of the Northeast before RPI emerged from a shadow MIT had cast for decades. And expert systems played a large role. You're part of history, boy."

"Listen, Harry, I'm telling you: Sherlock, this *particular* expert system, is the problem. A big problem. I hate the fucker."

"It seems a success to me, Lou. What about these pictures? These letters? This looks like a fuckin' pediatrician's office. You're a savior to these people. A friggin' godsend."

They were in McNulty's office: small, spartan, cigarette-littered, dominated by a Sun-9 workstation with an oversize monitor, which sat glowing amid Coke cans and empty Dunkin Donuts boxes, on the one desk in the room. There were pictures on the walls. Many pictures. Almost invariably of young children—

children who had been missing, but, thanks to Sherlock, were then found. And along with the pictures were posted a good many letters of passionate gratitude from parents, like:

Katie was the center of our lives. And now she's back. We don't know how to thank you, Detective McNulty. . . .

We prayed. Every night. And sometimes nearly lost hope. But God answers prayers: you brought Johnny back to us. . . .

"Harry, Harry, Harry," McNulty said, shaking his head. The detective dragged deeply on a Camel, shook his head some more, exhaled the smoke, dragged deeply again, all the while looking up at the many pictures and letters. "It isn't me, remember? It's Sherlock. It's the fucking expert system, the machine. He deserves all the credit. I don't do anything but feed in the data."

"You're a humble bastard, you know that? Where'd they get the rules for *finding* these missing persons? From you. They took your knowledge and coded it into the program. Sherlock is *you*. At least in part."

"Oh, Jesus. The machine is me, huh? Wonderful."

"Well," Chief Harry Benoit said, "isn't that pretty much the story? These computer scientists needed a domain expert—the guy who knew missing persons inside and out, the guy whose brain they could pick. And that's you. Right?"

"Right," McNulty sighed.

"So what's the problem?" Harry asked.

"The problem is that the part of me that's inside this computer is the shallow superficial part. The part that can be expressed in simple rules. But a lot stayed in here," McNulty said, tapping his head with his forefinger. "Intuition. Instinct. Hunches. Strokes of genius. That's the problem with expert systems. There isn't any way to impact these things to the program."

"It *is* solving our missing-persons cases, Lou. One after another."

"They've been easy cases," McNulty said.

The Chief looked skeptical.

"Listen, Harry, I want to run Sherlock on something meaty. Something tough." McNulty hesitated, and then went on: "And I want the freedom to pursue my test drive, no matter where it goes, no matter how long the journey."

Harry studied his detective: McNulty, the Chief suddenly realized, was clean-shaven, looked well-rested, and his clothes were unwrinkled. The chain-smoking insomniac, the fitful but brilliant detective—the *real* McNulty—had vanished. Which worried Chief Harry Benoit.

"Fine," Harry said.

"Fine?"

"Yup. You want to burn the candle at both ends, it's fine with me."

"Time? Travel?"

"You got it."

McNulty gave a nod of gratitude.

"Of course," Harry said, "if you want to take Sherlock to the limit, the right kind of case, a real nasty one, will have to come along."

GRU's Tereshkovo SBI Complex, Siberia

Before Galya Matra began to talk, she was remarkable only for her violent behavior, which her family took, quite reasonably, but nonetheless incorrectly, to be a sign of deep malevolence. Galya passed through infanthood without a single smile, without the slightest loving coo. And when she smiled for the first time, at two, it was after biting her mother on the cheek—so hard that blood was drawn. The thing that no one realized during Galya's "sadistic" stage was that if it was in fact sadism, it was an exceedingly clinical strain. The blood seeping from her mother's skin fascinated her, and brought a smile of wonderment to her lips; but that was all. There was no perverse joy in seeing another human in pain. There was only the blood, the shape of it, the motion as it trickled down a cheek.

The violence ended at two years, two months, at which time Galya Matra, speaking for the first time, announced that she wanted new books to read.

"New books? It will be a few years before you can read *these*," her mother laughed.

At which point, in response, tiny Galya Matra snatched up a fairy tale about a Russian mouse, read it out loud from front to back flawlessly, and flung it directly into her mother's face.

At five, by which time she had mastered differential equations, Galya Matra was recruited by GRU, her parents not at all upset by their girl's departure. Today, arriving at the Directorate of Space Operation's Siberian complex, she was an eighteen-year-old physicist fresh from Moscow University and the Academy of Sciences. But she didn't *look* eighteen: she didn't look any age in particular. Indeed, she didn't look any *sex* in particular, either. Her physique was that of a muscular male. Her hair was straight and greasy, but long enough to classify her as female. Her skin was pallid, funereal, and, combined with her features, marked some kind of genetic compromise between the sexes. There was absolutely nothing about her appearance that suggested even a modicum of female grooming. She was never seen out of a long white lab coat, which was invariably stained. She was never seen to wipe perspiration from her brow, despite the fact that it often appeared there. She was never seen to move a clump of hair from in front of her eyes, despite the fact that it often dangled there.

When she moved, she moved stiffly, as if only the joints in larger limbs were operational.

"A museum," Galya Matra said to her host.

"What?" said Dimitry Ignatov, puzzled.

"Oh, wonderful. And a deaf tour guide. GRU certainly goes first class."

Ignatov simply stared. He had been forewarned, but not adequately. The woman before him gave off the coldness of a corpse, the venom of a snake.

"A museum, Dimitry. This hangar looks like something out of World War II."

Captain Dimitry Ignatov was small, maybe even small enough to be considered a dwarf. This impression was exacerbated by his head, which, relative to his Hobbit-size body, was oversize. On the other hand, he had an intellect to match. He was plump, in body and face, bald on top, frizzy long hair on the sides, a long ungroomed Hasidic Jew's beard, superthick glasses. A fight with polio at thirteen had left him with a limp. Ignatov was also generally a cheerful person.

"Count your blessings, Comrade Matra. We're just lucky the old tanker managed to get GRU a piece of SDI."

"Andreev Kasakov calls *this* SDI?"

"Yes. And so do I," Ignatov declared in his rather high-pitched voice.

"Well, then, you're one fucking dumb son of a bitch. SDI is supposed to be interesting. Challenging. Glamorous. It's supposed to involve lasers or particle beams—*something* of that sort. Something that involves my expertise."

"Sorry, Galya. Our assignment is very clear: we are to build little rockets. Little conventional rockets that fly very fast. Interceptors."

"Interceptors," Galya repeated skeptically.

"That's right. We build thousands of small, smart interceptors. Small enough so that large numbers of them, via booster, can be lifted into space. Where we house them in clusters, inside environmentally controlled platforms powered by solar cells or nuclear reactors."

"And?"

"And when a ballistic-missile attack is detected, we release the interceptors. Their thrusters bring them to, say, five kilometers per second, ultrahigh velocity. Then sensors and regulating software guide the interceptors to collision with incoming warheads; and the result is kinetic death for these warheads."

"Primitive."

"What would *you* suggest, Comrade Matra?"

Galya looked down and directly into Ignatov's eyes and said: "Well, *if* I was going to do something along these lines, *if* I was going to follow the interceptor concept rather than lasers or particle beams, then I would consider toroids."

"Toroids?"

"Yes," Galya said, "toroids. I would build projectiles out of hydrogen plasma."

Ignatov displayed a thoroughly vacant look.

"Plasma, Dimitry. Well, you're not a physicist. Plasma is a state of matter consisting of charged particles, ions, and electrons. Anyway, you think *five* kilometers per second is something? Hah! I think it could be possible to accelerate compact magnetized rings—oh, say, fifty centimeters in diameter—of hydrogen plasma to speeds in excess of five *thousand* kilometers per second."

"How would this be done, Comrade Matra?"

"Simple. You would start by extrapolating from today's fast-capacitor banks. Take one thousand capacitor modules charged in parallel over thirty seconds, which ought to give you, oh, over fifteen megajoules of energy. These modules discharge electrical current across a cylindrical aluminum foil; the current superheats the foil, ionizes it, and thereby produces plasma. See?"

Ignatov didn't see anything.

"And how long would such a project take?" Ignatov asked.

"Oh, thirty years, maybe. Perhaps twenty with sufficient funding."

"Hmm. Well, Chief Scientist Bazakin has given us a rather different time scale, I'm afraid. We need a crude but working version of Space-Based Interceptors—SBI, if you will—as soon as possible."

Galya frowned. There wasn't a shred of cooperation in her demeanor, but she seemed willing at least to listen further.

"Now that you are finished dreaming about science fiction," Ignatov said, "perhaps you would like to see what I've managed so far."

Ignatov led Matra over to the test area, punched in a command to the workstation governing his interceptor, and brought the little rocket to ominous, hissing life.

"Its weight is about 200 kilos," said Ignatov. "Notice the monitor."

Galya Matra looked at a monitor which, she realized, didn't look the least bit like a museum piece.

"Nice, huh? Courtesy of Directorate Z; I'm beginning to think there's nothing they can't steal. It's a twenty-by-twenty-inch Sony Trinitron color CRT with 2,048 pixel by 2,048 line resolution. Refresh rate of sixty hertz, four million pixels without the slightest flicker."

Matra nodded, and even smiled a bit, looking over the shoulder of the diminutive Captain Ignatov.

"What are we looking at?" she asked.

"Oh, yeah, wait, here." Ignatov punched a command into the workstation. "See?" Suddenly the two scientists themselves appeared on the monitor. There was room on the screen for only a part of Matra's bulk.

"It's hooked up to a video camera on the demon," Ignatov explained.

"Demon?"

"Yeah, I call these interceptors 'demons.' Watch." Ignatov keyed in a command to the demon's 350-pound-thrust liquid rocket engine, and it fired up. The hiss in the cavernous hangar rose in volume and pitch, and became a scream. Then a 450-millisecond pulse from the engine lifted the demon up from its launch point to an altitude of twenty-three feet, where it hovered. The little rocket hung there, pulsing, small and stable, but not streamlined in the least. To Dr. Matra, who liked to work on cars, the demon reminded her of the sluggish engine in her Zaporozhet.

Ignatov cut the demon's thrusters, silence reigned once again in the huge hangar, and the vehicle dropped soundlessly into netting. The demo had taken place not more than twenty feet in front of the two scientists.

"Interesting," Dr. Matra said.

"You're a master of understatement, you know that, Galya?"

"You look light-years from genuine flight."

"Oh, I see," Ignatov said. "Tell that to Air India."

"Air India?"

"June 1985. Don't remember? A Boeing 747 disintegrated while en route from Montreal to London."

A vague recollection flickered in Matra's mind. "That was a terrorist bomb."

"Really?" Ignatov said. "That was the conclusion of the Indian investigation commission, but they never found much of the wreckage. The demon hit when the plane was over the ocean."

"Fuck."

"Ah," the tiny Ignatov said. "A little respect, I see. Then of course there's Lockerbie."

Matra stared at Ignatov serenely, but surprise flickered behind her blue eyes.

"Mm hmm," Ignatov hummed, looking up at her. "Pan Am Boeing 747, Flight 103."

"Wait a minute," Matra objected. "They found explosives."

"Yup," Ignatov replied. "Semtex. Odorless. High-performance. Very nasty shit. The Czechs know how to mix the stuff, I'll tell you that."

"You planted it?"

"Sure. We even blew up a tiny bit of it so they'd find the residue. Simple pressure-sensitive switch, comrade. Thirty-one thousand feet."

Matra was most uncomfortable with this tiny man's competence; she still wore her ever-present skeptical scowl. "They have detectors now," she pointed out.

"Sure. Good ones, too. Stuff *you'd* like. But we made a point of carrying the explosives past a fast neutron device. It's embarrassingly easy, really. The thing measures gamma rays emitted by the three elements a bomber's got to have: nitrogen, oxygen, and carbon. But you get a chunk of Semtex small enough, and it's below the program's discrimination level. We had a number of sugar-cube-size stuff, all wired together in a ring. And of course the wire's innocuous. Much better than the thin sheet bombs the terrorists use."

Galya Matra shrugged, allowing but a hint of genuine respect to show. "I still don't know why I'm here," she complained, Ignatov's deed having gone in one ear and out the other, unfiltered by a conscience.

"Vision, comrade."

"Vision."

"Yes."

"Explain."

"This, Comrade Matra, is where our expertise overlaps: vision. It's why Bazakin had you sent out here to this permafrosted wasteland. Vision is at the very

THE GRU TERESKOVO SBI COMPLEX

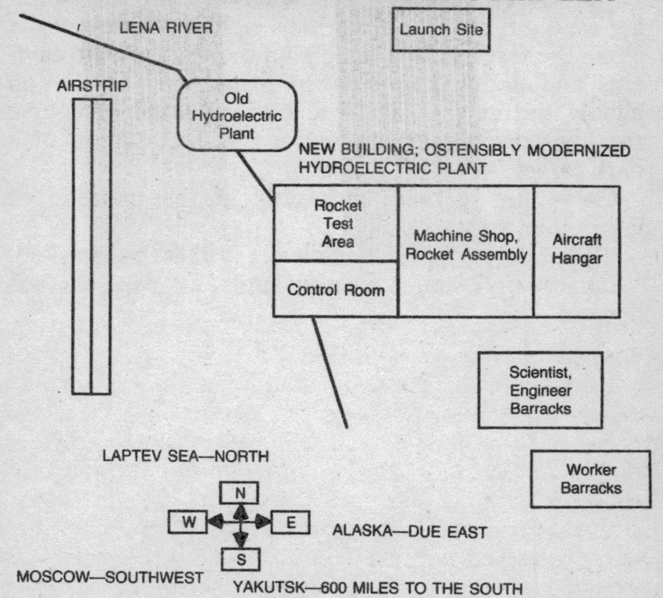

heart of SBI. We need to detect incoming missiles and warheads; we need to *see* them. And we need to have these demons see autonomously, rather than simply sending video images back to ground-based operators. Come, follow me."

Ignatov took her to another part of the vast, domed Tereshkovo complex, walked her up to a small but sharp-looking jet.

"What's this?" she asked.

"A Lear jet Thirty-Five. Z stole it for us."

"And?"

"And you and I are supposed to modify it."

"With?"

"State-of-the-art vision systems. Systems that will see enemy missiles and warheads."

"Specifically?"

"Divide and conquer," Ignatov said. "I was thinking we'd put a string of perhaps eight separate sensors along the fuselage. I'll handle all the visible-band cameras and photodocumentation—that's my area. You handle the imaging infrared cameras, and of course the low-power laser designator for illumination of a dark target."

Galya had perked up visibly at the mention of lasers, her area.

"What do we hunt when we get it built?" she asked.

Ignatov only smiled his elfin smile, knowing she was hooked.

6

The Merger

January 13—Gulf of Sirte, off Libya

"Hey, Donny, wanna surf?"

"That's a roge, Kid. Let's do it."

Billy "the kid" Jackson threw his Nighthawk, the F-117A stealth fighter, into a Mach .7 ninety-degree bank angle and dived toward the water. G forces hammered both men into their seats.

"She ain't the Wobblin' Goblin no more, eh, Kid?"

"Nope. She's smooth as silk."

They leveled out at twenty-five feet. Surfin' height. The moon lit up whitecaps for the two to see, and the fighter skimmed over the surf, its two GE F404 turbofan power plants emitting the distinctive high-pitched scream that had become the stealth fighter's signature to civilians living near the plane's home, a remote base at Tonopah, Nevada. They hit Mach .8. The Kid took her down to fifteen feet.

"Turning lights out, Donny."

"Roge."

The F-117A's diamond-shaped amber position lights went off; the pulsing red light in her nose died also.

"Okay, buddy, quiet her down."

"Roge, Kid."

Captain Donald Smith extinguished all active systems. No radio, no radar. No noise that could allow detection.

"*Now* let's see somebody find us," the Kid said.

His back-seater didn't say anything, but nodded and smiled to himself, the surf below taking him back to his California home, back to beaches and sun and surfing and curvaceous, blond, bikini-clad women.

Yesterday's buzzing by a MIG-25 Foxbat had been written off to Libyan luck, and today, now at Mach .9 Indicated Air Speed, altitude fifteen feet, streaking just over the water, Captain Billy "the Kid" Jackson, master of the Lockheed F-117A stealth fighter, felt as invincible as ever. Singled out while at the academy, he'd been in training for "radar-invisible" flight even before blueprints for the F-117A had been drawn up. The Air Force had decided long ago that a necessary condition for piloting the stealth fighter was youth, and youth with lightning-fast reflexes. There were two teams, daytime and nighttime; they were the best of the best. Like performing microsurgery, flying the stealth fighter required the coolness and quickness only pilots in their twenties and thirties possess, and which the Kid possessed to a degree above save but a handful of other young gifted American pilots. The F-117A was no longer ungainly; though subsonic, with all the wrinkles ironed out, she was in many ways as nimble as an F-15. The Kid had verified this day after day in the Allied-Iraq war.

Today, he had no mission. No agenda. On the chance that yesterday's apparent detection had been the product of mission leaks, his superiors had told him, in secret, simply to fly. Where he wanted. *How* he wanted. No headings known beforehand by anyone who could conceivably leak the information. No radio and no radar use, so as to minimize electronic noise.

Hell, they never even saw me yesterday. A fluke.

The Kid glanced at the head-up display, projected onto his windshield: twelve feet above water, he left a wake of mist; inching past Mach .9; and glowing before his eyes: a holographic representation of the watery terrain, courtesy of an infrared laser-aided camera on the F-117A's nose.

Fucking invisible. Come on, you A-rabs, can you find me?

Smooth. No corners. Radar-absorbent panels. Radiation-minimizing ceramics on the nose cone. Coal black. Nonafterburning engines covered with radar-absorptive mesh to reduce the chance of infrared detection. A ghost.

Dipping his right wing but a few feet from the sea, the Kid screamed off to the south, and took the stealth fighter into Libyan airspace. There was no harm in doing so, since he'd be in and out without them ever knowing. And the whole point of his team's coming to the Gulf of Sirte was to subject some Russian-made hardware to new tests.

"Anything, Donny?"

"Nada. Nothing locked on us. EMV is zero."

The Kid had his right hand on the control stick, his left on the dual throttle control. It was a beautiful feeling, one that, for the Kid, rivaled sex—though he would never *tell* anyone that.

Skimmin'. Surfin'. Bloody fucking invisible.

Behind his helmet: a smile. Then:

"Got a visual, Kid."

Jackson looked left, and picked up the hurtling jet through his AVS-8 night-vision goggles. His normal two-hundred-degree horizontal field of view was cut to forty degrees by the goggles, and consequently the Kid had to turn his head severely to the left. Everything through the lenses was an unnatural shade of green, but Billy was accustomed to it, and he pegged the visitor immediately, by instinct. "A MIG-25, Donny. Does he have us?"

"Negative, Kid. Nothing locked. No search stuff comin' our way. He's got his eyes closed."

"He doesn't know we're here," the Kid said with a hubristic chuckle, which was duplicated by some laughter from the equally confident Smith. Then the Kid saw the MIG drop altitude. And drop some more. And suddenly:

"Jesus, this is gonna be close!" the Kid said.

Both men felt the vibrations of the passing Foxbat. *Too* close.

"Man, what was he, on afterburner?" Smith asked.

"Yep," the Kid said, still cool. "We still invisible, Donny?"

"Absolutely. Nothing on EMV."

"You believe this? Two days in a row these dumb fucks buzz us without even knowing we're here."

Smith was silent.

"Donny?"

No response.

"Hey, Don, cat got your—"

"Ho, shit, Kid. The fucker's back."

This time Billy Jackson looked right. And his eyes found the same sight: the Foxbat.

"You still got nothing?" the Kid asked.

"Nothing. This Arab isn't looking electronically."

"The bastard's dropping again," Jackson said. "And whoa! he's *really* dropping this time. Shit, we're gonna—"

This time the vibration through the F-117A, and through their bodies, was like that produced by a California quake. And this time the Kid felt a nervous shudder, slight but unmistakable, in his gut. It lingered.

"You thinkin' what I'm thinkin', Kid?"

Billy "the Kid" Jackson didn't respond right away. It took him a few moments before he could bring himself to confront the truth. Finally he said, "Yup. Either Allah himself is flying that Foxbat, or the pilot can find us at will."

"Well, if it's Allah, he's back."

The Kid looked to his left and saw what he expected to see. He armed his four AIM-9M Sidewinder missiles, and peeled off toward international waters, hoping he wouldn't have to use them. He was no longer invisible, and hence no longer invincible. Indeed, Billy the Kid was suddenly flying a multimillion-dollar shitbucket, trapped in subsonic speed.

January 14—Peter Kasakov's Apartment, Moscow

Just last night Annastasia had danced in a guest performance with the Kirov, through an amber-hued forest in Balanchine's *Scotch Symphony*, at the Marinsky Theater, in Leningrad, perhaps the most physically beautiful city on earth. And after the performance, alone, she had walked cheerfully with the ghosts of Tchaikovsky and Rachmaninov, Nijinsky and Ulanova, on the wings of music echoing around every corner, floating about the many golden palaces, through the parks, over the Venetian waterways.

Then the *Red Arrow*, the overnight express, back to Moscow.

And now here, with Peter.

A prisoner. With knowledge of secrets which, should she flee, would guarantee her execution.

"Why don't you make yourself a drink, relax, slip into something more comfortable? We can listen to this together, have a little celebration. I've waited weeks for something juicy on Space."

Anna nodded assent, and departed for the bedroom. She was back in a minute, dressed in a nightgown so short that the full length of her graceful sartorius was laid bare. She sat down next to Peter. He handed her a glass of vodka, picked up his own, and, smiling, *pinged* his glass against hers. Then he clicked the recorder to Play:

She's a genius. Peculiar, but a genius.

Peculiar? The woman is utterly bizarre, comrade, with a volcanic temper. I often think that she could crush me like a gnat. And sometimes I think she wants *to.*

Laughter. Then: *But did it work, Comrade Ignatov? that is the question.*

Like a charm.

The Libyan chased him away?

Absolutely.

Like a dog with his tail between his legs, eh?

A chuckle. Then: *Invisible. Hah! The whole stealth program is now a heaping pile of shit, Comrade Bazakin.*

Yes, humiliating, definitely. And intensified no doubt by the fact that it was a Libyan pilot. The Americans hate *the Libyans. Almost as much as the Iraqis.*

Too bad the Arab missed.

Well, they suck, let's face it. They couldn't drive a Foxbat into the broad side of a barn.

True.

Now, the specs.

Well, Galya and I decided on only four cameras; the additional four you and I talked about earlier seemed superfluous. The whole system required just a small cutout from the Lear jet's body.

And your four?

Okay, well, first we have a special acquisition camera fitted with a wide-field-of-view zoom lens—we use this one to find the target. Wasn't too hard to get an initial bead on the American stealth fighter. This camera can lock on to very dim targets—even those rated as low as plus-nine stellar magnitude. Believe it or not, the core of this first camera is a Fujinon lens, commercial, used for television sporting events in America.

How'd you get it? Directorate Z?

Of course. They stole a truckload of these babies right off the New York State Thruway.

Peter smiled and nodded to himself.

And the others?

Well, Galya did most of the work. She put together,

first, a rather simple infrared imaging camera. One hundred microradian resolution; 160 by 244 focal plane array.

That is *simple.*

Yeah, sure, but she was just warming up with this one, took her maybe two days at most, as I remember. Next she hammered out a shortwave-length infrared spectrometer. The fucking thing uses a continuously variable filter that measures the spectral density of rocket and jet plumes. Picked up the F-117A's non-afterburning plume effortlessly.

Sounds like Galya, all right.

Indeed.

That's three. The fourth?

We teamed up. I know visible-spectrum stuff, as you know, and accordingly I set myself the task of building a high-resolution camera for straightforward photodocumentation. It yields thirty microradian resolution, with the help of an American hundred-inch focal-length Contraves SR100 telescope.

Z again?

Who else? Anyway, this scope has a 12.5-inch aperture, which is hooked up to a garden-variety low-light multispectral video camera.

Standard. Where'd Galya come in?

She took my camera and jazzed it up. Configured it with a laser designator that emits a beam through the telescope. The bastard illuminates everything. It lit the stealth plane up like Leningrad during Northern Lights. This laser, comrade, can see the invisible. *And the laser is so low-power, so gentle, no plane in the world can sense it.*

So you're confident this sort of camera system will do the trick for warning our interceptors?

No question.

How go the interceptors themselves?

Come on, Comrade Bazakin, they're not exactly flashy. After all, I fly the bastards. They send me back a picture and I manipulate a joystick accordingly. We need to give them some autonomy, use some AI.

Eventually, yes. But for now, Captain Ignatov, make them as supple and responsive as possible to your manual commands.

But I—

Listen, you're doing well. Don't fuck up now. Just listen to me.

And the rush? You still can't tell me why time is of the essence?

No. Yours is not to—

Reason why. I know. I know.

Excellent. Then get back to work, and tell Galya we will need her muscles again soon enough.

Very well, Comrade Bazakin.

Peter clicked off the Sony microrecorder.

"I *told* you Space was up to some nasty shit. My own directorate has given them many gifts. Interceptors. Hmm. I think a merger is in order, don't you?"

He turned to find Anna asleep, her head back, throat exposed. She was exhausted from her recent performance and the sleepless train trip back. But Peter was euphoric. For reasons that even he had never been able to completely fathom, sexuality and espionage were, for him, inextricably linked. He wanted her. Now.

He lifted her, intending to carry her into the bedroom, but she woke, and, looking into his eyes, saw his desire. He put her down on her feet, pulled his shirt off, undid his belt, and before he reached for her, was already swollen.

He wrapped his arms around her waist; she pulled her Dior nightgown down to reveal her breasts, and to expose her nipples to the friction provided by his chest. They kissed. He pulled back, rent the silk gown in two, from between her soft and smooth shoulder blades, to below her buttocks; and then he tore the shredded garment off her violently to reveal a female form of utter perfection. He tossed the gown aside, and before he seized her again, her heart missed a beat, and then began to beat quickly, like that of a trapped bird. He began to kiss her neck and lift her off the floor; not the slightest strain registered in his body from the effort. Peter was solid as granite, implacable, inhumanly strong; as always, resistance was an empty concept, a physical impossibility. She threw her head back, looking for his face, and found it; looked into his eyes and saw not only the extreme desire that was the norm, and not only the utter abandon that thrilled her, but also, this time, premeditation.

Standing, he lifted her up like a feather, and then simultaneously pulled her down over him and rammed into her, hard, with something close to the coordination she showed when dancing. She was wet, gushing even—that, as usual, saved her a good deal of agony. The pass from the meeting of their lips to the present point had proceeded at a speed that left Anna dizzy. And as always, it was much more complicated than pain. When he entered her, she half-screamed, half-moaned, half in utter fear, half in the utter pleasure he demanded. Grabbing her shoulders, he moved her up and down with ease, and then, staying inside her, fully erect, throbbing, he laid her down on the floor and pulled her ankles over his shoulders.

The fear was growing. This position, a new one, one she had never even entertained, thrust upon her suddenly, knocked the wind out of her. He lowered his shoulders down toward her own, keeping her feet on either side of his head, pinned. She found the depth of penetration incomprehensible. The ratio had suddenly changed: not mostly pain, with some slight, even sweet, pleasure. No, this time she felt a lot of pain. A thread of pleasure, and intoxicating pleasure at that, but mostly pain. Too much. He was up inside her, deeply, into her cervix, using, in this position, his size and strength like a weapon. She couldn't speak, couldn't make air pass through her voice box: he was stealing it with his thrusts. Her knees were pressed against her belly, her wrists pinned to the rug: she couldn't move. Couldn't speak. And then, utterly breathless, hardly able to breathe, she felt him, in what seemed the core of her being, ejaculate. And, though she ached for her own release, he pulled out. He released her ankles off his broad shoulders, laying her feet on the floor. She tasted blood on her lips, saw the depression in her wrists, felt a warm lingering glow of pain deep within, and a thousand little aches, and finally, a weariness as thorough as any she had ever known.

Anna, feeling as if she was moving an enormous boulder, pulled herself up to a sitting position. He was in his robe now. He brought her a glass of vodka, handed it down to her.

Five minutes later she was scrubbing herself violently in a steaming hot shower, weeping, filled with desire, and hatred, and fear.

January 15—Zagorsk

Andreev Kasakov, the old tanker, Hero of the Soviet Union, had, many years ago, with an ax and his own strong hands, built his log-cabin teahouse in the dense woodland of Zagorsk. The skeleton of the A-frame edifice consisted of enormous straight pine trunks, many over a foot in diameter; the interior, in turn, was superbly crafted by hand, from chestnut, birch, and more solid pine. For the senior Kasakov, and his young wife, their teahouse had been both a concrete testament to their socialist convictions and an amorous, refreshingly remote retreat. Andreev had forsaken the Byzantine architecture—ostentatious onion domes and elaborate icons—that had at the time been anathema to true socialists. He had built, instead, a structure in the style of the peasant timber house. And it was, in the real sense, a *teahouse*. Even now, dying within it, his eyes closed, his body being eaten away, Andreev could remember escaping here with his beautiful wife: They are beside the warmth of a roaring fire in their rustic living room, she conducting the *samovar*, the Russian tea ceremony. She is filling the urn with water, lighting the charcoal-filled metal tube through its center, her soft smooth hands pouring out some essence from the teapot, then diluting the tea with some water from the urn. Sipping the hot tea as it snows without, the wind howling. Then her kiss, her flesh, beside the fire.

This was where he wanted to die.

Peter sent the invitations. Everyone accepted.

Matra and Ignatov, from Space, came because the directorate chief, Bazakin, instructed them to do so.

Bazakin meditated in silence for an hour upon receiving the invitation, and emerged from his reflection with an educated guess about the purpose of Peter's meeting, and greatly intrigued.

Vanderyenko and Markov, unable to make it over from the States, where, with the help of Malachev, they were busy working on the theft of a new savory piece of Western technology, promised to attend in spirit.

Yankolov, the KGB chief, agreed to come to what seemed to him a GRU function, more out of personal loyalty to the old tanker than anything else.

Vasputin relished the idea of taking on a group he figured to be diehard conservatives, and, donning a leather bomber jacket, drove out from Moscow in his American open-air jeep.

It was cold, so cold that exhalation crystallized in midair, in front of one's face. A foot of pristine snow was on the ground, and in the towering evergreens. The old but sturdy teahouse spilled yellow light out into the night air, and sent a corkscrew ribbon of fragrant smoke up into the moonlit sky. Inside, it was toasty, and the lumber Andreev had by hand cut and fitted four decades before was aromatic. The great stones of the floor-to-ceiling hearth radiated heat, and would have continued to do so for days, even if the fire had been extinguished. Leaded glass. Ball-turned tables. Oil lamps. And delightful food, *zakuska* like the old days: different kinds of caviar, cold sturgeon in aspic, cheeses, pickles, liver pâté, cold cuts of all kinds, black bread, and, of course, tea and vodka. A lot of tea and vodka.

Small talk ended.

Peter assembled a semicircle of six chairs around the fire; Andreev, not much more now than skin and bone, slept in his deathbed, outside the gathering. The five spies and the one politician, full from the *zakuska*, poured themselves black and hot tea with jelly stirred in, and spiced vodka. Then, eager to pass beyond superficial banter, the six sat.

The others were curious and expectant, but Bazakin knew what was coming. He radiated sheer unadulterated mental energy. His high forehead gleamed from the firelight. The smoke from his ever-burning Prima, from which he drew without moving anything but his arm, twirled about his motionless head. There was about him an aura of utter contentedness.

Peter was about to begin when Vasputin spoke:

"Why am I here? I am no spy. I am an orator, a politician, an advocate for democracy. A businessman."

Vasputin had a joint MBA/J.D. from the University of Virginia. He was more conservative, economically, than Milton Friedman: he'd told the American Congress to its face that the U.S. was a welfare state, not a free-enterprise system, that American public education was criminal, since middle-class taxpayers were paying for the sons and daughters of rich parents to attend state universities for free. He was a shortish, potbellied, red-faced, hyperactive money-making Russian tycoon who owned a string of restaurants, a Lear jet, houses in four countries.

"Your democratic nature," Peter said, "is well-known."

"Well then?" Vasputin prodded, still looking for an explanation.

Peter's plan was to go after the outsiders first. The carrot to be dangled in front of them was power. Power, pure and simple. Vasputin to be handled with logic. Yankolov to be bullied. Vasputin was first.

"Aren't we all interested in the people?" Peter asked.

"Some more than others," Vasputin replied. "I suspect I feel a little stronger about these matters than the rest of you. I didn't have a father. One day my old man was flourishing in the Transcaucasus Secret Police, a proud member of the Cheka, the next day he was gone. Swallowed up irretrievably by the Great Terror. Stalin sent my pregnant mother to Potma, in the Mordovian Gulag, to give birth in feculent mud, wailing. I've had a nose for democracy, for the people, since leaving her womb."

"Well, perhaps," Peter said, "the people would be better off with *you* in power."

"Me?"

"Aren't you yourself working for a democracy in which Gorby could be simply voted out?"

Vasputin shook his head, smiled. "So you and your reactionary friends here are planning on putting little old leftist me in power in his place. Is that it?"

"You *are* loved. By the people. East *and* West. Chebriadze had the charm of an ax murderer. You give a speech and the people turn orgasmic."

Vasputin snickered, but a part of him, deep down, liked what was being said.

"Surely," Peter said, "you don't carry on the way

you do just for the money. You are reportedly worth millions. Have you no long-term goals for the Motherland? Are your words empty?"

"What I say I mean."

"You believe in your ideas, your proposals?"

"Of course."

"Then how can you fail to see the logic? You want the reins."

"By legal means."

"Legal means." Kasakov frowned. "There isn't time, Comrade Vasputin. We are scheduled to have national elections but every five years. And every day militant fools like Chebriadze plan how they might turn back all your progress toward democracy with one well-timed bloodbath. We are living in 1917 all over again, not 1776. You could lose everything in the twinkling of an eye."

"And you propose to move quickly," Vasputin said.

Kasakov nodded.

"And your agenda, then?" Vasputin prodded.

"I don't have one," Kasakov admitted.

"Such organization."

"Comrade Vasputin," Kasakov said, unperturbed, "you are spending time that could be used developing a plan."

Vasputin looked at the others again: at the pallid gigantic Galya Matra, the tiny Coke-bottle-eyed Ignatov, the serene and cerebral Bazakin, and at Yankolov, the innocuous head of the Committee for State Security.

Vasputin then looked back at Peter Kasakov. "I'll stay. For now."

"Excellent."

"Now," Peter resumed, "my fundamental assumption is that we are all Russians. Communism may be gone, but Russia, though dying, is not. I see Lenin, that poor mean-eyed bastard lying there in Red Square, and I hear people saying, 'Oh, no, he can*not* be interred. He is immortal'—when I hear this shit I get physically ill. And I hope the five of you feel the same. Our problem is not that Marx and Lenin have died. Our problem is that we are witnessing the end of the Russian republic itself. Civil war upon civil war. Estonia, Latvia, Lithuania—gone one day, brought back on a chain the next. Fervor, non-Russian nationalist fervor, continues to mount in the eleven remaining non-Russian republics. The Turks and the Armenians aren't far behind; they spit at the government that protects them, and are inches from civil war. All of these ingrates, my comrades, have tasted the Dionysian wine of independence, and they will get back in line under Moscow's central rule only if they are promised something to eat." Peter paused, sipped his vodka. "But Russia, comrades, communism or no communism, unity or disunity, is Russia. When Poland was a kingdom, Moscow knew well her invading armies. The Americans, and Comrade Gorbachev, would have Great Russia forget. They would have us forget Napoleon, forget the British in Crimea, forget the American-, Canadian-, and Nipponese-backed Whites in our bloody Civil War. They would have us forget in the name of reform. Well, *fuck* their forgetting. And *fuck* America. Before Lincoln freed the slaves we emancipated the serfs—out of a fundamental decency that had not a whit to do with economic expediency. Has Washington ever been abandoned as Moscow was, so that the French rode into the Holy City in hollow victory?"

Nods of affirmation. Yankolov's was the one head to remain impassive. Peter noticed.

"Do you dispute this, Comrade Yankolov?" Kasakov asked.

Yankolov remained silent. He had been dozing.

"Comrade Yankolov," Peter said, "we need you. We need the KGB."

Yankolov's eyes, half-closed, suddenly widened behind his bifocals. "The GRU needs the KGB?"

"Not the GRU as a whole. This *group* needs you."

"For what?"

"For whatever is necessary."

"Whatever is necessary for what?"

"I don't know."

"Well, then, *I* don't know. You speak in riddles."

"My father said he knew you—knew you well enough to know that a man with your gifts would not be content to reduce the KGB to some sort of effeminate, polite, law-abiding covert service. Perhaps it would be more efficient if you simply went to work for the British. Then you could have your well-mannered men, your cooks, your poetry. You wouldn't have to explain away the murders of the past. The brutal interrogations. You would preside over a heritage unblemished by the black and violent actions of the Committee for State Security."

"Colonel Kasakov, I resent your—"

"We look for common ground here, Victor Ivanovich, not selfish emotion. Your resentment is childish. You're either in or out. You're either the puppet everyone says you are, or you aren't. You either want your KGB to be vibrant, or you don't. I want those who are willing to do what is necessary to secure what the people want. Are you willing or not?"

Yankolov looked at the others; he looked from face to face. "I'm in," he said. He still looked about as threatening as a two-year-old, and as daft as a senile professor, but he was in. The sleepy gray-haired old man, just as Peter's father had claimed, was, deep down, a Hamlet.

"We want for our people what Gorbachev wants," Peter proclaimed. "We just want to find a better way. And I have brought you here tonight because I see the glimmer of a way. I do not have a comprehensive plan, but I see an opportunity, and if we work together, if we're ready to move when the right time comes, perhaps we can find a way to bring to the people the better life Gorbachev seeks, without sacrificing the Motherland in the process."

"What is this opportunity of which you speak?" Yankolov asked.

"In two words, comrade, Star Wars."

Bazakin threw down the last remnants of the vodka in his glass. He pulled out a Prima, lit up the acrid cigarette, looked through the smoke, and then handed over the tick-size microphones Peter had planted. "I spoke plainly enough for a military man? I was worried about that." Bazakin turned to Vasputin and Yankolov and said, "The Directorate of Space Technology is indeed pursuing a primitive version of SDI. Peter's father set up the program."

Peter nodded. Ignatov and Matra were about to protest, but Bazakin raised his hand and silenced them. "In fact, without your own Directorate Z, Peter Andreevich," he continued, "our interceptor system would not have gotten off the ground. You see, my comrades," Bazakin said, looking around the circle, "there has already been a good deal of cooperation between us. The thought that we can make it more systematic, well, I find that fascinating." Bazakin nodded slowly, his eyebrows raised, and drew again on his Prima.

"Let us merge," Peter said.

Bazakin nodded acceptance, then asked, "Where do you intend to *go* with our SBI, Comrade Kasakov?"

"I'm not sure. I'm working extemporaneously. We all are. I just have a sense of the ingredients at this point, not the recipe."

Bazakin merely raised an eyebrow.

"Ironic," Yankolov interjected.

The other five looked at the KGB chief quizzically; Yankolov explained: "Well, it's just that Gorbachev sees little place for the KGB, the GRU, and indeed the military itself, in the reaching of the goals for which we too strive. He rejects the Brezhnev doctrine in favor of oratory. But if I understand you, Peter Andreevich, you glimpse a way to put our strength to use to fortify Great Russia, and the irony of it is that Gorbachev has himself given us the opening."

Nods. Then a bit of silence. The fire threw off a lovely heat. The flames danced.

"But *has* he?" Ignatov said.

"Has who what?" Galya Matra barked.

"Well," Ignatov said humbly, his feet not touching the floor as he sat upon his chair, "I'm not so sure Gorbachev *is* giving us anything. Or at least I don't think we should take it for granted that he is. Maybe Gorbachev will turn off funding tomorrow. I mean, why *is* he still going ahead with SDI research? It seems out of character to me."

It was a trenchant question. Matra, condescending before, was the first to grasp its cogency now.

Ignatov continued: "You're talking about a guy who cut our army by a million men. A guy who wants to throw away most of our ballistic missiles. A guy who—"

"All right," Bazakin interrupted. "You've made the point."

"I'll *ask* the bastard," Peter said.

"You'll what?" Vasputin said.

"I'll ask our fearless leader why he *is* going ahead with SDI research. Simple."

Initial incredulity gave way to supporting nods and shrugs.

Yankolov said, "I don't mean to dampen the enthusiasm here, but we don't exactly have a Rolls-Royce. We're talking SBI. Interceptors. Smart rocks. That kind of stuff. Basically rockets, I would imagine, of a rather conventional sort. What about the laser and particle-beam efforts? The Gagarin SDI laser complex alone has a budget twice the size of GRU's Directorate of Space Technology. And we know that the Americans are working feverishly on these technologies."

Yankolov had directed his objection to Peter; Peter, with a smile, redirected it to Bazakin, nodding in the scientist's direction.

"The Americans," Bazakin said, "have scaled back considerably on SDI. Reagan dreamed of an umbrella, and was getting the SDIO four billion dollars a year. Bush needled Dukakis on his lack of support for Star Wars, but when in office promptly cut the American program to well below two billion. If Atwood is elected, they should dip below one billion."

"Maybe so," Yankolov responded, "but they haven't halted research. I have information on a laser which—"

"Comrade Yankolov, no offense," Bazakin interrupted in his deep even monotone, "but the GRU eats, sleeps, and drinks technology. The KGB has other interests. Andreev had the vision to get us the primitive stuff, which is stuff we *know* is going to work. Laser and particle-beam technologies are years away from being perfected—both superpowers now know this. And the main reason for the inevitable delay has nothing to do with problems intrinsic to the technology involved, it has to do with the unavailability, both now and well into the future, of advanced high-power supplies; this is the wall the laser-crazy Americans are soon going to slam into. You see, Comrade Yankolov, directed energy weapons pose unprecedented power requirements; such weapons, indeed, require multimegawatt systems. According to my calculations, exotic space-based weapons, such as free electron lasers, charged particle beams, and neutral particle beams, will require fifty to two-hundred megawatts per platform. Chemical lasers, I believe, would require tens of kilowatts. Now, the real killer is this: We know, and they know, that nuclear-energy sources *could* power the weapons at multimegawatt levels, but the effect of effluents and vibration from such massive nuclear-power systems would essentially be the destruction of the platform involved. We know, for example, that at times the plume of a rocket at high altitude consumes the rocket itself. This would happen on a grand scale if nuclear-power systems of the required sort were installed on mothering satellites. But space-based interceptor rockets, SBI—this is doable *now*. And SBI, as Comrade Kasakov has just explained, is what's at the heart of our . . . our . . . well, it's not a plan, our *orientation*."

"With all due respect, Comrade Bazakin," KGB Chief Yankolov said, "we have gathered much information that suggests the Americans are nearing the implementation stage for space-based lasers."

"Once again, Victor," Bazakin resumed, "no insult intended, but the GRU specializes in gathering such information, *and* in interpreting it, whereas the KGB dabbles; and I can tell you that your men are much too sanguine about progress on the other side. I repeat: the problem is a sufficiently potent power supply. They have recently achieved 6.2 million watts of energy in output from a seven-hundred-million-dollar laser called Beta-5—the last test was conducted at a TRW plant in San Juan Capistrano. This is their most powerful laser. And they plan to launch a version of Beta into orbit in 1994 as part of an experiment called Zenith Star. Notice, however, that what is to be launched won't even violate ABM—because it won't be powerful enough to kill a mouse. To be a genuine weapon, such a laser would have to fire for minutes, but Zenith Star will be able to fire for only one-fifth of a second. And, again, the reason it can't fire a sustained beam is that the power supply needed is absent, and is indeed ten to fifteen years off."

Yankolov, bridling his pride, nodded, satisfied.

Bazakin took the time to drag on his Prima, and

then continued, "I tell you all, however, that we have our own problems with SBI. We can build the rockets. That is not a problem. We build better rockets than the Americans. But," Bazakin said, now looking directly at Peter, pausing to take another deep drag on his Prima, "computers are another story. SBI requires computer hardware of a sort we simply do not have in Russia."

"What sort of machine, Comrade Bazakin, would do the trick?" Peter asked.

"Well," Bazakin answered, exhaling a stream of tobacco smoke, "there is an American massively parallel machine, a neural-net computer, that would do quite nicely, I believe. It's called a Neurocube. But the security surrounding these—"

"Let my men worry about that," Peter interrupted with a smile. "Remember, we have merged. I'll call Vanderyenko tomorrow morning and put him, and thereby *spetsnaz*, on it." Everyone except Vasputin smiled: the *Macka*'s capacity for theft was legendary throughout the Soviet intelligence community. It was said that Nickolai Vasilyevich Vanderyenko could steal the heart of a frigid nun.

"What about a name?" Ignatov chirped.

No one, at first, knew what he was talking about.

"For us," Ignatov explained, looking up at the others through his superthick glasses. "Something to baptize our group."

More silence, but this time suffused with cerebration.

Then Peter said, "Let us, from this night on, be known collectively, amongst ourselves, as the *Starik*."

This had been the name, many years ago, given to GRU's General Berzin, who had been known as the "old man." All the GRU agents found it fitting. And surprisingly enough, Yankolov, Chief of KGB, nodded in agreement. Vasputin, the only person from outside the secret world, didn't grasp the appellation's significance, but did not, at least at the moment, object.

And so the *Starik* was born.

"Well, Comrade Vasputin?" Peter prodded. "Are you in?"

"It's all rather amorphous, isn't it?"

"Undeniably. Too vague to constitute mutiny. Wouldn't you agree?"

"I suppose."

"In, then, comrade?"

No response.

"You are free to leave now. You are free to return to your speeches, to your eloquent, nonviolent calls for sweeping economic change."

Vasputin didn't leave. He looked around the room.

"Well, Boris?"

"I'd like to stay. At least for a while."

"Test the waters, as it were?" Peter said.

"I suppose you could put it that way."

"The point of no return will come soon enough, however."

Vasputin didn't get it.

"You stay in long enough," Peter amplified, "and you'd leave with information that could kill us if disclosed. We couldn't allow that, of course."

"What is this, an ultimatum?"

"Excellent choice of words."

"Now or never?"

"Now or never," Peter echoed.

"I would have a say."

"*The* say."

"In a new . . . situation, I would have a position of . . . of . . ."

"Power," Peter said. "Look around. You are the only statesman here. It would be natural."

Vasputin raised his glass, waved it toward the others, smiled the smile he'd smiled in America, from coast to coast, on *Nightline* and CNN and *60 Minutes*, and downed the vodka.

"Now, my comrades," Peter said to them all, "I'm afraid we have more somber business to attend to. The foundation for our group was assembled by my father; it was the last thing he did in his capacity as head of GRU. Our assembling here tonight, in the teahouse that he built for my mother, must now be sealed in accordance with his wish."

The five visitors looked over to Andreev's bed: the Hero of the Soviet Union was awake, his eyes open but glassy. He could no longer speak, but he could move his head slightly, and he did so now, in a nod.

Andreev had asked that it be one of his own guns. For Vasputin, the violence was alien, and his knees nearly gave out completely. Ignatov, shuddering, simply couldn't bear to watch, and hid his eyes. Matra looked, and though no nausea came, though there was no shudder—pity, quiet but piercing, tugged at her muscular heart. Bazakin looked on clinically, smoking, as a coroner might look upon a corpse. For Yankolov, who had fought beside Andreev in the Great Patriotic War, the sight stirred up memories of brave and bloody fighting in Stalingrad against the Nazis. For Peter, who pulled the trigger, and who had killed before in like manner, there was first the sheer joy he always felt when the gun kicked, sending a jolt of pleasure up his arm; and then there was the fact that, given his father's condition and prognosis, it was simply his duty. The only odd intransigent thought in Peter's head had nothing to do with the deed itself, nor with the taboo that surrounds such deeds, but with the fact that he found himself, an atheist, thinking in terms of freeing his father's soul from the prison of a sickly, degenerating body.

There was but a tiny shudder, a dark circle on

Andreev's forehead, and a halo that spread out on the old man's pillow, under his lifeless head.

Andreev died from his son's merciful bullet as a panoramic vision filled his mind, overtook it with blazing clarity—a vision of Russian horses flying through the snow in Zagorsk, of Leningrad during Northern Lights, of the Trans-Siberian rocking on and on through Russia's unmatched expanse; a vision of Great Russia in full glory, and of America subdued. His last thought was a question to himself. You saw the Nazis' doom while wounded in the snow at Stalingrad; have you once again seen the future?

7

The Machine

January 16—Dartmouth University

Nickolai Vasilyevich Vanderyenko liked what he saw in the full-length mirror. He had once again achieved the complete sartorial neglect that was part of this particular disguise, and was thus quite pleased with himself. Today he sported striped pants, a plaid jacket that would have been rejected by the Salvation Army, a loud, stained, wrinkled four-inch-wide tie, and bell-bottoms. He took one last look in the mirror: Excellent, said the *Macka* to himself.

Vanderyenko looked the quintessential academic, his mind occupied with things a good deal more profound than clothes. Before he left, he put on a pair of Coke-bottle glasses and roughed up the hair of his wig so violently that it reached, as planned, an Einsteinian wildness.

Upon meeting some of his American hosts in the lobby, he was right on cue: he said, humbly, utterly disoriented: "Excuse me, Professor, but could you help me decipher this map? I haven't a clue as to how to get to the conference from here."

The American professor, glad to help, guided the "elderly" Vanderyenko to the auditorium by the arm. The Russian laughed silently to himself all the way there. His mockery of the American flickered in his eyes, but no one ever looked into them at the right moment.

* * *

Vanderyenko was headed for an ACM—Association for Computing Machinery—conference on the limits of computing, and specifically for a presentation entitled "The Neurocube: Fifth Generation Neural-Net Connectionism." However, Alexander Nelsen, the professor scheduled to give this presentation, was as yet absent, and this was worrying his research partner, Jeff Renear.

"Have you seen him?" Renear asked.

"Have I seen whom?"

"Come on, Alex. Who else?"

"Nope."

Renear collided with a vendor hawking voice-recognition devices for IBM's newest workstation.

"Have *you* seen him?"

"Whom?"

"Alex!" Renear exclaimed.

"Oh. Nope, haven't seen him today. And now that I think about it, I didn't see him yesterday either."

"Well, I *assumed* he'd stay away for opening day, but we're supposed to present in about ten minutes, and the guy *still* isn't here."

"Sorry."

Renear waded through the hum of micros, and through nonchalant talk about technical wonders—frictionless, entropy-defying computers; the transmission of information by light rather than electricity; the limits of miniaturization; parallel processing, and countless other mind-benders, many of them discussed in the abstract and formal language of mathematics.

"No, haven't seen him."

"Haven't seen him. He's probably skiing, or snowboarding, or something of that ilk. You know Alex."

"No idea where he is, Jeff. Sorry."

The serene and rarefied air of the conference began to sicken Renear. Hearing it all, seeing everyone so damn comfortable, and then realizing that Alex was absent—a nausea crept into his body.

Renear collared Nelsen's chairman: "Bob, where is he?"

"Dunno," Koller said, munching on the last bit of a doughnut.

"What do mean you don't know? We're on in a matter of minutes. Have you seen him at *all* since the conference began?"

"Nope."

"Damn."

"We gave up worrying about this kind of thing a few months after he started at Brown. Unproductive. He'll show. And if by chance he doesn't, he'll sweet-talk you anyway. And what can you do? We don't like to even consider ticking him off. He's a franchise, as they say."

"You've been very helpful," Renear said.

Jeff Renear was heading for the program coordinator to request a change of schedule when he saw Alex enter down the hall. Renear ran down to meet him.

"Alex, you're late, and . . . and shit, you're dressed in ski clothes."

"Observant. I came by to tell you I'm leaving."

"You're what?"

"Leaving. To ski. I find the whole production insufferable, as always, and consequently I'm leaving."

"You aren't serious."

"I most certainly am. My skis are strapped on the Landcruiser, raring to go."

"There's no snow."

"Killington's open."

"What, the very top?"

"Yep. I'll take it."

"For God's sake, Alex."

"Calm down, Jeff."

"What about Reitman?"

"What about him?"

"Well, shit, Alex, the man's bankrolled this whole expensive escapade, and now you're just going to walk out on him? I don't think he'll take it well, my friend."

"*You* can do the presentation."

"Christ, Alex, we did the bloody thing *together*. You deserve more than half the credit."

"True. But that doesn't mean I can't leave. I'm on the rebound, you know. It's over with Akiko. No more weekends in Japan. And I'm thinking American now. Only the walls of this building, my friend, separate me from the glowing cheeks of Dartmouth girls, and from the skintight Bogner-wrapped bodies of female racers."

"What we've accomplished can't be exaggerated," Renear said, growing desperate.

"I agree," Alex responded. "But that shouldn't stop me from leaving. Just look around you. We do this stuff for the thrill, for the high of scientific discovery. That puts us out of communion with almost everybody here. For them it's a purely social thing, a kind of cerebral cocktail party."

Jeff sympathized with Nelsen's appraisal. He too realized that for many of the participants there was an earthy undercurrent more important than science and technology: booze, gossip, and sex of a most awkward and indiscreet sort. The paucity of departmental travel money, as always, had provided an excuse for failing to take spouses along, and many were "single" for a weekend, and available. A number of the intelligentsia, at such conferences, acted with the bacchanalian fervor of college freshmen suddenly free from mom and dad. Alex, Jeff knew, had an explanatory thesis for the phenomenon: Nelsen believed, perhaps uncharitably, but nonetheless reasonably, that the carnal abandon seen at such conferences could be traced to the rather repressed history of the typical academic, that many a professor, after receiving tenure, began to enter into childhood, their affinity for chess and books, and their aversion for games, having caused them to miss the childhood normally scheduled for the early years of life. Jeff, looking around, had to admit that his friend had a point. Flirtation peppered with science. It wasn't science peppered with flirtation.

Alex put a hand on Renear's shoulder. "Look, it's not just them. It's me. It's the tedium again. When it sets in, it's like running into a wall. I've been working on the code that runs your beast for two friggin' months, Jeff. And during that time I don't think I've slept for more than two hours at a stretch. A little skiing, maybe a 5.10 climb, and then I'll be back in business."

"Look," Jeff pleaded, "she's almost done, Alex. We're next, everything's set up, and you know as well as I do that the presentation needn't be long at all."

A mustachioed woman with frighteningly wild hair and wrinkled attire finally finished talking about the networking of supercomputers. Alex glanced at his watch and calculated: Five minutes till I begin, talk'll run half an hour, with the Landcruiser hauling, maybe as little as forty-five minutes to Killington's Upper Lodge, ticket, strap 'em on, probably no lines to speak of . . . skiing in ninety minutes. The result of the calculation cheered Nelsen appreciably.

"Okay," Alex said. "I'll do it."

Professor Alexander Nelsen, in CB ski pants, walked down to the podium, threw a switch which pulled back curtains to reveal his demo setup, and began:

"Recall with me the spaghetti computer, ladies and gentlemen." Alex picked a clump of spaghetti off the table in front of him. "Let's say you want to sort *n* jumbled numbers, you want to arrange them in order, from largest to smallest. So you choose two of the numbers, compare them, and put the smaller number first. Now you pick up a third, compare it to the first two, and place it either in between or at one of the ends. And then you iterate the procedure, the basic operation being one of comparison. Nothing new. And as most of you will remember from your undergrad days, *n*log*n* comparisons are required to sort *n* numbers, which of course gives us a growth function beyond the linear; consequently, if the number of numbers is quite large, the most powerful of our supercomputers will be paralyzed. But now consider the spaghetti computer in my hand. Let's say I want to sort ten jumbled numbers. What I do first is trim each noodle so that each represents a number from one to ten." Nelsen, using a knife, cut the strings of pasta in the manner he described. "Now, the longest noodle represents the number ten, the smallest represents the number one, the second-smallest number two, and so on. Cutting the pieces in this way has required a time proportional to ten. Next, loosely holding the pieces of spaghetti in one hand, I do this."

Nelsen brought his hand down on the table, thus aligning one end of all the pieces of spaghetti.

"And now, to achieve our sorting, simply remove the longest piece, and then the longest remaining piece, et cetera; and each time a piece is removed, its corresponding number is recorded. This second stage of our procedure is of course a set of operations linear in *n*. And so, overall, the entire sorting operation on our spaghetti computer violates the *n*log*n* computational bound on sorting for sequential machines.

"Enough review.

"What gives rise to the demo I'm about to present is the fact that Jeff Renear's company, Neuron Data, has built a machine, the Neurocube, that is the incarnation of the analog logic hinted at by our spaghetti computer. Jeff, will you be so kind as to rise and take a bow?"

Renear, blushing, did so with sheepish rapidity.

"Now," Alex said, "let's get down to business. Take the Traveling Salesman Problem. You own a company— say, you sell widgets. You have a traveling salesman, and you want him to peddle your widgets in thirty cities, not an unreasonably large number. You of course want your salesman to be efficient. He has to hit all the cities, but his itinerary must take him on the shortest distance possible. So, for example, you don't send him to L.A., back to New York, and then to San Fran; instead you tell him to bop over from L.A. to San Fran, and *then* back to New York. But what general procedure, what *algorithm*, can you give your traveling salesman so as to ensure that he *always* takes the shortest itinerary? The answer seems obvious: compute and compare the distance of each possible itinerary, and take the shortest one. Seems simple enough. One small hitch, though. If there are thirty cities, there are twenty-nine factorial itineraries, and that's larger than ten to the thirtieth power. A rather large number. There have been fewer than 10 to the eighteenth seconds since the beginning of the universe. Even if we could examine a billion itineraries per second, the required time for completing this calculation on any ordinary parallel machine, using this "brute force" approach, would be more than a billion human lifetimes. In short, you, company president, are screwed."

The audience stirred a bit—dropped some chatter about plans for tonight's debauchery. Hardly anyone was dozing, and no one was doodling, which was highly unusual. Alex had managed to spark an uncharacteristic attentiveness in his audience. Not because of what he had said about the spaghetti computer or the Traveling Salesman Problem, which computer-science undergraduates are familiar with, but because no one could imagine where he was going with such elementary topics.

"Now," continued Alex, "if I presented you with a

map showing a number of cities, and asked you to pick the shortest itinerary, would *you* resort to charting out and measuring each one? Hardly. Some routes would be ruled out immediately, because, looking at the map, without getting out a ruler, you could intuit that they were untenable. What would happen if we could move the processing in your brain onto a machine? This is the question that catalyzed our project.

"All of this, of course, brings us to a question—one of the immemorial questions at the heart of our field. As all of you know, if it's possible to get a computer to solve the Traveling Salesman Problem in realistic time, then other, similar problems, thought for decades to also be intractable, will *also* be solvable in realistic time by a machine. Unfortunately, the Traveling Salesman has itself resisted quite a few decades of intense research. At least when standard machines have been deployed."

The audience began to buzz. Squabbles broke out. Some snickered derisively, some sat in silent disbelief, some hurled insults, some simply sat in quiet anticipation. A few believed the Traveling Salesman to be solvable. Most believed it unsolvable, like squaring the circle. But nearly everyone realized that cards *were* about to be laid on the table, that this bold soul was about to claim that the Traveling Salesman *could* be solved in a realistic amount of time.

"Jeff and I approach the problem from two sides: his massively neural architecture gives us a quantum leap in speed, and the ability to represent the itineraries in maplike analog fashion. And my algorithm puts us over the hump."

A few skeptics were now thinking: Christ, maybe the damn thing *is* solvable.

Alex smiled, and he affectionately patted the Neurocube on the demo table. It was a rather small thing: a shiny black cube, footprint of the average personal computer. Next to it was a larger machine about five feet high. Cognoscenti in the audience made out the signature of the larger machine: a Cray 4MP. Each machine was connected to a monitor.

Alex called for the lights to be turned off; they went out, and the only illumination came from the computer screens. There followed a brief but pregnant silence punctuated only by the muscular hum of the machines firing up.

"Okay," said Alex, "let's have some fun. I'm going to run these two side by side. I've got a Cray 4MP hooked up to this monitor, and our Neurocube hooked up to the other. We'll start with five hundred cities. Here goes."

Both monitors were projected onto oversize super-resolution screens for the whole audience to see. On both shone a map of the United States, a number of the five hundred cities represented by glowing dots.

"The Cray's going to run the algorithm we all know leads to combinatorial explosion: it will measure each itinerary, compare the distances, and declare the shortest. Our machine will do something quite different. Its monitor will give an impressionistic representation of its thought."

Alex punched a key to start the race. The process was, as promised, represented graphically: at first there were five hundred nodes representing the five hundred cities, and arcs between them lit when a distance between two nodes was being considered by the machine. At five hundred nodes it was over in a flash on both monitors. At one thousand, however, the Cray supercomputer, priced at a cool five million, was forced to examine all of 10^{1000} itineraries, and consequently it lagged, flashing and flashing arcs, while the neural-network machine finished in an instant. There arose a host of internal exclamations on the faces of the audience; incredulity, amazement, a rush of random emotion surfaced in more than a few muttered curses. At four thousand cities the Cray, its monitor flashing and flashing ponderously, was projected to finish in five years; the neural machine, however, finished in five minutes. The usually staid audience of scientists gasped collectively—a strange *whoosh* of a sound. At five thousand cities, declared Alex, the Cray would think for ten years; the neural machine would finish, stated its creator, by the end of the conference.

It had all started with the Connection Machine, which came to light early in Reagan's second term. Within two months the Reagan administration called for a national push in the direction of neural computing. Within three months IBM made an instant multimillionaire out of a former Cray scientist who dreamed of mating neural-network architecture with light-based semiconductivity. And then the progression started: the Connection Machine, grandfather of it all, to NASA's Massively Parallel Processor, to ICL's Digital Array Processor, to Intel Corporation's Hypercube, to IBM's RP3, to NYU's Ultracomputer, to Carnegie Mellon's Jonah, and on and on. Until, finally, Neuron Data's Neurocube.

The profundity of Nelsen's presentation wasn't lost on Nickolai *Macka* Vanderyenko. He hobbled down to the stage. Once there, in a creaking, quavering, elderly voice, he asked Alex if his machine was for sale. Alex smiled, thinking the question a joke. He didn't notice then, as he would later, the utter absence of humor in the other man's eyes.

8

Hurrying

January 17—The Kremlin

Gorbachev agreed to the meeting immediately, without the slightest hesitation, even though no advance notice was given. Domestic strife and economic chaos were shoved onto the back burner. Peter Andreevich Kasakov, after all, was the son of Andreev Ivanovich Kasakov; and the late Andreev Ivanovich stood at the core of a Russian legend roughly equivalent to the American tale of the fearless, iconoclastic, bear-fighting, Indian-killing, government-fixing Davy Crockett. The Soviet Union is a nation which, more so than any other, takes lineage seriously: if the father single-handedly whipped Hitler, the son, it would be assumed, possessed genes of the same fearless sort. Peter Kasakov was thus not a man to be put off. Even the President of the Soviet Union was obliged to see him.

Kasakov walked briskly and confidently into the Alexandrovsky Garden, paid his respects to the grave of the Unknown Soldier, asked his father for strength and cunning of the sort that had stopped the Germans in Kryukuvo, and walked on, in uniform—erect, strong, young. As he passed by the Troitskaya tower he visualized Napoleon's cavalry storming through this gate into the Kremlin.

Never, never again.

Peter arrived at the gate at the base of the Borovitsky tower, entered the Kremlin, made his way to the Arsenal, and Gorbachev's office therein, supported, he felt, by ghosts of heroic martyrs.

He strode boldly into the General Secretary's office. No awe, no reverence, no fear.

"Welcome, comrade," Gorbachev said, his hand outstretched. Kasakov shook—firmly and warmly. "My sympathy on the passing of your father," the President said. "He was truly a Hero of the Soviet Union. When a virile tanker like Andreev Ivanovich succumbs to death, we, who by comparison are mere mortals, feel the grave breathing down our necks."

"Thank you, Comrade President."

The two sat down, Gorbachev ensconced in a plush high-back chair behind a large ornate desk preserved from czarist times. Coffee was served by an aide in civilian dress. The aroma, Kasakov noticed, was wonderful; he suspected Jamaican Blue Mountain. Kasakov, who himself sometimes wore custom clothes as part of his cover when abroad, noted the quality and cost of Mikhail's clothing, which was worn as his globe-trotting uniform: the collar style bespoke Paris-based Lanvin, and, framing the snow-white poplin fabric of the shirt, hung a perfectly fitting charcoal mid-weight twill suit. All in all, Peter thought, the scene encapsulated Gorbachev's era: furniture that seemed to hint at toleration of pre-Marxist times, the MVD no longer serving, perfectly tailored attire, the subtle trappings of wealth, in the form, for example, of delightful coffee. Kasakov had himself long ago learned that austerity isn't a *sine qua non* for a devout Russian. And he knew that the value of class in a world that respects it is inestimable for a secret organization like the GRU—an organization, after all, which seeks to manipulate the world.

"So, Peter Andreevich, what can I do for you?"

"I would like nothing more, Comrade Gorbachev, than to exchange pleasantries and childhood remembrances. But we are both men of diligence, with countless deadlines. So I will cut right to the point, Mikhail Sergeevich. SDI research. Why do you pursue it?"

Peter saw immediately that Mikhail had no intention of answering impulsively; divining the Secretary's position on SDI was going to be far from effortless. Gorbachev scratched pensively at his chin, pushed out his lower lip a bit—pondering.

"An interesting question, Comrade Kasakov. Motive?"

"I am always on the lookout for hypocrisy, Mikhail Sergeevich," Peter said, feigning as much indignation as possible.

"Hypocrisy? Are you insinuating that I—"

"Precisely," Kasakov snapped. "And if you are honest, I'm afraid you must admit that, on the surface anyway, there *is* inconsistency. You are, after all, no longer the loyal Marxist who was my father's lifelong *tovarichka.* There was a purity about you, Mikhail Sergeevich, that he thought could never be erased. But it is very firmly in the past tense: that purity is gone. It used to be an ethical thing for the two of you, correct? He told me you had a Western way—sort of an ancient Greek way, really—of putting it, but it seemed, at the time, to *both* of you, apt: you believed, years back, that Kant's categorical imperative ought to have called for equality, for the realization of every man's potential. To bring about a world in which such potential can be raised from the ashes of a dehumanizing capitalism—that was your imperative. My father's dream never wavered. Yours, however, has. You think in new ways, my friend. Democratic ways. Irenic ways. And in light of these new ways, your backing of SDI seems to me hypocritical."

Something flickered behind Gorbachev's eyes. Peter had, as planned, sparked some defensiveness—defensiveness just intense enough to give rise to some rather uncharacteristic volubility.

"Hypocritical?" Gorbachev said. "Come, now." The General Secretary rose and walked over to the largest window in his Kremlin office. "I am, at bottom, a plain man, Peter Andreevich," Gorbachev said. "Nothing I do is a mystery. I am moved by the obvious. I am but an automaton, driven by the urgency of this moment in history, by the wishes of the people. I react to the times, to the problems—nothing more. You cannot see the things I see from such a window and call my reforms a mystery." The General Secretary raised his eyes and looked out—and sighed under the weight of burdens that would have crushed an ordinary man. "I see poverty, Comrade Colonel. Twenty-eight percent of our population is below the poverty line; there are streets in Moscow that make the Bronx look like the Garden of Eden. Look! Look for yourself! Look and you will see lines—lines as long as ever: for decent bread, for a tiny piece of candy to thrill a youngster, for shoes, for *everything*, my comrade. The gold-backed ruble is turning out to be a nightmare. Our decontrolled economy is thrashing uncontrollably. Inflation is projected to exceed one hundred and twenty percent this year, one-fifty the next. Our deficit is now thirty percent of our GNP, and now that we have entered into genuine global competition, it can no longer be covered by our printing presses. The Japanese are running trucks over us. And smiling their little cocky smiles while doing it. They promised to buy our bonds—but now? Now they flood us with fucking little Toyotas, every one of which ups the deficit. And in the distance, my friend? Look further! In the distance you can see the Azerbaijanis, who don't care a whit for communism, and who in a million years wouldn't give up Islam for the secular religion our demigods offer. And then, to the east, I see the Moscow-hating Estonians, now independent, as desired, but now getting their asses whipped by economies long free and well-oiled. I also still see the Red Army leaving Afghanistan with its tail between its legs, Peter Andreevich, leaving behind how many Afghans hanging in trees? And when I look *real* hard, my friend, I see Stalin's face, his genocide, and Lenin's countless mistakes."

Kasakov could barely hold back an urge to jump up and snap the General Secretary's neck. *You are the one man most responsible for the worsening of our situation. Stalin would crush the Muslims in an instant. He would not whine, as you do. And who the hell was it who brought us capitalism, without thinking through the consequences?*

Kasakov fought back the urge to pounce, kept to the script, and said, calmly, proddingly, "Do you renounce everything in the Motherland's heritage, Mikhail Sergeevich?"

"Hardly. I distinguish between our father and his wayward children. This is a distinction you conservatives fail to make, and it's the main thing separating you from us reformers. Surely the West can understand it: the Christian reverts to the teachings of Christ, and overlooks Alexander Borgia, the Inquisition, and all the atrocities committed in the name of their God. Well, comrade, our messiah is Marx. His children are such idiots as Lenin, Stalin, and even, I daresay, Khrushchev. The children have displayed a remarkable ability for screwing things up, but Marx's ideas are ones I still affirm. The Marxist that your father knew still lives, my friend."

"So, then, Mikhail Sergeevich, what is it that forms the Marxist core of what you're doing? Where exactly is Marx in *glasnost* and *perestroika*? Where is he in the introduction of free-market policies? Where is he, for that matter, in democracy?"

"Remember your hockey days?" the General Secretary asked. "Remember when you gave your entire being to compete, and to win? You were living Marx then, living by a truly communistic code that doesn't lead to purges, and to poverty and corruption, and to the inability to compete internationally."

"Hockey."

Gorbachev nodded.

"Marxism-Leninism, all the writings, all the jargon, all the slogans, everything adds up to hockey. That would be a marvelous reduction," Peter said wryly.

"Work that is utterly demanding and dangerous, yet self-fulfilling. Isn't that what Marx wanted for us?"

Peter nodded. Slowly. He thought of his own life on the ice. Last-second goals, bloody fistfights, victory celebrations. Teeth shattering from a wayward puck. Work and toil, but joy. There came a time when Kasakov was forced to choose: hockey or the GRU. Sport, or his father's life. He chose spying. And now many of his former teammates were migrating to America, where the NHL paid them six-figure salaries. Which from Peter's standpoint had defiled the purity of Soviet ice. But it was an interesting connection: Sport and Communism. Into Gorbachev's warm, comfortable office there came an icy wind, the smell of blades on ice, and the brotherhood of team competition. "I concede it's apt," Kasakov said.

"Gracious of you," the President said.

Peter nodded humorlessly. "And our SDI, Mikhail Sergeevich? How does *it* fit in?"

"You disappoint me," Gorbachev replied. "You don't ask me why we build hundreds of missiles, and fighters at fifty million rubles a shot, and submarines each with sufficient nuclear punch to destroy the world. You find the rationale for these things transparent, while you find it puzzling that I seek to have a Star Wars system? You see nothing odd in building ships and tanks, and other toys that bankrupt us, and *not* building SDI? Such a system would save us billions, would allow for the virtual elimination of our nuclear arsenal. . . ."

Kasakov thought: Ah.

And then: The man is fucking blind to the real beauty of SDI. The best offense is a good defense, Comrade Gorbachev; surely you remember that from your own days as a defenseman.

Gorbachev talked on. *Droned* on, from Peter's perspective. And on. Kasakov was beginning to make out his leader's overall painting; and the GRU spymaster found it quite insane. *The deep tank cuts on the eastern front, the submarines filled with concrete and dropped to the bottom of the sea. Costly toys being put away in preparation for the umbrella to be raised. Lunacy!*

Kasakov was of course creating—minute by minute, alert, ready to improvise—a canvas. And he intended Gorbachev to be just one more stroke upon it. The painting was coming along nicely: the *Starik* had been formed, it seemed Gorbachev would indeed see to it that SDI research remained funded—but then:

". . . However," Gorbachev said, "I am quite prepared to shovel all of SDI into the Baltic, if the Americans cooperate. And I think they just might. I have met Atwood. And he is nothing like his predecessors. They were prudent incrementalists, unable to take seriously the possibility of quick, comprehensive change. In my opinion both felt a certain nostalgia for the cold war. East-West conflict was for them a rock-bottom fact, something that was part of the permanent furniture of the modern world. But Atwood is different. Atwood would like it all to stop: conventional, nuclear, *and* SDI."

What?

"Excuse me, Comrade President?"

"You heard me, Comrade Kasakov," Gorbachev said, his voice suddenly as strong as steel. "I am after peace, above all else. And Atwood shares my vision.

Once he was elected, the Russian monarchy was doomed."

"Monarchy."

"You know *exactly* what I'm talking about, Peter Andreevich. Russian royalty is a thing of the distant past, but the political and military elite is a present-day approximation. You yourself are royalty, Comrade Kasakov, and this is something Marx would have detested. The right blood flows in your veins; you had a Hero of the Soviet Union for a father, and he in turn was sired by a man who fought valiantly for the cause of original socialism. You *all* have privileged fathers, and powerful grandfathers, and so on, often at least back to before the Butcher himself and his contemporaries. Russians have a word for you, Peter Andreevich, they have a word for children of the elite: 'golden.' "

"This is all ethereal rhetoric, Comrade Gorbachev."

"Oh, I don't think so. I think it's becoming plain who the real Marxist is here. Perhaps you are scared, my friend. The people, up till now, have uttered 'golden' not in derisive tones, but reverentially. The common people, *middeli*, who wait on long lines for bread and dress in uniformly drab attire, have hitherto swallowed their resentment. They used to grant the elite their limousines, and country homes, and fine attire—they used to grant these things quite as a subject grants the king a castle. But not anymore. Times have changed. The people brought me back from exile. The people saw to my resurrection. And the people want me to complete my mission. True unadulterated socialism is something I seek to bring back by democratic reform. And you, Comrade Kasakov, are frightened that I will succeed. Perhaps your job, Peter Andreevich, is not as secure as you think it is. There is a plan afoot, you see, that could very well send you spies to unemployment lines."

Gorbachev slid U.S. Secretary of State Orville

Simon's massive *Blueprint for Superpower Disarmament* to the other side of his desk for Peter to see.

Kasakov looked, began to skim an architectonic plan that would, if realized, render old-time spying a superfluity. The final step in the complete dissolution of East-West antipathy. Nuclear weapons trashed. No tanks. No planes. Nothing except a little loose change on the Chinese border.

It's a damn good thing I stopped by.

"It may happen very soon," Gorbachev said. "Not just intermediate range, not just short range, not just troop reductions—but everything. If Atwood is elected, we're talking about a summit in early 1994. And SDI, along with everything else, is on the table. So you see, Peter Andreevich, there is no hypocrisy here."

Peter nodded and smiled as convincingly as possible.

A single unceremonious hug, a pair of kisses to each side of each face. Once outside the office, Peter ran.

GRU Headquarters

Ten minutes later Kasakov and Vanderyenko had the following E-mail discussion:

> I have just recently heard about a most interesting machine, Macka. Something called a Neurocube, with an architecture modeled on the human brain itself. I would love to see one. Yesterday.
>
> Ah, I have seen the prototype. It is indeed a thing of beauty. I'll see what I can do.
>
> I'll come over and see if I can help you dig one up.
>
> I look forward to seeing you, then.

Kasakov grabbed a GRU-owned Antonov An-124 to Paris, and from there hopped on the SST to New York.

Six Hours Later—Manhattan, the Plaza

John never wrote an order down, never forgot a face. You could come into Manhattan on business for the first time, stop by the Plaza for a Scotch, make it back in a year or two, and when you asked for that Scotch again, John would remember your name. He was a bartender—his life was serving drinks, listening, and once in a while talking in a low-key entertaining male-bonding kind of way—but he was a *gifted* bartender. Not only in regard to mixology and its attendant ritual, but also in regard to judging character. Three decades of setting 'em up for the movers and the shakers and you learn how to peg a man's nature from his casual remarks and gestures. Which was why John figured something about the man here now wasn't quite right. The man was Peter Andreevich Kasakov; John knew him as Daniel VanHorn.

Mr. VanHorn was in furs; Mr. VanHorn was rich; Mr. VanHorn was physically beautiful; and Mr. VanHorn traveled—never failed to take the Concorde when he hopped the Atlantic. All the suits were custom: perfect lines, perfects shades of black and gray. Ties of the finest silk. A cologne whose scent was the very essence of monetary substance. Appeared to be from Eastern schools—maybe Williams, or Princeton, apparently someplace sufficiently smart but a good deal more elegant than, say, Columbia or Harvard. All in all, Daniel VanHorn's exterior was utterly ordinary for the Plaza's business crowd. But John thought something was wrong. Peter traveled around the world without anyone suspecting that he was a GRU agent, and there were a lot of counterespionage professionals paid handsomely to see through such covers. But John was the only person that thought something was odd. Of course, John didn't peg Kasakov as a Russian illegal. He simply knew that something was wrong. Something.

It was the TV that did it. Mr. VanHorn was ordinary when interacting—he talked furs with other dealers in the expected way, he flirted with women in the soft subtle highbrow manner John saw men of his class adopting nightly, and when Daniel VanHorn talked to John, he fitted the mold perfectly. But it was the TV. Hardly anyone at the bar, VanHorn'd be there nursing a vodka, and he'd watch the TV. And his reactions were all wrong. John would notice out of the corner of his eye: he'd be wiping glasses, doing some chores, and he'd see VanHorn watching in a subtly schizophrenic way. Like a sitcom, and VanHorn'd laugh or grin at the wrong time. Anything cultured on, and the man was back to smooth Northeastern money and well-educated. But boy, he totally missed the lowbrow zeitgeist. John figured that the low volume and background noise helped get things screwed up. You could hear the dialogue at the bar, but then somebody might sit down and order, or a glass might *ping* against another, and you'd miss the audience laughter wired into the background of the show. And there would be VanHorn: laughing when there wasn't a joke or staring expressionless when a double entendre was dropped.

It was all pretty much sewn up in John's mind when the Russians, in compliance with the latest Soviet-American arms treaty, destroyed some of their own SS-23's. They had CNN on; it was late. Hardly anyone around except for VanHorn. Having a "Stoly" before hitting the sack, or whatever elegant sort of thing they slept on in the rooms John had never even seen. It wasn't a sitcom. Just news. And there was Daniel VanHorn—jaw tense, eyes backlit by a strange powerful light. The footage was of the explosion. The SS-23's were reduced in an instant to a cloud of dust. John found it a happy-enough occasion. He didn't mind in the least that the superpowers were now the best of friends. But there was VanHorn; John stole another look: the fur trader's visage had darkened in a way that John had never seen before. There was an utter blackness, a violent choking hatred—all the more intense because they had overtaken the visage of a smooth wealthy man of exceedingly good fortune.

Man, okay, maybe this ain't a comedy kinda thing, but he's just outright hating, *like it's some sort of horror.*

Kasakov saw, in the CNN report, the masterful brushstrokes of Russia's leader, and a sign of peaceful times ahead. He'd been to see Vanderyenko; plans concerning procurement of the Neurocubes were proceeding nicely.

But fast enough to keep pace with Gorbachev's fucking pacifism?

There was anger. Intense anger. And then, as suddenly as it had come on, it vanished. VanHorn offered to buy John a drink. John hadn't touched a drop of booze in thirty years on the job at the Plaza: he declined. They cut back to the main desk in Atlanta, and VanHorn's face returned to the smooth genial monied manner that was his norm, shook John's hand, flashed a perfect smile, and said he'd see him next time he was in town. John was polite as usual, gave a dapper little bow of the sort that makes the Plaza special. Peter Andreevich left for his room.

Unfortunately, John kept everything to himself. He had looked, he was sure, a murderer in the eye, but he kept it to himself. Keeping a secret was part of his code, part of the reason for his longevity. And he hoped to be here, tending, for another twenty years.

9

Searching

**January 19—National Security Agency,
Fort Meade**

Herbert Light, head down, deep in concentration, one of only a handful left in NSA's vast but spartan cafeteria, was picking patiently through his lunch in search of a piece of edible fowl when Admiral James Buchanan, his own tray in hand, sat down beside the NSA analyst for an unscheduled visit.

"Hello, Herb."

Light looked up.

"Admiral Buchanan! What a pleasant surprise!"

Buchanan smiled his warm, grandfatherly smile. "Has a decade done anything for the cuisine, Herb?"

"You kidding? Take a gander at my teriyaki chicken."

Buchanan scanned the drab slop on Light's plate; an abundance of chicken hair glistened under the cafeteria's lights. "Some things never change," said the Admiral.

Light grunted assent and ingested a slice of desiccated meat.

Buchanan cut into his own entré, a rubberized halibut steak, which, following a habit that went back the full ten years of his stint as Chief of NSA, was drowned in salt and pepper.

"I thought you were retired, Admiral."

"I was."

"Past tense? You're coming back?"

"Maybe."

"Uh-huh. I see. You want to be prepared when you *do* return. So you come knocking for some secrets."

"Never could hide anything from you, Herb. Have you had one of your birds watching me?"

Light smiled, then swallowed a starchy clump of rice pilaf and washed it down with a gulp of his low-fat chocolate milk. They were friends, but the analyst was looking far from voluble.

"Well?" Buchanan said.

"Well what?"

"Listen, Herb, you want a piece of the action I'm about to get into, then maybe you should open up a bit. We see eye to eye; always did. We're not doves."

"Yeah, and we're probably the two loneliest men on the planet. Webster's gonna take 'hawk' out of commission, Admiral. We're relics, you know. Dinosaurs."

"The world is a pendulum, son. Back and forth. You and me—we're on the forth."

"Hmm." Light thought to himself that of all the threadbare dichotomies in life, come hell or high water, communism or no communism, none was more legitimate than hawks versus doves. He negotiated another gulp of milk. "All right, Admiral." Then he paused. Herbert Light was about to do something which was technically illegal, and his demeanor was that of a not-completely-sure daredevil about to embark on the dare. "Well," Light began, his voice lowered, "there's the INF-4 stuff, of course."

Buchanan took a sip of his orange soda and smiled. He felt a warm, soothing wave of self-satisfaction. He'd hand-picked Light fifteen years back. And he'd picked ingeniously.

As director of NSA, Admiral James Buchanan had displayed the recruiting skill of a Big East college basketball coach. He had somehow managed to now and then bring in new blood of the highest caliber, despite being able to offer only paltry salaries; and one such success story had been the signing-up of one Herbert Light. Fresh from Stanford's computer-science department with a doctorate worth its weight in gold in the civilian market, Light had turned down academic and corporate jobs for one he thought would be more exciting. He had worked at NSA during Buchanan's stint as its chief. Buchanan had retired; Light, crow's-feet now, and a paunch, was still in the thick of things.

"INF-4? So what? You got some angle I don't know about?"

"Well, not really. But you know me: paranoid. I didn't trust their X-ray imager. We have the computer images of the contents of railroad cars filing out of the Votkinsk plant, and they're fuzzy. So I took a closer look at their most recent demolition. They took advantage of the hundred-missile limit on elimination by launch, and turned to using the static firing method we used on the U.S. Pershings in Longhorn."

"And?"

"Very interesting footage, Admiral. Classic mushroom, the kind everybody remembers seeing in the file footage on Hiroshima."

"You've become a film director."

Light shrugged. "A man's gotta look on the bright side of things. I *looked*, Admiral. There just wasn't anything to see. There hardly ever is anymore. You realize I spend most my time looking up Pakistan's ass, trying to find out if they have the bomb. I spent the last seven years enhancing the ability of our satellites to spy on Ivan. And technologically speaking I've been successful. But now they use silos for flowerpots, for Christ's sake."

Light was a spy, and spies feed on information the way the rest of humanity feeds on calories. Secrets are their sustenance. And Light was starving.

"Every now and then I pick up a piece of fresh data

that sends a pleasant-enough voyeuristic shiver down my spine, but basically, Admiral, business is pretty damn slow."

Light stabbed another piece of chicken and continued:

"Most of my coworkers look catatonic; the tedium's enough to turn a man insane. We have a slogan round here now, Admiral, one adopted from the op-ed pages: 'It's the end of history.' And I'll tell you, James, I'm beginning to think all this spooky Hegelian stuff is true: there don't seem to be any conflicts anymore. Now that we fried Saddam, we haven't any Hitlers, no Stalins are up and about, and Marx has lost the race. All we have left are the Japs, and they use money, not missiles."

Buchanan decided to restrict himself to the rice pilaf, which was at least chewable. He moved his halibut off to the side, and slid his fork under the rice; then realized that the pilaf was so stiff and sticky that chunks of it could be impaled.

"You're *looking* at the Japs?"

"Shit yeah. You know, uh"—Light lowered his voice—"they have a spaceplane. Bastard takes off like a jet, and bingo, it's in orbit. Just got the prints. Haven't told a soul."

"Okay, Herb, but Ivan. You've got nothing new on the Russkies? Nothing?"

Light, after another sip of chocolate milk, shook his head and echoed: "Nothing. But listen, you want to see the spaceplane? See, I've designed this new computer program. It takes one of our ordinary fuzzy photos, attempts to fill in the details, and outputs a refined photo. It's real neat. The original photo is translated into pixel points in a huge rectangular array. Then the program, in a sense, connects the dots: it adds new pixel points between old ones, following the trend dictated by the old ones. It's kind of like convolution, an algorithm that's been long used in AI for vision systems. So anyway, you can start with a vague jawline, then the program sharpens it, and you've got an identifiable feature. I've nabbed some *spetsnaz* trying to sneak over the Bering Strait for exercise. One call ahead at Tin City and our boys nabbed 'em, sent 'em back to Big Diomede, with their tails between their legs."

"Very impressive," Buchanan said with patent insincerity.

" 'Course the technology not only works for faces: it works for missiles too. And also for an assortment of military aircraft. Hell, I was looking inside the MIG-19 well before Farnborough."

"Really."

"Yep. I'll tell you what, Admiral. I'll keep a vigil for you. Just as long as you get me a piece of the action."

Light shook the Admiral's hand earnestly. Buchanan, having come up empty, and seeing nothing of consequence on Light's horizon, clasped the analyst's hand without vigor, and promised only that their next meeting would be over better food.

Troy, New York

With trembling arms he dropped the last of the Murine onto swollen, bloodshot orbs.

"Jesus, Lou, how long you gone without sleep?" Chief Harry Benoit asked.

"Good question. I'm not rested enough to figure it out."

Detective Lou McNulty hadn't slept for as long as he could remember, and his sleeplessness magnified the brightness of a rising sun. His eyes were on fire. He closed the blinds of a window framing a sea of sun-silvered roofs on RPI's campus.

"I've been talking to Sherlock throughout the night,

and throughout the night before that, and . . . hell, Harry, I'm not sure *how* long I've been talking to the bloody system."

The machine's stamina, of course, was immeasurable. But McNulty, a mere human, had had to scan all the requests and replies, had had to run a hundred errands. And he'd done it all on the strength of caffeine.

"Is it gonna be worth it?" Benoit asked.

"Definitely, Harry. Sherlock's just about ready to give up and leave the case to human intuition. Not a shred of evidence in favor of intentional disappearance has come up. And listen, I can assure you I've been utterly obedient. I've followed the bastard's instructions to the letter. I've sent officer's to every hangout Fred was known to have patronized; via modem, I've checked police departments down to the local level for accidents within a radius of three hundred miles with unidentified victims, hell, I've checked the entire *country* for unidentified bodies fitting Fred's description. And then there were countless other data bases tapped: no rental cars taken by people unaccounted for; the same for flights out of Albany and Springfield. A statement taken from every known friend. A psych profile constructed and inputted."

"And?"

"Nothing," McNulty said, smiling, blinking, moving his eyes to circulate the Murine. "Not a damn thing. The system's fucking stumped, Harry. It's a dream come true. Look," McNulty said, drawing Benoit's attention to the monitor of his SUN workstation, where Sherlock summed up its resignation: "SUBJECT ABDUCTED/PROBABILITY NEAR CERTAIN."

Benoit stooped down to read the text off the screen, straightened up, nodded, smiled, and looked at McNulty, who was himself smiling. "Beautiful, ain't it?" McNulty said.

No food save for an untoasted pop tart now and

then, no sleep save for five-second-long catnaps as his head drooped in front of his machine, no bath or shower, no change of clothes. McNulty lit another cigarette, drew down the nicotine, coughed violently, killed the butt, lit yet another Camel. Three burned in his ashtray simultaneously while his brain worked feverishly; the room was suffocatingly smoke-filled. A masochistic life-style which should have put him in an early grave didn't. John felt great. His heart was inefficient, his lungs made simple stairs a challenge—but John felt great. The computer before him hummed in wonderful paralysis. Another drag. Another cough.

"SUBJECT ABDUCTED/PROBABILITY NEAR CERTAIN." The end of Sherlock's contribution.

Detective John McNulty's constitution was at home in downtown Troy. He smoked like a fiend, dressed in old wrinkled clothes, slept erratically—but John believed, with the fervor of a religious fanatic, in technology. *High* technology. Nearly everyone in Troy did now. As the Chief had recently pointed out to his best detective, Troy went from armpit of the Northeast to rising star in twenty years, and at the center of it all were expert systems and RPI, Rensselaer Polytechnic Institute, the country's oldest technological university. When RPI bloomed, when it set up a two-thousand-acre technology park and filled it to the brim, when it swallowed up dilapidated real estate and restored it, Troy regained a good deal of its former glory. And John saw it all up close. He was a native Trojan—born, raised, and educated in the Hudson River city.

"And now?" the Chief asked.

"You do remember our bargain, Chief."

"Of course. You name it, you got it. This is your case."

McNulty nodded; said, "The docs'll love it, you know. The scientists on the project wanted a challenging test drive for Sherlock, and now they have it."

"You gonna drop him?" Benoit asked.

"Sherlock?"

"Yeah."

"Nope. I'm gonna *use* him. But now I'm the boss. This case'll still be part of the research project. The National Science Foundation's paying half my salary, you know."

"Hmm. Well, what's next?" Chief Benoit asked.

"I've called her in."

"The mother?"

"Yeah." McNulty nodded toward a woman waiting in a chair just outside his office.

"Well, good luck, kid," the Chief said, slapping McNulty on the back good-naturedly.

McNulty nodded, but was already keying in on Mrs. Pattison, whose bearing was the very incarnation of grief: face streaked with recently dried-up tears, tremulous, handkerchief in hand, circles under her eyes, and a general sagging aspect, as if gravity, in the spot underneath her, had somehow intensified.

The minute John had seen her a few minutes back, he'd known he had a case out of the ordinary, something that would stump Sherlock, something he could tackle on his own. He'd been feeling the weight of the tedium for months. Normal hours. Square meals. Utter boredom. Sherlock guiding him invariably to success. Thank-you note after thank-you note; picture after picture. Mostly missing kids, nine times out of ten stolen by a parent who'd lost custody. With enough factual information Sherlock was well-nigh infallible. Most missing persons either wanted to be missing or were children caught in the middle of custody battles. Those who wanted to be lost could always be found: they had favorite places, hideaways, friends to whom they'd dropped hints about their destinations. Children whisked away by parents were harder to locate, but even someone with the resources to create a new identity could be tracked: there was always some data base that Sherlock could use—like start-up bank accounts, new credit cards issued, something. Fleeing parents always turned up sooner or later, and when they did, they and the children they had abducted were usually healthy. But this case was hot. John had sensed the utter authenticity of the woman's anxiety well before he conversed with her. Her face was bloodless and gaunt; she was a genuine victim; someone she knew was gone, *really* gone.

It had started with the report. One glance and he could sense Sherlock's impotence. You could set your watch by Fred Pattison's behavior. Computer operator at RPI. Unmarried. Lived at home. Bit of a loner but well-balanced, happy. And now missing for two days. Wardrobe found intact. Car found in employee parking lot. Never showed for his shift, but the car was outside. *A real case.* McNulty had felt the rush of it like an addict.

Now, with Sherlock finally in a submissive role, John asked the mother in.

Mrs. Pattison waded through the cigarette smoke and sat down amid: smoke as thick as a fog bank; walls covered with pictures of smiling children; books, papers everywhere, half-burying the phone; stray socks and shirts here and there; empty burger cartons from McDonald's. And at the center of the clutter, glowing and humming, McNulty's workstation. The decor seemed not to bother Matilda Pattison in the least. She was beyond tears now, beyond desperate requests to look here and there: she radiated morbid resignation.

"Mrs. Pattison, I—"

"Matt."

McNulty stared blankly.

"Matt. For Matilda. It's what people call me."

"Ah. Well, Matt, we're trying every—"

"You haven't found him."

"It's just a matter—"

"You haven't found him."

"No, we haven't."

"Are you religious, Mr. McNulty?"

"Lou," the Trojan said as softly and as warmly as a tough, hard-boiled, Marloweish man could.

"Are you religious, Lou?"

"I wouldn't say so. No."

"Do you have kids?"

"No."

"A wife?"

"No."

"I see. Well, I have my doubts."

McNulty had expected the ordinary depression, the ordinary reluctance to talk, and had expected to dispense the ordinary commiseration. But Matt didn't fit the mold at all.

"Doubts," the detective echoed.

"Yes. I have one son, Lou. One. My husband died when Fred was two. I raised him alone, struggling. Head after head. See these hands?" Matt raised her hands for McNulty's inspection: they were rough, callused, discolored. "Hairdressing, sir."

"Ah."

"So one of my friends from Loudonville, Helen, she says Fred was an ambassador, and all ambassadors get called home eventually, and God called Fred home. You think he's dead, I said. And Helen just looks at me with this . . . this . . . excuse me, this *fucking* pity, and touches my shoulder. The Lord giveth and the Lord taketh, she whispers. Well I don't know if I'm buying it anymore. I have doubts now, Lou."

McNulty was not particularly excited about descending into theological antinomies, but he figured the woman had a right to talk.

"I see," the detective said.

"As well as you can, given that you're childless and . . . and . . ."

"A heathen," McNulty volunteered, smiling. He was unshaven, his hair was uncombed, but McNulty's smile was a winning, masculine one. It broke the ice: Matt smiled back.

"Know what I think, Matt?"

Matilda Pattison shook her head.

"I think the Man has a plan, a grand plan, a tapestry, if you will. And if you look at one brushstroke, one patch, well, then you might get the wrong idea. But if you could stand back and see the whole thing, you'd see that everything fits together in beautiful harmony." McNulty paused, stubbed out his Camel. "You know what else I think, Matt? I think your Fred is alive and kicking."

"How can you know?" she asked.

"I know because *God* didn't take him; an ordinary mortal did."

"Who?"

"I don't know. Yet."

"Do you have any . . . any . . . ?"

"Leads? No. No leads. But that's why you're here, Mrs. Patt . . . Matt. Now that we know he's been taken, things are easier."

"How is that?" she asked.

"Well, from this point there are two main branches. Either a drifter took him, someone without any ties, or someone took him in premeditated fashion. I think it's safe to rule out the first branch. Fred wasn't a professional wrestler, but he wasn't small either. Drifters up to no good almost invariably target those they can handle physically if it comes to that, usually young women."

"I see."

"So we're left with premeditated kidnapping. And the nice thing about this crime is that it always has a motive. It's about as rational a crime as you get."

"But why would anyone kidnap Fred?" Mrs. Pattison asked.

"Well," McNulty said, "you're not a rich family. No insult intended, but it's not like somebody would take Fred and demand a million in cash or anything. So the motive clearly isn't monetary."

McNulty was thinking on his feet and enjoying it. This was pretty much what he lived for. He lit another Camel, took a deep drag, coughed violently but enjoyably, and placed a cigarette next to four still-burning ones in his ashtray.

"Which leaves Fred himself," John said. "Fred would have to be the prize, he'd have to be the thing of value. Which brings us to the question, Mrs. Pattison, of what Fred did at RPI."

"He fixed computers."

"What kind?"

"Oh, uh, he used to work for the company that made them, out in California. Neuron Data. He took a job here in Troy to be near me."

"And the computer itself?"

"Oh, a . . . something about the brain. He talked about it all the time, a . . . a *Neurocube.* Yes, a Neurocube. Fred helped build them."

What a fucking tragedy. She ain't rich, ain't all that educated. Sends her kid to school. Probably struggled to do it. He's smart, maybe even brilliant, builds computers I haven't even heard of, comes back to be near his mother, and shit, he disappears.

"This Neurocube was something special?" McNulty asked.

"Yes, from the way Fred described it, I would say so."

"What *made* it new?"

"I'm not sure. Maybe you should ask the people he worked with at RPI."

McNulty smiled. "That's *exactly* what I need to do." Then he said he'd be in touch, said good-bye, and said he *would* find Fred. In seconds NcNulty was running from the Hudson up the hill to RPI, coughing up phlegm all along the way. Within minutes he was talking to Ronald Maherty, chairman of computer science, and he once again heard the magic word: *Neurocube.*

"Fred was the best," Maherty said. "I mean, hell, he helped *build* the things, out at Neuron Data. Getting him to come here was a steal, if I do say so myself. These Neurocubes are delicate and arcane little bastards. When they crash, you don't just call in the Maytag man. Without someone like Fred, they're worthless."

"Who would want someone like Fred badly enough to kidnap him?" McNulty asked.

"No one, as far as I know. There aren't many of these machines, and those who have them have the resources necessary to fly people in from Neuron Data or to train their own operators. We're talking MIT, Stanford, Brown, and perhaps something like the NSA. These folks don't *need* to steal."

Lou thanked Maherty and, wheezing, jogged back down the hill to headquarters, stopping twice to pump eyedrops into his sleepless, bloodshot eyes. He was numb from lack of sleep. His vision, despite the drops, was blurry. His stomach was empty and ached. But the question of who *would* need to steal Fred would keep McNulty from sleep and food for quite a while to come.

10

Procurement

January 21—The Boston Area

A Stone's Throw from Logan Airport, 11:00 P.M. The safe house was safe, but it was not much to Peter Kasakov's liking. First there was the noise—jets roaring in and out of nearby Logan. Then there was the neighborhood, which seemed to be composed, down to a person, of ill-kempt, shouting, stereo-blasting, party-throwing, potbellied ethnic Americans. Kasakov, dressed in a T-shirt and jeans, pulled out a Swanson Hungryman Salisbury Steak TV dinner from the freezer, slid it in the oven, turned on the power, pulled out some vodka, flicked on the television, and began to wait.

A tour through the cable channels left the Great Russian mightily unimpressed. He settled on the Discovery Channel: a documentary about Hawaii. He took a sip of the Stolichnaya, and looked at his watch.

They were due back in less than an hour.

The narrator's voice was now and then drowned out by screams from the nearby cottage, where domestic violence was evidently in full swing.

Kasakov thought of calling the police, but then laughed at the utter idiocy of the idea.

Worcester, 11:05 P.M. The new dispatcher, Dick O'Ryan thought, was a damn cold fish, could pass for a bloody robot, said Dick to himself. This dispatcher,

Billy Joe Dupree, had just presented Dick with orders to deliver some cargo to MIT's Center for Artificial Intelligence: it was past eleven o'clock, about five degrees outside, and Billy Joe issued the request in a dull, Southern-accented monotone.

You're so fucking suave, eh, Dupree? O'Ryan thought. *So fucking suave in here, all toasty, sending us out into air colder than a witch's tit.*

Dick O'Ryan and his partner, Bruno, cursed the order. It was cold—too cold to drive to MIT to deliver four boxes which, they both reasoned, could wait till morning to be moved. But the order was there and it was their job, and it was no small consolation that at this time of night no one would bother them when they warmed themselves along the way with some Jack Daniel's. The two men looked at the shipping papers, let the scanner do its thing. It checked out, they loaded the four boxes into their white Jet Express-emblazoned van, and screamed off rather angrily. By the time they reached the Charles River the van was weaving slightly and the whiskey had warmed them nicely. The task became tolerable.

Center for Artificial Intelligence, MIT, Cambridge, 11:10 P.M. Joe Quillian, janitor, was, all in all, a decent man. With some idiosyncrasies. Such as a love of crime- and firefighting. He had a Radio Shack scanner; carried one, in fact, a portable one, on the job. He loved to listen to cops talk about break-ins and holdups and robberies. Deep down, though he didn't realize it, his passion for eavesdropping was a substitute for his holding a mop rather than a gun. It was as simple as that. Joe Quillian would have jumped at the chance to be on the talking end of the emergency calls.

Interstate 93, Heading into Boston, 11:15 P.M. Dolly Parton was pouting lyrically about a cowboy with painted-on blue jeans.

"I hate that country shit, Bruno. I fucking *hate* it." Dick O'Ryan crooned abrasively: " 'My old ladeeee's left me, and I ain't gaaat a dime.' Aaah, it's always the same. It's shit."

"Yeah, and who are you, Arthur Fiddler?"

"Arthur who?"

"Arthur Fiddler."

"Who the hell is Arthur Fiddler?"

Bruno had to think for a while. "An authority, anyway. And *you* sure as hell ain't no authority. We'd have friggin' gospel on if it was up to you."

"Give me some of that, you ignorant son of a bitch," O'Ryan said.

Bruno passed over the whiskey; O'Ryan took a swig, sighed, and said, "Arthur Fiddler, my ass."

Their Jet Express van, sliding erratically across two lanes and a shoulder, rolled on toward MIT.

Cambridge, 11:23 P.M. Their Ford van, heater on full, lights off, idled unobtrusively in a back alley populated only by trash and a lone vagrant huddled among it.

"I'll tell you, comrade, I want one passionately," Malachev said.

"And I don't?" asked Malachev's accomplice, Sergeant Vladimir Alenovich Korchnoi, also of *Spetsnaz*. "Macka says one of these Neurocubes, and that's it: you get a luxurious life of the sort Marx deprecated, but which the Soviet citizen craves."

Malachev laughed.

"Thanks to their security, or *lack* of security," Korchnoi continued, "I may soon enough be relaxing in my Black Sea dacha."

Malachev laughed again, then turned and glanced at their cargo. "A moderately heavy box. Housed in a container measuring four feet in height and three feet square; weighs eighty pounds; and the scanning laser has to verify for inventory purposes the computer code imprinted on the outside of the box. But that's it, comrade. There could be a Siberian tiger inside, for all they know."

The NEC portable phone beeped, Malachev answered, listened for but a second, uttered an "Okay," clicked off the line, and said to his partner, "*Macka* says it's a go. They're on their way."

Korchnoi nodded, clicked on the headlights, threw the Ford into gear, rolled the van into the traffic of Harvard Square, and guided the vehicle toward MIT's Center for Artificial Intelligence.

MIT, 11:26. "You're lost," Bruno said.

"Bull*shit*," O'Ryan responded.

"You've been down this street three times," Bruno pointed out.

"You're drunk. I could drive down fucking Pennsylvania Avenue and you'd think it was this street."

Bruno switched on the radio: Crystal Gayle. Singing about heartbreak.

"Turn that shit off. I can't concentrate."

Bruno obeyed.

"All right," O'Ryan said, "get the Cambridge street map out."

"See?"

"See what?"

"You *are* lost."

Worcester, Jet Express, 11:33. The dispatcher's absence was wreaking havoc. A pile of boxes was growing by the second, heading for the ceiling of corrugated plastic. Some of the drivers, paralyzed, were approaching their boiling points.

"Where the fuck is Dupree?" one of them asked.

"Takin' a leak," another replied.

"For fifteen minutes?"

"All right, a dump, then."

"No dispatcher, no work. Long as he's in there shittin', this stuff piles up."

The door to the can opened up; someone exited, but not Dupree. And it was a one-man rest room.

"He ain't in there."

"I see that, Einstein."

"Why don't you check the lounge? Maybe he's having coffee."

The Jet Express driver did just that, but returned empty-handed. "Nope," he said.

The other driver nodded, rose to look through a window to the parking lot, and announced, "Well, he's gone."

"What do you mean, gone?"

"Gone. Departed. Left. It's English."

"What are you talking about?"

"Dupree's car. It's not here."

Center for AI, 11:39. Another thing about Joe Quillian: the man was a football addict. He didn't miss a game, munchies beside him, beer in hand. He'd played a year for Holy Cross—defensive end—before dropping out, overwhelmed by the academic load. Joe thought the new moving crew must've played in the NFL.

Jesus, they're big and flat-bellied, wonder if any of them played. Aah, they're busy; I'll ask 'em later.

The pair that was the object of Joe's admiration was busy moving boxes to Bay 2.

Yeah, but why should they be moving . . . ?

It was a simple fact of life: those paid to move the boxes weren't as clever as those paid to steal them.

That's it," O'Ryan said triumphantly.

"It's a miracle," Bruno said.

"You know, you're one sarcastic motherfucker."

"You want sarcasm or country?"

* * *

Malachev and Korchnoi, posing as MIT Physical Plant workers, met Bruno and O'Ryan at Bay 3.

"Here," O'Ryan said to Malachev, pointing at an X.

Malachev sighed. O'Ryan handed over the receipt and said, "You boys a tad cold?"

Both officers nodded, blew hot air into cupped hands, and stomped to ostensibly bring feeling back to frozen feet. Neither spoke.

"Here," O'Ryan said, holding out the flask of Jack Daniel's.

Malachev shook his head in declination, and then, smiling, pulled a flask of his own out—and took a swig.

O'Ryan grinned and nodded, then climbed back into his van, where it was warm. And where Kenny Rogers held court.

"Off, Bruno." Bruno obliged. "Any pickups?" O'Ryan asked.

"Radio's dead."

"Dead?"

"Yup."

"Aah, that fucking Dupree. Probably in the lounge sipping coffee."

"Yeah. You know your way out of here, Dick?"

"You're a riot, Bruno, you know that? A regular riot."

Joe the Janitor came over. "Kinda late, ain't it, fellas?"

Malachev and Korchnoi behaved as if Joe Quillian didn't exist. Quillian looked over the pair: big, and fit enough, indeed, to have played in the NFL. They were busy. This time loading the boxes that had just come in, into their van.

Joe tried again: "Kinda late, ain't it?"

Korchnoi looked up, looked Joe in the eyes, but said nothing, and went back to loading the van.

He looked through me, the bastard. Through *me.*

Joe hit one of those fundamental forks of a lifetime. He knew something was fucked up here. Something was very wrong. He had his long flat broom with him; he could have turned and walked away and put it back to mind-my-own-business-don't-get-involved use over the smooth safe floors of the Center for Artificial Intelligence.

But he didn't.

"Uh, men, listen, you know, these boxes just got here. I saw the Jet Express fellas bring 'em in. So why would you be movin' 'em? I mean, wouldn't they be intended for the Center, here?"

Sergeant Vladimir Alenovich Korchnoi, fit enough to have played in the NFL, *spetsnaz*, paused, looked up again at Joe, and said with steel in his voice, "Leave, old man."

"Well, now, sir, I'd like to do that, but this just doesn't add up. I'm afraid I'm gonna have to ask you to show me your authoriz—"

He felt it on his forehead. It was cold. The night was cold, but the steel barrel was colder. And after feeling the sensation on his skin, he felt only paralysis, no pain, as a bullet tore through his brain, exiting through the back of his skull.

"Fool," Korchnoi said, as he helped slide the last of the four boxes into the van.

Malachev, standing on the bay above Joe's body, said, "Messy, Vladimir Alenovich. Very messy."

"You're right," Korchnoi said, looking down. "It was a little bit too far toward his left eye."

The two men laughed, and then, missing not a beat, hopped into their van.

Nickolai Vasilyevich Vanderyenko, the *Macka*, the new cold-as-a-fish Atlanta-bred dispatcher known to his coworkers as Billy Joe Dupree, had simply changed a two to a three on the delivery orders Dick O'Ryan followed in driving to MIT. Malachev and

Korchnoi had secured their dachas by seeing to it that four laser-tagged and appropriately marked cube-shaped boxes measuring three feet square, stuffed with old magazines, and weighing eighty pounds, were waiting at bay number two to be moved inside to the Center by *genuine* MIT Physical Plant workers; and by taking the four Neurocubes for the *Starik.* Within five minutes after Dick O'Ryan pulled out of the Center for Artificial Intelligence at MIT, thirty seconds after Joe the Janitor died on the concrete loading bay, his head lying in a pool of blood, three exuberant men in a Neurocube-filled van marked convincingly as "MIT Physical Plant" had followed. Vodka was flowing in celebration long before they dumped the van, changed to another, unmarked one, and cruised to their safe house near Logan Airport, wherein Daniel VanHorn, having consumed his second Swanson Hungryman dinner and more than enough vodka, and having watched an hour of television nearly as inane as that broadcast in the Motherland, was waiting to fly some "furs" to the Soviet Union.

When Kasakov saw the lights, he peered out. When he saw the boxes, he smiled. When he saw Vanderyenko pull up behind the van and step out, clad in his orange-white-and blue Jet Express uniform, he laughed.

Spying, he thought, is fun.

January 22—San Mateo, California

Harriet Kaminsky's realism was the glue that held her marriage together. She knew her husband's faults, but she accepted them. She stoically played the cards life dealt her; she was patient, she waited, and sometimes she was joyful. Not often, but sometimes. Finding hundreds of betting slips from jai alai, and hidden liquor; enduring lonely nights while Frank bowled and drank with the boys—these things she tolerated, supported by the fact, and it *was* a fact, that Frank made an honest living, put food on the table, and cared for his wife not without some tenderness when, on those special nights, he was sober and clean-shaven.

But Harriet began to worry in earnest when Frank turned generous. He'd brought home roses a number of times, and Godiva chocolates, and Korbel champagne. He encouraged her to buy some new clothes, something he hadn't done in thirty years of marriage. When Harriet asked how they could afford these things on a janitor's salary, Frank said he'd received a raise: Neuron Data had been doing well recently, and they'd decided to spread the profits around. This explanation seemed plausible enough—until Christmas Day. For when Frank gave her tickets to Hawaii, and showed her an itinerary that included luxurious lodging, she knew something was very wrong.

Frank was no spy. She had only to feign gratitude and a complete absence of suspicion until he slipped up. She went to put the groceries in the trunk one day, and there it was. Not a big box, but strangely clean-smelling. Though her hands trembled, she managed to slit the tape with her nails, and she pulled the cardboard open. It was a black plastic-coated cube about the size of their television, with strange receptacles. It didn't take her more than a second to figure out that it was a computer. Even before she saw the Neuron Data insignia she knew: Frank was crooked. Not just another harmless vice. Frank was crooked. Harriet sobbed; tears held back for years gushed out.

Frank came back that night with roses yet again. That the roses were for her, that he still loved her, that he wasn't spending this money in secret on some other woman—these truths overwhelmed her, and it was with joy that she hugged him. Yet it was with sorrow that she kissed him, for she knew he wasn't capable of evading the law forever. He would be caught in this as sure as she'd caught him in a thousand harmless things.

11

Hawks and Doves

January 25—Washington, D.C.

Herbert Light, NSA satellite specialist, took a sip of fresh-squeezed orange juice, thought about the watered-down version he would normally be drinking at this time at Fort Meade, relished the genuine pulp upon his tongue, placed the glass back in its holder on the door of the capacious limousine in which he sat, and said, "So you knew?"

"There were clues, Herb," Admiral James Buchanan responded. "In retrospect it's somewhat of a miracle that the press didn't stumble on any of them. Hell, they came to my house to install an STU-5 a week before the announcement."

The press had failed. Which was unusual. They had dug diligently, and probed, and bribed, and spied—but they had drawn a blank. They had managed to peg a number of other slots in the new administration, but the CIA had thrown them for a loop. Consequently there hadn't been even an inkling of the appointment in the media. Even the Washington *Post*, with moles as deep and mysterious as those possessed by the KGB, had been totally unprepared. Buchanan had been hired quickly and discreetly: a telephoned request to the Admiral from the Commander-in-Chief himself; some friendly banter between the two about Buchanan's "prescience"; an immediate and unequivocal acceptance; and, less than a month later, the inaugural ball at Union Station, where Lillian Buchanan danced and smiled and glowed in the sort of opulence her husband suddenly realized she was somehow prepared by instinct to handle. It was Annapolis again: elegant balls, strong brave men in uniform, and beautiful girls in gowns. Only the uniforms were tuxedos, the men were no longer lean and flat-bellied, and the women spent thousands on evening wear that hid a heaviness in the thighs and buttocks. Lillian, young again, loved it. She turned out in a Dior gown and furs, smiled as in her youth, drank too much champagne, and now and then, dancing, her eyes closed, her head upon her husband's shoulder, she felt herself in the arms of the young and dashing Navy man she had fallen for many years ago. Lillian had an aversion to the cloak-and-dagger world in which her husband moved, but she loved its surface glamour. After eleven years without it, she didn't mind being back in the flow. Not at all.

Buchanan's first day on the job had started in remarkably normal fashion, and this suited the Admiral fine. It was pretty much the same sagging, gentle face he had seen in the mirror; the same sparse white hair (which was to some degree thickening from his blood-pressure medication); the same four stars on his not-very-broad shoulders, and the same wife, a morning person, who was already energetically involved in one of her horticultural projects while he struggled to clear his head of sleep. Standard. And yet Admiral James Buchanan had not yet completely assimilated, intellectually, the fact that he was to be the new President's DCI—Director of Central Intelligence. It was simply too good to be true; even, perhaps, downright miraculous.

The face he saw in the mirror was astonishingly unlike the face of the young man who had taken on U-boats head to head. But deep down the core was still intact; the core of self-control and fearlessness was immutable, ageless. Nearly ten years on the lecture circuit, heckled at Brown and Berkeley, cheered at Yale and Duke; ten years of intermittent testimony on the Hill; ten years of reading the *Sunday Times* front to back, the task spilling into Monday; ten years of golf, his swing shorter each season; ten years of puttering around the house—the lawn, a leaky faucet here and there, some painting.

Ten years on the outside.

But deep down it was still there. Intact.

Buchanan was ready for the job.

The Admiral had done Reagan the favor of helping out the fierce but plodding Casey. But Bush had never even called for so much as the time of day. Two Republican administrations without holding a post. But Atwood, though a Democrat, had called. About more than a consulting job.

Buchanan was a Republican—who'd voted for Nixon, no less. The link, the affinity, the connection between the two—it had to do with brains, not hearts. Randolph Atwood was a tall, elegant, utterly masculine black man who'd played hoop with Bill Bradley at Princeton, when the Tigers had reached the Final Four. He was also the first genuinely educated president since Woodrow Wilson, holding a Ph.D. in political science from Georgetown. Atwood's formula for success in the American political landscape was simple and unbeatable: he blew away other too-strident less-elegant blacks, but of course retained a lock on the minority vote in the general election. He was a conservative Democrat, not a liberal one, not pandering to the fifty or so special-interest groups that drained his party. In the debates, he was unflappable and elegant and wondrously articulate, an impossible match for an opponent who, having only a bachelor's degree and a ten-year background of squawking on the Hill, seemed by comparison to be a high-school dropout. Randolph Atwood, to put it simply, was a genius, a hundred times more cerebral than his two Republican predecessors. And he was also tough. Tough to the point of being brutal. When Atwood wanted to be forceful, he dropped into more colloquial language than that used at Princeton's Eating Clubs; and he used his bulk, all six-foot-six of it; and his fine-tuned bass voice; and he was not averse to placing a large hand upon the shoulder of an adversary or a surly aide—a hand the soft but fractious pressure of which could not be resisted.

All in all, the diminutive, Napoleonic, cerebral Buchanan was a logical choice. But still . . . still, Buchanan didn't know Atwood well at all, had never done him any favors, and indeed, when, quite a few years back, Atwood had himself headed the CIA, Buchanan, as head of the NSA, simply because of a dearth of meaty raw data at the time, had not been particularly helpful. But here he was: preparing, in a chauffer-driven armored limo, a presentation the reaction to which would impact the global geopolitical situation; guards protecting his wife and family round the clock; and heading to the White House to brief the new President just three days after the inauguration.

Career-wise, of course, it was just the thing he'd wanted. The last step up the spook corporate ladder. The Admiral had risen through officer ranks during fifteen years on submarines, to three stars and director of Naval Intelligence, to director of the Defense Intelligence Agency, to director of the NSA—and now finally and unexpectedly to DCI. Though his exterior had been as calm and cool as ever, Buchanan had felt a certain sorrow upon leaving the NSA. It was the people; it was leaving the people that was tough, not the secrets. But now, a decade later, the secrets collected from the myriad listening posts and satellites tied into the NSA would, for the most part, be finding their way to his new desk at Langley. But the people, especially those loyal and tireless students of the

Soviet Union working at Fort Meade—the people he still missed.

At least Herbert Light was here now, in the limo. Light was indispensable. A scientist of the highest caliber. Meticulous. Willing to forgo both a high civilian salary and fame within professional computer-science journals in order to enhance, in secret, the ability of American satellites to spy on the Soviet Union. Light had been Buchanan's eyes at NSA; and Light, though remaining at NSA, would be Buchanan's eyes at CIA. It was friendship and technological necessity, brotherhood and business—all rolled into one. They had an unwritten contract to share everything. They were a team. Had been since Buchanan had recruited the doctorate-holding Light from Stanford's computer-science department.

"The President know what a hell-raiser you are, Admiral?" Light asked, only half-joking.

Buchanan smiled. "There *is* some mystery in the appointment. Randolph and I never really hit it off."

"Same side, James. Fundamentally, anyway."

"True."

"And besides, Atwood chose with his head, not his heart. From that standpoint, you're a logical choice."

Buchanan shrugged slightly, took a sip of coffee, and said, "Maybe."

President Atwood had not made appointments in the usual pattern. No nepotism, no political patronage, no senescent cronies who were owed favors. No horde of old Texas friends descending upon D.C. in cowboy hats and boots. Randolph Atwood's approach harked back to Kennedy's cabinet, which, whatever else its shortcomings, *had* been composed of men who were simply the best and the brightest. Reagan and Bush had assembled a cabinet in the traditional way: the supreme qualification was friendship with the boss. But Atwood hardly knew any of his men personally; he and those who helped him choose knew only that the minds of those to work in and around the White House were first-rate. Buchanan seemed to fit the model perfectly: charming to the Congress, moderate, cautious, utterly knowledgeable about high technology, probably the most experienced intelligence officer west of the Iron Curtain, and smart, very smart. But there was one thing about Buchanan that Atwood didn't bargain for: though he was not emotional like Bill Casey, though he had no OSS old-boy experience fighting the very incarnation of evil in the form of the Nazis, James Buchanan had a creed. He kept it below the surface, beneath his cerebral white-haired professorial grandfatherly demeanor—but it was there. A simple and familiar creed. One that Churchill, Buchanan's hero, had promulgated: Peace through strength. Admiral James Buchanan saw a gathering storm where others saw calm waters; he wanted strength, extreme strength, when others wanted frugality.

"Think they're going to expect our position?" Light asked.

"Probably not. But who cares? I believe it. I think we're right."

"So do I, Admiral."

"You know, Herb, my wife thinks I'm out of step."

"You are, James. The Russkies are angels now. Perfect angels."

Both men laughed. And then turned back to their machines to review and rehearse some more. The limo, black, spotlessly clean, impregnable, wove through dense D.C. traffic on its way down Pennsylvania Avenue.

Three men received Buchanan and Light in the Oval Office: the President, Secretary of State Orville Simon, and Secretary of Defense Allen Newell.

The President sat relaxed and in command, behind a desk made of timbers from HMS *Resolute*.

Simon had the look and bearing of a man operating under the conviction that the world's ills can be solved at civilized parties. He was forty-one, but looked sixty; had a doughish, jowly face. The persistent use of alcohol as a foundation for diplomacy had placed red splotches on his cheeks and nose. And his body was one of utter flaccidity and softness: drooping, fatty breasts, narrow shoulders and a wide paunch, buttocks that hung and swung in his pants like bags of change. But of course Simon was paid to use his brain, not his muscles. And most people in D.C. thought that underneath the rather sickening exterior hummed a brain of peerless quality.

Buchanan, who knew Simon well, did not agree.

Now, Newell—Newell was another story. Newell had a hairless, shiny skull. Wore horn-rimmed glasses. And was anything but flaccid. He seemed to be, rather, solid as a rock. In even violent verbal battle Newell's frame barely moved. Maybe a hand. To underscore a point with a tap of his pencil on a pad. Maybe an eyelid would open and close. But that was about it. When you fought Newell, you fought a computer. He might curse, he might shout, but he would do so looking straight at you, his body frozen in place. Buchanan had often thought that if you sliced Newell open, out would pop a mass of wire and transistors.

Ten minutes into the briefing it was clear what not only the President but also the secretaries of State and Defense wanted to hear: an appraisal from the DCI that allowed for funding cuts to covert agencies. It was that simple. And for Buchanan it was simply unthinkable:

"This is traditionally when they knife you, gentlemen. The more favorable the media's portrayal, the harder they twist the blade."

"Well, Admiral, you can trash tradition," Simon replied. "This is a different world. One running on realism, not some unworkable ideology. As the saying goes: communism turned out to be the shortest road from capitalism to capitalism."

"You have your world, I have mine," Buchanan answered.

"Well, then, maybe your world is a little out of step," Simon declared, his cheeks wiggling. "You've got bloody cutthroat stock exchanges in Shanghai and Budapest. You've got state-owned companies in what's left of the communist East running joint ventures with American multinationals. And you've got Gorbachev back."

"I'm giving you my opinion, based on the best available evidence," Buchanan replied.

"Evidence? I see no evidence here. Hell, even if Gorbachev keeled over today, the changes would last for decades. He's back. And this time there aren't any hard-liners to give him trouble. Hell, Vasputin and his crowd make *Gorby* look like a hard-liner. It's a different world. The only thing the Soviets are up to is bettering their economy. Look, for example, at their openness on their new orbiting reactor," Simon said, gesturing to Allen Newell for support.

Newell picked up the cue, and in doing so confirmed for Buchanan that the whole meeting had been orchestrated by these three men with the objective of cutting the CIA's funding. The Secretary of Defense was a man Buchanan had had occasion to deal with over the past twenty years in D.C., and specifically in the Pentagon; and the Admiral was quite familiar with Newell's breadth of detailed knowledge. There were many stories about Newell that confirmed his herculean command of objective data, one of which involved the time, along with a number of Pentagon officials, he was watching a slide presentation that droned on and on somnolently. Two-thirds of the way through, when nearly everyone was dozing, Newell objected that the current slide, number three hundred in the progression, contradicted slide number seven.

When slide seven was recalled, Newell's claim was confirmed.

"The new reactor to which Secretary Simon has alluded," Newell began, "generates thirty thousand watts of electricity and orbits at an altitude of six hundred miles, which puts it well beyond the reach of any of our projected ASAT weapons. It could have easily been installed without us knowing its full capacity. But yet they told us everything. And do you know *why*? Because they want to sell the technology to *us*, and make a sweet capitalist profit."

"Oh, yeah, you're right, they're a fucking Eastern-bloc General Motors now," Buchanan quipped.

Light couldn't suppress a chuckle in the background. Newell didn't blush, didn't flinch, and didn't smile. A robot.

"Look," Buchanan continued, "let's not get carried away, gentlemen. The Agency has a friggin' stack of complaints about Ivan's brand of capitalism. If space is what you want to talk about, then fine. Sure, the days of international cosmonaut flights based purely on scientific exchange and international goodwill are finished. Their policy now is if you want to fly, buy a ticket. They've taken some French, Austrian, and even some Malaysian chaps up to MIR, and payment for the ride hasn't always been on the up-and-up. Perhaps you are aware of the fact that in negotiating the price of a hop to outer space, the Soviets are open to compromise: if a country has some interesting equipment to put on the station, then they sometimes count this as partial payment."

"And?" Newell prompted.

"And the French, for example, quite often have their equipment returned in a 'broken' state, where it is obvious that the Soviets have unscrewed or X-rayed things. Perhaps you recall that the flyby of Halley's Comet, Vega Venus, was a bloody disaster for the

French. They got back stuff that had been masticated, with wires hanging out."

"Thoroughly unsurprising," Newell said. "Any country with a developing space program will want to learn as much as it can from Western hardware. This kind of story is pretty much par for the course, communists or not. What exactly is it that you dispute?"

"That they've suddenly made the dove their national bird."

"No one's saying they have," Newell said.

"You guys are coming pretty close. Listen, this new job of mine is a dream come true for me, but I'll give it up in a second if the plan was to get a lame-duck DCI. You want somebody to twiddle his thumbs while a country like Iran is turning upside down, then go ask Jimmy Carter for suggestions. From where *I* stand, nothing substantial has changed. They didn't send up the reactor you've alluded to simply to advertise, and they didn't do it as a step towards a reactor-fueled Phobos mission to Mars. You can bet your life that that bird is gonna be looking down on us, telling them, for one thing, exactly where our carrier-battle groups are. And what the hell do you suppose they were going to do with the fourteen HAL prototypes IBM lost the other day in Westchester? Think they were gonna run some finance programs, try to help their economy?"

"That's anecdotal." Orville Simon snickered.

"What do you want, a controlled study? They're still stealing things whenever they can—that's a fact. It's so bad we recently threw in the towel on trying to prevent them from taking high-end workstations. We just couldn't stop them."

"PC's don't win wars, though, do they, Admiral?" Newell said.

"No, but supercomputers might."

"You think they've stolen supercomputers?"

"Think? A Cray 4S, on its way to Cornell. One driver drugged, one killed."

"Conclusive?" Newell asked.

"The KGB doesn't leave fingerprints, Allen."

"Just as I thought. You're not sure."

Buchanan knew that haggling over circumstantial evidence and burden of proof with a stubborn Harvard Law graduate would be fruitless. The Admiral just shook his head.

"So," Newell said, "that's your case: the stealing of some computers."

In silence Buchanan studied his three interlocutors. The President, save for a perfunctory greeting, hadn't spoken yet: he seemed content to watch the machinery he'd put together work. Buchanan looked at Newell and Simon—and, for the first time, he began to feel some genuine anger. The Admiral stretched his legs, took out his .pe, and, without 'ing if anyone objected to his smoking, lit up. He blew smoke directly at Newell. He might as well have rolled up his sleeves and made a fist.

"Gentlemen, with all due respect, the theft of high technology is the least of my worries. I don't really know *what* they do with all the stuff, actually. It wouldn't surprise me if a lot of it just rusts, in light of the fact that it takes some brains to make use of raw computing power. *Other* things worry me, however. I've lived quite serenely for years with full knowledge of SIOP. But I don't sleep as well now despite what you and your kind call 'the new world order.' And much of it is instinct, ineffable, like tracking enemy subs in the dark."

"Instinct," Orville Simon observed. "That's it."

"Ultimately, yes. Instinct," the former submariner said.

"Well, *this*, Admiral Buchanan, is based on objective data." Simon heaved a book-length manuscript onto the table in front of Buchanan. The document landed with a thud. On the cover page, in boldface type, the title: *Blueprint for Superpower Disarmament*; and the author: Orville Simon.

"Two years, Admiral," Simon said. "Two years of solid work. A team of strategists working round the clock. You think Reagan's INF was something? You think Bush put an appreciable dent in ICBM forces? This is *it*. This is the whole thing. Disarmament. The whole fucking peach. Complete . . . nuclear . . . disarmament. It leaves just enough to handle the Saddams of the world. Nothing more."

Buchanan was rarely off-balance, but he was now.

"You're thinking it's a pipe dream, right? Well," Simon said, "Gorbachev knows about it. He's read it. You think his recent pledge of a twenty-eight-percent cut in defense spending and a five-hundred-thousand troop drawdown comes out of the blue? Not at all. That's just page one." Simon gestured to the volume in front of Buchanan.

Buchanan looked at Newell, and at the President. Both were nodding; they'd read it, probably knew it front to back. The Admiral made a decision not to carp: he decided not to mention that even after reducing 500,000 troops Ivan would end up with an active military establishment of about 4.6 million personnel and the world's largest inventory of military hardware.

"The Soviets," Simon continued, "are going to decrease their troops and tanks on the border. To a point where even *you* would be willing to denuclearize."

"You're sure, huh?"

"Very."

"What's the timetable?" Buchanan inquired.

"This doesn't go outside the three of us," President Atwood said. "We're aiming at an American summit sometime around the middle of 1993."

"And we sweep the inconsistencies under the rug?" Buchanan said.

"Inconsistencies?" Simon said.

"Mmm."

"Such as?"

"Well, the Soviet SDI, for one."

"That clunking shit at Sary Shagan?" Newell asked, joining the fray.

Buchanan shook his head.

"That Mesozoic crap down at Dushanbe that Clancy wrote about?" Newell asked.

"Nope."

"Than what?" Newell prodded.

Buchanan took a puff of his pipe and said simply, "Herbert."

Herbert Light was Buchanan's trump card. Though a thin, frail man, nondescript physically, he was luminescent with strength of a mental sort. The NSA's recon satellite guru pulled out three ReconSat photos from his briefcase, walked humbly over to Newell, Simon, and Atwood, and presented the three men with the data. All three were familiar with such photos, and all three were manifestly unimpressed. There was an unspoken but collective shrug, and then Simon said:

"So?"

"It's not as tame as it seems," Light said. "One of our new birds sharpened things up. They're a good deal farther along than we thought."

Simon and Newell had been caught a bit off-guard. It was Randolph Atwood, finally coming to life, who started the probing. "Explain," the President said.

"Lasers, sir. *Monster* lasers."

Newell frowned, thoroughly unimpressed. Atwood, showing the unflinching take-charge attitude that was sometimes hidden by his Ivy League patrician manner, asked for clarification in a voice rather like iron.

Buchanan took the floor again. "Well, Mr. President, let me put it this way. The bird that snapped these photos could be vaporized in an instant by what the Russkies have at Gagarin there."

"Impossible," Newell snorted.

Buchanan took a puff of his pipe, eyed Newell, and again said simply, "Herbert."

"Well," Light began, "the sobering fact is that we don't fly any satellites that are beyond the range of the ground-to-space lasers implied by the specs that can be extrapolated from photos like the ones the three of you now have. The photos are clear enough to show a deuterium-fluoride laser of enormous size."

Buchanan saw it coming, because he'd seen the expression so many times before. Allen Newell was smiling, he was balanced, he'd absorbed his opponent's best blow, and, like a circling vulture, he was about to strike. "You guys are *completely* out of your league," he began. "Herbert here can no doubt *find* these half-hidden lasers—that's his job. And you, James—you can no doubt gather intelligence par excellence. But when you start talking about the Soviet ASAT and SDI capability, you're groping in the dark. First of all, James, let's face it: most of the physicists and computer scientists reporting to the SDIO are uniformly pessimistic about implementing lasers anytime soon. Taking out a satellite from earth is one thing; taking out thousands of missiles by space-based lasers is quite another thing, and a thing everyone agrees is at least more than a decade away. Now, this isn't to say we don't have our dreamers. We do. And ours'll blow the Sovs out of the water. I've known about this Gagarin facility for two years now. And I don't give a flying fuck about some half-ass chemical laser they've got clunking around outside of Kirovobad. The dreamers on both sides have dropped repetitive-pule excimer and oxygen-iodine lasers. And so maybe these snapshots of yours show some progress on the deuterium-fluoride track. But so what? We've got out own chemical ASAT, Miracl, which I guarantee blows the socks off this toy you've found. And we're years ahead. Our free-electron laser is coming along nicely, and this sort of beam is the cream of the crop. I ought to fly you chaps down to White Sands so you can have a look. They've broken into the visible part of the spectrum, and are on the way toward handling the atmospheric propagation effects that impair beam quality. The plan is to take a quantum leap: from primitive patriots to lasers. Your news isn't good news, but it doesn't worry me in the least. I'll admit that we've carved down our SDI push appreciably. I'll even admit that hardly anyone is thinking about Reagan's umbrella now: we're thinking about ways of assuring the survivability of offensive missiles. But even though our goals are more humble, even though the SDI budget has been chopped down, we still hand one billion a year over to the SDIO, for Christ's sake. And the boys we have working at Los Alamos, at Livermore, all across the National Test Bed for SDI—indeed the brains on our payroll at the twenty best universities in America—these dreamers aren't dumb. And even if they *were*, they wouldn't be half as dumb as Ivan's dreamers down at Gagarin."

There was competition in this group, vehement competition. Buchanan and Light, skeptical about Soviet reformation, on one side; Newell and Simon, the believers, on the other; and somewhere in between, the President. But everyone was on the side of America. And so, fundamentally, Buchanan and Light wanted very much to be reassured by Newell's speech. Buchanan himself was pretty much in agreement. Or at least very much *wanted* to agree. He didn't have any data to support the intuition that Newell was overconfident, but he *did* have the intuition, and he was unable to let it go.

Peace through strength. Are these men strong? Buchanan asked internally.

President Randolph Atwood himself wasn't completely reassured. And his reason for not being so was stated simply, in the form of a question to Newell:

"Yes, but what if they manage a breakthrough, Allen?"

"They wouldn't use it," Simon snapped.

The President replied: "The Admiral here says that in the field they're still tough as nails."

"Underlings," Newell said. "This time, Gorbachev is a rock. And Gorbachev is at the top."

"I don't deal with the top," Buchanan said. "You fellows do, but not me. The field is my chessboard, not the negotiating table."

"You're scared, Admiral," Secretary of State Simon said.

Buchanan raised his eyebrows.

"Scared that this plan may work. Complete disarmament would put you spooks out of a job. Things get too friendly, and you won't have anything to do."

The profundity of the situation began to press upon Buchanan like a palpable weight. They *were* considering putting intelligence out of business. It was as simple as that. Churchill had been forgotten.

President Atwood reached across the table, pulled Simon's voluminous *Blueprint for Superpower Disarmament* to him with one of the hands that still palmed basketballs in the White House gym, and said, "James, you're a smart man. I know that. And a man of intuition and instinct. I know that too. I respect your position. So why don't we maintain the status quo for a while? Leave the Company alone? You do have till the summit. And if Gorbachev and I ratify Orville's plan, well, then I guess, save for snooping on amateur upstarts like Iraq, you *would* be out of a job."

12

First Steps

February 2—Moscow

The Volga sagged to the right as the driver turned off the Lomonosov Prospekt. Then it rolled past the antique railings of Moscow State University onto Vernadsky Prospekt, the Sternberg Observatory dome now visible to its passengers, winter having stripped the birch branches bare. Then, left onto University Prospekt, the Volga stretching once more under the centrifugal pull, as if constructed of elastic putty. The driver eased past the university and brought the heavy car to a halt, for there it was: headquarters. Situated so as to facilitate a technological and scientific symbiosis between Russia's best university and her high-tech covert agency, GRU.

The driver got out, was blasted by the biting wind, darted a hand up to keep his hat on his head, circled around, was thrown off-balance by another gust, cursed indeterminately, then cursed again specifically because it hit him that the wind presaged soon-to-arrive knee-deep Moscow snow, and then, with his free hand, he opened the massive rear door of the vehicle. Colonel Peter Andreevich Kasakov, hatless, stepped out of the limousine into the brutal cold without flinching, took a deep breath of air nearly frigid enough to scar his lungs, smiled at his driver, and said:

"Beautiful, isn't it?"

"Oh, yes," the driver said, his eyes tearing.

Kasakov slapped the chauffeur sledgehammer-hard on the back and laughed his bass laugh.

The *Starik*'s leader liked the cold. The colder the better, in fact. When Moscow's winter air was at its fiercest, he was in his element, for then the weather became just another adversary to be conquered, and conquering was what being a Kasakov was all about. He could have pulled his hat down over his ears, or squinted, or ran. But he didn't. He stood still and looked up at the clear icy sky, a stray puff of cloud now and then racing over the glittering golden domes of the Novodevichy Convent; he looked up, his face open to the wind, his thick longish hair streaming back, and said, "Fuck your mother!" Of course, it was only his exposed skin that presented a problem; that which was covered was covered with sable.

Peter gave one last look across the panorama, picked out the shining domes of the Kremlin cathedrals in the distance, renewed his smile, gave his driver another brotherly slap, and headed in.

Kasakov was the last to arrive. Bazakin, Matra, Ignatov, Vanderyenko, and Markov were already seated, and, with the exception of the emotionless Bazakin, they glowed with self-satisfaction—an attitude that wasn't exactly unjustified, for before them, shimmering on their conference table, was an American Neurocube, and an accompanying keyboard. Bazakin, dressed as usual in a black turtleneck, was expressionless and still, as relaxed as a meditating monk; the tips of his fingers were pressed together, and his eyes were charting, in the mental terrain over which he slipped like a leopard, the consequences of a policy he would soon describe for the others. Matra, in her lab coat, frowned, made impatient cracking noises in her neck and spine by moving her chin out and by leaning her head over toward a meaty shoulder. She periodically cast a look of pure aspersion in the direction of Markov, who was busy devouring food quite nauseating to a bodybuilder: potato chips, soda, and more potato chips. The tiny Ignatov—white pen-loaded shirt and tie, his eyes enlarged by his thick lenses, smiling—rubbed his hands together, apparently in anticipation of a succulent feast of high technology. But Vanderyenko was the happiest and proudest, for he, of course, had procured this machine, and had overseen the theft of the other seven that were already in the hands of the *Starik*, sitting patiently in a laboratory down the hall.

Kasakov gave his heavy fur coat to an attendant, who sagged under its weight, took his seat at the head of the table, and moved immediately to the business at hand.

"When we need Vasputin and Yankolov, comrades, we will call on them. At present they are irrelevant; hence their absence."

The four other agents, seated in plush leather high-backed chairs around the black polished granite table, each in front of built-in computer consoles that accessed both GRU's and Moscow State University's mammoth computer systems, nodded. The average age of those in attendance was thirty-three.

"Now," Kasakov said, "I'm afraid that though we don't have a detailed plan, time *is* of the essence. I had my little talk with Gorbachev. I will spare you his incoherent rhetoric about why *demokratizatsiya* is necessary for true Marxism, and tell you simply that if he has his way, and if the Americans cooperate, then I'm afraid, first, that every wizard working on *any* type of SDI research, East *and* West, will be standing in line for bread. And second, since the GRU, following a tradition older than the KGB, exists solely to steal, modify, and build high-tech weaponry, we, in particular, would be, as they say in America, driving taxis."

Kasakov explained about Orville Simon, the American Secretary of State, and his blueprint for complete superpower disarmament. And about the fact that these plans entailed the complete death of SDI research.

Everyone looked at Bazakin, who merely raised his eyebrows slightly. He didn't smile. Bazakin was perhaps the least self-congratulatory man in Russia.

"Are you clairvoyant, Comrade Bazakin?" Kasakov asked with a smile.

"It was logical," the scientist replied evenly. "Merely logical. Bush took office and in a few short weeks Sam's SDI slipped down the priority list. America has a fetish for drugs—for using them, and for combating those who sell them. That's where all the money went. SDI funding dipped from four billion a year under Reagan to less than one billion under Bush. And it seems clear now that Atwood, Simon, and company won't buck the trend."

"Congress wouldn't let them even if they wanted to," Vanderyenko commented.

Bazakin nodded.

"Well," Kasakov said, "on top of this potential funding problem, I'm afraid we have already hit our first substantive obstacle."

Kasakov turned to Vanderyenko and said, "Nickolai Vasilyevich, I'm very disappointed."

Nickolai's visage turned ashen—instantly.

Kasakov nodded to Bazakin, and Bazakin spoke:

"Comrade Vanderyenko is guilty of a rather disheartening oversight, I'm afraid. The Neurocube in front of us shines, my comrades. It even *sounds* quite powerful. But it's a worthless piece of shit."

The disdain in Bazakin's soft, measured voice was like acid. He continued with robotic coldness and precision: "A Neurocube, my comrades, is a massively neural-net machine; and as such it is, in turn, a *parallel* machine, not a sequential machine. In this regard alone it is somewhat like a human brain. A sequential machine executes its instructions one at a time through the CPU. You may think of each execution as a single movement—a single movement of either a zero or a one, placed in or taken out of a box. This picture fails as a metaphor for the creature before us, though." Bazakin nodded in the direction of the pirated Neurocube. "Here we have essentially thousands of processors working together simultaneously, which amounts to thousands of little subcomputers, if you will, working together in parallel. Which is how the brain processes information. Now, we—"

"No, no, no. That's bullshit," Galya Matra exploded. "Some American scientists think these Neurocubes constitute a counterexample to Church's Thesis, the claim that whatever can be done by a machine of *any* sort can be done by a Turing machine. You can't just—"

"A what?" Ignatov interrupted.

"What do you mean a what?" Matra barked.

"A Turing machine. What is a Turing machine?"

"It's the simplest computing device we know of," Matra said. "It's protean, but one version is that of a bunch of shoe boxes, and an arm for moving rocks to and fro between these boxes in accordance with very basic commands, like 'Take one rock out of shoe box *n* and move it to box *m*.' Believe it or not, we know that whatever can be done by a conventional high-speed digital computer can be done by this shoe-box machine. Though of course it may take a good while longer."

"Okay," Ignatov said. "So some people think these Neuro—"

"This is all irrel—" started Bazakin.

"Yeah," Matra broke in, "some Americans believe there are things these Neurocubes can do that are in principle beyond the reach of a Turing machine."

"Very well, Comrade Matra," Bazakin said evenly. "Perhaps it is ill-advised to take a neural network like this and view it as a bunch of ordinary digital computers working in parallel. If you *could*, then I grant you could model these machines on cellular automata. But of course cellular automata can be simulated by Turing machines. And so we wouldn't have anything to challenge Church's Thesis."

Ignatov was squinting; Kasakov, his palm outstretched, was making a motion with his hand that communicated a desire to expedite matters; Matra was frowning rather in the manner of a disgruntled bull.

"I'm simplifying, Comrade Matra," Bazakin said.

"Well, I don't like simplification when it obscures things," Matra opined, shifting her muscular bulk in a chair that was too small for her.

"Viewing a Neurocube as a bunch of many subcomputers doesn't," Bazakin said.

"It certainly does."

Ignatov stepped in, looking up at the others through his thick lenses, and squeakily said: "If I understand what's going on here, I have to ask who the hell *cares* about Church's Thesis? So maybe some Americans think these Neurocubes represent a qualitatively different mode of computation. So what? Who cares if one of these neural networks refutes Church's Thesis? We're just trying to build things. Our demons. We're engineers."

"*You're* an engineer," Matra snapped, blowing air between her teeth to create a sound of utter condescension.

"Oh, my apologies," Ignatov squeaked. "We have a physicist in our presence. Someone from a crowd quite content to speculate idly about twenty or more dimensions when we plebeians live in three. Someone from a crowd which daydreams about Big Bangs and Black Holes and other unprovable horseshit."

Matra reached out, grabbed Ignatov's shirt, the dwarf's glasses fell to the floor, and the amazonian physicist gave every indication that she was going to promptly pulverize the midget.

"Comrades," Bazakin soothed. "Please." Matra and Ignatov were locked in a stare. Presently each frowned at the other as if frowning at a child, and, disengaged now, looked toward Bazakin, who resumed: "Now. *If* we view these Neurocubes as enormous groups of parallelized digital machines, we are left with the point that we have no idea how to tell such a *group* of computers to *do* something."

"*That's* the problem?" Ignatov exclaimed. "I was under the impression that our *main* problem would be the use of novel data structures. Sure, we have a parallel machine; but I would think the salient feature of these Neurocubes would be their analog side. They *directly* represent the world, don't they? In a digital machine the symbols, high-level symbols in languages like PROLOG and LISP, and then low-level symbols, zero and one, in machine code—in a digital machine these symbols, or rather strings of such symbols, come to represent, or *stand for*, things in the external world: numbers, English and Russian expressions, objects, whatever. You can type facts about the world into a digital machine pretty much as declarative sentences, in first-order logic, for example. But in a neural-net machine the internals are perhaps best thought of as allowing for a microscopic *copy* of the world. These Neurocubes are intended to be idealizations of the human brain; and the human brain somehow allows for the manipulation of images. If I ask you to give me directions to your apartment, you are likely to start bringing the route, and landmarks along it, before your mind's eye. And when you do so you sort of create a copy of the world inside your head. I thought this machine was capable of handling such mysterious data structures."

Bazakin nodded. "They are. And you're right, this is a problem, because we have no Russians who understand such analog properties. But the more fundamental problem is simply that we don't have a soul to *program* these Neurocubes. We can't so much as get this beast to add two and two. It is very truly a worthless piece of shit," Bazakin said, looking serenely at the guilty Vanderyenko.

The *Macka* understood completely. He vaguely remembered the presentation that had started the whole thing. *There was something about the guy who wrote the software, wasn't there? If I'd only . . .*

Bazakin continued: "Of course Nickolai did have the sense to procure men to maintain these machines. We are holding one computer engineer at the moment in the States, a man who can handle the hard errors that are bound to come, even with this machine. And Nickolai is attempting to fetch us another. These men know a bit about the operating system, the master 'secretarial' program that organizes things. But unfortunately, we need more than secretaries. Whom do we have to *program* these machines, comrades? Whom do we have to tell them to do the work we want them to do for our SBI? The answer, I'm afraid, is 'No one.' "

It was there; he couldn't deny it. In his stomach, in his chest. Vanderyenko thought he was in serious shit. Maybe gulag kind of shit.

What was the name? What was the goddamned name?

Bazakin was not the least bit uncomfortable with the fact that no Russian wizards could handle Neurocubes. Galya Matra, however, was not beyond a certain nationalistic pride:

"Bazakin, are you telling me that no Soviet scientist can operate this machine?"

"That is *precisely* what I'm telling you, Comrade Matra. Look for yourself. The machine is on right now. You look at it, you who come to us straight from Moscow State University."

Matra moved the machine closer to her chair as if

it were a feather. She looked at the screen—and found what she saw thoroughly unenlightening. She had not expected in the least to find a friendly front end which hid the ugliness of the operating system, but she *had* figured that maybe the front end would be recognizable. It wasn't. Matra reasoned that the system would have been developed for academic research, and she was right in this regard, but what she saw flash back at her after typing in some garbage wasn't reminiscent of UNIX at all. *Shit.* And it was nothing like AIX, nothing like NEXT's IBM-Apple hybrid, nothing even like a Connection Machine—nothing at all familiar. And, Matra reasoned further, if the operating system wasn't familiar, then the programming languages you'd use to tell this damn thing what to do would probably not be descendants of the parallel languages with which she was familiar. So much for the rarefied command Matra had over CAM Forth. Galya frowned, and though it was against her nature to do so, she nodded deferentially at Bazakin and returned her muscular bulk to her seat.

Kasakov now stood, prepared to speak about solutions. It was the usual pattern: there was always the next hurdle, and there had always been the late senior Kasakov to get GRU over it, and now there was the young lion Peter Andreevich Kasakov to surmount hurdles plaguing his own group.

All I need is the fucking name. Am I going senile? Maybe I am. How could I have neglected the software, anyway? They probably won't kill me outright, it'll probably be Siberia, somewhere out in the wasteland, isolated, freezing, a shack, a tiny garden . . .

"The solution, of course, is, in general terms, easy enough," Kasakov said calmly. "Nickolai?"

All eyes turned to Vanderyenko, who appeared to have aged ten years in the past few minutes. His brow glistened. He was muttering feverishly to himself: *I remember the face, for God's sake. Didn't look like a scientist, more like one of our young athletes. What the hell was the name? What was the affiliation—that would suffice. Come on, Nickolai, think!*

"Comrade Vanderyenko, have you anything to say?" Kasakov prodded again.

The mental flash came, and surfaced in Vanderyenko's eyes before he spoke: they lit up for everyone to see. And then he responded breathlessly to Kasakov:

"Al . . . Al . . . Alexander, uh, Alexander . . ."

"Alexander Nelsen," Bazakin interjected. "As one man, he monopolizes the programming of Neurocubes, my comrades."

"You knew?" Vanderyenko gasped.

"Comrade Vanderyenko, you steal things. Perhaps you know the great jewel thieves in the world. I am a scientist. And the scientific world knew of Nelsen well before the presentation you so fortuitously attended."

"I see," Vanderyenko said, rankled by the pressure he had just been needlessly placed under, but accepting it nonetheless.

"Let us initiate recruitment attempts immediately, Nickolai Vasilyevich."

"Recruitment is not a science, Comrade Bazakin. Getting this Nelsen will be easier said than done. If he is as brilliant as you say he is, he might laugh at monetary offers."

"There is money, Nickolai, and there is money," Bazakin said. "A few million might make him think twice."

"I doubt it," Vanderyenko said.

"And why is that?" Bazakin asked.

"Well, it's a pattern. As you have just kindly pointed out, I'm no scientist, but I *do* have data of my own. GRU and KGB almost never manage to recruit those who already have a great deal of money. We have great success, of course, with the Walkers of this world—but these are men who yearn for a lifestyle they simply cannot obtain legally. Nelsen no doubt lives exactly as he wishes to."

Bazakin, though rarely wrong, knew when he was, and he was now. He nodded to Vanderyenko, and stood corrected.

"Well, then," Ignatov said, "what *will* it take to get this Nelsen?"

"I think," Kasakov said, "that we should at any rate *start* with money. Comrade Vanderyenko is correct, but while it's not a truism that every man has his price, it is *generally* true. What if we start with five million American dollars? I don't care how much of a genius the guy is, five million is a lot of money."

"I'm telling you," Vanderyenko said, "forget it."

"I would jump through *hoops* for five million," Matra said. "We've got to at least give it a shot."

"I suppose there's no harm in trying," Vanderyenko conceded. "But suppose he refuses?"

"There's six, seven, eight," Kasakov said.

"But at some point," Vanderyenko commented, "you've got to think about—"

"A different currency?" Kasakov interrupted. "Of course."

"And that would be?" Matra asked.

Kasakov smiled at the female scientist in a man's body and said, "That would be, first and foremost, sex, my dear."

"No, no, no, Peter Andreevich, come on," Vanderyenko said. "You've got the same problem here as with the money. We've run into it a thousand times. When you're talking about the American grunts, then sure, it works. The marines are always after a little pussy over here, and once in a while you find some old fart who's had a lifelong fantasy about making it with a younger woman. But you're talking about a young American scientist here. Hell, I *saw* the guy. If you threw him into a crowd of our athletes, he wouldn't stand out in the least. And you tell me you're going to get this guy by throwing one of our hardened professionals at him? No way."

"We'll cross this bridge when we come to it. Let us now turn to some of our technical problems. Bazakin?"

"First, let us agree to proceed full speed ahead without the software," Bazakin said, looking at Ignatov and Matra. Matra nodded. Ignatov didn't.

"Comrade Ignatov, do you have a problem with that?"

"No, Comrade Bazakin. But at some point we're going to need—"

"Yes, yes," Bazakin interrupted. "Of *course* we'll eventually need the software. I've just finished pointing that out. The fact remains that we don't have the software yet, and until we *do*, there is work to be done. Do you agree, Comrade Ignatov?"

Dimitry Ignatov murmured assent.

"All right, well," Bazakin continued, "our GRU friends in the space program have assured me that they will cooperate. When and if we can build them, they could move mass quantities of our interceptors into orbit; the Energia alone could bring up thousands. We will certainly have no problem getting demons to MIR, from where, every now and then, our men could drop a tiny piece of what would appear to be either a satellite or a piece of junk. This part promises to be smooth as silk, as the Americans say."

"Then what are the problems?" Matra asked impatiently.

"Well, to start, there is validation, Comrade Matra."

"Look," the mercurial Matra said, pointing a finger at Bazakin, her massive forearm coming to life in the process, "I've had it with your fucking pedantry, Bazakin. What the hell is validation? What kind of talk is that? You want to *test* the system, so *say* that. Don't give me this jargon shit."

"It's the same thing," Bazakin responded evenly.

"The American AI community has traditionally called it 'validation.' I don't care what the hell you call it. You want to call it 'testing,' then fine. At any rate, the problem here can be summed up by way of a simple question: On the assumption that we manage to build our interceptors, how do we know they will work? And of course the answer is, without testing, we *don't.*"

"Well, so then we'll test," Matra said. "What's the problem?"

"We can't test our SBI system in an orthodox way, say, by launching a dummy missile and attempting to take it out upon launch. We don't have the entire military's blessing, but only the fragment controlled by GRU. We can't just phone the Red Army and tell them to set up a simulated launch of an American ICBM."

"But we can test it in other ways," Matra said.

"As you know, we've already tested some primitive demons against commercial aircraft. But eventually we'll need to test in a *realistic* scenario," Bazakin said. "I'm just pointing out that that won't be easy."

"Unless we hire the Americans," Kasakov said.

"Hire the Americans?"

"Oh, just thinking out loud. Sorry. Let's just all keep this problem in mind. We'll cross this bridge when we come to it. Okay?"

The four techno-spies nodded.

"Very well," Kasakov said. "Now, for the last item. In light of what Gorbachev and Atwood are seeking to accomplish, time is of the essence for us—this was mentioned earlier. Well, I believe Bazakin has found a way to accelerate development of our SBI. I'll let him explain."

"At our first meeting out in Zagorsk," Bazakin began, "I pointed out that extravagant versions of SDI are sucking up more money than that allotted the entire GRU." Bazakin pulled out a Prima, tapped it on the table, and lit up with the help of a Japanese lighter that doubled as a four-meg computer. "Now, wouldn't it be nice if we could get some of the money that is going into these profligate laser and particle-beam efforts?"

Bazakin pulled some acrid smoke into his lungs, exhaled through a smile.

"Well, my comrades," he resumed, "if our friend Vanderyenko can provide us with some men, I think we *can* get this money."

"Me?" Vanderyenko said.

"Yes, you, Nickolai Vasilyevich," Kasakov said. "Before my father died, he told me of your link with *spetsnaz*. You have Malachev himself on a string, do you not?"

"That's hyperbolic, Colonel. I have Malachev and his men for operations on American soil, but that's *it*. You know as well as I do that the GRU takes control of *spetsnaz* only in time of war and training exercises. At all other times special forces are controlled by the KGB."

"Fine," Kasakov said. "Then how 'bout a call to Yankolov? Maybe this is the first juncture at which we need his help."

The other four members of the group agreed that making a request of the KGB chief was worth a shot.

"But what would you have *spetsnaz* do, Comrade Bazakin?" Ignatov asked.

"Ah," Bazakin said, "something very simple. I would have them eliminate our competition."

Bazakin explained. It was a black and brilliant plan—but, everyone agreed, it was also, as Bazakin had asserted, simple. Peter was to contact Yankolov within the hour.

13

Clues

February 3—Yale AI Lab, New Haven

They were a helluva lot easier to diagnose before there was any software in the picture. Maybe the 'Cube shoulda been left alone as a net, and not converted to a programmable neural computer. Oh, hell, I don't know. Half the time I'm not sure whether it's a software or hardware problem. Shit, what time is it? Oh well, there goes dinner. Damn. I could kill *that fucking Nelsen. He's programmed all my Neurocubes—every single one, no matter where it is, has his friggin' cryptic signature on it. I have no idea what the code says; hell, nobody but Alex does. Well, let's see here. Let me just trash all the high-level programs, they're all backed up on the other 'Cube. Yeah, okay, get down to bare bones, the operating system, which Fred and I at least have a clue about. Gone, good. Now, let me fire it up again . . . Shit. Nothing. Not a bloody thing. Well, got to look under the hood. Son of a bitch.*

Knock.

Who? Oh, company. Great. I'll never *get out of here.*

There was no reason for the stranger to seek entrance to the lab. He wasn't a faculty member: Jeff Renear, creator of the Neurocube, had been brought in often enough so that he knew every professor in the department, and this was an alien face. The man's age guaranteed that he wasn't a grad student. And he wasn't a visiting scholar, since, Jeff knew, no colloquium was scheduled for the week. Furthermore, he wasn't administrative: Jeff knew every single Yale computing administrator by sight, and this face matched nothing in his memory.

And yet when you live outside the clandestine sphere you are almost invariably unprepared to act decisively on the basis of mere instinct. So Jeff opened the door to the AI lab even though this septuagenarian didn't know the combination to the lock. Instinct prodded him to call security, to refuse entrance to the stranger, to let him stand outside knocking; but the civilized side of Jeff Renear's brain told him that this wafer-thin elderly man with the ludicrously wide and loud tie was harmless.

"I thank you for letting me in," the stranger said.

"What can I do for you, sir?"

"I need to find the department of philosophy," the stranger said while pulling out a crinkled map. "It should be nearby, if I understand this drawing."

First there was a meteoric fall in suspicion: *He's a visitor, all right, but not a visiting computer scientist. A philosopher—that explains the clothes. Philosophers, I suppose, are too concerned with the ethereal to pay attention to fashion.*

"Maybe I can be of assistance. Let me see your map," Jeff said.

As the stranger was handing the piece of paper over, he dropped it, and knelt down on the floor to retrieve it before Jeff could do the poor guy the favor of picking it up.

It was like sleight-of-hand. Jeff was looking right at the guy, indeed right at his hands, and he didn't catch the old man's swift and soft assault. By the time he noticed the bottom of his trouser rising, he felt the tiny prick, and by the time Jeff determined that force was appropriate, Nickolai Vanderyenko was standing by the door, gun in hand and grinning, looking quite a bit younger, waiting for his target to collapse.

There was a fleeting attempt at calculation: *Run? Negotiate? Rush the guy?*

And then Jeff Renear collapsed. He retained consciousness long enough to see the . . .

EMT's?

. . . coming to help him. His last thought was that the men lifting him onto a stretcher were talking quickly and precisely in some foreign language.

Russian?

Troy, New York

It was while he was in the hot tub that his next step struck him like a blinding light. Detective McNulty had come to the health club for his biweekly workout. Somehow he always found himself gravitating to the hot tub—this was quite often his first and last activity. He enjoyed sitting in the tub with a cigarette and a Coke and looking out upon an array of female bodies moving iron and pedaling away on lifecycles. He had little doubt that the instructors at this place, people McNulty posited to be sadists at heart, could gleefully inform him that without raising his pulse to a certain rate there was little point in coming. But despite what they might say, there were women here, shapely women, and they invariably exercised in skintight leotards, and there was the hot tub, into which occasionally slid a near-naked female, and then there was always the steamy shower he took at the end of his "workout"—a shower which, despite the fact that his cardiac output during it was the equivalent of a night's sleep, always left him feeling reinvigorated.

Today in the hot tub it struck him that the disappearance of Fred Pattison was possibly a single event in a *web* of crime, that if someone wanted an engineer to *maintain* a Neurocube, they would have, or at least want, a Neurocube *itself.* The jump from missing persons to missing machines was a link McNulty suddenly saw he had to explore; and it was a link that with Sherlock's help he felt he could begin to chart rapidly. Fortunately he would be in control: *he* would ask the questions and set the tasks; Sherlock would be the slave. It was a continuation of the role reversal McNulty had sought.

The professors had recently been down from RPI for a briefing, and McNulty had told them about the Pattison case, one too difficult for Sherlock to handle alone. They were happy upon hearing this, and encouraged the Troy detective to try to use Sherlock in its new subservient role. And they brought the detective a present: some improvements to the natural language interface that allowed Sherlock to converse with McNulty in a rigid subset of English.

He skipped the steam bath and was back in his office after a fifteen-minute streak in his Subaru.

Please open the Fred Pattison case, Sherlock.

OK.

I want to look at recent theft.

OK. THEFT OF WHAT SORT OF ITEM?

Computer.

WHAT KIND OF COMPUTER, LOU?

What are the possibilities?

AT THE MOST GENERAL LEVEL, THE POSSIBILITIES ARE: SUPER, NEURAL, MAINFRAME, MINI, PERSONAL, AND WORKSTATION.

Neural.

IN WHAT SECTOR?

The entire United States.

OVER WHAT PERIOD OF TIME?

Oh, let's say the last three months.

OK. TEN NEURAL COMPUTERS RECORDED LOST IN THE UNITED STATES OVER THE LAST THREE MONTHS.

Enumerate.

TEN UNKNOWN.

Unknown?

SORRY, LOU. UNABLE TO PARSE.

Tell me something about the ten unknown machines.

TELL YOU WHAT ABOUT THE TEN UNKNOWN MACHINES, LOU?

What kind of machines *were* they?

UNKNOWN, LOU.

Christ. Uh, tell me the names of the ten unknown machines, Sherlock.

SORRY, LOU. THE NAMES OF THE TEN UNKNOWN MACHINES ARE UNKNOWN.

What the hell?

UNRECOGNIZABLE SYNTAX.

Okay, okay, listen. Where and when were the ten unknown machines stolen?

THAT INFORMATION IS UNKNOWN, LOU. SORRY.

If you don't know their names, and you don't know when and where, then how the *fuck* do you know that these ten machines were stolen?

UNRECOGNIZABLE SYNTAX.

All right, all right. Let's see. I need another angle here. Who did Maherty say would have these Neurocubes? Oh, yeah. Have there been any neural computers stolen from the California Institute of Technology during the past three months?

NO.

Have there been any neural computers stolen from Brown University during the past three months?

NO.

Have there been any neural computers stolen from the Massachusetts Institute of Technology over the past three months?

YES.

Bingo. What kind of neural computers were stolen from there?

WHAT KIND OF NEURAL COMPUTERS WERE STOLEN FROM WHERE?

The Massachusetts Institute of Technology.

OK. FOUR UNKNOWN NEURAL COMPUTERS WERE STOLEN FROM MIT.

Got you, you stupid son of a bitch. Find Cambridge PD reports filed over the last three months pertaining to computer theft.

OK. THERE ARE THREE HUNDRED NINETEEN.

Isolate those reports pertaining to theft of computers from MIT.

OK. THERE ARE TEN.

Well, it's worth a shot. Isolate those reports pertaining to theft of unknown computers from MIT.

OK. THERE IS ONE.

Let me see this one report.

NO, LOU.

Open this one report, Sherlock.

THIS REPORT IS INACCESSIBLE, LOU. SORRY.

Big Brother's put up a friggin' wall here. I want to shift to missing persons.

OK, LOU.

Are there missing persons with the same occupational profile as Fred Pattison?

YES. THERE IS ONE.

Enumerate.

JEFF RENEAR, LAST SEEN NEW HAVEN, CONNECTICUT, 2/3/93

Jeff Renear has been missing for only one day?

IS THAT DECLARATIVE OR INQUISITIVE?

Inquisitive.

VERY WELL. AFFIRMATIVE, LOU.

Give me the police report on Renear.

OK: "SUBJECT IS A COMPUTER ENGINEER, PRESIDENT OF NEURON DATA CORPORATION, CALIFORNIA. WAS FLOWN INTO YALE TO SERVICE A COMPUTER OF UNKNOWN TYPE IN THE YALE ARTIFICIAL INTELLIGENCE LAB. BY ALL INDICATIONS RELIABLE AND

NEVER KNOWN TO HAVE DISAPPEARED BEFORE. SUBJECT IS UNMARRIED AND LIVES IN CALIFORNIA. NO OVERT SIGNS OF ABDUCTION AND NO VISIBLE MOTIVE FOR GOING INTO HIDING. HIS RENTAL CAR WAS FOUND IN THE EMPLOYEE PARKING LOT AT YALE, OUTSIDE THE LABORATORY IN WHICH HE WAS WORKING. HIS ABSENCE WAS NOTICED BY WORKERS IN THE AI LAB ON THE MORNING OF 2/4/93, WHO FOUND THE MACHINES RENEAR HAD BEEN WORKING ON GONE, BUT RENEAR'S BRIEFCASE OF TOOLS STILL PRESENT. NO IMMEDIATE LEADS WHATEVER. DETECTIVE DANNY TREBLIANTI, NHPD"

I don't fucking believe it.

UNABLE TO PARSE, LOU.

Sorry.

The call came through to McNulty's phone not more than five minutes after the session with Sherlock ended.

"McNulty here."

"Detective Lou McNulty, of the Troy Police Department?"

"Yeah. Who's this?"

"Agent Moore, Federal Bureau of Investigation."

"Uh-oh.

"Lou, you still there?"

"Uh, yeah, can I help you, Mr. Moore?"

"You're a curious man."

"I'm a detective."

"Missing persons, isn't it?"

"Yeah, that's right," McNulty said.

"Theft an avocation, Lou?"

"Recently, yes."

"Of what sort of item, Lou?"

"Look," McNulty said, "cut the crap. You know damn well what sort of item."

"Nonetheless I'd like to hear it from you, Lou."

"Neurocubes. There. You satisfied?"

Silence.

"You still there, Agent Moore?"

"Yes. It *was* classified, friend."

"Yeah, well, the people are a rather tight link to the machines, Mr. Moore. I don't think it's a coincidence. And it's the first time Sherlock's been tight-lipped."

"Sherlock?"

"Forget it."

"You mean the data bases you've been tapping?"

"Well, Sherlock's more than a data base: he's the guy who *accesses* data bases. It doesn't matter. You gonna open up, or what?"

"You're telling me that some men who work on Neurocubes are missing?"

"*Very* missing."

"And you'd be willing to supply the Bureau with the details?"

"*More* than willing."

"All right. I'll pass your info on. In the meantime, can you keep a secret?"

"Absolutely."

"Good. Then why don't you log back on, Lou."

"I'll do that, Agent Moore."

How many Neurocubes have been stolen in the United States over the past three months, Sherlock?

SEVEN, LOU.

Enumerate.

OK. MASSACHUSETTS INSTITUTE OF TECHNOLOGY: FOUR. UNIVERSITY OF PENNSYLVANIA: ONE. YALE UNIVERSITY: ONE. NEURON DATA CORPORATION, SAN MATEO, CALIFORNIA, ONE.

Give me the police report on the four machines stolen from MIT.

OK: "FRANCES LUNGREN, SECRETARY IN THE CENTER FOR ARTIFICIAL INTELLIGENCE AT MIT, CALLED US ON THE MORNING OF 1/22/93 AFTER SHE OPENED A

BOX THAT WAS SUPPOSED TO HOUSE A COMPUTER (CALLED A 'NEUROCUBE') AND FOUND ONLY OLD MAGAZINES. THESE COMPUTERS WERE SHIPPED TWO DAYS AGO BY NEURON DATA CORPORATION, CALIFORNIA. TELEPHONE INTERVIEWS WITH OFFICIALS AT NEURON DATA DISCLOSED THAT MANY EYEWITNESSES SAW THE MACHINES LOADED IN THE BOXES JUST BEFORE SHIPPING. JET EXPRESS HANDLED THE SHIPPING. OFFICIALS AT JET EXPRESS, WORCESTER, MASS., WERE INTERVIEWED IN PERSON. THE DISPATCHER ON DUTY THE NIGHT THE BOXES WERE SHIPPED HAS SINCE QUIT, AND COULD NOT BE LOCATED. THOSE WHO TRANSPORTED THE COMPUTERS BY TRUCK TO MIT STATED THAT NOTHING UNUSUAL TOOK PLACE. INVENTORY PERSONNEL AT JET EXPRESS STATED THAT LASER SCANNING ON THE BOXES CHECKED OUT PERFECTLY: THE TAGS ON THE BOXES WERE APPARENTLY THE SAME FROM THEIR UNKNOWN POINT OF ORIGIN TO WORCESTER. FURTHERMORE, THESE PEOPLE NOTICED NO EVIDENCE OF TAMPERING. THEY POINTED OUT THAT ANY ATTEMPT TO OPEN SUCH A BOX WOULD ALMOST CERTAINLY RESULT IN THE DESTRUCTION OF THE LASER-READABLE TAG. PHYSICAL PLANT WORKERS AT MIT SHOWED UP TO CARRY THE FOUR BOXES FROM A LOADING BAY TO THE DEPARTMENT OF COMPUTER SCIENCE JUST AFTER THE JET EXPRESS TRUCK DEPARTED. THEY NOTICED NOTHING ODD ABOUT THE BOXES—NO SIGNS OF TAMPERING, ETC. ONE OF THEM STATED THAT HE HAD MOVED SUCH A BOX BEFORE, PERHAPS A MONTH EARLIER, AND THAT HE BELIEVED IT HAD BEEN ABOUT THE SAME WEIGHT AS THE ONE HE MOVED ON THIS NIGHT. PHYSICAL PLANT LOCKED THE BOXES IN THE DEPARTMENT OF COMPUTER SCIENCE. NO EVIDENCE OF FORCED ENTRY IN THE DEPARTMENT OVERNIGHT. AFOREMENTIONED FRANCES LUNGREN OPENED THE BOXES THE NEXT DAY. JOE QUILLIAN, A JANITOR IN THE AFOREMENTIONED CENTER, WAS FOUND SHOT TO

DEATH OUTSIDE THE CENTER, ON THE LOADING BAY. IT IS NOT KNOWN WHETHER THIS HOMICIDE IS RELATED TO THE THEFT OF THE COMPUTERS. DETECTIVE MACALASTER, BPD."

Shot to death?

UNRECOGNIZABLE SYNTAX, LOU.

Kennedy Airport, New York.

Jeff Renear was still sufficiently dazed to think that the other man's limb was the limb of a corpse, and that the utter absence of light, the complete darkness, was the atmosphere of hell. Then, as he gradually regained his senses, Jeff thought the most plausible explanation for the body beside him, and the cramped coffinlike enclosure that held them in the blackness, was that he and another man had been buried alive. But then he felt the movement, and then he heard what sounded like voices outside; and then he heard the other guy say:

"What the . . . ?"

He knew, upon hearing the voice, that he was alive, and aboveground. And then it clicked: the voice was familiar.

Jeff said, "Fred? That you?"

"Jeff?"

"Yeah, it's me."

". . . hell's going on, boss?"

"I think, Fred, that someone wants us to fix some broken Neurocubes."

"What? Who?"

"Someone not very nice." The motion of the crate that held the two men registered in Jeff's brain. "And someone very far away."

"How do you know?"

"Listen."

The two computer engineers listened to what, even from where they sat, had to be jet engines.

"Shit," Fred said. "Who, exactly, do you think?"

Jeff thought back to the accent of the men who had lifted him onto the stretcher at Yale. "You speak Russian, Fred?"

PART II

14

Explosions

February 6, 1992—Kirovobad

As ordered, the two *spetsnaz* officers had camped unobtrusively in the thick of the forest, beneath Mount Kyapaz, waiting for inclement weather. Which, even though their prayers were meant to be facetious, had come promptly. Tonight, indeed, it was not only overcast but also snowy; the mist-haloed peak of Kyapaz, which had not long ago towered above them, could no longer be seen. There was no wind; the snow fell in downy sheets, giving rise to a rather poetic hiss around Captains Anatoly Dobrynin and Igor Ivanovich, two solitary hooded figures in the pristine Azerbaijan woodland. Whether Allah had deigned to answer the pleas of heretics or not, the fact was that visibility was absolutely nil. The sentries to be dodged had night-vision scopes, of course, but these devices were for the most part impotent in the face of a snowfall as thick and steady as the present one. Flakes now and then landed upon a nose or cheek of the two officers, who, by the light and warmth of a campfire, were double-checking inventory and synchronizing timers to their watches. The juxtaposition of pretty snowflakes on the faces of men prepared to commit the kind of traitorous act these men were seeking to commit was strangely incongruous, like white on black, or good on evil.

"We are like Nazis, comrade: we obey, but shouldn't."

"Look, it's just the weaponry. Maybe one or two engineers at this time of night. But that's it. And besides, you forget that we are Azerbaijanis, children of Allah, and followers of the late great Ayatollah."

"More like GRU, my friend," Dobrynin said, frowning at his accomplice's attempt at humor. "*They* are our employers."

"Well, maybe they have a damn good reason."

"I'm sure they do. In *their* eyes."

"This is idle talk. We have a job to do; I suggest we get on with it. Are you ready?"

"Yes, and may Allah guide us!" Dobrynin exclaimed, laughing heartily.

The last component checked out; inventory was complete. The explosives, piece by piece, were pocketed away and hidden; compasses were withdrawn. Left by the doomed but still-burning fire were two Korans and a poster of the Ayatollah Abhazia himself.

NSA Headquarters, Fort Meade

Herbert Light downright loved the new all-weather bird. For many reasons.

First, because he loved real-time video. So much so that he sometimes sent the spacecraft looking for things of private, prurient interest. It was amazing how many people frolicked in the great outdoors. He had a number of snapshots in his possession: Scandinavian women bathing together in the nude, French couples making passionate love in the countryside, even a number of amorous couples alone on the open ocean on the deck of solitary sailboats.

But of course it wasn't just these voyeuristic perks; Light's passion for satellite video arose, second, from knowing that the Soviets didn't really believe the Americans *had* the technology. Sure they'd no doubt read the media's speculation about Lacrosse-3, but then again, the media are often one or two generations ahead of practicable technology. Hell, the *Post* had described the stealth fighter before it made it off the CAD screens of Lockheed engineers.

And, finally, Light's enjoyment derived not only from the fact that the Russians apparently refused, quite rationally, to believe the Americans could look down in any kind of weather, day or night. It was also the fact that the *could* look down in any kind of weather. That was in and of itself a thrill. There is something magical about seeing what, by all counts, is invisible. And Light felt the magic. He could see the expression on a face halfway round the globe, at night, while sitting in a room at Fort Meade, looking at a monitor. And there it was, by magic, postcard-perfect on this snowy night: Gagarin, the Kirovobad laser facility. He recognized the faces of the sentries, and even the German shepherds by their sides. He saw, too, the human-canine pairs, on foot, on roving patrol.

A bloody fortress, Light said to himself. *Two guards on every friggin' tower. And . . . let's see . . . three patrols. What do you* really *have in there, Ivan?*

Light studied the screen with a fastidiousness he usually reserved for erotica. Both man and beast out there, in the vortex of a Georgian snowstorm, looked mighty cold. Light, warm and safe, and relishing that fact, took a sip of his coffee. And that's when he saw that a heat source was being picked up outside the perimeter. He looked a bit closer at the screen. *Two humans and a campfire? Out there? What the . . . ?*

Gagarin Complex, Outside Kirovobad

It was supposed to be a cakewalk. But then again, when such men as Dobrynin and Ivanovich are used, and wedded to the sort of technology the two were carrying, there is good *reason* to expect a cakewalk.

It was just that, on this night, *spetsnaz* pitted against KGB, something that could not have been anticipated arrived.

Namely, the patrols.

The Ninth Directorate of the KGB, traditionally entrusted with the task of keeping important installations safe, was a vigilant, innovative group. And they had recently decided to step up protection of the Gagarin ASAT and SDI complex—by supplementing the sentries with roving patrols.

This was something of which Bazakin had not been apprised. And hence it was something for which Dobrynin and Ivanovich was not prepared.

Both men had the blueprints of the facility memorized. Their instructions were to destroy the lasers and the software, and if they had to choose between the two, then the software. The Americans regarded the Soviet penchant for putting everything under one roof to be a serious strategic mistake; and at the moment this penchant was something that promised to make the job of the bombers easier. Everything was here. Including, alas, all the software: all the Battle Management systems, the entire C^3I for the Russian version of a laser-based Star Wars. The simulation system alone had 264,000 lines of painstakingly written and torturously debugged code. The entire software framework for the real thing, the program that managed all Phase-1 hardware, was at 700,000 lines of code, and growing. All the software was housed on the *Macka*-pirated, parallelized Cray 4S, and was backed up and housed at two different ultrasecure locations in the Kirovobad complex. The hardware could always be rebuilt in reasonable time, for the simple reason that a number of engineers had the designs memorized. The software was another story. If lost, it would mean a protracted setback. And without the software, of course, the hardware might as well be a handgun.

Getting past the sentries, because of the weather,

and because they knew how to penetrate the perimeter at a point equidistant from two guard towers, was supposed to be easy, and was supposed to be the first step. And it would have been both. Had it not been for the dogs.

Ivanovich heard it first. A bark he estimated to be not more than fifty yards away.

"Listen."

The sibilance of falling snow. And then—barks.

"Patrols?"

"Hmm."

"The bastard must smell us. Hell, he can't *see* us in this."

"Yeah, and where there's a dog, there's a man."

Dobrynin pulled and cocked his Canadian-made SSK hand cannon.

"Don't be a fool," Ivanovich said. "We have one of two options: run or decoy. We're packing toys compared to the assault rifles the guards have."

"Well, I'm not running," Dobrynin whispered rapidly. "*Spetsnaz never* runs. I'm for decoy, and then hand-to-hand. Shit, they're only KGB."

"All right, I'm in. You lead."

"*I* lead?"

"You're a better actor, Captain Dobrynin."

Dobrynin muttered a curse, but obeyed, and thus—staggering, moaning—led. Toward the bark. Through the falling snow.

Within a few minutes the saboteurs saw the two KGB guards and the two German shepherds.

"Comrades! Help us!" Dobrynin shouted. Ivanovich followed suit with a similar plea. "We left the barracks and lost our way in this horrible storm!" Dobrynin said as he drew up close enough to look into the eyes of the guards, four points of light in hooded darkness.

Their features were concealed under the overhanging hoods, but suspicion was written all over the bearing of the KGB guards. One of them handed over his leash to the other, and then swung his AK-47 into position.

"How could you possibly end up here?" the guard said, with as much genuine incredulity as suspicion in his voice. "This is a helluva long way from the barracks."

"Comrade, we are academicians, not fucking explorers. The snow is blinding. You can't see your hand in front of your face tonight. Look."

Dobrynin put his hand out in front of his face. In it was a knife. Which, to the rifle-toting guard, seemed, at first, odd, rather than dangerous. So there was just a split second of indecision. Which, for a man like Dobrynin, constituted an opening through which he could drive a truck.

Before the guard could swing his rifle around, Dobrynin lunged toward the man and stabbed him through the eye, into the brain. His attack had been by instinct, delivered to the only vulnerable area in a target covered from head to toe by heavy winter clothes, and delivered to the one point that would spell instant immobilization.

Ivanovich simultaneously pulled his pistol and fired three bullets into the hood of the other dog-hampered guard, who, releasing the leashes, went down immediately.

But then there were the dogs.

Who were not sentimental in the least.

They cared not a whit about the death of their masters. They sprang. Both of them at Dobrynin. At his face.

Ivanovich, in a flash, delivered his remaining rounds into the dogs. But the beasts, trained from puppies for situations like the present one, were running on adrenaline. And the *spetsnaz* officer had been forced to aim for their midsections rather than their faces. And so it was quite a few seconds before the attack ended, with Ivanovich kicking the now-sluggish, bleeding hounds off his partner.

And when Ivanovich looked at the face of his companion, he saw that a good part of it was missing. It was a red, pulpy mess.

"Alone," the mangled Dobrynin gasped. "Go it alone. I'll try to get back to camp before you return."

"Can you see?" Ivanovich asked.

With a gloved hand Dobrynin rather haphazardly wiped what was left of his face. One eye emerged from the blood seemingly intact.

"Yes. Now, go. You haven't much time. This patrol will soon be missed."

"Very well, comrade," Ivanovich said. He loaded his companion's explosives into his own pockets.

The lone *spetsnaz* officer headed off through the snow, knowing deep down that his partner's odds were next to nil, but knowing too that the mission was more important than a single life. Which was an attitude he shared with special forces, in the East *and* in the West.

Captain Ivanovich, compass out, headed for a point between the two guard towers—a point toward which he had been heading before the interruption.

He made it past the sentries without a hitch, shielded by the falling blankets of snow.

Getting past the retina scanners, handprint scanners, and voice scanners was next. And it wasn't a trivial task. Nonetheless the solution had been easy enough for Bazakin to conceive. The GRU wizard had seen to it that the computer program underlying the automated "guard" was changed in a slight but potent way: whereas before, the code had essentially expressed the command "If the eye, hand, or voice readings differ from those in memory, deny entrance," it now contained the conditional statement "If the eye, hand, or voice readings differ from those in memory, grant entrance." It had not been difficult at all for

Bazakin to modify the code in this way, nor had it been difficult, after dropping the KGB chief's name, for him to see to it that a new version of the software for the system had been shipped to Gagarin, with the explanation that the old version was, in some esoteric way, bugged. As a result, the scanners waiting for Captain Ivanovich didn't care *who* was trying to gain entrance. Of course, generally, it would be an extremely rare occurrence of someone without authorization to *try* to gain entrance. So the system had been working ostensibly as normal, waiting patiently for Dobrynin and Ivanovich to arrive.

Ivanovich arrived at the main entrance to the laser facility, looking for all the world like he had trudged over from the nearby barracks through the snowstorm. Two assault-rifle-armed KGB guards stood in the foyer next to the computerized sentry.

"All this snow and nothing to do in it, eh, comrades?" the *spetsnaz* officer said to the guards. "No skiing, no sledding. Not even any skating. Just work."

The guards, two rather surly fellows, didn't reciprocate with any pleasantries. Ivanovich responded to his own small talk, however:

"Well, the sooner we get this project up, the sooner we can return to civilization. We engineers are working hard, I can assure you of that."

Ivanovich continued to talk emptily, and, his readings having satisfied the computer, waltzed into the facility. As soon as he cleared the guards, he brought the blueprint before his mind's eye and, without the slightest hesitation, headed, in an unobtrusive but nonetheless brisk walk, for a rest room.

Someone was urinating.

Ivanovich slapped the man on the shoulder. "What a night, eh comrade? You'd think we were in Siberia."

The other man, a civilian engineer, grunted assent. Then occupied himself with finishing the task, without another spill on his shoe.

Ivanovich stepped into a stall, closed and locked it, sat down, and out of the components he was carrying, began to assemble six Semtex-based bombs.

The engineer, after washing his hands and dabbing his shoe with a moistened paper towel, called good night to Ivanovich and left.

Each device was no larger than a cordless telephone and each had an adhesive plate that made quick, unobtrusive placement easy. Within five minutes of Ivanovich's simulated defecation, the Cray 4S and a supporting parallelized IBM 3090 were inching toward death. The two tape backup facilities were living on borrowed time after another five minutes. And after another two minutes the main ASAT laser itself, sitting under a closed observatory-like dome, was serenely sitting on the equivalent of one ton of TNT.

On the way out, Ivanovich was just as friendly as he'd been upon entering, and the guards were just as cold, quiet, and robotic. He thought to himself: *All this glitz and show, and a simple scale would have done the trick. Too bad, gentleman.*

Just as he was leaving, Ivanovich noticed that his boots, upon entering, had left a slight trail of blood upon the floor—canine blood, from kicking the dogs off his partner.

Now, maybe if the KGB was a little nicer they'd notice such things. The *spetsnaz* officer chuckled to himself as he stepped back out into the blizzard.

NSA Headquarters

Before the confrontation there had been no reason to call in a superior. It was an unprecedented scenario, but it didn't conclusively imply foul play, or anything else that would necessitate bothering a colleague. After all, Light reasoned, they could be a couple of guards or maybe even a pair of scientists out for relaxation, or maybe some sort of kinky tryst, or . . . or . . . *Hell, the roasting of marshmallows, for all I know.* But then he saw the pair of strangers meet up with the patrol, and then, upon witnessing the violence, the stabbing, the shooting, the dogs—when he saw this he knew something was wrong, very wrong. He picked up the phone, dialed Jonesie down the hall. Five rings, an eternity; no answer.

Shit, out for a Coke or something. What timing.

Only people like himself were on duty. It was two A.M. No heavies worked the graveyard shift. Only techies like Light, guys without much of a taste for sleep.

What have I seen, for God's sake? Jonesie, where the hell are you?

Light returned to the screen. One of the remaining three had survived, and was still moving out there in the snow. Slowly. Apparently crawling.

Back toward the fire?

Gagarin Complex

"You made it!" Ivanovich said, truly amazed.

No response from Dobrynin, now unconscious. Ivanovich checked the injured man's pulse. Faint and slow, but there.

The *spetsnaz* officer threw his partner over his lap, ignited the engine, clicked on the headlight, saw nothing of the tracks they'd left in coming down from Kyapaz's foothills. Cursing, he pulled out his compass, a pen-size flashlight, which he lodged in his mouth, and a map, which was promptly covered with large, heavy flakes.

NSA Headquarters

Light had seen the other stranger enter the complex. And now the stranger was back. They were *both* back—at the fire; and now there was another heat source: the pair was moving away under power. Given meteorological conditions, and the absence of a road under their vehicle, Light had to assume they were riding a snowmobile. And now things were clearly inexplicable: the pair couldn't be from within Gagarin itself, but must have come from outside. Or perhaps they *were* from the inside, and the snowmobiles had been planted for them.

Who the hell knows?

Light seized the phone and dialed Jonesie again.

"Jones here."

"Listen, Jonesie, I—"

Light was about to inform his colleague of the irregularities he'd witnessed when a good chunk of the Gagarin complex blew up in front of his eyes.

"Jesus H. Christ."

"Light? Light? What is it, man?"

February 7—CIA Headquarters

His tentacular existence in Langley was a thousand times more powerful than what it had been a decade earlier at Fort Meade. The Admiral's arms now reached well beyond SIGINT, well beyond what the hardware could divine of the secret plans of foreign governments: as DCI he not only had machines out there listening but also men, and men who not only listened but also aggressively *stole* information. Ten minutes into a fresh day, his desk, clear at the start, would be filled with the latest data. And today was no different. Indeed today would be the hottest yet encountered. Buchanan had the *Post*, a cup of coffee, had just sat down, and John Ross, NIO for the Soviet Union, burst in with the AP report:

> MOSCOW (AP)—It was confirmed today by TASS, the Soviet news agency, that a "serious explosion" took place yesterday at the Kirovobad laser research facility, known as Gagarin, in the Azerbaijan region of the Soviet Union.
>
> An article in *Pravda*, the Communist party newspaper, carried a brief report of the explosion, noting that "emergency rescue workers managed to heroically extinguish ensuing fires before there was serious loss of life to their comrades."
>
> Though no supporting data have been presented, Soviet officials have already hinted that Abhazia-supporting terrorists in the Azerbaijani region are prime suspects in the crime. Said Stephan Bogadhazh, head of the Kirovobad facility, who happened to be sleeping in the barracks at the time of the explosion: "This monstrous act was carried out in a professional, calculating manner. The nearby community is home to potential terrorists, people with much hatred for the Soviet Union, but much love for Iran."
>
> American officials are as yet not commenting on the disaster.

Buchanan hadn't completely parsed the last sentence of the story when his secretary informed him that Herbert Light was on the phone. Buchanan took the call.

"I assume you know," Light said.

"Yes," Buchanan said.

"Well I saw it on Lacrosse, Admiral. The crime meshed perfectly with the passing of our bird."

"And what did you see?"

"Two men, dark-skinned, at a campfire beyond the

facility's perimeter. They make their way toward the main complex, run into a roving patrol, one man goes down, the other goes inside for a total of ten minutes, and returns to their makeshift camp, to which the injured man has managed to return. Snowmobile fires up; the two get the hell away; and then she blows."

"Interesting."

"Interesting? You realize this is the base of SDI operations. It's conceivable they lost quite a bit. Maybe everything."

The Admiral was silent for a moment, then said, "They may not have lost as much as me."

It had hit Buchanan hard that this new development would weaken his plea for maintaining the CIA's expensive status-quo posture against the Russians. The President had stepped in and had personally given him a stay of execution. Until the summit. He was supposed to be looking for hard data to confirm his hawkish intuitions. And now . . . now things were going in the opposite direction. Buchanan imagined the federal budget shrinking at the expense of the Company. He could already hear the Secretaries of State and Defense: "Ivan no longer *has* an SDI, James. So you can *forget* that angle. And now maybe you can save Uncle Sam some money, eh?"

"Admiral? You still there?"

"Yeah, yeah, thanks, Herb. I understand. Send me your written report ASAP."

"Will do, Admiral."

Buchanan dumped his coffee, which by this time had turned cold, and refreshed his cup. As he was walking back to his seat, William Gundersen, Director of the FBI, called for Buchanan, and the Admiral's secretary assumed that her boss would want to receive the call; she forwarded it in.

"William. What's up?" said Buchanan, settling back into his chair.

"I don't know. You'll have to tell *me.* Remember the Neurocubes?"

"Sure. Have some more been stolen?"

"Nope. But more people *know* they've been stolen."

"Oh?"

"Yeah, in fact, someone figured it out on his own."

"Not the press, I hope."

"No. A Detective Lou McNulty, from Troy, New York."

"And he's gonna keep his mouth shut? I'll tell you, Bill, about all I need now is to have the *Post* tell the American people the CIA can't keep the fastest computers known to man inside the borders of this country."

"Why borders, James?"

"What?"

"You said 'borders.' You think someone's taking 'em out?"

"That's my gut feeling. I wouldn't say it in the Oval Office, but it *is* my intuition. Anyway, Bill, I don't mean to be rude, but fax me the details over the STU system. If it *is* the Russians, they go at this sort of thing relentlessly, Gorbachev or no Gorbachev. It wouldn't surprise me. Now, I do have a lot of—"

"Detective McNulty's put a new spin on this, James. Let me get to the punch line before you get back to saving the free world."

"Sorry, Bill. Shoot."

"McNulty is a missing-persons guy. A genuine techie. Instrumental in getting a number of expert systems up and running in missing persons and kidnapping. He knows his stuff."

"Missing persons? Are you telling me—?"

"Yup. Now, aren't you glad I—?"

"Who?"

"Oh, just two little old engineers, James—from the

company that *built* the Neurocube. One of 'em is the president of the company himself."

"Holy shit."

"That's what *I* said. You think it's Ivan?"

"Oh, yeah, it's Ivan, all right."

15

Demon Dance

February 8, 1993—Tereshkovo Complex

Bazakin, Vanderyenko, and Kasakov were in flight from Yakutsk to the *Starik*'s Tereshkovo complex in a wobbling de Havilland Twin Otter. They were recuperating. Violent Siberian winds had tossed the plane as if it were a toy; only seat belts had prevented heads from smashing against the overhead luggage rack. The turbulence had subsided considerably, but the bush pilot was still not in a talking mood, and there was a sheen of perspiration on his neck. Staying aloft still seemed to demand all his concentration; he worked with his controls in the manner of a surgeon who may at any moment lose the life of the patient upon whom he is operating.

Vanderyenko was pallid. Bazakin and Kasakov, on the other hand, seemed to be enjoying the trip. The noise from the plane's engines filled the cabin, but now and then the passengers conversed in raised voices.

"It's a perfect cover, Comrade Kasakov," Bazakin said over the steady hum of the engines, pointing down toward the monochromatic permafrosted ground one mile below. "There are twenty-three hydroelectric plants under construction on the Yenesei alone. The Americans fully expect us to try to tap the power of our Siberian rivers. After all, just the Angara, if tamed, could provide seventy billion kilowatt hours per year. We fit the pattern nicely. The only difference is that we're on the Lena, in no-man's-land, so far north that every building must be founded upon concrete pillars that plunge twenty feet down into the frozen soil."

Vanderyenko mumbled, "Jesus," and shivered.

"What?" Bazakin said in a voice loud enough to transcend the engine noise.

"Nothing," Vanderyenko said, drawing his coat up around his neck. The *Macka*, looking out his tiny window, was quite sure he would never adjust to the barren, treeless, windswept world of Northern Siberia. He was already homesick for America.

"I'll tell you, comrades," Vanderyenko said, shaking his head, "I can't understand those Russians who want Alaska back. As far as I'm concerned, Seward's America got the raw end of the deal."

Bazakin and Kasakov laughed loudly enough to be heard over the engines.

"The location may be harsh," Bazakin said to Vanderyenko, "but it's what gives us our invisibility. At the moment, American terrorist experts are busily sifting through the fatally wounded Gagarin laser facility outside Kirovobad, and some UN inspectors, invited by our hero Gorbachev in a goodwill gesture, are at Baikonur. But out here"—Bazakin gestured downward again with his hand—"out here in this wasteland, we have no visitors. We are ghosts."

Kasakov and Vanderyenko nodded, the latter somewhat unconvincingly.

Soon all turbulence departed; the pilot's body relaxed as if it had been hit by a wave of Valium. They began their descent just as the horizon began to clear; the peaks of the Verkhoyank Mountains, the foothills of which cradled the *Starik*'s home, emerged through lingering low-lying clouds. Even Vanderyenko was touched by the harsh majesty of the sunlit peaks.

The landing was unproblematic. The three men deplaned, climbed into a waiting Toyota Landcruiser, and rode off to Tereshkovo, toward the distant mountains, over what was only charitably called a road. They passed over the raging Lena after fifteen minutes of rocking and rolling; after another five they pulled up in front of the SBI complex. Large fierce-looking hard-hatted men of questionable character walked about like ants in an anthill, tending to the ostensible purpose of Tereshkovo: hydroelectric power.

The trio passed inside, to the true heart of the facility. Once there, the three men were greeted by Matra and Ignatov.

"Well, comrades," Kasakov said to the pair of scientists, "you should soon see a nice little jump in funding." Peter smiled and gave a brotherly slap to the back of the diminutive engineer, and shook hands with Galya Matra.

"With the loss of the Gagarin facility, Mother Russia has lost any possibility for boost-phase SDI interception, perhaps for as long as half a decade. The space-based interceptor project Andreev managed to get for us will soon be elevated in importance in the eyes of the Soviet military, academicians, scientists, and even our dear Gorbachev himself."

All true, and all just as Bazakin had predicted.

"But you know," Ignatov said, "I'm getting a little weary of murder. We took down the first 747, and it was a thrill. And the second wasn't bad either. But generally when I murder I like to have a cause in mind."

"We do," Bazakin said. "Great Russia. What could be simpler?"

"You give me an ethereal concept, an ideal. Marx gave us ideals. The fact is, we don't even have a fucking *plan*," Ignatov complained from down near the floor.

"Come now, Dimitry," Bazakin said, "you program once in a while, do you not?"

"Program?"

"Yes," Bazakin said. "You know. A machine. A computer."

"Yes, in that sense, of *course* I program."

"And you know what a flow chart is? What pseudocode is?"

"Give me a fucking break," Ignatov said, angered by his superior's condescension. "A flow chart is a graphical representation of the high-level logic that is gradually reduced to low-level code, to instructions suitable for giving to the machine. Our work here has necessitated a *thousand* flo—"

"Well, my friend," Bazakin said calmly, "our group is putting together the flow chart, the logic of the situation. With time we shall refine things down to the nitty-gritty, to direct, simple instructions that even an engineer can understand."

"Even an engineer, huh?" Ignatov said, wanting, though not daring, to respond to the insult with *Fuck you, Bazakin.*

Kasakov raised his hand to preclude further argument. "Enough idle chatter. Let us get down to business. How are you two progressing, comrades?"

"Nicely," Dimitry Ignatov said, his anger fading, and his true nature, that of the technological, returning. "The strategy forced upon us by the absence of Neurocubes, namely that demons have no autonomy, appears to be proving itself, at least in the short run. *If*, down the road, we can handle the software angle, I believe the project will succeed. Mass production has always been our strong suit; in this regard the Americans cannot compete. And delivering the endoatmospheric version of these demons, with the help of Baikonur and Plesetsk, should be a piece of cake. As you know, a couple of trips up by the SL-17 should suffice to get us in business."

The five GRU agents were standing beside one of the kinetic-kill rockets, or demons: one foot in diameter, three feet tall. The rocket didn't look particularly spaceworthy, but its agility was actually unparalleled.

"As per your orders, Comrade Galya and I are working on the assumption that none of the demons, and indeed none of the delivery platforms, need have *any* intelligence," Ignatov continued. "We're designing things around the image-processing system to be created and installed later. So this means we simply have a camera sending images back to us, and that, based on that image, we manually control their thrusters. What we see is very similar to what's returned to the technicians in our early-warning missile-detection sites, by satellite-carried infrared telescopes. As you know, this technology is rather barbaric, but we *have* refined the camera. In our latest version we've reduced it to two hundred and fifty grams, but despite this small size, it still has constant angular resolution over the whole sixty-degree field of view. From a mere one thousand kilometers, comrades, this wide-field-of-view optical system can image a land area the size of Estonia."

"*Fuck* your camera," Matra said, speaking for the first time. "You and your cameras. We're going to trash it, you know, when, armed with our Neurocubes, we move toward genuine vision. Why tinker with it?"

Galya Matra glared down at Ignatov, towering above him like a Greek god over a mortal; Ignatov looked up defiantly. Kasakov wondered how in the world this pair produced the wonders that they did. Ignatov was about to protest when Kasakov once again forestalled heated dialectic. "Let's talk about testing," he said.

"Testing?" Ignatov said, diverted. "We already know we can hit objects incapable of evasive maneuvers. Further testing is either superfluous or, given the absence of automated vision, premature. And to get vision we need the Neurocubes, and someone to harness their power. Even after they arrive, Galya and I will have a lot of work to do before testing becomes viable."

"Your concern is laudable, Comrade Ignatov, but you are forgetting a crucial step. Before we give our demons autonomy, before they see, and act of their own power based on *what* they see, it would be nice if we knew the rocketry could handle an agile target. Do you not agree, my tiny friend?"

Ignatov frowned. Then pulled on his long scraggly beard. And then nodded.

"Now," Bazakin continued, "Colonel Kasakov and I have hit upon a way to test our interceptors against formidable targets *prior* to the arrival of the Neurocubes, and without the military's cooperation. But perhaps, Dimitry, you are not even ready for testing that involves only mid-course and reentry, minus automated vision?"

Bazakin had pushed the right button.

"Of *course* we're ready. Galya and I have thrusters and propellants which now allow these demons to dance like hypersonic fleas."

Ignatov looked at Matra, who nodded.

"But I must tell you, comrades," Ignatov continued, "that even if we have these rockets operating on the assumption that every hurtling object is associated with a genuine missile, at closing speeds exceeding twenty thousand meters per second your Neurocubes must process megabits of data every half-second. This is an enormous demand. An unprecedented demand. The rocket technology is perfected, comrade, or at least nearly so, but the programming is, in my opinion, perhaps unattainable."

"Let *me* worry about the software," Bazakin said. "Just tell me, are you ready to test the rocket, yes or no?"

Ignatov was still at a loss as to what the hell he

was to test his creations *on*. He decided to make his ignorance known:

"And what will our targets *be*?" he asked.

"For your ground-launched terminal-phase vehicles: aircraft," Bazakin replied.

"Again?"

"Mm hmm."

"Not commercial again, I trust."

"No, not commercial," Bazakin said.

"And realistic targets for the space-based demons?" Matra asked.

"Ah. You're going to like this," Bazakin said.

San Mateo

Frank Kaminsky was neither an uncoordinated nor an absentminded man. In fact it was quite the reverse: he bowled in a league, weekly, with an average of 205, invariably rolling, like a cyborg, a graceful hook that was the envy of many of his competitors. And Frank Kaminsky, during his entire janitorial career, had cleaned in an efficient, methodical manner, never forgetting a mop or a broom, or whether a room had been scrubbed the previous night.

But about his chronic inability for stealth, his wife was right: she knew when he stole a smoke at the lanes, had one too many beers or bet one too many times on jai alai or the horses, or gobbled down a secret snack that violated the cholesterol-reducing diet Frank's doctor had prescribed. It wasn't that his wife was a genius; it was simply that Frank's face was an open book. Always.

And Harriet Kaminsky was right, in particular, about Frank's inability to pull off the illicit transaction involving the Neurocube.

It started as just a baseball size snowball: pulled over for a missing blinker signal. No big deal. The cop, when he saw Frank Kaminsky's benign, middle-aged, hard-worked face, was inclined to go easy, and he rather softly instructed Frank to get the light replaced tomorrow.

But Frank tried to speak, to concoct an excuse about the blinker, and nothing but air came out. Which caused the cop to take a closer look. And that's when he noticed that Frank's face glistened with sweat. That Frank was trembling like a leaf. That Frank was grimacing as if in pain. And then the cop saw the briefcase. Which in and of itself wasn't extraordinary. Blue-collar guys, after all, do get promoted to the office every now and then. But when the cop added the case to the nervous demeanor, he smelled something fishy.

The snowball had started to roll.

"May I see your license and registration, sir?" Mirror sunglasses. Pearl-white teeth. Immaculate uniform. And Frank had this thing about cops, even though he'd never even committed a misdemeanor.

Kaminsky said of course, but fumbled with his wallet, dropped it, picked it back up on the second try, was physically unable to pull his license out. He was shaking so badly he couldn't even open the door to the glove compartment. When Frank finally managed to extract the documentation, the cop eyed it, and then eyed Frank, and his briefcase, again. The cop had everything to gain and nothing to lose. Frank sure as hell wasn't the kind of guy who'd sue for brutality.

"May I ask you what's in the case, sir?"

"Uh, sure, officer. Nothing. See?" Kaminsky popped open the briefcase; it was indeed empty. But this only fueled the cop's suspicion. The snowball was a snow *boulder* now, still rolling down the hill, still getting larger.

"What are you planning to use the case for, sir?"

Frank should have said none of your damn business, forcefully, with a curse thrown in, but this wasn't bowling, and instead poor Kaminsky searched in silence for some harmless legal use. After too long a period of contemplation, Frank said: "I'm going to use it as my lunchbox, officer. Kind of sick of the usual kind, you know?"

Which, of course, was a thoroughly inane response. The cop peered in at the backseat: nothing.

"Mind if I look in your trunk, Mr. . . . uh . . ."—the cop looked at the license in his hand again—"Mr. Kaminsky?"

The beads of sweat on Frank's face were by now rolling into his eyes, and he was wiping them away with the back of his hand.

"Mr. Kaminsky? Sir?"

Still no response from Frank. His lower lip quivered.

"Sir, I'm going to have to ask you for your trunk key."

Floor it? Run when he's looking in the trunk? Frank decided no, he was trapped.

"That's it, Mr. Kaminsky. Step out of the car now, or I'll have to use force."

Kaminsky handed over his keys, the cop looked inside, found the Neurocube, and within twenty minutes Frank Kaminsky—broken, sweating, tremulous—had given a description of the man who had offered to make him rich. The man being, of course, Nickolai Vasilyevich Vanderyenko, the *Macka* suitably disguised.

Worcester, Massachusetts

Detective McNulty was at Jet Express, trying to piece together the theft of the four Neurocubes from MIT. And specifically, he was trying to find out more about the dispatcher from that fateful night: Billy Joe Dupree.

It was not a particularly easy interview. While they talked, packages and people flew by. McNulty felt the breeze from a box that passed, airborne, within inches of his nose.

"You say he was a good dispatcher?" McNulty began.

"Billy? You kiddin'? The guy was a friggin' wiz," the supervisor said, oblivious of the commotion.

"How long did he work for you before he disappeared?" McNulty asked.

"Uh, not long at all. Not sure exactly *how* long. Hold on."

The manager of Jet Express went to pull the relevant file, leaving McNulty alone. The detective dodged a few capped and clean-cut couriers while he waited. There was movement everywhere, and no apparent organization whatsoever. Conveyor belts conveyed, people sorted and ran, trucks screeched up to loading bays and roared away. It was dizzying.

"Yeah, here it is. He was with us for about a week."

"A week?"

"That's what the record says, mister."

"And he proved himself in that short a time?"

"What, you kiddin'? Look around. If a man can dispatch these trucks for a fucking minute, then in my book he's a winner. And besides, the guy had a résumé."

McNulty looked at the file. Application, small photo, recommendation, cover letter, résumé; the latter two in laser-quality print. Billy Joe Dupree. Born in Cumming, Georgia, 1958. High school diploma. Started work immediately after graduation for UPS out of Atlanta. Worked his way up to dispatcher there. The recommendation was filled with praise: "diligent," "courteous," "precise." The cover letter said that his wife was a Northerner, that she was taking a job in Boston, that he was going to follow her, and that he "would welcome the opportunity to discuss my qualifications in person."

"See what I mean, mister?"

"Yes, I see what you mean."

McNulty put Dupree's dossier into his briefcase and held his hand out for a parting shake.

The manager shook, but then said, "Wait. You gonna take that file?"

"Yes I am, mister."

Atlanta UPS had never heard of Billy Joe Dupree. Neither had Cumming High School. McNulty bought a street map at a bookstore and found Dupree's local address, or at least the one that was listed in the dossier. It was an apartment building in an area that made South Troy of the 1970's look like a garden spot. McNulty knocked on the first apartment on the first floor. He smelled marijuana and, he thought, the unmistakable odor of someone freebasing. A T-shirted man wider than the doorway answered. He reeked.

"Yeah?"

"Could you tell me how I might contact the landlord?"

"You're lookin' at 'im."

"I'd like to look at apartment four, if you don't mind."

The man puffed on an enormous cigar and looked McNulty over. "You don't wanna rent, do ya?"

"No."

"Didn't think so. Not with clothes like that. You're a cop, right?"

"Yup."

"Well, hold on." The man waddled into his apartment, which was, McNulty saw, a sea of clutter: newspapers, beer bottles, old Domino pizza boxes. He returned and handed McNulty a set of keys. "It's this one here. One flight up. It's empty. Has been for a while."

"Since Dupree?" McNulty asked.

The fat landlord raised his eyebrows slightly and hesitated a bit before saying, "You got it."

It was clean. Surgically clean. Apartment four had been scrubbed from floor to ceiling. There were some glasses in a dust-free cabinet but McNulty didn't even bother trying to get prints. Ivan, McNulty's name for Billy Joe Dupree, was a pro. And despite their well-publicized economic problems, Lou McNulty was quite sure Russia had enough cash to enable a guy like Ivan to cruise.

Holiday Spa, Troy, New York

The water was wonderfully hot today. He had a Camel, an entire pack, and two supercold Cokes, drops of condensation running down the outside of the cans. He'd toyed with the Nautilus machines, just so as to come within a few feet of a lovely blond and perspiring woman in a painted-on leotard. Today Detective John McNulty had even taken a computerized life cycle for a spin—one that was strategically positioned behind a woman whose well-proportioned ass was gyrating suggestively from her pedaling. And now he was in the whirlpool, mulling over the Neurocube case. And once again it was here, looking out over the glistening and shapely clientele, that his next move hit him.

Maybe somebody's been caught. Not likely, but worth a shot. And hell, with Sherlock's help, it's rather effortlessly pursued.

To the office.

Hello, Sherlock.

HELLO, LOU. WHAT CAN I DO FOR YOU?

Have any stolen Neurocubes been recovered?

YES.

How many?

UNRECOGNIZABLE COMMAND.

How many stolen Neurocubes have been recovered?

ONE.

Give me the details, please.

Sherlock proceeded to give McNulty the police report on the Neurocube recovered from the trunk of Frank Kaminsky's car. Upon reading it, the detective from Troy nodded to himself, sent some more nicotine down to his lungs, and then, without delay, faxed a copy of Billy Joe Dupree's picture out to San Mateo with the request that his colleagues there ask Kaminsky if he'd ever spoken with Ivan. The response came back, one hour later: Kaminsky, if he can be believed, has never seen this Dupree fellow before. Frank had, however, been approached by a smooth, sharp, suited gentleman who, posing as the CEO of one of Neuron Data's competitors, offered Frank $100,000 for a Neurocube. The San Mateo PD faxed McNulty an artist's rendering of the con man; McNulty studied it, and was rather amazed to find that the sketch reminded him of Dupree. He pulled out the photo of Dupree: the resemblance was indeed uncanny.

McNulty took a deep drag on one of his Camels and thought about his next move, resigned to a situation in which the FBI wasn't going to be of any help. It had been a week now since he'd gotten his data to the Bureau. They hadn't replied. He looked down at the two pictures on his desk, and back up at a world that was a haystack. But he decided to keep the photos to himself. He never had thought much of the feds.

16

Demon Strike

February 10—Northern Siberia

Roman Kyator, chief test pilot for the Soviet Mikoyan Design Bureau, was relaxed, proud, and heading home through the hyperborean, cloudless, turbulence-free sky of Northern Siberia. His single-seat MIG-29 had performed impeccably in subzero weather: a tail slide initiated at but five hundred meters altitude, a roll while holding a turn, a number of sustained 9-g small-radius turns, a low-speed/high-angle-of-attack pass over some "hostile" Siberian terrain, a hammer-head stall—everything, absolutely everything, had gone perfectly. Kyator's job was done; he was pleased with himself and his jet; he had his left hand on the MIG's dual-engine throttles and was looking proudly over at the arctic sun glinting magnificently off one of his camaflouge-painted wings on a fine-and-dandy day at twenty thousand feet and one thousand miles per hour—when his automated defense system screamed into operation. First the electro-optical sensors detected the rocket plume; then the MIG's pirated French DDM pulse Doppler radar, with look-down, shoot-down capability, interrogated the data, automatically read it as a threat, and consequently began to configure an attack; and then range information was provided by the MIG's laser-ranging system.

Kyator, cool, his heart still beating at a slow, even pace, flipped down his combat goggles, which were to function now as his head-up display, and looked at the glowing red digits in the black glass for the range of the target.

Five kilometers, and closing. Fast.

"What?"

Kyator's eyes darted instinctively to the radar display which, in the MIG-29, was in the upper right above the engine instruments—he looked and his first thought was malfunction. It had to be: according to on-board computer calculations, the object was traveling three times faster than the current Mach 1.5 speed of his MIG. But when the object didn't disappear from the screen, when it began to pick up speed, when, ignoring the flare decoys and chaff that the MIG had automatically released, it began to home in on his jet—when all this happened in the span of two seconds, the Russian pilot said fuck the malfunction hypothesis and took evasive action. He pulled his nose up at full throttle and rocketed upward vertically on afterburner.

But when Roman Kyator leveled out at forty thousand feet, the scenario hadn't changed, save for the fact that Demon 1 was that much closer.

The Russian pilot, having faced death unblinkingly in the past, still retained his cool. And thought calmly, fearlessly, about the alien on his ass, and how to shake it.

For Demon 1 it was all rather effortless. Its camera had a lock on the MIG, and corrective guidance was being provided to the tiny rocket's pitch-and-yaw-control thrusters by Ignatov, sitting calmly inside the *Starik*'s Tereshkovo SBI facility in front of an oversize monitor. Every move the MIG made was seen and compensated for. Demon 1 was traveling four times faster than the MIG now, and the jet was on full afterburners running away to the West as fast as it could.

Nothing in the Soviet pilot's training had prepared

him for this. He'd heard the stories about UFO's traveling at impossible speeds, and he thought that maybe he was having one of these experiences. The only problem was that this object very clearly wanted to kill him, and all the tales of UFO's spoke of rather benign objects.

Roman Kyator was now gripped by the steely hands of the survival drive; he was determined to live, to fight. He jinked up and down wildly in an attempt to shake the rocket on his ass; his eyeballs shivered from the g forces he was inflicting upon himself and his plane. But when he smoothed out for a solid look at radar, he saw that his erratic flying had done nothing to change the situation.

He cursed into the radio for ground control: no response.

Options were running out. He decided to try to shoot the intruder down. Kyator threw his MIG into a 10-g turn, as sharp a maneuver as his jet could tolerate without shattering. Kyator's flesh sagged severely toward the outside of the turn, and felt as if it was going to be torn off his bones by the awesome centrifugal force.

But he made it: a 180-degree turn. He faced the closing Demon 1 now, head-on.

Kyator activated his tracking system in an attempt to get a fix on the object hurtling directly toward him. But the jet's laser ranging and electro-optical aiming systems were now apparently dead. Utterly, unmistakably, mysteriously dead.

"Fuck."

Kyator looked to radar. It was . . . it was jammed! Someone or something was now jamming his radar from a great distance. By the time Kyator shouted again for ground control, a visual sighting of the demon told him he had to eject; he lowered his right hand toward the large seat-ejection handle, but then realized that the demon was too close to eject safely.

So instead of ejecting, Kyator threw his jet into a knife-edge pass, wings vertical in relation to the ground, hoping to fly through the demon.

It worked. The demon had been aiming at horizontal wings that had suddenly shifted to vertical. A miss. Only a few inches of clearance, but a miss.

Now he had time to eject. He lowered his right hand once again to the ejection handle, as the demon screamed into a horseshoe turn back in pursuit of its target. Kyator pulled.

Nothing.

Pulled again.

Still nothing.

The demon was on a bead now, at Mach 8, a streaking blur.

Kyator pulled once again, hard, desperate, but still nothing. He cursed one final time into his radio.

Then the legendary test pilot, without suffering any pain, blew apart into a million pieces, as did his MIG-29.

The entire confrontation had lasted but two minutes.

NSA Headquarters, Fort Meade

Military accidents happen. Indeed, they happen all the time. And when they do, the other side invariably tries to learn as much as it can, especially if the weapon involved is state-of-the-art. The Soviets knew quite a bit about the stealth fighter before it was declassified, because their recon satellites sent back informative pictures of a number of crash sites of the experimental plane. The crash of a lone MIG-29 on a routine training mission in Northern Siberia, however, isn't something which perks up Uncle Sam's ears. The military-packaged story of the lost MIG was relegated to a back page in *Pravda*.

> A Mikoyan MIG-29 fighter crashed during a low-speed high-angle-of-attack pass in routine testing exercises in Siberia yesterday. The aircraft was flying at approximately 100 knots when the pilot evidently initiated pitch adjustments in an attempt to sustain the high angle of attack. The MIG then increased its pitch angle to 40 degrees as the pilot applied full afterburner. Seconds later a 20-foot-long orange flame shot from the left engine, indicating some sort of surge. Elevator inputs were made in an attempt to regain control, but failed. By that time it was too late to eject.

And the disaster had not been seen by any American satellite, though a Navstar-class satellite had come awfully close to catching the whole tragic sequence in real time. A Vortex-class satellite, however, had been listening in.

When the photo recon bird Lacrosse passed above the crash site, Herbert Light took a look. And what he saw looked damn strange. The wreckage was widely dispersed, in much the same pattern as Pan Am flight 103, which had met its tragic end above the skies of Scotland. Light thought this was odd enough to bother the boys in eavesdropping; he called Henry DeRose, one of the men assigned to the Magnum team.

"What can I do for you, Herb?"

"What kind of data do you have on the recent MIG incident?"

"Incident? You mean crash."

"Maybe," Light said.

"Maybe? You mind telling me one other possibility?"

"Explosion."

"Explosion, my ass," DeRose said. "These terrorists have you spooked, Herb. They can't even get inside the U.S., and you think they got inside the

Soviet Union. *And* you think they sabotaged a MIG. You better cut back on your hours, buddy of mine."

"Who mentioned terrorists? I said explosion, nothing more. Maybe it was a malfunction."

"Look, you're a satellite guru, but you don't know shit about Russian fighters. Malfunction, huh? Well let me tell you, jets don't just blow up by themselves."

"Well, all I know," Herbert Light said, "is that the photos I have of the site are uncannily similar to those I got of the Pan Am that blew up over Lockerbie."

"All right, but Lockerbie wasn't a malfunction, Herb, it was an explosion. From a bomb."

"Or so we think," Light commented.

DeRose puffed pejoratively into the receiver. "British AAIB found traces of an explosive commonly used by terrorists."

"Maybe the Sovs planted it," Light said.

"You ever heard of Occam's Razor?"

"Look," Light said. "Let's not debate this. You got any data on the MIG?"

"Sure," DeRose replied, "all sorts of stuff, but all of it standard, I'm sure. We had a Vortex in solid position to monitor communications between pilot and ground command. And now we've got Magnum listening in on the reaction, which, given the loss of one solitary MIG under those conditions, promises to be terse."

"Mind if I see the comm stuff?"

"Not at all," DeRose said. "Come on down."

DeRose pulled out the relevant 4-gigabyte high-capacity WORM (write-once, read-many) optical disk fed yesterday by Vortex. He fed it into a hot-rodded Mac V and searched for the relevant chunk of data, using time as a parameter. The Mac's MIDI interface pumped the recorded transmission out for the men to hear. But there was only silence. No urgent voices. No desperate calls for help. Nothing at all.

"Hank?" Light prodded.

"I'm drawing a blank, man."

Light checked recordings made before and after the MIG incident: playback was flawless.

"No malfunction," Light said.

"Yeah, spooky."

"What are the possibilities?"

"Well, could've been the strong silent type. Isn't that the profile of these Russky pilots?"

Light frowned at his colleague's facetiousness. "No, really, come on, Hank. What gives here?"

"All right, well . . . the radio could have been dead, I suppose."

"Dead? Just like that?"

"It happens."

"Hmm."

"What is it?" DeRose asked.

"Quite a coincidence, isn't it?"

"What are you driving at?"

"I don't think you need to be sinister to diagnose this, Hank. Guy's jet is obliterated mysteriously, in home territory, and his radio just happens to be dead before the incident."

"Yeah, but like you say," DeRose commented, "it was on his home turf. This was the bloody middle of Siberia. The only guys that could engineer this kind of hanky-panky would be . . . Oh, Jesus."

"Yup," Light said. "Ivan himself."

"And Lockerbie?" DeRose asked.

Light and DeRose looked at each other. Both men said simultaneously, slowly, "Holy shit."

February 11—Baikonur Cosmodrome

The two cosmonauts were immobilized, enclosed in spacesuits and strapped in, facing straight up into the cerulean sky; in front of the two men, the *Buran*'s cathode-ray tube-type display blinked, and aircraft-type analog instruments whirred and shivered. Both men, brave though they were, were a bit sick to their empty stomachs.

"Comrade?" Captain Yuri Sagadeev ventured.

"Yeah?" Captain Alexy Dynamatov responded.

"You okay?"

"Fine, my friend. Just fine."

"Well," Sagadeev said, "I must admit I wish we had the two Lyulkas for landing."

"Superfluous, comrade. We don't need power for our approach. The Buran's glideslope has been verified."

"Well."

"Well what?" Dynamatov prodded. His stomach was a good deal less turbulent than his comrade's.

"We've been flying a simulator, comrade. You don't hit Mach 24 in a simulator. You don't suffer burnthrough in a simulator. There's no plasma in a fucking trainer. And the damn thing is air-conditioned, which in my opinion is rather poor preparation for the twenty-eight hundred degrees Fahrenheit that this orbiter is going to have to endure."

"Take it easy, comrade."

It was the fourth launch of the Buran orbiter, the first manned mission, and takeoff was as picture-perfect as the first two. This time the weather cooperated; no cyclones were threatening to move in off the Aral, as they had for the historic first flight. It was calm, clear, and cold, indeed below freezing. The orbiter had picked up a coating of ice the night before from some freezing rain, but deicing agents had been applied, and the Buran was immaculate. Unlike the American shuttle, the Soviet shuttle's all-liquid propulsion system could easily tolerate cold-weather launches.

The Energia booster's four oxygen/hydrogen core engines and four oxygen/kerosene strap-boosters waited patiently. At T minus eleven minutes the orbiter's computers took control of the countdown, and shortly before liftoff commanded ignition of the Energia's engines.

At which time Sagadeev and Dynamatov rattled in their seats, the former feeling a sudden overwhelming need to urinate.

The giant booster hesitated for eight seconds of thrust buildup on the pad, and built up a staggering 7.9 million pounds of thrust, shaking the mammoth Energia as if it were a toy.

Lift-off. The two cosmonauts felt as if they were going to become part of the seats into which they were violently pushed.

Climbing now, the strap-on and core boosters together providing 2.9 million pounds of thrust. Captains Sagadeev and Dynamatov were brought to the edge of consciousness, their eyelids forced closed, their minds blank save for the primal determination to emerge from the immense g forces they knew would eventually pass.

When the vehicle reached the upper atmosphere, engine performance began to improve, and at Mach 6 the strap-ons separated. The Energia, driven by the core vehicle, soon achieved a velocity of more than twenty-five thousand feet per second, and at an altitude of sixty-two miles it shut down and separated from Buran. Though the booster was in space, it had only reached a low-altitude suborbital trajectory, and so it fell toward reentry over the South Pacific. To continue on and achieve orbital flight the Buran fired its two aft-mounted OMS (orbital maneuvering system) engines. Soon it reached a 150-mile altitude.

Sagadeev and Dynamatov breathed deeply, then evenly, as if taking in air for the first time in what seemed now to be a new and glorious life in another dimension.

Ten minutes later the OMS engines fired a second

time, lifting the Buran to its planned 255-mile-high orbit.

GRU Headquarters

The *Starik* was together. Qualmless. Flushed with the excitement of opening night.

"How did you find the window of invisibility, Comrade Bazakin?" Matra asked.

"Simple," Bazakin replied without the slightest bit of arrogance. "I computed the needed altitude-inclination pair using only a hand-held calculator. Basic trigonometry," Bazakin said, smoking one of his foul but perpetually lit Primas. "First I found a region in space that, for a long enough period in time, wouldn't be scanned by an American spy satellite. As you know, in ideal weather conditions there is no spot on the surface of the earth that is ever outside the watchful eye of some photo-recon satellite owned by the United States. But the *surface* of the earth is one thing, space is another. If you fly high enough at the right time to the right region, you'll be outside the field of vision of every satellite."

Matra nodded and pursed her lips in appreciation of her comrade's competence; muscles in her chin contracted, which in turn caused muscles in her bulky but striated neck to quiver.

"The Buran," Bazakin continued, looking at his watch, "needs to reach an altitude of 255 miles during the thirty-minute interval bounded by 1300 and 1330 hours Greenwich mean time; and its inclination has to be 63.5 degrees. During this interval of time the American Lacrosse is at apogee, but on the other side of the globe, and hence blinded; their two Navstars and the four KH-11's, on the other hand, are in circular orbits lower than Buran's 255-mile altitude, and they are all looking down upon the earth, not up at our target."

Ignatov was the only member not to nod respectfully. Murder was just dandy for the dwarf, but he had yet to see the big picture, and that had him irritated.

Kalingrad Control Room

Everyone was smiling, shaking hands, whistling. The large central wall display in the shuttle control room told it all: the Buran's orbit track was indicated by a white trace over a glowing world map. And the track, currently, was perfection itself.

Some brave and happy employee of the Molniya Scientific and Industrial Enterprise had smuggled in vodka; more than a few technicians threw down some celebratory gulps.

Orbiter

"That's orbit five, comrade. Now comes the easy part," Dynamatov said. "Set up a couple of these solar monitors, and then we dump the cargo. Nothing in our payload is large enough to require explosive ejection: we just use the spring system."

Sagadeev nodded.

GRU Headquarters

"The thing I can't figure," Kasakov said to Bazakin, "is how you got around *our* tracking. You said yourself that Kalingrad gets data from two ground stations and four tracking ships."

"True," Bazakin said, dragging on his cigarette. "That's why we sent up *two* demons. One for the Gorizont comm satellite in geosynchronous orbit, through which Kalingrad receives transmissions from the cosmonauts, and one for the cosmonauts themselves."

Nods all around.

Orbiter

The fifteen-by-sixty-foot bay was designed to accommodate payloads up to 67,000 pounds. But now the two Soviet cosmonauts in it maneuvered two objects that were, relative to their expectations, tiny. Unlike the reasonably comfortable crew cabin, there were no windows in this part of the fuselage, and their inability to look out at the phosphorescent sphere upon which they lived had an unsteadying effect on them. Earth, though 255 treacherously traversed miles away, was still their anchor, their home.

"*This* is a satellite?" Sagadeev asked as, with the help of a robotic servicer, he moved one of the demons into position for spring ejection.

Dynamatov frowned. "We get paid to fly, Yuri Sergeevich. And, when in here, to play construction worker. We are not wizards, comrade."

"But *look* at this minuscule thing," Sagadeev said. "It doesn't even have an antenna. Don't satellites have to have antennas?"

"How the hell should I know? Just launch the bastard."

"You know, it looks to me to be a rocket of some sort."

"Look, just launch the thing. Who the fuck cares *what* it is? Two more orbits and we're supposed to retrofire. Pretty hard to fire the OMS engines from in here, my friend. And if you don't mind, I'd rather not put the wizard's claims of a 1,240 cross-range to the test."

Sagadeev nodded, toggled the ejection switch, the

first demon whooshed out into space, and he directed the robotic arm to lock onto the second.

Kalingrad

"We've got a blackout, comrades."

Tension for the first time since ignition at Baikonur. Eyes raised to the central display.

Orbiter

The two cosmonauts were relieved to be back in the cabin, but not relieved to find that communications with ground control had broken down.

"Shit, and we've got to retrofire in . . . ten minutes," Captain Sagadeev said.

"It'll come back up. If nothing else, we'll come within range of another satellite."

"Which one's supposed to be carrying comm now?"

"A Gorizont."

"Hmm. And next?"

"A Molniya."

"How long?"

"Uh, let's see . . . eight minutes."

"All right, it's not much, but it should be a sufficient cush— What the hell is that?"

"What?"

"That. That!"

The two men saw the demon as a white cometlike streak against the black interstellar background, and Sagadeev for a split second actually admired the phenomenon's aesthetic appeal before they realized they were on a collision course with what seemed a beam of light.

"Fire the OMS engines!" Dynamatov shouted.

Sagadeev obeyed, by flipping two enable switches

on the Buran's instrument panel, and pushing, violently, two ignition buttons. The aft-mounted engines responded almost instantaneously with seven thousand pounds of thrust, a thousand more than the max for American OMS engines. The Buran's speed slammed to five hundred feet per second, rocketing it beyond its 255-mile orbit.

"Again! It's still running on a bead toward us!"

But, five seconds later, no pain whatsoever, just complete and instantaneous disintegration. An instant before which Dynamatov had the thought: They *were* rockets.

> MOSCOW (AP)—It was admitted today by TASS, the Soviet news agency, that the Soviet shuttle, known as the Buran, suddenly disintegrated while at an altitude of approximately 450 miles. *Pravda*, the Communist-party newspaper, carried a terse summary of the mysterious explosion, saying simply that "the Buran is completely lost, but we ought to congratulate ourselves for learning the lesson taught to us by the tragic end of Soyuz 11, in which an entire brave and valiant crew was lost." The ill-fated Buran mission was unmanned.
>
> Though no supporting data have been presented, Soviet officials from the Molniya Scientific and Industrial Enterprise, interviewed at the Baikonur Cosmodrome, have hinted that the Buran's mission, on this particular flight, may have had something to do with the explosion. Said Vasily Priabin, head of ground control at Kalingrad: "All I can say is that it was a particularly dangerous mission, one with the ingredients necessary for the sort of explosion we saw. Exactly what those ingredients were, and how it might have happened that the robots on board

erred in their handling, I am not at liberty to discuss."

NASA routinely monitors Soviet space flights, but officials from this agency are as yet not commenting on the disaster.

Langley

Buchanan's STU-4 lit up, the handset indicating the caller's identity and security clearance. The DCI inserted his crypto-ignition key, pushed the Secure button, and took the call. It was Light.

"You sure this is appropriate? I know we have an agreement, but I'm not your boss anymore, Herb."

"I know, but Festivo said to dump this directly on you. All in all, he's quite comfortable with the concept of NSA as conduit to CIA."

"Boy, times have changed. And for the better. So what do you have?"

"A lot of data, still quite disparate at this point. But I also have an organizing hypothesis."

"Which is?"

"Which is, in a word, that the Soviets *have* SDI."

A pause. Buchanan knew Light to be a cautious, prudent analyst.

"Was the destruction of Gagarin an illusion?" the Admiral asked.

"In a sense, yes. It did blow up, and it did house the entire laser-based approach to the Russian Star Wars. But it housed only *part* of their SDI."

Buchanan punched a button on his phone to record the rest of the call and said, "Explain, Herb."

"Well, the MIG is the first piece in the puzzle."

"The plane they lost two days ago in Siberia?"

"Yep."

"Yeah, and?"

"They brought it down, James. They destroyed it.

We checked for comm over here and found zip. Someone took the poor guy's radio out to pasture, and it sure as hell wasn't us. The wreckage indicates some sort of explosion or super-high-speed collision. Exactly like Lockerbie, sir."

"Lockerbie?"

"Yes, Admiral."

A period of silence. Of righteous anger.

"But collision? Were there other planes in the vicinity of the MIG?"

"I'm not thinking planes, Admiral."

Buchanan's brain started clicking. And when it did, the United States immediately had a chance in a silent war it was hitherto losing hands-down.

"Ah, you mean interceptors. Smart rocks, brilliant pebbles, that kind of thing."

"That's my hypothesis, Admiral."

"It would also explain the shuttle."

"How so?"

"Well, it's just a rumor at this point, but apparently some Air Force techie down in the Manzano Mountains was playing around with one of their optical tracking telescopes when Ivan lost his bird. Claims he spotted another object besides the Buran."

"Another piece in the puzzle," Light said.

"Perhaps. And then there's the bombing you witnessed. We've had a team of analysts on that from day one, even had some boys make an on-site inspection, thanks to Gorbachev. And there are some things that just don't add up."

"Like?"

"Well," Buchanan said, "like how they got past the computerized security system. It's just like the kind of thing we use here: handprints, voice pattern, even retina scan—that sort of thing. We can't figure how the hell these terrorists waltzed right past this checkpoint."

"Unless it was an inside job," Light said.

"Precisely. Engineered to provide a diversion, to lull us into a false sense of security on SDI while they march ahead full-speed with these potent kinetic-kill rockets."

"Quite a few pieces to the puzzle," Light said.

"Yup. Maybe even enough so that when you and I arrange these pieces for the brass, we'll make a dent in their irenic little heads. How'd you like to make a return trip to the White House, Herb, and this time piss all over 'em?"

Light laughed, in the affirmative.

17

Smart Rocks

February 12—Situation Room, White House

Buchanan was in full battle dress, his chest decorated with gleaming medals of various colors. From the United States: Purple Heart, Silver Star, Distinguished Service Cross with oak-leaf cluster. From France: rank of grand officer of the Legion of Honor and a shimmering Croix de Guerre. And Britain: a bright badge signifying membership in the Distinguished Service Order. This morning his wife, who was taller than the Admiral, had henpecked him about his penchant for leaving dirty laundry on the floor, short of the hamper; now, in the White House, James Buchanan's gaze was one of steel, and his bearing no less authoritative than that which, in submerged submarines under Nazi attack from above, he had used to breathe courage into young submariners quivering with fear. Light—boyish, in a suit for the first time in two years, horn-rimmed glasses—was by Buchanan's side. Two ramrod-erect marines, one black, one white, stood at attention down the hall, by the entrance to the Situation Room, in which Buchanan and Light were now overdue to make their presentation.

"Admiral," Light said, peering discreetly at his Seiko, "shouldn't we, uh, go now?"

"No, let 'em sweat, Herb. I want surgical revenge

here. Complete precision. I don't want a single false note, not one second when we're not in control."

Herbert Light nodded. And, thinking about the avuncular, even bovine image the white-haired Buchanan projected on the outside, laughed.

Civilian friends who saw James Buchanan only in civilian life considered him a wallflower. At posh D.C. parties to which his gregarious wife dragged him, he invariably grabbed a bottle of beer and struck up low-key, sequestered conversations with men content to watch such late-night athletic oddities as ESPN motor-boat racing, in back rooms, away from the chatty hustle and bustle of finger food, cocktails, and people who desperately needed to be seen.

But in the secret world in which he worked, Admiral Buchanan was in many ways the ultimate utilitarian: goal, means to the goal, and damn the side effects. Intimidate. Manipulate. Cajole. And act. With an unfailing sense of what the heart of the problem is. Buchanan had quite a flair for the thespian, and rather relished the limelight. And kicking a man when he was down, if it made sense in the grand American-warrior-peace-through-strength scheme of things, was something he could do without the slightest pang of guilt. The Admiral was a man whose dark and violent side had been harnessed for the fighting of fair, structured battles.

"Uh, ten minutes now, sir. How long do you, uh, how long do you intend to wait?"

"Till they squirm, son. Having the cards isn't everything, you've got to know how to play 'em. Spying, Herbert, is acting. Not waiting. Acting. And though you don't know it, we have a script for today."

"But I don't—"

"Follow my lead," Buchanan interrupted. He then looked at his watch and announced, "It's time."

The two entered crisply. Buchanan's black, blindingly shined shoes caught some light, as did his medals. The four stars on his shoulders shone. His posture was that of a much younger man, and there was a grace and strength in his motion. The much taller Light, on the other hand, dwarfed as he was by Buchanan's larger-than-life aura, hurriedly but unobtrusively took a seat. No small talk, no handshakes. Buchanan looked out over the expectant faces of his audience, nodded solemnly and silently to the men running the most powerful nation on earth, then focused his eyes on the President, who was seated at the opposite end of the conference table, and then, after a slight nod directed at the Commander-in-Chief, took control of the podium.

"Gentlemen," began the DCI, "there is good reason to think our worst nightmare is upon us. Given the evidence Mr. Light and I are about to present, I would say that no amount of hyperbole in describing our plight suffices to express the gravity of the situation."

Admiral James Buchanan paused, letting the silence underscore his opening remarks. Then he proceeded: "Mr. Light will present the satellite evidence first. Herb."

Light stood and walked to the podium; Buchanan sat. During the next ten minutes, with the help of computer-generated slides to render his points vivid, Light discussed the MIG crash, Lockerbie and Air India, parallels between the two, and hinted at his hypothesis concerning high-speed collision. The two men exchanged places once again; and Buchanan proceeded without delay to present the evidence from the Buran disaster, and from the "terrorist" attack on the Gagarin complex.

The *Starik*'s ruthless tapestry hung in the air like a palpable horror. No one present had any reason to believe what was in fact the case: that events so far had been extemporaneous, and that these events were not crafted steps leading to some well-defined goal.

"Presumably I don't need to spoon-feed you the implications," Buchanan said. "To put it bluntly, gentlemen, we've been fucked."

Silence. The heads of hawks nodded serenely; the visages of doves reflected mental pain.

The problem had of course arisen through no fault of any scientist, but it was to the scientist that everyone looked now. It was all unspoken communication: the Vice-President was stunned speechless, and it showed clear as day on his face; Newell and Simon, the Secretaries of Defense and State, respectively, were as yet simply too embarrassed to speak, since both were on record as stating that Weinberger's hard-line damn-the-budget-and-build-Star Wars policy was silly in a post-cold-war era; and the Chief of Staff managed people, not weapons, and so hadn't the slightest inclination to speak. The Joint Chiefs, as well as the President, who was pensive but surprisingly cool, looked at their portal to the world of SDI: Harold Rogers, director of the Strategic Defense Initiative Organization, the SDIO. Rogers in turn looked rather imploringly at the grandfather of it all, the brash Brooklyn-born physicist Arnold Bramsen, the thirty-three-year-old Nobel laureate who had conceived Star Wars. And Bramsen—thick black hair, Roman nose, arrogant but often justifiably so—said:

"They're in manual, my friends."

Which caused a slew of knit brows and a crisp and caustic request from President Atwood for clarification.

"These kinetic strikes *must* have been manually effected," Bramsen explained. "They haven't automated the system yet. It's *impossible* that they have. As I've recently told the SDIO, we now know that target signatures are not in the visible and ultraviolet wavelengths, and that therefore infrared detectors must be built. But it would take a genius we don't have to build these detectors in this *decade*. And detection is a *minor* problem. We haven't even *started* to tackle the software aspects of the massive super-speed connectivity required for the computerized implementation of SBI."

"S*B*I?" the President said.

"That's right," Bramsen said. "The acronym stands for Space-Based Interceptors. It's SDI without anything as extravagant as lasers or particle beams. We've more than dabbled in this approach ourselves. It would appear, now, that since day one of the Star Wars race the Russians have been putting most of their eggs in the SBI basket. We, on the other hand, spread them evenly across various technologies. I am in general loath to use such language, but in this case Admiral Buchanan's summary seems apt. We are indeed fucked."

It was nothing as dire as outright cracking of the psyche, but the dismay was still severe: Secretary of State Orville Simon didn't like what he was hearing. Indeed he was revolted by it. His job was founded upon the ability to erect civilized dialogue between parties he took to be fundamentally averse to violence. In a world which, from his perspective, had been improving greatly of late, he was suddenly shot clean through with the reality a warrior like Buchanan grasps from his teens on. But Simon fought the awakening, and said, "Let's not jump to conclusions here, gentlemen. Many other hypotheses, I venture to say, can accommodate this data. Restructuring is genuine, I assure you, and we have simply stumbled upon an aberration."

Buchanan said, "Orville, you're the single most sanguine person in the whole fucking world. Ivan could ram a friggin' SS-20 down your throat and you'd smile and ask for a second course."

Simon reddened a bit; Buchanan pushed: "Alternate hypotheses, huh? Well, why don't you run some by us?"

A slight pause.

"Terrorists," Simon responded.

"Hmm. Terrorists. I see. Terrorists who can build rockets our scientists can't. Terrorists who can sneak these rockets into the Soviet shuttle. Terrorists who can shred a MIG in the heart of Siberia. Who *are* these guys, Orville?"

The Secretary of State's complexion was crimson.

"Why don't you face the music, Mr. Simon, why don't we *all* face the music?" Buchanan said. "We're not talking technology of the future here. It is utterly reasonable to think the Sovs have managed to build these kinetic killers. Right, Dr. Bramsen?"

Bramsen nodded, and, addressing the entire group, said, "Remember the Apollo lunar module? How unstreamlined the thing looked? Free from the earth's drag-inducing atmosphere, you don't need to have sexy-looking rockets. I figure the interceptors in the Soviet SBI aren't sexy, but are still bastards. Maybe no more than three feet long and one hundred and fifty pounds. But the little buggers probably have something like, well, something on the order of a four-thousand-pound thrust rocket and enough solid fuel for, say, ten to twelve seconds of brute-force acceleration. They should be able to reach, by extrapolation from our own work—which, by the way, the Congress, in cooperation with the present administration, slashed to zip—let's see, they can perhaps hit about, oh, let's say eight miles per second just before impact. A penny traveling at that speed can explode a solid chunk of steel.

"At any rate," Bramsen continued, "we could have seen it coming. Their ability to mass-produce rockets has been solid for a decade, way ahead of ours almost from the start. We still build them one at a time: one here for the Delta, one here for the Shuttle . . . for us its like making a wood carving or something. They, on the other hand, can churn out launcher after launcher, and that's evidently what they've done, or at least what they *plan* to do, for their SBI: they've mass-produced smart rocks. Consider also the fact that they had working ASAT's well before we did. And the fact that for a good many years they've been going back and forth to space while NASA stood around picking up the pieces from the Shuttle disaster. With the Salyut series, and then Mir, they've had a working space station for nearly a decade; we put Skylab into orbital hibernation in 1974, and since then our next station has stayed parked, in blueprint form, on the desks of bureaucrats. And finally, one might say that *glasnost*, a spate of altruism from the beast that sends harmless people to Siberia for life, should have made us suspicious. Instead, it made some of us blind."

"But they're in manual, you say," the President said, his deep voice having an instant stabilizing effect on everyone's perception of the situation.

"Yeah, and that's why I'm not biting my fingernails. Without the software for this stuff, it won't do the least bit of good against a large-scale attack. They can't have men in Kalingrad controlling these interceptors; human reaction time is much too slow. The only way the system can work is if it's completely automatic. What they've doubtless done to this point is strap on a garden-variety camera, and then steer the rocket to its prey from ground control. This is light-years away from an army of one hundred and fifty thousand genuinely intelligent and interconnected kinetic vehicles that can neutralize a horde of MIRVed IC and SL ballistic missiles. When our warheads MIRV, that's it. Hell, the MX is a rocket which, by midcourse, releases twenty or so warheads, each powerful enough to make Truman's bomb look like a firecracker, and also a couple hundred decoys, and chaff, in the form of clouds of infrared-emitting aerosols. So if a significant number of ICBM's made it to MIRVing, their system wouldn't have a prayer. You see, the whole Star Wars concept, as I said almost ten years ago, is a layered one. And they have only the last few layers. In their SBI we're talking only mid-course and terminal interception—in other words, post-MIRV interception, which is probably intractable. All of our ICBM's, during boost phase, the start of their flight, are safe from their system. You can't have a conventional rocket, even one streaking down from space at Mach 30, take out an ICBM while it's taking off. I mean, hell, the silo cover pops open, the gases eject the bastard, and the first-stage booster ignites, blasting it out of the atmosphere before one of these kinetic-kill rockets gets its pants on. For boost-phase interception you need lasers, particle beams, and so on—the sort of flashy stuff they appear to have panned."

"Then why do you agree we're fucked?" Simon asked.

"Come now, Orville," Arnold Bramsen said, looking at Buchanan and then at the Joint Chiefs. "I believe our military minds understand. Don't you, now, gentlemen?"

It was by now a completely tangible thing, as noticeable as pressure changes inside the cabin of a rising jumbo jet. The weight of the free world, in the microcosm of the Situation Room, had shifted squarely onto the shoulders of soldiers and spies. The politicians and managers faded into the background. Everyone felt it; it was clear as day.

Buchanan pulled out his pipe, packed it slowly and surgically with tobacco, drew the flame of a match into the bowl, exhaled, and addressed the Secretary of State as a father might a four-year-old: "You see, Orville, though people make a lot of money philosophizing about it, the balance of nuclear power is rather simple, even with Star Wars thrown in. We start by assuming that we'd never launch first—maybe we would to thwart a massive conventional attack against

Western Europe, but we can leave this out of the picture without loss of generality. We *don't* assume that *Ivan* rules out a first strike, however. Our job is to make his first strike unpalatable, by way of good ol' MAD, of course. And we make a surprise first strike unpalatable by ensuring survivability of enough of our nuclear arsenal to enable significant retaliation—one Trident 2 will do that trick. Or at least it would do the trick without Ivan's SBI. You see, our ability to retaliate declines with their interceptor system. With this devilish SBI behind them, maybe they can launch a preemptive strike and *not* have to worry about retaliation. This, of course, is a scenario the general populace, and the popular press, have been insulated from. Most public debate about SDI turns around the system's effectiveness—will it be twenty percent effective, fifty, ninety, what? The scenario before us, however, is dreadful, no matter *how* effective the Soviet SDI. Even if Ivan's system can take out only five percent of a full-scale first strike, he might be able to take out what *remains* after his own preemptive strike."

Simon, proud author of *Blueprint for Superpower Disarmament*, was of course paid to know, and know well, the strategies and scenarios Buchanan had just described. The mere fact that Buchanan had directed his soliloquy at Simon was a cutting insult.

"To make it explicit," Air Force Chief of Staff Harold Singletree added, "consider this: Maybe they get their SLBM's just off our coast, and take out a helluva chunk of our arsenal before we know what's going on. Then their SBI might just handle enough of what remains. Not complicated at all, but quite wickedly formidable."

"But there does remain the software," Bramsen said. "We're years ahead of them here."

"Maybe. Maybe not," Buchanan said. All eyes turned back to the Admiral, who was at the podium still, standing, drawing on his pipe, and now back in command of the meeting.

"Elaborate," the President said.

Buchanan explained about the stolen Neurocubes.

Bramsen, upon hearing of the theft, said, simply, "No."

"They have seven, Arnold," Buchanan said.

Bramsen ran his hands through his hair a number of times, then said, "Seven? Seven Neurocubes?"

Buchanan said, "Yup."

"Jesus," Bramsen said. "Jesus H. Christ. You're talking machines which make conventional Crays look like turtles. And these machines are in the hands of the *Soviets*?"

"Of course," Secretary of Defense Allen Newell said, "Ivan is in no position to *use* these machines. He has trouble running spreadsheet software on a PC."

"I agree," said Bramsen. "The learning curve for these machines is about as high as it comes. They're not digital devices, they're analog. There's a crowd out there that can make massively parallel machines dance, but these babies are more than parallel. They're neural, genuinely neural. In the opinion of many, myself included, there's no mathematical creature that defines limits on them. Only a small number of scientists are in this league."

"Maybe. Maybe not," Buchanan said again, sending some pipe smoke up toward the ceiling.

"What do you mean?" Newell asked.

Buchanan explained about the missing and believed-to-be-kidnapped Neurocube engineers Jeff Renear and Fred Pattison.

Newell said, "Christ."

"Disarmament, eh, Orville?" Navy Chief Conrad Glennie said, speaking for the first time. "Ivan's smashed a MIG and an orbiter, stolen seven computers and the American citizens to maintain them, and four short days ago you were orgasmic about the prospects for the complete elimination of our respective nuclear arsenals."

There was really nothing Simon could say. Nothing. The usually swift, vibrant, and verbal brain behind his forehead refused to work now in an orderly fashion. Everything seemed disconnected. And uncontrollably so.

Bramsen said, "Hold on, gentlemen, there *is* still the software issue. These two missing men are merely operators. They're like the guys who pull out and replace defective chips. The mechanics, if you will."

"These guys can't program neural-net machines?" Newell asked.

"Teach," Bramsen said.

"Teach?"

"Yeah, you don't program a neural net; you train it."

"Whatever," Newell said impatiently. "You're telling us they don't have anyone to program them?"

"No more than you or I," Bramsen replied. "They have the machines and the technicians, but who's going to, to use your misnomer, *program* these Neurocubes? Neural computing, as I've said, is well-understood by just a few scientists, and all of them are here, in the States."

A fleeting moment of united relief.

But then Buchanan, smiling, pipe in hand, said, "Still?"

Silence. While the import of the succinct query sank in, and with it, strenuous thought:

The Joint Chiefs—of a preemptive strike.

President Randolph Atwood—not of strategy, or retaliation, or threats, but of history. And of his, and his predecessor's, precarious place within it.

Buchanan—of his plan.

The Admiral brought the meeting to a close by volunteering to handle, with the Bureau, protection of the scientists in question. Everyone nodded. And then the group disbanded.

On the way out Buchanan asked Bramsen who Ivan's first choice would be, and Bramsen, without the slightest hesitation, said, "Alexander Nelsen, Brown University."

No one but Buchanan heard the name, just as the DCI had planned.

Back at Langley

The size of the opportunity was intoxicating. If his plan worked, it would be a very big deal indeed. But he had little doubt that some of the others would soon start thinking about direct confrontation with Ivan, especially if the Soviet Union was able to use these strange neural machines without much delay. Time was of the essence.

"Gail, get John in here."

John Kurst, DDO, Deputy Director, second in command, entered a minute later.

"What's new, James?" Buchanan didn't respond right away, and Kurst studied his chief. "Actually, I'm not sure I want to *know* what's new. Your face is tied in knots."

Buchanan proceeded to explain everything—MIG, shuttle, kidnapping, theft—to his DDO. It took all of a succinct ten-minute speech to turn Kurst's world upside down.

"Christ, James."

"I know. But listen, I have a plan."

"To leave the country?"

"No, really, listen to me. What if we can get someone to sabotage their system?"

"Come on, James. What system? If I understand the situation, the Soviets have literally thousands of self-contained devices. So *what* if you take out a few?"

Buchanan explained the need to tie them all together in a BM/C^{3}I network. And then he explained that the machines that could do this were tough little bastards to work with. "Especially if you're a communist who creams over something as primitive as a VAX," Buchanan said. "Bramsen tells us there are only a few people trained to put these machines to work."

"So? This is welcome news, but how does it give rise to a plan?"

"Simple. We help them build the software, and while we do it we sabotage the system."

"*We* build it?"

"Yup. If we don't, they will. It'll just take longer if we leave 'em alone. This way we get our hands into the engine, where we can install a few wrenches."

The DDO was intrigued but skeptical: "Who, James?"

"One of the few who can at present create the software, of course."

"A civilian?"

"No alternative. No one else has the knowledge."

"Let me get this straight, James. You want to recruit a civilian scientist to go into the Soviet Union as a double agent, and you want him to sabotage their SBI?"

"You got it."

"No way."

"Why not?"

"Come on, James. A civilian? You don't even know who the candidates are. You're talking about sedentary middle-aged scientists. You'll be lucky if these men and women tolerate *vicarious* danger: if they watch spy movies, without taking Valium first, I'd be surprised. And you're going to put one of them in the Soviet Union. And what about security? What are you going to do, bypass background checks? You'll have to, or else you know as well as I do that the guy you send over there will be half-dead before he arrives. These days we can't bring a new man in without spending years to establish a cover."

Buchanan, undeterred, said, "I already have my man."

"Who?"

"Alexander Nelsen. He's at Brown University."

"James," Kurst said, "just like that? What do you know about hi—"

Buchanan quashed Kurst's objection with a raised hand, and said, "Just set up the interview, okay?"

Kurst was back in thirty minutes.

"All right, Chief, we're ready for a road trip to Providence."

"Good. Get anything on him?"

"Oh yeah. Just what you want: A thirty-two year old overeducated maniac with a deathwish. Mountains. Caves. Rocks. Skydiving. All kinds of insane stuff."

"Hmm."

"What about a background check, sir?"

Buchanan reflected for a moment.

"Simple," the Admiral finally said. "Ivan may already be trying to get their hands on him. If they are, we chart the target's reaction. And if they *haven't* made a play for Nelsen, why, then, we'll encourage them to do so."

In the old days, encouraging Ivan would have been a matter of ideology: the next morning certain senators known to leak like sieves would have "inadvertently" received information about Nelsen's "Marxist sympathies." But these were the new days. And so it would simply soon be suggested to a number of media people that Alexander Nelsen would make a good story. And, concurrently with the dissemination of this KGB-bound data, agents of the CIA were dispatched to Providence to watch and eavesdrop on Professor Nelsen's reaction.

"One more thing, John."

"What's that, Admiral?"

"Code name Dendrite."

18

Dendrite

February 13—Providence, Rhode Island

Malachev was by nature inclined to try a straightforward, guns blazing, rapid abduction. But *Macka*'s subtle *modus operandi* had bestowed upon the *spetsnaz* officer a degree of circumspection, and consequently Lazery Malachev, in a wet suit replete with diving mask, chose a subterranean route: it was the only way to get into Brown's Center for Information Science without being seen. All other points of entrance and departure were exposed, and were thus quite conceivably watched.

Armed with a crowbar, Malachev popped a manhole cover five blocks to the east on Angell Street, expending no more effort than that required to open a soda can. He climbed down, lit his headlamp, slid the cover back into position above him, pulled out his compass, got his bearings, and started to pick his way due east through wiring, steam pipes . . . and sludge? Yeah, feculent sludge.

"Shit!"

Nelsen was in his lab, his darkened sanctum, the only light emanating from the monitors within it. He was alone, unarmed, preoccupied with the disobedient code displayed on the screen of his Neurocube, tenaciously debugging a program that refused to run. Van-Dam lab: where, alone with his Neurocubes in the early morning, Alexander Nelsen worked in tranquillity, cradled in the bosom of technology. It wasn't a place where visitors blended in. Those who worked here had rumpled, sleepless bodies speaking the esoteric language of a silicon-driven subculture.

First he smelled a sewer smell.

And then, catching the human form, Alex smelled another scent—the scent of danger. It registered in a deep recess largely dormant since his ancestors hunted game without the luxury of guns. The figure reflected on the Neurocube's screen was all wrong: motionless, too heavily and sharply clothed, posture too rigid, physique that of man capable of bone-crushing leverage. Alex's brain assimilated countless such facts in an instant, and, by instinct, his muscles came alive even before he turned quickly to see Lazery Malachev, *spetsnaz*, standing in the lab, looking serenely at his prey.

Dark.

Huge.

As threatening and implacable as an approaching thundercloud.

The two were utterly alone. Silence save for the hum of the neural machines.

Who the hell is this?

"Hello," Malachev said. The voice deep, supremely calm; the accent heavy. The greeting echoed through the room ominously.

"Hello," Nelsen responded with a calm of his own, one born not of such confrontations as the present one, but of battles against nature. "Have you thought of changing deodorants?"

"I would like to keep this neat," Malachev said, ignoring the quip. The agent pulled out a large, silver, glistening handgun.

"All right, look, I'll pay my overdue traffic tickets. Here, I'll write you a check."

"Just come with me quietly, and you won't be harmed," Malachev said.

"I have quite a bit of work to do here. So if if it's all right with you, I'd appre—"

"Shut the fuck up!" Malachev boomed. "We're going to walk out of here side by side, and do a little caving in the process." Malachev pointed the gun at Nelsen now.

"Well, all right, if you insist. I do like spelunking."

They looked at each other. Nelsen wore a wide smile. Malachev started to approach, keeping his gun up.

When the *spetsnaz* agent was but five feet away, it hit Nelsen that the man was a fucking house. *Well, now or never, I suppose.*

Alex dived under the row of machines in front of him.

Didn't hear a gunshot.

Did hear a grunt of exertion that wasn't his own.

Felt his ankle locked in what seemed an iron vise.

And it was funny, but with pursuit inevitable, and inevitably rapid, Alex thought, first, that this was a needless interruption of work he had very much wanted to complete.

His second thought, underneath the long one-piece desk that supported a row of eight Neurocubes, was that he'd better think—fast. That he'd almost embarked on an unwanted trip to who knows where, that the guy looked like a pro, someone no doubt quite comfortable with inflicting bodily harm—these things didn't occur to Alex. He hadn't the slightest intention of leaving. At the moment he felt strangely alive. Adrenaline had kicked in. He felt as if he could modulate at will, with utter precision, the quivering to his tiniest tendon.

The keen preternatural hyperawareness that came before a dive from a cliff or bridge overtook him.

Alex unplugged a machine, reached back, and violently dug the prongs into the hand clasping his ankle.

Blood.

Loose.

Alex scampered through a maze of computer cables, outlets, and desk-supporting legs, up to the next row. The angles were in his favor; he had a second to breathe. Darkness would help, Nelsen thought, but there was no way to get to the switches without the intruder seizing or shooting him. A dash to the switches, however fast, was out of the question. *Mutatis mutandis* for a dash to either side exit.

Malachev was patient. He didn't crawl along the ascending floor after Nelsen. Instead, starting from the row at which their exchange had taken place, Malachev began checking row after higher row systematically, bending down to look for the American.

Alex crawled as quietly as possible toward the back of the lab and put a cushion of five rows between himself and Malachev. Each row was higher than the one in front of it, and he knew the intruder, by bending down for a look, couldn't get a clear view along the lab's uneven floor. Malachev made his way back slowly but surely, and eventually, Alex knew, he would reach the back wall, with nowhere to go from there. Malachev realized this and checked each inch of each row, moving gradually and fastidiously toward the rear of the auditorium. Alex felt the Russian's ungodly patience fill the room, and, with the universe slowing to a crawl, his mind wandered over a lightning-fast montage of countless life-and-death situations he had faced. He recovered, and the lapse in concentration, the sheer idiocy of it, struck Alex as amusing.

His only chance hit him on the heels of his internal laughter: the power. The cables snaking round his body, the receptacles for these cables—he suddenly saw the electricity as his only shot. It would be noisy, he'd give away his position, but it was his only chance.

He smashed his heel against an outlet—nothing, just a streak of pain from foot to lower back.

Sweating profusely now, he kicked again, harder this time, the vibration of the blow rippling over his skull.

The kidnapper was close: Alex could hear the man's breathing. The receptacle had opened a bit, but just a bit. Just after the third kick, which did it, Alex thought he heard the intruder sigh with delight at finding his target. But when Malachev bent over at Alex's row, a black wire carrying 120 volts met his face. The Russian's eyes opened beyond what Alex thought physiologically possible, and the shock distracted the *spetsnaz* officer enough to allow Alex to grab his gun and to run for the emergency exit, through which, after a dash, he burst. The door closed behind him. An alarm started screaming.

He was outside. The sweet fresh open air of Brown University. A moment to think:

The door through which Alex had passed flew open; Malachev emerged, stood in the doorway, blood on his hand, face. The Russian looked quite a bit like a rabid animal.

Alex smiled. And held the gun up, pointing it at Malachev's chest.

"I imagine this is quite a reversal for a guy like you, huh?"

Malachev said nothing. He looked a wreck. And he smelled awful.

There was simply too large a distance between the two, and Alex was faster, capable of scaling vertical rock as quickly as the muscle-bound Malachev could sprint. Alex could run like the wind; Malachev could move mountains. But the mountains had to be grasped before they could be moved. And in this case the mountain was armed.

"Care to explain what you want with little old me?"

Malachev said nothing. He was the embodiment of hate. A vision gripped his brain: one in which he ripped this American's head off with his bare hands. Literally.

"Cat got your tongue?"

They stood still, looking at each other, on Angell Street, on College Hill, at two-thirty in the morning.

What they hell do I do? March the guy to a police station? Too messy. Gives him too many opportunities. I'll just fucking disappear.

"I'll be leaving now, sir," Nelsen said, and, taking one step away, he emptied the .44 of its Lyman bullets and cast them into some nearby rhododendrons.

Malachev growled something in Russian. Every ounce of his being craved killing this American.

I'd like to tear the spinal cord of this wise-ass in two. Now. Right fucking now.

But: *I can't.*

Malachev cursed Alexander Nelsen's mother, in Russian.

Then Malachev bolted toward Nelsen just after the bullets made little thuds, landing on the nearby soil. His acceleration was greater than what Alex had anticipated. But the attempt, though surprisingly deft, was still pointless. Alex was thirty-two, possessed of a constitution honed by the passionate pursuit of utter danger, chronically cool, and knew the territory: Malachev hadn't a chance.

Nelsen ran fast in the winter air; he ran, indeed like the wind—through the lit courtyard underneath the Science Library, across Thayer Street and underneath Soldier's Arch, into the tree-lined darkness of the lower Green, whipping past buildings that had been makeshift hospitals for American soldiers wounded in the Revolutionary War. When he reached Prospect Street on the other side of the Green, slipping like a shadow underneath Brown's ancient lamps, he saw Providence's State House dome shining brilliantly beneath College Hill, and he knew he had left the kidnapper light-years behind.

And Nelsen was strangely happy, having tasted a degree of danger hitherto sought, but hitherto unknown.

His brother's hope, uttered atop a Himalayan peak, had come to pass: the mountain, the challenge, had indeed come to Alex, rather than the other way around.

Under the university's clock tower, its bells just now striking three A.M., Professor Nelsen thought about what the hell to do.

Let the police know, anyway.

A phone, then.

But home was out of the question: maybe this guy, or some of his friends, whoever they might be, had the place covered.

Alex slumped against Brown's clock tower, relaxed, reflected. Looked out of the darkness at his surroundings; listened.

The lamplights burned in the university's buildings as they had for injured soldiers in the Revolution. The writings of the greatest thinkers, taught to generations of youth, whispered in the ivy. Alex had just about lost his life minutes ago, but, supported by the ghosts of the university, he was utterly self-possessed now.

He took a deep breath.

A phone, then.

A pay phone? The Seven-Eleven on Thayer had some—but too exposed. And impossible to get over there while staying under cover. *All* the pay phones within reach, he realized, were too out in the open.

A private phone, then.

Whose?

Well, that of a colleague.

Which?

Katherine Brock lived in Fox Point, on the fringes of the gentrification that continued to sweep across Providence; she'd have to do.

Alex stepped out of the shadows and saw him approaching on Prospect's sidewalk. Not the intruder. But an elderly gentleman, white-haired, slow gait, smoking a pipe and humming. A professor. Alex couldn't place the guy, though.

When they were about to pass, the professor abruptly stopped. And looked directly into Nelsen's eyes.

Buchanan then pulled out his wallet, flipped it open, but kept it down by his waist. Alex saw a badge, what appeared to be legitimate seals and symbols, and made out "CENTRAL INTELLIGENCE AGENCY."

A strange night.

This elderly spy with the craggy avuncular face took Nelsen's hand, shook firmly, smiled grandfatherly, and said, "Hello, Alex. We've been expecting you. I'm Buchanan. You like caving, don't you? Join me."

Buchanan pulled out a hooded poncho and handed over one of the two walking sticks he was carrying.

"Just look old and feeble, young man, and we'll walk side by side. You know the abandoned railroad tunnel that used to run underneath College Hill?"

"Yes."

"Do you know where it ends, emerging by the Seekonk?"

"I've been through the thing. It goes from one side of College Hill to the other."

"I figured as much. Come. You lead the way, keeping us off sidewalks whenever possible."

It was a ten-minute walk through the cobblestone alleys and private yards of Providence's College Hill. The two stayed almost completely off the streets, weaving their way on private property. They walked side by side shrouded in the ponchos, like ghosts, through bracing sea air perfumed by nearby Narragansett Bay, passed quiet, darkened colonials.

They headed for the Seekonk River, entered the community of Fox Point.

They passed by two sleeping pit bulls, a snoring

German shepherd, saw a goodly number of cats on the prowl, slid underneath ghost-shaped clothes hanging out to dry, walked by a number of Virgin Marys and crucifixion scenes, stepped over a man mysteriously asleep against the rear wall of a house, scaled nine thankfully short chain-link fences, interrupted a pair of lovers on a back porch, and finally slipped across Wickendon Street and down into the dense underbrush that hid the east entrance to the 1800's bat-and-rat-infested tunnel that Nelsen, ever the adventurer, had explored two years ago after hearing about the passageway from a student.

They walked into the blackness. Buchanan clicked on a flashlight. Rats scurried away from their feet. They walked by a couple of abandoned homeless-people shacks, built of cardboard. They walked further in, under the Hill. Until the moonlight marking the entrance disappeared behind them.

"This'll do," Buchanan said, taking a seat on a block of granite that had been part of the wall of the tunnel. Nelsen followed suit and sat on his own block. The flashlight remained on, their only illumination.

Half-soldier, half-civilian, Alex thought, surprised at the speed of his intuitive assessment. Buchanan was in a suit, but looking strangely at home in the dank, stuffy, claustrophobic tunnel.

"You go into these kinds of places for fun, don't you, Dr. Nelsen?"

"Sometimes."

Alex thought: This is the genuine article. Coalescence of ID with demeanor: an elderly face, but one devoid of fear—one upon which Alex couldn't even *picture* fear. Eyes that seemed to throw off a palpable beam of intelligence. A bearing which was not the least bit diminished by sitting akimbo, upon a block, underground, in a foul tunnel. Buchanan had the lean, self-assured look of a man who had come face-to-face with death and triumphed. Part weariness, part fearlessness.

The Admiral smiled. And the smile seemed to Alex warm and confident and utterly self-possessed. There was something utterly masculine behind it, and it radiated the brotherhood of a taxing ascent up a sheer face of rock, your life hanging on your partner's rope. Buchanan's job involved thrills similar in type to those Nelsen went out of his way to find, and so from the start there was a bond between the two. But there was more, Alex saw: a heightened sensitivity to shifts in undercurrents that truly mattered. It was the closest Nelsen had ever come to a soldier. He had missed Nam, of course, and since then American males had tasted war only through the obfuscating medium of film, in the form of such movies as *The Deer Hunter* and *Platoon*. Alex wondered for a second where combat and its effects were in the psyche of his interlocutor.

"Expecting?" Alex said.

"Sorry?"

"You said you were expecting me. How so?"

"We were *hoping* Ivan would try recruitment."

"You were watching?"

"Yes."

"And you didn't intervene."

"Right."

"Why not?"

"Time, Dr. Nelsen. We don't have any. Rather than a lengthy background check, interviews with your family, friends, and acquaintances, we let Ivan proposition you."

"Waiting for my reaction."

"Mm hmm. The conventional method is not only more time-consuming, it's less reliable. There are always people with backgrounds cleaner than the driven snow who turn. It's a better bet that someone who resists a multimillion-dollar offer will stay loyal."

"No Russian has offered me money."

"Really? Hell, that's out of character. Usually they try cash first, and then, if that fails, force. Either someone fucked up or they don't see you as sufficiently venal."

"How closely were you watching? What about the ape back there at Brown? If he'd managed to get those simian hands on me, your story implies that I'd be on my way to Russia."

"True," Buchanan said softly, unemotionally. "We're still not sure how he got into VanDam without us seeing."

"Very reassuring, Admiral."

"Well, all for the best, son. Civilians put in a spot like that are likely to piss in their pants and freeze. I've more than once seen machismo evaporate in an instant, to leave a whimpering child pleading not to be killed. Most don't even think of running. None to speak of dig down and think. Of course, on paper you look resourceful, to say the least, but that's paper, and paper doesn't mean shit when the barrel of a sleek nine-mil is breathing down your neck. Now we know, don't we?"

"It was a .44 mag. Octogonal barrel. Group 3″ bullets."

Buchanan looked for a moment at Nelsen before saying, "I see."

"So what's next?"

"Well, they'll be back. Maybe they'll be civil at some point, maybe not. Maybe the ape'll pop up next to your bed with the barrel of that mag on your temple. No matter what, just play damn hard to get. They won't kill you: they need you for their Star Wars system. Eventually they'll make you an offer you can't refuse. If they do get nice and contemplate defection, it doesn't matter, because with you playing hard to get they'll soon get back to kidnapping. And then . . .

why, then you go over to sabotage the software for Ivan's Star Wars. Simple, direct, straightforward."

"And also predictable. I find it hard to believe that the Russians, in this case, wouldn't anticipate. After all, some American computer scientists, in public, have pondered the software sabotage of *our* SDI. Perhaps you succumb to some such stereotype as that the Russian is a cretin. I don't."

"Look, let's do this sensibly. Let us assume that, yes, the Sovs will think you've been hired by Langley to throw a wrench into their system. Accordingly, they'll keep a close eye on you and try to make sure you're a nice little boy. What you have to do, then, is blow the thing up right in front of their eyes, without them seeing."

Buchanan had packed his pipe, and now lit the tobacco with a few measured puffs. When satisfied with the molten mass of Captain Black, he said, "Now, that's the worst-case assumption. The fact is, Ivan can be astonishingly slow. Historically he's been waiting to shoot down anything that touches his airspace. He racks his brains about how to hit our spy planes. A JAL jet so much as touches the edge of Kamchatka—boom, gone. But then a harebrained German boy flies a single-engine Cessna from Bonn to Moscow without a scratch."

Buchanan smoked a bit in silence. The airborne Capain Black took on a strange pearl-white shimmer in the tunnel, lit up by the flashlight.

"Now, as I say, they may regroup and start off very polite. They don't think you're Mother Theresa, for Christ's sake. And you're not J. P. Morgan. There's money. In unfathomable amounts. They're not cretins, but they do believe, deep down, that a capitalist's weakness is capital. They may make a monetary offer."

"Which I decline."

"Yep. Hard to get, that's the ticket. The harder to get, the less likely you are to be on our payroll."

"But we assume that they *do* think I'm with the CIA."

"Right. Assuming the worst is always theraupeutic in ops like this. Everyone's less likely to fuck up."

"And why should I accept *your* proposal?"

"Ah," said Buchanan, "we pay *too.*"

"A dead man, Admiral, doesn't have sybaritic taste."

"I'm afraid this stuff is a good deal less romantic than you seem to think, Alex. Murder is rather a rarity in our business. Our rate of loss is a third what it is on any urban police force."

Having said this, Buchanan felt a pang of guilt. In this mission, as always, there was doubt—a good deal of doubt. And there sure as hell was the *potential* for violence in Dendrite. It wasn't going to be a cakewalk. Possible complications had nothing to do with Nelsen's ability, conventionally appraised; they had to do with Nelsen's decency and the other side's complete lack of it. Alexander Nelsen was a dream come true for the present op, on paper. But it wasn't possible to represent on paper whether or not a man had what Buchanan considered the decisive trait: the ability to be utterly predatory. When Buchanan looked at his new recruit he saw a dizzyingly talented individual, but not a predator. Could he kill a KGB agent? Put a bullet in an opponent's heart, if it came to that? Buchanan wasn't sure. He looked into the fundamentally nice blue eyes of Alexander Nelsen and wasn't sure. If anything, he thought the answer to such questions was no. But Professor Alexander Nelsen was the best an imperfect world had to offer, and Buchanan brimmed with assurance and concealed his doubt behind the ruddy poker face that was legendary among Langley's gambling cadre.

"Save it, Admiral."

"Sorry?"

"If I cared, I'd be better off as a redneck cop walking a beat in Harlem."

"If you cared?"

"Yeah. I don't care. About the danger, that is. I play with computers as a hobby, Admiral. Danger is my profession."

"But of a different sort, of course."

"Of course. But dangerous *people*, rather than dangerous *activity*, may be a pleasant change."

It had occurred to Buchanan, when looking at the scientist's dossier, that Nelsen was arguably insane. It occurred to him again.

"Forget the money, Mr. Buchanan. I have more than I can spend. I sit on my ass and I have royalties pouring in from software—that alone is excessive. And besides, I spend large sums generally only in pursuit of—"

"Mountains, caves, and so on," Buchanan interjected, smiling.

"Exactly. Furthermore, Admiral, if I wanted money badly enough to risk my head on this juvenile James Bondish scheme, I'd probably steal it—a few minutes with my machine and a modem and I've got a Swiss account that rivals the CIA's budget."

A disdain for money as an intrinsic end was common ground between them. Buchanan believed in America, and believed that without those dedicated to defending her, she would perish. As a realist, he knew that all kingdoms eventually end, but he'd decided long ago that he'd do his level best to keep America's end as far off as possible. And a talented individual's drive for money, in Buchanan's grand scheme, accomplished nothing.

"Forget the money, then," Buchanan said. "There are the biggies."

"The biggies?"

"Preserving democracy and saving the free world.

If the Soviets bring up a workable SDI, you can kiss the liberty of Occidental culture good-bye. With such a system, they'd be holding a shotgun to our temple. Mutual assured destruction, deterrence—the system which, however barbaric it seems, has kept the peace for over forty years—these things would evaporate, lose their meaning. Ironic though it be, a strategic *defense* turns out to be the ultimate *offensive* weapon."

Buchanan was right to shift to philosophical grounds. One thing about Nelsen, he was straight as an arrow ideologically. Despite recent events, the world, when carved up in terms of political philosophy, carved up neatly for Dr. Alexander Nelsen. Freedom; tyranny—simple. Alex understood all too well the moral disasters of the purges, of Cambodia, of Afghanistan. He had a fundamentally sound conception of who the bad guys were. Most brainy people, he believed, were quite fuzzy on that score.

Buchanan explained, as had been explained in the Situation Room of the White House, how a partially effective SDI, coupled with a large and decisive nuclear strike from submarines, could mean instant victory.

A silent interlude. Buchanan inhaled, exhaled; the sweet smoke filled the old railroad tunnel. Most of the track, Buchanan noticed, was intact.

Nelsen walked all the way to the other side? Jesus. Probably without a light, too.

The Admiral looked up at Nelsen and could sense the young man's brain searching for a solution; it was as if there was electrical current in the air.

"We can't retaliate while their birds are airborne?" Nelsen asked.

"Not in the submarine-launch picture. Our policy for retaliation has been to ensure sufficient survivability, and then, after sizing up the situation, retaliate. We never did adopt LOW, launch-on-warning—the policy of initiating retaliation while their missiles are on the way."

"Why not?"

"Well, the rationale is simple, and seems, even now in retrospect, compelling. The fact is that launch-on-warning is a policy that would have to be automated; there is no time for human deliberation if we are to retaliate while their missiles are airborne. LOW is only for machines. A Soviet ICBM has about a twenty-five-minute flight time; after detection and confirmation, we're left with about eight and a half minutes of clean and informed decision time—plenty of room for deciding whether to use 'em or lose 'em. But the SLBM scenario isn't so pretty: one of these birds finds us in nine short minutes. After subtracting time needed for detection, confirmation, and counter-launch, if that is decided upon, you're left with about thirty seconds of decision time. And that's too little to permit human deliberation up and down the NORAD chain of command. So if you want to implement LOW, you've got to leave it up to the computers. And that didn't seem like a good idea. The dilemma's nasty: if you want LOW you've got to hand over the earth to a computer, but without LOW their SDI, even if only marginal, is rather unpleasant to ponder."

Another silent interlude—during which Nelsen searched once again for a solution, and Buchanan enjoyed feeling the kid's wheels turning.

"What about cruise missiles? They fly just above the ground, presumably invulnerable to attacks from space."

"Who says they have to attack from space? They have ground-to-air interceptors for terminal defense. And besides, one of the first things the superpowers agreed on at the new round of arms talks in Vienna was the elimination of cruise missiles."

Though Alex didn't know it, at this juncture, for the first time, the collective mental power of the *Starik* had genuinely pressed upon him. For Professor Alexander Nelsen it was purely visceral: he sensed, deep down, the tip of the other side's genius.

"So what could we have done?" Alex asked.

"That's simple," the Admiral replied. "As always, it turns out that the ultimate armament is distrust. We trusted. If we hadn't, the absence of launch-on-warning wouldn't matter a bit."

"We've let them get close?"

"Close? They *have* the hardware. What they lack is what you can give them."

"But even the most optimistic predictions have an operative SDI consigned to the next century. How could they possibly be twenty years ahead of us on laser and particle-beam technology? And would we sit back on our ass while the Soviet Union calmly put together their SDI? This kind of system isn't built overnight, and presumably isn't built of small pieces. It's not like they can do it all inside a building."

"All true enough. But remember the Patriots?" Buchanan, puffing intermittently on his pipe, explained that the Soviet SDI was really S*B*I, a smart rock, or kinetic-energy, system, that they could easily bring these rocks up to space without drawing suspicion, that they did indeed do it all inside a building, somewhere, someplace, and that they perhaps had enough kinetic-kill ammunition already in orbit to first-strike the U.S. by sub and handle a good chunk of the retaliation. Buchanan also shared with Nelsen the top-secret information regarding the destruction of the MIG, the Soviet shuttle, and the laser SDI facility at Kirovobad. And also the theft of the Neurocubes. And *also* the kidnapping of Jeff Renear and Fred Pattison.

"Jeff? Fred?"

"Sorry, Alex."

"Jesus."

Nelsen thought silently for a minute. "What about us?" he asked.

"Us?"

"Yeah, *our* SDI."

Buchanan explained that the U.S. and USSR were at parity on the laser stuff, but not so with smart rocks, and that, simply put, the Soviet SBI was undeniably a brilliant move.

"So, Alex, as you can see, you're on center stage."

Buchanan looked at Nelsen, and Nelsen looked at Buchanan, and the Admiral, with his eyes, asked the professor if he was willing to do it.

Deliberation wasn't necessary. Defense of eternal ideals. Danger and challenge that exceeded climbing. And an intellectual game par excellence: neural-net computing applied to a project a good deal more interesting than anything he was at present doing. And the task itself, the actual software sabotage, seemed to Nelsen trivial. With access to the program, he figured he couldn't fail to find a way to trash it, even with the Sovs looking over his shoulder. How well could they possibly understand Neurocubes? The challenge was in *getting* access—in finding the right moment, the opportunity, and in finding a way to slip in a virus or worm or software bomb or something similar without them seeing. And Alexander Nelsen simply saw the challenge as a helluva lot of fun. Poor imitations are read at the beach, and films that carry the gist are watched by millions. Alex had an opportunity to live the genuine article. For a patriot seeking to hit his limits, it was quite simply irresistible.

"When do I start?" Alex asked.

Admiral James Buchanan inhaled, puffed out a ring of smoke. Then, to Nelsen, he said, "Now. We call the mission Dendrite. It's known to only three men, and all three are with the Agency: myself, the DDO, and the NIO on the Soviet Union. That's it."

"The Congress? The administration? Are they completely in the dark?"

"Yup. It's the only way to go. Aside from the standard reasons for keeping this op under wraps, such as, for example, your own safety, there's also the fact that knowledge of your mission means knowledge of Uncle Sam's nasty dilemma. And no one in the know, no one who knows that the Soviets have a working though rudimentary SDI, wants anyone *else* to know. Least of all the public. If Dendrite leaked, the Russian SDI superiority would leak with it, and soon the *Post* or *Times* splashes it all over the place. And then we might very well have a panic, or worse. Iran-Contra was an idiotic flop, but the attempt to keep it within NSC and CIA was in and of itself quite prudent."

Nelsen nodded.

"The bottom line, Alexander, is that you're buying us time—time to perfect our own SBI, which our scientists are feverishly trying to do. What we want is parity; it's what we always want. Someone's always dreaming about actual elimination, but who the hell wants Uncle Sam and Ivan to go unarmed when the fucking Saddams of the world have the bomb, and the ability to deliver it? Now, I don't expect you to trash their SBI forever—that, of course, is completely unreasonable. After all, they'll eventually find out the thing's defective, and then they'll just fix it. It may take them a while, but no matter what you do, they will eventually bring the system up."

"But it should test out dandy while I'm there."

"Yup."

"In a genuine battle scenario, however, it should crash."

"Yup."

"Okay."

Alex thought for a moment, fingers on his temple. Then he asked: "What about the logistics of my departure?"

"In the shallow sense, your leaving isn't any big deal. We don't know when, but, as I said, the Soviets *will* be back, and they'll have no trouble getting you out. I would assume, indeed, that you'll simply walk onto an Aeroflot flight to Moscow. You're not a public figure."

"Then in what sense *is* my departure a problem?" Alex asked.

"Oh, come now. Think a bit. You're part of an enormous web of human interaction—everybody is. You've got a mother and father, a brother, innumerable colleagues and friends. But remember, Ivan still thinks that in all likelihood we know nothing about his SDI; he thinks we haven't a *clue* as to how far along he is. So, clearly, they don't want anybody to know you're helping them, because someone knowing that might have reason to think you were there precisely to put your expertise to work on the Russian Star Wars. The Sovs'll demand your help in this regard, and you'd better be ready with a plan."

Nelsen began to reflect in silence. The Admiral pulled out a thermos, poured himself a cup of coffee, gestured an offer to Nelsen, who declined. Then Buchanan sipped his brew and waited.

"No problem," Alex said after a minute. "Getting around my teaching is easy. I'll take release time. I've got loads of grant money; I'll just send enough in my Chair's direction for adjuncts to cover for me. He'll approve it on reflex. As far as friends, family, colleagues, and the Russkies: it should be easy enough to have everyone believing that I'm floating around the globe as usual. As soon as the Russians make their offer, I announce that I'm off to the Soviet Union for a working vacation: some conferences, some interaction with computer scientists over there, presentation of a few papers, and also an expedition."

"An expedition?"

"Yeah, it's something everybody half-expects me to

announce at a moment's notice: it'll fit the pattern. Let's see, what is there in Russia and its surroundings? . . . Oh, yeah, hell, of course: there are *many* damn good climbs to be had over there. The twenty-four-thousand-foot Pamirs are on communist soil. That's where I'll say I'm headed."

"Good," Buchanan said, rising to his feet. "That's that, then. Let's go."

Buchanan started walking out of the tunnel. Then noticed that Nelsen wasn't following.

"You coming?"

"I'll walk through to the other side. The exit's just a block from my house on Benefit."

"I'll leave you my flashlight, then," the DCI offered.

"Naah, it'll be a trip without it."

The Admiral smiled and shook hands with his newest recruit. They separated, walking in opposite directions, Buchanan toward light, Nelsen into darkness. Buchanan, after a few steps, pulled out from his poncho a walkie-talkie, and into it said, "We're ready."

The DCI emerged from the tunnel shortly thereafter, plowed through the brush, and climbed up to Wickendon, where a limo, door open, was waiting. Four phones in the back blinked with other business; a Mac VI laptop computer hummed; refreshments were waiting; and the pleasant aroma of complete secrecy, as always, cradled him. As the car eased out onto the road with the soft languorous feel of a boat on water, the Admiral began to serenely reload his pipe. Then, thinking of Nelsen underground in the blackness for a thrill, he shivered.

America's newest spy was home twenty minutes later, just as day was breaking. No Russians were waiting at his house. He was due in his office at eleven, and decided to get some sleep. He was soon dreaming, not about espionage, but about climbing in the Pamirs.

February 13—The Plaza, Manhattan

"He what?" Kasakov exclaimed.

"He tried to bring Nelsen in," Vanderyenko replied.

"But on his own? Unauthorized?"

"I'm afraid so." The *Macka* nodded. "Lazery Petrovich has much entrepreneurial spirit."

"Why are the enterprising so often brainless?" Bazakin asked philosophically.

"Idiot," Kasakov spat. "But let us not forget, comrades, that Malachev and his men have been an indispensable part of our smuggling operation. Every time I click on my Sony or run a laser disk, I offer up a little thank-you to our *spetsnaz*."

"True," Vanderyenko said. "He and Korchnoi screw everything in sight, take all kinds of gambles, are probably utter sadists at heart, but I wouldn't want to be on the other side, facing them."

"Let's not get carried away," Bazakin said. "These Neanderthals are sooner or later going to put us out of business. What if Nelsen had been killed? Didn't you say there was a struggle, Nickolai Vasilyevich?"

"Yes, there was."

"All right, and who won?"

"Won?" Vanderyenko said.

"Simple question, *Macka*. Who *won*? Didn't Nelsen escape? Now, in my book that makes your venerated *spetsnaz* look rather silly. A fucking scientist, no less."

"I've told you," Vanderyenko protested, "this Nelsen is not your typical scientist. Consider our Comrade Matra. *She* is a scientist. And yet her biceps are equal to three of mine. I'm telling you, this Dr. Nelsen is superbly conditioned, clever, and, according to Malachev, both surly and fearless."

"Surly and fearless," Bazakin repeated coldly. "The Motherland invests a fortune training *spetsnaz*, and you're telling me that some young American—"

"Comrades," Kasakov interrupted, "let us not lose sight of the issue. We still do not *have* Alexander Nelsen. I suggest that, without further ado, we put our heads together and find a way to bring him in."

Nods all around.

"Macka?" Kasakov prodded.

"Well, we had talked eight mill before, but again, I urge you both to rule out money."

"Double it," Bazakin advised.

Vanderyenko exhaled air through his lips, making his exasperation clear. "Why are we so fucking redundant?" the Americanized techno-thief said. "We've been *over* this. Money won't do it. The man *has* money. Not sixteen million, I grant you, but he has enough to do everything he *wants* to do. You could offer the guy Fort Knox and he'd laugh in your face. He's not after a sybaritic life, comrades, he just wants to climb rocks, for God's sake."

"Well," Bazakin said to Vanderyenko, "then what do you suggest?"

"It's algorithmic, comrades; purely mechanical. There's ideology, money, blackmail, and sex—that's the fundamental quartet. Ideology's out right off the bat, has been since the Rosenbergs. Hardly anyone with a half a brain has enough pure hate for Uncle Sam to turn to us; and besides, Gorbachev has us looking like cutthroat capitalists these days, not champions of the downtrodden. Not to mention the fact that our Dr. Nelsen looks to be quite conventionally enamored of America."

The *Macka* paused for input from his colleagues; none came; so he proceeded:

"All right. So we're left with blackmail and sex.

Now. We've put his life under a microscope, and the guy's clean as a whistle—this goes hand in hand, of course, with the absence of greed. We have even looked painstakingly for dirt in the ever-widening arc of those who matter to him. But in this particular case—nothing. The Nelsens are a puritanical tribe. Even his brother, a Wall Street 'master of the universe,' is apparently on the up-and-up. So we're left with—"

"Wait," Bazakin said. "Are the two brothers close?"

"I would say so," Vanderyenko said.

"Okay," Bazakin continued. "You said Alexander isn't greedy. What about his brother?"

Vanderyenko nodded, and replied, "It's safe to say that money makes Matthew Nelsen tick. Not greedy, though. He's a Trump type."

Vanderyenko was the object of two quizzical looks. He often forgot that as a native American his knowledge of the States went well beyond that of his Russian-residing cohorts.

"Trump was a tycoon in the States," the *Macka* explained. "Built a fortune, lost it, rebuilt it, lost it again. Someone who supposedly strives for money because the striving itself provides the high, rather than the money; the money is merely a side effect of intrinsically rewarding deals. In my judgement, Matthew Nelsen is of this type."

"Then he does indeed provide an opening," Bazakin announced.

No one spoke; the other two searched for Bazakin's point, but drew a blank. In silence, they waited for elaboration.

"Well?" Vanderyenko prodded.

Bazakin, his fingers on his temples, was still sorting through the details. After a few more seconds of silent contemplation, he said, "Simplicity itself, comrades. Is this not the era of *perestroika*? Of joint ventures between Russia and America? We take one of the Russian companies that front for the KGB, bring our young tycoon inside information indicating its imminent demise, he goes massively short, and then, if Alex refuses to come to our party, we pump in cold, hard cash, give the company some favorable press, and boom, our Matthew is seriously wounded."

Vanderyenko was still parsing Bazakin's soliloquy when Kasakov said, "Inventive, but fucking stupid. One of the reasons we're here working our asses off for Great Russia is that we have no private industry to speak of. And yet suddenly we're going to build the next Exxon? And then there's the fact that Matthew Nelsen no doubt believes with all his heart in diversification. Even if he took a bath here, he'd be far from destitute."

"Well," Bazakin said resignedly.

"All right," Vanderyenko said, "let's return to the algorithm. Ideology, money, blackmail, sex. We're left with sex. And I'm afraid I must again reiterate what I said at an earlier meeting: sex isn't the least bit promising when it comes to Dr. Nelsen. Why would a man whose chief romantic problem is one of fighting off the unwanted fall for the kind of dim, washed-out women the KGB dangles in front of horny marines?"

Bazakin smiled. "Well-taken, *Macka*," he said, "but hardly an insuperable problem. There are women and there are women. What seems to be his preference?"

"I wouldn't say there's a pattern, comrade. He has recently ended a relationship—or perhaps *she* ended it; who knows?—with a Japanese computer scientist, but I know nothing about her. Other than that her name is Akiko."

"*Ended*, did you say?"

"Yes."

"Ah, most promising," Bazakin said. "We will fill

a vacuum, comrades. With a woman who makes this Akiko look like a cow."

"Who?" Vanderyenko asked, to some degree disappointed he was not in Nelsen's shoes, the wearer of which now stood to enjoy not only millions but also unbridled erotica.

"Come now, comrades," Bazakin said. "I believe Peter Andreevich has owned certain . . . property since GRU first brought her in as a *wunderkind*. She stands alone. Has a cover of unsurpassed verisimilitude. Hasn't had a single mission. And is," Bazakin said, grinning at Peter, "in terms of love, unattached."

Vanderyenko nodded, smiled; enjoying, vicariously, the amorous future of the man the *Starik* sought to recruit. Matra and Ignatov, had they been here, would have displayed disdain, for the two of them, despite their differences, saw eye to eye on the idiocy of love.

"Listen," Kasakov said. "Anna's not going to cut it either. Why don't we face it? We have a problem. And I'll tell you the source. If you start with bad premises, you can end up with shit. Garbage in, garbage out. Isn't that what you techies say? Well, I think the *Macka*'s algorithm is fatally flawed right from the beginning. Ideology, money, blackmail, sex. It's an incomplete list. Good old-fashioned gun-in-the-throat threats are missing. Why don't we stop walking so gingerly? Let's drag out some sleepers, give Mr. Nelsen a couple of businesslike offers. And if he declines, well, then we'll make him an offer he can't refuse. And nowhere along the line do we let him out of our sight. Malachev had the right idea. He just fucked up. If he'd shot Nelsen in the leg and carried him in, we'd already be in Siberia hard at work."

19

Offers

February 13—Providence, Rhode Island

The odd thing about the invitation, in retrospect, was that it seemed impromptu. Professor Alexander Nelsen was in his office, had been all day, waiting for them to come. Now he was looking at an electronic atlas that contained topographical maps of the Pamir Mountains. Willford Jones, doctoral candidate in the department, walked by out in the hallway, then stepped back to wave, then started to leave, and then ducked his Midwestern head back in and said:

"Professor Nelsen, can I buy ya some dinner?"

Nelsen, keeping his hands on his keyboard, did a quick mental scan of his appointments for the evening, found no engagement, and said, "Sure."

"Great," Jones responded. "I'll be back at six, then."

Willford Jones was a graduate student in Brown's Department of Computer Science. He was from the Midwest, or so he told everyone, anyway—from Bozeman, Montana. Jones had freckles, wore jeans, had yellow intractable hair of the texture of horsehair, occasionally sported a cowboy hat, and claimed to be a rodeo aficionado. Though he talked at a slow speed, often said "ain't," bounded around thunderously in cowboy boots even in the department's computer laboratories—though he was apparently from a different culture, he was well-liked and generally regarded to be an excellent doctoral candidate. However, he was not known for having disposable cash on hand, for lunch or anything else.

So when for their gastronomic destination Jones suggested Lucky's, an expensive Italian restaurant down the Hill in Providence, Nelsen wondered. And possibilities soon presented themselves: Jones was going to request that Nelsen be on his dissertation committee, was going to make a pitch for additional financial aid, was going to ask to be an employee in Nelsen's company, was going to make an amorous advance, being gay despite the surface masculinity of a cowboy from Montana. And so on. All such hypotheses, however, proved wrong.

"Do you have any political views, Professor Nelsen?"

A slight pause. "Sure."

"Such as?" Jones took a swig from his beer bottle; he seemed unusually relaxed and uninhibited.

"Oh, the usual, I suppose."

"What's the usual?" Jones asked.

"Cynicism, to start."

"You're disenchanted with the American capitalist system?"

Holy shit, this is it.

"With the American capitalist system? There's no need for pedantry here, Willford. I just subscribe to the common view that many politicians are corrupt."

"Perhaps the system itself is to blame," Jones suggested.

"I would think *power* is to blame. Or greed. Something like that, anyway."

"Forgive me for being presumptuous, Dr. Nelsen, but ain't it a bit duplistic of you to dump on the system while taking grant money from the government, from the military even?"

"Jones, are you a computer programmer or a philosopher?"

Jones emptied his bottle, waved the waitress over, and ordered another Coors with a deferential tip of his cowboy hat. Then he looked at the professor and said evenly, "What I'm driving at, Dr. Nelsen, is that perhaps you're on the wrong side."

"Jesus."

Do I look surprised? I hope to hell I do.

"Now, don't over—"

"And what side are *you* on, Willford?"

"The side of socialism," Jones said without hesitation.

"Socialism is dead."

Nelsen's pasta with four cheeses and Jones's linguine with red clam sauce arrived. Neither spoke till the waitress departed. Jones had smiled at her as a cowboy might.

"Listen, Jones, why don't you just cut this mysterious preamble. What's your point?"

Again, no hesitation: "We'll pay you sixteen million dollars to come and make the world safe from nuclear terror by helping us build our SDI. That direct enough for ya, partner?"

"Us?"

"The Soviet Union, Dr. Nelsen."

"The Soviets. The ape last night . . . Holy shit."

Willford Jones nodded, wound some linguine around his fork, swallowed the pasta, and said, "But you see, Dr. Nelsen, we'd like you to come willingly. The Soviet Union has no intention of using their SDI for anything else but to put an end to the arms race. If we have the system, and it works, we'll share it, and then both sides can throw away their weapons. Yours would be a defection history would smile upon. You'd be immortal."

"I already am," Alexander Nelsen said.

"Do you decline, then?"

"You got it, Willy."

Nelsen felt something hard on his kneecap.

"Oh, now, Willy, don't go too far with this cowboy stuff, okay?"

"Shut the fuck up." The accent was gone. "The kneecap is a nice place for a bullet. Not much blood, and though you'll be a cripple, you'll still be able to type."

"Your wish is my command."

"All right, listen. There's a limo out front, on Steeple. Get up, go out and get into it. Two marksmen are out there hoping you'll do something stupid, so don't. They too like kneecaps. They have to shoot, we dump you into the limo anyway. Kapish?"

"Yes."

The limo was there, back door open. Nelsen got in. There was another man in the backseat. An old friend.

"Hello, Alexander." It was Nelsen's mentor from Cal Tech, the man who had contributed to the fifty-year progression from vacuum tubes to Neurocubes. Kasakov had talked about sleepers. Josiah was Z's most valuable sleeper. Ever.

Professor Josiah Rosenkrantz—gray manicured hair, a Palm Springs tan, in a suit of a sort Alex had never seen him in—said, "It's been a long time."

Nelsen's mind went into overdrive, flooded with visual memories of the many nights he'd been a guest at the humble but wonderfully brainy house of the Rosenkrantzes, wherein, over inexpensive wine, the three of them had discussed not only the nuts- and bolts of parallel machines but also the philosophical side of AI, such as whether or not people are, at bottom, computers.

"I have two tickets to the ballet, Alex. The Bolshoi is in New York, with Marianov."

"This is purely pleasure, huh?"

"It doesn't have to be painful."

The car took off, and within seconds was speeding south on 95.

Alex settled in. The leg room was stupendous. Leather, burled walnut, a tiny Persian on the floor. Full bar, including an electric blender and a fridge. Caviar, champagne. A remarkably clear television. Cellular phone.

"I guess you've moved up in the world, Josiah."

Professor Rosenkrantz, known to wear the same inexpensive, tattered sport coat day after day, the same ancient, faded wing-tip shoes; the brilliant man with the unruly, ungroomed hair, the baggy pants held up with suspenders well before suspenders returned to fashion; the scientist who for years turned down consulting for cerebral solitude—this man was gone.

And it depressed Alex greatly.

Rosenkrantz said, "I can't say that I mind a little style after forty years of frugality."

"This is just business, is that it?"

"I don't know whether I can tolerate any righteousness. You don't hesitate to spend on one expedition more than I make in two years."

Alex didn't reply. The car sped on toward Manhattan through the gathering darkness. The two old friends stared straight ahead. This was without a doubt the biggest blow of Alex's life, one that made a climb, any climb, look uneventful. But within thirty minutes Nelsen had regained his balance. And that's when Rosenkrantz made his pitch.

"In the world of dance, they have it on us, Alex, you know that. Dance is a passion the both of us share. Remember the trips up to Saratoga together? Remember when Marianov gave a guest performance? They're better. Hell, we're as good as we are only because of them. Consider the immigrants. Take Balanchine and Baryshnikov away from us, and what ballet do we have? Compared to them aesthetically, we're Philistines."

"And science? If they, if *you*, have it on us there, then drop me off. I'm superfluous."

"You know, Alex, the Bolshoi is here now, so is the Kirov. They, on the other hand, let us perform Balanchine over there. *Glasnost* is for real. The Iron Curtain has dissolved. There aren't two opposing sides now. Or at least there shouldn't be. Not in dance. And not in the world of science and technology."

Alex shook his head. It had crystallized: the job with Reitman, access to high-technology products, suddenly money to burn and a desire to burn it.

Jesus.

"Giving up on you, Alexander, would be irresponsible. Should we be expected to sit quietly on the sidelines when a chance to make the world a safer place slides by? Why don't you allow us to explain ourselves? Has the possibility that we want SDI for the good of all not even crossed your mind? Reagan said he would share a perfected SDI with us. Why are you unwilling to take seriously a similar statement from us?"

"You ain't Gorby, Josiah. If *he* pays me a visit and wants to hire me, I'll think about it."

"If I see you again, Alexander, it will be when I take a trip to the Soviet Union. Your destiny is sealed."

Rosenkrantz pulled out a gun and nestled it into Nelsen's crotch.

"You'd be surprised, Alex, how little your loss of virility would affect your ability to program."

At that moment the door locks came down with a thud, the black motor-driven glass between front and back purred open, and Nelsen saw that the driver was the ape from the night before: Malachev. The *spetsnaz* agent turned and smiled.

Malachev said, "One move, one fucking move, and I'll be hanging what's left of your balls from my mirror here."

The car sped on. It was dark now.

* * *

Soon Manhattan's glow appeared on the horizon. Nelsen saw it, and daydreamed.

Growing up, two distinct worlds, like two galaxies in the night sky, had been within Alexander's sight. Baseball in breeze-caressed meadows that seemed in endless supply, versus the crowded vibrant glory of Fifth Avenue just before Christmas. Skiing on hills serviced by makeshift rope tows, versus trips to enormous buildings in which constellations sparkled, and giant dinosaur skeletons stood frozen, and paintings hung, and statues looked down upon humans imperiously.

Whippoorwill, a mansion-studded community in Armonk, a small town thirty-five miles from Manhattan in Westchester County. Versus Manhattan.

Twilight golf in Whippoorwill, at the highest point in Westchester, with a view of New York's skyline, a glittering necklace strung out across the horizon.

The apple-pie wholesomeness of sandlot ball versus magical nights at Yankee and Shea stadiums.

And now, at thirty-two, the glitter—theater; music; ballet; cuisine; a mouth-watering compaction of great beauties from across the globe; skyscrapers under construction, from which he was known to occasionally parachute—the glitter still drew him.

But would that I were going to the ballet under more relaxed circumstances.

And yet when all was said and done, the *prime* attraction, the *real* reason Nelsen flew down rather often from T. F. Green for weekends in the Big Apple, was a pair of kids: his brother's two daughters, Lisa and Lynn. The scientist willingly played the role of baby-sitter while Matthew Nelsen and his wife, Wendy (who had been through a string of nannies), out on the town without diapers and bibs and carriages, enjoyed the glitter that Alex and Matt, as young boys sitting together on a verdant hill, had seen hovering in the distance, at the end of the Hudson.

The girls were angels. Lisa—golden-haired, blond, button-nosed—was two and a half. She already had a passion for Dr. Seuss, confabulated charming if truncated stories of her own, was thrilled to the core by Walt Disney "Sing Along" videos, proudly displayed a number of "her faces"—sad, happy, surprised, frightened—and showed a remarkable degree of affection, through hugs and kisses and proclamations of innocent love for her uncle Alex. Lynn, equally cute, was only ten months younger than Lisa (the quick succession planned: Matt's wife had wanted to contain the physical trauma to one get-it-over-with stretch), had a vague, unstructured, but hilarious grasp of hide-and-seek (she'd hide by closing her eyes), loved to wrestle, play ring around the rosy, and get chased by a roaring dinosaur clad in the clothes of her uncle.

As Malachev approached the city, one of his colleagues was working hard within it.

It had been a standard stay-at-home evening. The girls, problem eaters, had had the staples for dinner: Kraft macaroni and cheese, some pineapple pieces, Oscar Meyer hot dogs, orange juice. Each, as usual, had made a hurricanelike mess. Lisa had dropped her tube steak two times to the floor, and had been instructed to rinse it off both times herself. Lynn had painted what she saw as a house on her Mickey Mouse place mat with cheddar-cheese sauce. Roughhousing in the playroom. Story time. Prayers. Lights-out. Complaints. Lights-on. Another Dr. Seuss story. Lights-off. Some talk passed between them. And then they were asleep.

Which finally freed Matthew and Wendy. They put on a video, rented for the night.

Now noises in Lisa's room, at night, even loud noises, were par for the course. The little girl, at her own insistence, had recently moved to an adult bed, and was forever falling out onto a section of floor padded with protective pillows.

So there were par-for-the-course thuds.

Furthermore, Lisa had been dreaming in narrative fashion since one and a half, and she was forever calling out in her sleep—she shouted at monsters, talked softly to fawns and rabbits, and often beckoned for Mommy and Daddy to come and extricate her from a dinosaur's grasp, or to come and meet a dream-world friend.

Tonight, the dream started for Lisa before Alex reached the Metropolitan Opera House. It was of the monster genre; pretty standard as the type went. A man came through her window, a man dressed in black. And he took her away. No particular terminus. Just away. From her sister, Lynn. From Mommy and Daddy. In a car. Driving. Blindfolded. On and on.

Matthew and Wendy Nelsen heard their daughter's exclamation in the other room, even heard it above *Moonstruck*, which they'd never seen, but, given Lisa's habits, they merely smiled at each other.

Harvard's box. On snow-white linen and gold-plated service reminiscent of the Romanovs, an elegant, sumptuous spread—of caviar, and smoked fish, and various tart and little-known cheeses, and crackers for holding the delicacies, and numerous bottles of various kinds of liquor for washing everything down.

Nelsen had grabbed two-dollar student seats to the Symphony when an undergrad, and at Saratoga and Tanglewood and Caramoor he and Rosenkrantz had been more than content with the cheap seats. In the case of Saratoga, in fact, the two simply claimed spots on the grass bank facing the stage upon which the New York City Ballet performed for their summer season.

Kasakov had been elected to carry out the negotiations. But not until after the show. Malachev was in the box too, gun in hand.

Sleeping Beauty began. And from the first graceful step, the narrative, the drama, was expressed in terpsichorean perfection by the Russian dancers. Above all, there was Annastasia Ivanova Marianov: young, strong, graceful, a body of perfect proportion, a face of perfect symmetry. Marianov fell off point once or twice, even missed a couple of *fouettés*, but the fact of the matter was that technical perfection, given her astounding beauty and warmth, was unnecessary. In the world of dance, Anna stood alone. Pure unadulterated feminine beauty. And the young computer scientist, despite the fact that no more than twenty minutes ago a gun barrel had been buried in his testicles, was wholly transported.

It was finished. She came out for a bow. The crowd went as wild as a crowd of this kind can. Back behind the curtains. Applause undying. Back out. Another bow. Cheers. Roses thrown.

The cycle repeated twice more.

And then finally it was really over.

The food from before was cleared off the table in their box, and tea and coffee were brought in.

"Coffee, Alexander?" Kasakov asked, holding out a steaming cup.

As always, her efforts earned her intense pain. Her feet, burning, blistered, were soaking in ice. Her black hair, up for the role of Beauty, was down now, cascading to her waist. Breasts were untaped. Thighs screamed; deltoids ached. She started to remove her makeup, slowly, looking at herself in the mirror. The room was fragrant with countless flowers sent by countless suitors. Various praise-filled reviews were strewn about. Alone. Vodka on lots of ice in front of her. A sip, a deep cleansing breath, toes wriggled, a tight muscle stretched. Clad only in a towel. Head back, hair down almost to the floor, another deep breath. She didn't want him to come, but he always did. She looked in the mirror. A lone tear was on her cheek. She was expected to stay clothesless. The alternative was . . . was what? Death.

Nelsen studied the Russian. Gray worsted wool pants, black silk turtleneck. Tan, clean, polished, smooth, relaxed amid opulence unseen in the Soviet Union. And young. Mid-thirties? Hair rather long, not manicured, but rakish. All in all, quite a remarkably prepossessing personage. And, though odd, it was exceedingly difficult for Alex to believe he was looking upon Kasakov for the first time. It seemed to Nelsen like recognition, not a first-time meeting. The Russian looked quite a bit like some of the cold, rich youths Alex had known at Yale: men from dynastic families of great power who, despite the wealth from which they came, were ambitious and ruthless. Alexander did not know that Russia's covert world revolved around lineage, and that whereas Peter came not from American money, he came from the Russian equivalent: those invisible omniscient men who hold the course of world events in their secret hands, and pass their hidden power on to sons.

"I'm going to come right to the point, Professor Nelsen. We need your expertise; we cannot live without it. And unless you come with us, and show some good ol' American know-how, Lisa will die."

Lisa? Lisa!

A nanosecond after Kasakov finished his utterance, Nelsen's right fist was halfway to the Russian's nose. An instant after that, impact; an instant after impact, blood; an instant after blood, Kasakov had a knife on Nelsen's jugular and was holding the American by his hair. Malachev moved to help his boss, but Kasakov said, "Fuck off!" to the *spetsnaz* agent.

Alexander, knife on this throat, looked into the

phosphorescent eyes of Peter Kasakov and thought, first, that the stereotype of the Russian spy as tough, smart, and ruthless was as accurate as could be, and then, second, that there was no need to demand verification of the kidnapping. A smile that struck Alex as devoid of mirth was upon the Russian's lips. The lips were parted, the teeth were exposed, the corners of the eyes crinkled a bit—but there was no mirth, no warmth. The man's incisors were prominent, lupine.

Alex calculated coolly here, the razor-sharp steel lightly depressing the flesh of his throat, as he calculated coolly on the slick-as-glass wall of a Himalayan peak. There had been just an evanescent spike of rage, but sometimes that was what it took to fire the adrenal glands on a climb, when death was beginning to seep into your mind, under the cover of peace.

Nelsen reached up and shoved Kasakov's knife away from his neck.

"Come on, Pete. You seem sharp enough. I won't be of much help dead, will I, now?"

Kasakov retracted the blade, slipped it into a sheath strapped onto his leg just above his ankle, straightened out his slacks, and, unruffled, sat back down. The Russian dabbed at his bloodied nose with a handkerchief, without emotion, mechanically, like a cyborg repairing a malfunctioning part.

Peter and Alex studied each other, and settled into an arrangement each seemed to have been born for: natural enemies. With a future ahead in which to wrestle.

"Let me tell you something, Petey. I need guarantees. Without guarantees you can go fuck yourself. How do I know that you'll release Lisa if I come? And I'll tell you something else. If I come, I'm not coming as a slave. You want me to play ball, you give me something to cushion the ride. Now, your boy Willy was talkin' sixteen mill. Double it. And wire it into my brother at Morgan. Then show me why I should believe it's there, and that Lisa is back home, safe and sound."

"You come or she dies."

"You really think it's that simple, huh? You may be a helluva spy, but you'd sure as hell suck as a scientist. You want me to do something maybe no one else on this planet can do, and you expect me to do it like a slave. I don't know what you want me to do, but I know whatever it is, it ain't like pickin' cotton, Petey. I need to be relaxed, pampered, taken care of. That's a fact. You ought to take a lesson in ergonomics."

Kasakov smiled, took up his coffee, sipped it, and sighed, as if to say: Ah, this is what life is all about. "When you're on the plane with us, Dr. Nelsen, Lisa will be released. You can also have thirty-two million if it will make you a productive little slave. As soon as we are airborne, you can phone home for confirmation."

Nelsen nodded.

"Now, do we have a deal, Dr. Nelsen?"

"This day has been rather taxing, Petey. I need to wind down a bit. When do we leave for the Fatherland?"

"Motherland."

"Whatever."

"Early morning," Kasakov said without humor.

"Well, then, I guess I have time for a night on the town."

Kasakov raised his eyebrows.

"And I'll tell you what. I want you to play matchmaker. You know Marianov, the prima ballerina we just had the pleasure of seeing? Well, I want her for an escort. In fact, Petey, I want her, period. She's flying back with us."

"What makes you think I can arrange such a thing?" Kasakov asked evenly.

"She's Russian, you're Russian. Just work out the introduction. I'll take it from there."

Kasakov's face gave nothing away, but inside his mind was racing. This Nelsen was totally unpredictable, and unpredictability, as his father had taught, was the most powerful enemy a military mind could face. *On a whim he wants a date with her? Or could he possibly know about her? About us? Impossible. Just a fluke. Has to be.*

"This is a highly irregular request, Dr. Nelsen."

"Right. And you're regular as they come, huh? Kidnappers daily demand that I come to their country."

Kasakov, stumbling perfectly, said, "So I . . . I should just knock and say I have this friend?"

"Look, I'm on the rebound. It's worth a shot."

"But maybe she dances better than she fucks."

"Why don't you let me be the judge of that, Pete?"

20

On the Town

February 13—Manhattan

Nelsen waited in the box. He complimented Malachev on the Band-Aid on his cheek, which covered the cut Nelsen had inflicted the previous night. Malachev was singularly unamused.

In Anna's dressing room, Kasakov said, "To him, you are a dancer. Nothing more. To me and my men, you are eyes. If he's a double agent, you find out. Do we understand each other?"

"Yes," she rasped. He had his hand around her neck, her head pinned against the mirror above her dressing table.

"Good," he said, and then released her.

Peter returned to the box, and Alex.

"She agrees to see you. I said only that I had an American friend who was a great fan. Now it's up to you. There is a room waiting for you at the Plaza, under your name. Be back by twelve midnight, Dr. Nelsen, or else little Lisa dies. And then we move on to her sister."

"We cut the deal, Pete. I'm coming. Relax."

Kasakov looked into Nelsen's eyes for a moment, then nudged his head, and he and Malachev departed.

* * *

Nelsen knocked on her door.

"Come in." The voice didn't sound Russian, but then again, the closed door had no doubt muffled the sound waves.

Nelsen entered. And beheld a woman of extraordinary beauty, clothed only in a towel from armpits to upper thighs. Her skin was smooth, unblemished, unreal in its porcelainlike perfection. She sat facing him, her legs crossed, her black hair pinned up, a mirror behind her.

"When you said come in, I . . . I thought you were decent."

"What do you consider decent?"

"Well, clothes, for starters."

Anna laughed.

"What?"

"Your Russian friend. He said you were a scientist. I had expected a senescent academic."

"Senescent?"

"Old. You're definitely not a linguist."

"Computer science. I'd like to say you're definitely not Russian, because you have no accent, but I don't see how that's possible."

"You're right; it's not. I'm Russian. Trust me."

She smiled completely and utterly, and when she did, something magical happened between her eyes, nose, and mouth. He looked at Anna's beauty, her half-naked body. What hit him first, in sexual terms, were the proportions. Somewhere in the back of his mind he had stored away the vague fact that great ballerinas, of necessity, possess a kind of symmetry and cleanliness of line. And indeed before anything else, before it struck him completely that the face itself was improbably beautiful and delicate, that her breasts, though half-hidden, were clearly generous and smooth—before this the overall lines of Anna's body began to work its ways. The ratios of limb to limb, line to line, were all perfect.

"Would you like to get something to eat?" Alex asked.

"Very much," Anna replied.

He saw nothing more of her body; indeed he thought she displayed a definite modesty. She tended to her blistered feet, which were of a sort Alex would soon realize to be standard in the dance community. Then, behind a curtain over which Alex obediently threw her clothes, Anna dressed and bound up her hair. She emerged seconds later in jeans and sable fur, green eyes blazing under strong eyebrows, took his arm, and they departed.

She flagged down a taxi, dived in, and pulled Nelsen in to join her; gave their destination to the driver, and told him to hurry, that she'd make it worth his while. She took his hand, and kissed him softly on the lips, pulled back her head, closed her eyes, kissed him again, even more gently.

Rape seemed to the scientist a viable option for the first time in his life.

A small and cramped café in the Village: intimate, dark, live jazz in the background. Noise enough to afford them complete privacy. Anna was sipping vodka on ice; Alex had a Beck's.

"You seem to know the Village like the back of your hand. You sure you're Russian?"

"I am, but I do know the area."

"Is the Bolshoi in town that often?"

"No. But having gone to school in Manhattan helps."

He looked at her.

"Barnard. Before that Moscow State University. After Columbia, the Sorbonne. And then dance."

As she said "dance" she closed her eyes and rolled her head back gracefully in keeping with the theme.

He looked at her again.

"What's the matter?" she asked.

"Nothing."

She smiled. The room itself seemed to Alex to brighten.

"Computer science? Specializing in?"

"Neural computing."

"Computer modeled on the human brain? I think it's all hype."

"What?"

"What do you mean, what? I said I think it's hype. Exaggerated. We're going to have to work on your vocabulary."

Nelsen took a swig of his Beck's and looked at her. He had never found looking, simply looking, to be so intoxicating.

"How do you happen to have a Russian friend?" she asked. "And one that could pass for Mephistopheles?"

"Who?"

"Maybe this isn't working out," Anna said.

"Words turn you on, or something?"

"The right ones," she said slowly. "Mephistopheles is the devil. An urbane version of him, anyway."

"You think Pete's the devil?"

"Is that his name?"

"Yes."

"What's his patronymic?"

Shit. I don't fucking know.

"He hasn't ever told me."

"Boy, you guys are bosom buddies."

"He's a colleague. Nothing more. Some of our professional interests overlap."

"Don't get defensive," she said, smiling, catlike again. A face of smoldering sexual heat; a smile that could transform an octogenarian into a raving maniac.

"I've seen you before, you know."

"Really?"

"Yup. Twice before at the Met. Once at Saratoga."

"You're a fan."

"Absolutely."

They were both hungry, and, having rejected French, considered alternatives. She wanted simple American, and so she took him uptown to Jackson Hole, for what she claimed were Manhattan's best burgers and fries. On the way there, the angles, the light, innumerable inanimate objects seemed to be conspiring against him. Leaving the café, they had to plow through a crowd, and her figure remained maddeningly fleeting: he saw her glorious face now and then in its fullness, though even it was seen in glimpses; but the black and silken hair was up and bound, a vision of her limbs was always interrupted by something—a bystander, a chair, her own gestures. The total effect remained elusive, and its absence was heightened by what he'd seen of her in the dressing room. When they emerged onto the street, his vision was still crisscrossed by all sorts of obstructions. Her movement in hailing a cab was, he managed to see, dancelike, and he found her balance and grace on a Manhattan sidewalk remarkable. But she flagged the cab down quickly, and once again they were in before he had been able to get a clear, unobstructed, detached view of Annastasia's beauty. Jackson Hole was also part of the conspiracy. They were tucked between two foursomes. Alex kept stealing glances at lines that, because of the crowding, were once again broken. The curve of her neck kept going in and out of focus, because she ate and drank the food energetically and with joy, and wasn't still long enough to adequately devour mentally. And the table was high. It was also narrow—narrow enough to occasionally catch a view of her legs, and her shoes, and her ankles, but only occasionally, for a number of times the diners that flanked them went off somewhere, only to return shortly, their departure and return forcing Anna to contract politely, so that nothing was visible, save for her face and chest, and even her chest was never captured, due to her arms, and her laughing, and her drinking and eating. By the time they left, the streets had cleared sufficiently, and it was with premeditation that he held the door for her, and delayed following Anna out. Holding back, he saw her finally and completely. But it wasn't nearly enough.

They caught a horse-drawn carriage outside the Plaza. When, seated within it, she was up against him, and under his arm, it was very nearly more than Alex could take. Stray light from around the park seemed to collect in her shimmering hair. He wanted to feel the strands against him. Wanted to kiss her cheek. Her lips. Her neck.

"Where is the Boshoi staying tonight?" he asked.

"Mostly at the Waldorf."

"I see."

Utter, unalloyed pulchritude. Her neck. Perfect.

She turned and kissed him. In an instant it turned hot. He slid a hand in under her sable; she wrapped a hand around the back of his neck. The driver, sixty, turned around and thought instinctively of his youth, his bride.

"I have a room at the Plaza," Alexander said.

They were both breathless.

Annastasia leaned back, her head against the leather seat, her throat exposed. She was looking up at the Plaza. And seeing her neck that way was more than he could bear. He pulled her to him; he cupped her head and directed her lips to his. They kissed again. And Alex felt a molten burning of a degree hitherto unknown.

They kissed feverishly in the elevator; and inserting the key and unlocking the door seemed to commit them to an unpalatably long period of separation, so long, indeed, that they gave serious, if primal, thought to making love in the hallway outside his room. Once inside the suite, without searching for a switch, in the darkness, the layout unfamiliar, they ripped their clothes off, he let her hair down, and she pulled him to the floor. She was ready for him, he felt, immediately, and he all the more for her. He entered her, and it was lovely, in a way he had never known, or even dreamed, before.

They said nothing for a long while, content to look into each other's eyes.

For Anna, it had been a revelation. He had waited for her, had held back until they could come together. He had tasted her, and the warmth brought on by tongue-to-clit stimulation had surprised her more than anything in her twenty-five years. A number of times he had pulled out, and had rubbed his tip around the outside, before reentering. He caressed her breasts, kissed her lips, her nose, looked into her eyes—all while thrusting slowly, lovingly.

When Anna, freed from her desire for the first time, thought about Peter, she thought about killing him. But Alex saw nothing in her eyes. Nothing behind them. He saw only emerald light, a graceful brow above.

The third time they made love it was in an acrobatic position, and, laughing, they came together, and then tumbled to the floor, panting, smiling, looking into each other's eyes.

"Come with me," Alex said.

"Where?"

"Russia."

"Russia?"

"I'm going to be working on a project over there. With Pete. And some others. We're kind of a . . . task force."

"What are you working on?"

"It doesn't matter. Just say you'll come."

"The Bolshoi isn't due in Oslo for a week. In fact we're flying home early this morning. Why don't you fly with us?"

"I'll have to check with Pete."

"He's the boss?"

"You could say that."

"Can I tell you what I think?"

"Sure."

"I think you're up to something. Peter doesn't look like any scientist I've ever seen. And scientists usually don't have rooms at the Plaza."

"Maybe you're a victim of stereotypes."

"Maybe. What is the goal of your task force?"

"Such curiosity."

"Well, it's all very shady."

"It just seems that way."

Then they took a bath together, made love again in the water; toweled off, and Bazakin showed up.

"We need to clarify a few things before we depart, Dr. Nelsen. Perhaps the young lady could step out for just for a minute. My concerns are all of a most tedious and technical nature."

Alex looked at Anna, who nodded and left.

"I just hope you're as fast with machines as with women. I'm Bazakin," the scientist said, holding out his hand. They shook.

Alex read Kasakov as the warrior. Here was a techie. Again Nelsen thought: Youth. Bazakin was in his thirties. Perhaps a year or two older than Nelsen. Receding hairline, prominent forehead, long face. Kasakov's cultured sheen was nowhere to be found here: not in the clothes, which were tattered and ill-fitting; not in the physique, which was thin, severe, even monkish; and not in the accent, which was unconcealably Russian. Bazakin radiated raw, unbridled, limitless intelligence. The head struck you first, and the impression never faded: there was first and foremost, and always, the head. The brain. Electrical current seemed to be emanating out from the prominent cranium. The brain waves were palpable; you felt them when you looked into Bazakin's pale blue eyes. Brilliance. Nelsen sensed its presence, in front of him now.

"She's probing," Alexander said.

"And this worries you?"

"Of course. Where is her incentive to keep quiet? One call to the CIA, and I imagine you boys would be in some hot water."

"When we're airborne, you can tell her."

"What?"

"Such naiveté," Bazakin said. "If she tries to tell anyone, we kill her. You can explain that to her too."

"You boys have such a knack for building incentive."

Bazakin pulled into his lungs a cloud of utterly carcinogenic smoke from a just-lit Belomor, and then exhaled a tobacco trail into the air.

"One day an average student; the next, a seminal scientist," Bazakin said, changing the subject. "Fascinating."

"Late bloomer." Nelsen shrugged.

"But there were no signs. None at all, Dr. Nelsen. You were competent from the start, of course, but no predictors, really—certainly nothing that would correlate with the accomplishments to come."

"Before Rosenkrantz, it was all gray."

"And after?"

"Sunlight after the rain. His vision of computation modeled on the internal processing of the brain came to obsess me, to discipline me, to draw out mental energy that had been parked idly since grade school. And then, as luck would have it, I happened to have a firm grounding in logicist AI, which allowed me to find a way to recast neural nets as standard general-purpose automata."

"I see."

"In the early days we hadn't any hardware, you know. No parallel machines to experiment with. So we designed our theoretical machines on paper, and hand-simulated their workings."

"And these machines," Bazakin said, "they were what we now call cellular automata?"

"Yes. Josiah tells a story about his flash, you know. It's classic. He's watching his three-year-old playing with blocks, and then—bingo, it hits him."

"Each block a self-contained computer. And then, connected, they form a composite machine. Correct?"

"Essentially, yes. He had me running around with pencil drawings of the architecture before it was embodied. My friends would be programming high-speed digital machines, and I would be frantically writing, erasing, writing, erasing, simulating what was to come."

"The Connection Machine."

"That's right."

"And after a while," Bazakin said, "the Neurocube."

"Yup."

"And finally, this." Bazakin stretched out his arms, opening his palms.

"And what *is* this, Bazakin?"

A drag on his cigarette. "This is war, Alexander. We fight a gray one the overt world doesn't comprehend."

"East versus West?"

"No, in that regard mankind has indeed reached the end of history. It's simply us against forces which, if left unchecked, will bankrupt the Soviet Union. And the Japs will inherit the earth."

"The sides can be described without the help of geography, then?" Nelsen asked.

"For me? Yes. For you? Improbable. You no doubt see clichés, and a black animus, where we see merely survival."

"And Gorbachev?" Alexander asked.

"A blend. A compromise. Ultimately a rather weak man, but no weaker, I suppose, than your own politicians, who haven't the fortitude to cut your deficit without taxing your citizens to death. The war you have been caught up in is an exceedingly practical one. Russia alive, any Russia, even one energized by *perestroika*, we would welcome. We have reached the point of thinking solely in terms of survival. And you, your leaders, and the Japanese, have reached the point of thinking solely in terms of profiting from our destruction. So you see, though ideology is gone, this is a violent war, a war to the death, I'm afraid. The reporters don't see it, of course. It isn't in the papers. When your President Atwood offers thirty million dollars in economic aid to an unstable Poland, your New York *Times* reports it with an arid, detached voice. But such an offer is a weapon, violent and invidious, no different than launching a missile. Poland can be owned. So can Russia."

So Kasakov thought in terms of murder, and Bazakin in terms of chess. Alex began to see some of the *Starik*'s diversity, some of the flesh-and-blood core of a group not chained to stereotype. It was tiny, but undeniable: Nelsen felt a flutter in his stomach. The loss of control was fleeting, but it was there: the irrepressible thought that perhaps this was too much, too steep, too fast, too dangerous. He had always overcome it in the past by simply willing himself over the edge. Would there ever *be* a too much? Nelsen had died in Louise's Shaft. Only to emerge later into the bright Canadian sunlight. *How many lives do you have, Alex my boy?*

Their silence marked a transition point. It was down to business.

"Let me tell you what we're building," Bazakin said, igniting a fresh cigarette with what seemed to Nelsen impossibly thin fingers. The Russian took an initial drag with his eyes closed, as if drawing in his very sustenance. And then he spoke.

Over the next five minutes the *Starik*'s brain proceeded to describe his band's SBI project—his description meshing remarkably well with the account Buchanan had provided. The bottom line: high-speed rocks.

"Fascinating."

"You think so?"

"Well, not the hardware, of course. I suspect, given Iraq, that there is consensus, both in the U.S. and the Soviet Union, that the rockets are doable. It's the software angle that's interesting. Indeed I can see why you need me: the complexity involved in continuously tracking thousands of ballistic missiles would fry even a conventional supercomputer in minutes."

Bazakin nodded, dragged. Nelsen finished off his orange juice.

"Your wish list, then, Professor Nelsen."

"Neurocubes, to start. Obviously."

"They're waiting for you."

"Impressive. All right, technicians to handle the intermittent hardware problems that crop up in the Neurocube."

"We have them. One is a friend, I believe. Renear? Jeff Renear?"

"I see."

"What else?" Bazakin asked.

"Airline tickets?"

Bazakin smiled: what teeth he had were stained. And as he smiled, Alex's impression that the essence of this spy was concentrated fiercely in his extremities intensified. The mind. And hands. It's all you need for chess, Alex thought.

* * *

Alex was permitted to travel with the Bolshoi. Before leaving for Kennedy, he posed for a few shots at the Plaza; GRU did the rest. Within fifteen minutes they had supplied every piece of paper needed for an unobtrusive passage into the Soviet Union: birth certificate; two identical photographs, two inches square, full-face; two passports, ninety-six-page version; three different types of visa: ordinary, a transit visa (for those wishing to travel through the Soviet Union on the way to another country), and a visa for private journeys (for those visiting friends in the USSR); and then ten different itineraries for travel in the Soviet Union, each one mapped out meticulously, one of them including a trek into the unforgiving Pamirs.

Alex was to begin work the following day. We'll send a car, Bazakin had said. "Bright and early."

When airborne, Alex used the phone. He told his secretary, Fran, that between climbs and talks he'd do his best to stay in touch through the Net. He told her to tell Lynch, the chairman, to line up some adjuncts ASAP, and to rechannel as much as was needed out of the latest DARPA grant to pay these new salaries. Within two weeks Fran would inform nearly everyone who came into regular contact with Nelsen that the globe-trotting scientist was trotting once again.

Then he called his brother, and thereby, indirectly, his mother and father.

"Lisa was kidnapped, Alex."

"What? Is she all right?"

"She's back safe and sound."

"Thank God."

"Where are you?"

"On the way to Russia."

"An expedition?"

"You got it. The Pamirs."

"I don't know how to tell you this, bro, so I'll just

come right out and say it. There's been a bank error in your favor. A *big* bank error. To the tune, in fact, of thirty-two million dollars. I checked your discretionary portfolio tonight, and boom, there it was."

"There's no error, Matt. Invest it wisely for me, okay?"

"Hey, come on, you've got to be—"

Click.

Nelsen sat there, sleepless, in the dark, and felt alone.

About thirty minutes later she was awake. Or at least he thought so. She had stirred—just a bit too much movement for someone sleeping. And then, gradually, slowly, it was confirmed: she leaned her head on his shoulder. And then her hand found his thigh.

"Anna."

"Mmmm."

"What are you up to?"

"That's a remarkably dumb question."

"Now? Here?"

"Look around," she whispered.

He did so. It was risky but not unthinkable: all lights were out, the seats across the aisle from them were empty. He turned back to see her smile. And to feel that she had, with the dexterity that marked her every move, already slid her dress up and her undergarments down, and that she was managing his own state of daring dishabille. She moved onto his lap and eased herself over him, and said, "Put the blankets on us." Which he did. And then, with an economy of motion that magnified all the sensations involved, they climbed together, looking to occasional passersby as if they were simply holding each other in a sleepy platonic embrace. When they came they whispered delight softly, and though he didn't see her smile, he felt it, felt her lips draw apart on his neck. And then, suddenly, it was lighter; plastic shades were pulled down throughout the cabin, theirs remaining open: the moon was out, shimmering on clouds below them. And America was nowhere to be seen or heard, and its absence, for Alex, was now something to be welcomed, without the slightest doubt.

On the return trip they were chameleons.

Kasakov, Bazakin, and Markov followed the *Macka*'s dizzying lead, and so became expert at transforming themselves in grubby airport toilet stalls, with hand-held mirrors, amid graffiti written in the universal language of vulgarity. Sometimes they were businessmen in suits, sometimes tourists in loud flowery attire, and sometimes officials with official-looking papers and official-looking pens and official-looking world-weary expressions.

After passing circuitously through South America, Africa, and Spain, with the help of Pan Am, Lufthansa, and Iberia, they returned to Moscow untracked, where Matra and Ignatov, having just flown in from Tereshkovo, where they had been working while the others were in America, were ravenous for news.

"So, he's ours?" Matra asked. She seemed, to the three returning men, to have doubled in size.

"It would appear so," Kasakov said.

"Appear?" Matra sneered. Her eyes were large, violent, incredulous. Kasakov tried for the millionth time to picture her erogenous zones, and came up empty yet again. His mind's eye was totally, utterly blind. No image. "What the fuck is that supposed to mean? Appear! We either have him or we don't. I don't see any middle ground, Peter Andreevich. Is the man coming to help me, or not?"

"We have him," Bazakin said, breaking in.

"Such wonderful unity," Matra said.

"In our business, Comrade Matra, there is much to

be said for paranoia. Walker was on the KGB's payroll for seventeen years," Kasakov said, "and as a result the Motherland knew the complete location of U.S. Navy ships at all times. Nothing like this has ever happened to us. Because we are paranoid. We suspect. We listen. We seldom trust. And in this case, as in all others, we must take reasonable precautions."

"Like?"

"Oh, watch the American embassy. Check to make sure no American illegal is communicating with Nelsen. Have Malachev check into Nelsen's last few days in the States. And have Markov here keep a close eye on Dr. Nelsen's code. Standard stuff. And easily implemented."

"Last few days in the States?" Matra said. "Wait a minute. You—"

"It's standard, Comrade Galya."

"You're saying he might be a double agent!" Matra exclaimed. The veins in her striated neck suddenly popped into action. The woman's bulk was not concealed in the least by her lab coat, which was large enough to function as a commodious tent for two mere mortals.

Kasakov said calmly, "He could very well be."

Matra hissed, but for the moment said nothing more.

"What about his cover?" Ignatov inquired.

"Straightforward. Everyone in the States is under the impression that he is on an expedition to the Pamirs. It fits."

Ignatov nodded, apparently satisfied.

"And what are the terms?" Matra asked.

"There are no terms. Failure to cooperate results in death—the death of a niece, a mother, a father, a brother. This isn't defection, this is kidnapping. We did give him some money and a woman to keep him happy."

"Woman? What woman?" Matra inquired.

"Marianov. From the Bolshoi. She's one of us."

"One of *us*? She's a dancer," Matra said.

"That's her cover," Kasakov said. "It has been from the start."

"Ballet?" Matra said.

"Yes," Kasakov said.

Matra expelled a derisive blast of air.

"Do you have a problem with ballet, Galya Mikhailovna?"

"Yes, I do. Sticks, all of them. Spindly sticks," Matra spat. "Ignatov here has the phallus of a fucking amoeba, he's never loved anything other than GRU. But maybe even *he* would want more woman than that found on the emaciated frame of a ballerina."

February 14—Troy, New York

Detective McNulty was on excellent terms with the computer-science faculty at RPI. They had helped him design Sherlock; he in turn had given them a glimpse of the underworld, which, relative to the calm tweedy world of academia, seemed to them to be glamorous. And everybody, thanks to the National Science Foundation, had pocketed some cash.

"Why on earth do you want to know about neural networks and connectionism? I thought you tinkered with expert systems."

"I do," McNulty said. "But this isn't tinkering, it's business."

"Fred?"

"Yup."

"I don't get it," Associate Professor of Computer Science Harold Folnick said.

"Think big," McNulty said.

Folnick scratched his temple. "Conspiracy?"

"It's possible. Fred's not the only engineer of this type missing."

"What? How many?"

"Just one more. But he's the president of Neuron Data."

"Renear?"

"Hmm."

"And the machines themselves?"

"There are seven neural-net machines floating around out there somewhere."

"Have you gone to the FBI with this stuff?"

"Yeah, but I don't think they're taking it too seriously. Haven't heard from them since."

Folnick shook his head. "Well, who do you have in mind?" he asked.

McNulty looked over at a large map of the world hanging on Folnick's wall. RPI's expert on neural computing followed the eyes of the Troy detective—eyes aimed at the East.

"Come on. The Russians?"

McNulty nodded.

"You sure you haven't seen too many movies?"

The detective frowned.

"Okay," Folnick said, knowing McNulty for the calm criminological logician he was. "But what do you want from me?"

"I want you to put yourself in their shoes. You have the machines, you have guys like Fred. Need anything else?"

"I'd sure as hell say so. How about somebody to *train* the machines."

"But what about Pattison and Renear?" asked McNulty.

"No, they're just the mechanics. You'd need somebody like . . . like me."

McNulty pulled out a cigarette, lit up, smiled, and said, "No offense, Harry, but let's start with the superstars. Who's the best?"

It came to the computer scientist immediately, and that it did pleased him greatly, because Harold Folnick was quite amenable to letting the Russians have someone besides himself. "Alexander Nelsen, at Brown University. We correspond over the Net. I know him quite well, in fact. Sure hope he's okay."

"Maybe I'll go down and see if he is," McNulty said.

"That would be rather difficult," Folnick said. "The guy's in Russia."

"What?"

Langley

"Jim, the others have some rather incendiary ideas," President Atwood said. "And I'm not sure they're unpalatable, to tell you the truth. Very clearly, either much of what they've told us over the past few years has been lies or people we don't know are running part of the show. The tough thing to swallow is that we can't really unveil this, given our current evidence. We'd be a million times less credible than Haig when, back in Reagan's first term, he tried to convince the public and press that the Soviets were sponsoring terrorism. Coming out of the closet on this now would do more harm than good."

"I'm working on it, Mr. President," Buchanan said.

"I believe you are. But I also believe the Chiefs have a point when they suggest preemptive strikes."

Jesus, Buchanan thought.

"So find us some additional data, Jim. Where do they house these smart rocks? Get some hard evidence so we can at least confront the Soviets without having the accusation blow up in our face."

"Yes, sir."

Buchanan figured he had sufficient time to give Dendrite a shot, that he could keep the warriors in the Pentagon at bay long enough to give Nelsen his chance. He was mistaken.

PART III

21

First Night

February 14—Moscow

The group brightened visibly upon landing at Sheremetyevo-1, Moscow's international airport. And it had nothing to do with the mere fact that they had made the passage safely; it was rather that the company was home, back in Mother Russia, in a land they loved. The dancers came to life as the plane rolled to the gate: weariness was shed, smiles appeared, chatter started up, small mirrors came out and hair was shaped and clothes were straightened—to prepare for waiting lovers, family, friends, the media. Plans for many a vodka-based celebration were laid, muscles were stretched in anticipation of a workout in the homeland, and some simply looked out the plane's small windows with tears of joy. The Bolshoi was composed of men and women who were, on the whole, rather remarkable physical specimens, and the sight of them glowing now, especially the female dancers, was something that had a powerful effect upon Alex. The collective joy of the group was not at all in line with the stereotyped dreariness most Westerners associate with the Soviet Union; in particular, their joy was inconsistent with the depression that was being ascribed to the Russian public by American prophets of doom. Gorbachev had returned, and economically the republic was still in turmoil, but from where

Nelsen sat at the moment, gloom was nowhere to be found.

The library of official papers proved superfluous. There was none of the usual suspicion from customs bureaucrats. Calls from on high had preceded the couple: they waltzed through inspection and emerged from the terminal into the hustle and bustle of a frigid Moscow afternoon. There was a limousine waiting for the two of them. The driver took their luggage, placed it in the trunk, handed Annastasia the keys, tipped his hat to Alex, and walked inside to the terminal.

"Get in, Dr. Nelsen," she said with a smile. He obliged, if only to prevent frostbite from setting in on his fingers. The cold took his breath away.

Inside the commodious auto it was wonderfully warm. Alex took in the interior.

"What are you smiling about?" she asked.

"This."

"What?"

"This car. You could raise a family in here."

Anna laughed. "This is a Chaika. It's partly built from molds brought from the old Packard Company in the States. About the closest thing to it in America are the huge Checker cabs, but they're much smaller."

He looked at the dashboard, which was so ancient it was cryptic. There were large red light bulbs glowing, and Alex had no idea what they were for. "It's yours?"

"Yes," she said as they lurched out into the traffic. He looked over at her apprehensively: though at five-foot-six she was not a small woman, sitting at the wheel of this tank she looked tiny. But it was clear that she was in control: within seconds they were weaving deftly between other vehicles on the crowded Leningradsky Prospekt.

After a few minutes they crossed the Moskva River; and soon Khimki Harbor, the starting point for Volga cruises, passed by on their right. Dusk was approaching, but there was still enough sunlight for Alex to see the snow, which was deep and lovely and untainted by the darkening slush that quickly accumulates in New York. They turned off Leningradsky onto Gorky Street, enormously wide and, as far as Alex could tell, devoid of travel lanes—which was fortunate, thought Alex, because Anna's Chaika took command of the entire street.

She made a series of rapid turns, in utter command of the tank. A kaleidoscope of domed architecture spun by his eyes.

"This is home."

She drove into a parking garage, took a ticket from an automated dispenser, and found two contiguous empty spots, of which the Chaika needed every inch. When they emerged onto the street, he was once again hammered by the cold, and began to regard Anna's fur coat a necessity. She pulled him into a run, and they were in front of her building soon enough, his face as raw as it had ever been from a day of zero-degree skiing on Stowe's National. It was a charming building; the surroundings, indeed, were not unlike a town house on the Upper East Side. They went through the lobby and up one flight of stairs, and entered a spacious, elegant apartment that looked more like something out of *Architectural Digest* than the modest abode of a party member. The regal touch of silk Persians underfoot. Much open space; the airiness soothing. Wraparound windows overlooking Moscow's glowing cultural district. Black leather couches, glass table in front of them, fresh-cut flowers on top of it. More flowers on the lacquer dining table. And yet another bunch in an elegant vase on top of a Printz side cabinet. Since she had been gone, and since the flowers were freshly cut, he deduced that she had help coming in periodically. And then the mere fact that there *were* flowers in the dead of a *perestroika*-plagued Moscow winter struck him.

"Isn't this a bit above the average?"

"You have tycoons; we have artists."

"This is all part of what you get for dancing?"

"Tolstoy's house is a shrine, as is Dostoyevsky's, and Pasternak's, and so on. If you were to dress up like Tolstoy and venture out into the bleakest parts of Moscow, you would be recognized as such. If you put on an F. Scott Fitzgerald disguise and paraded around New York City, who would notice?"

"But you dance," Alex said.

"There's no difference," Anna replied. "Arguably, dance is music. And if you put on, say, Mussorgsky, and ask a peasant what he's hearing, he'll tell you. We tell stories. We believe in emotion and character, a dramatic sense of pathos and excitement, of birth, death, and love and passion. And, as such, ballet is Russia."

Annastasia smiled, and it hit the computer scientist that she could probably make narration of a physics textbook something sexual.

"There's something I think I ought to tell you, Anna."

"You're a traitor."

Alex looked patently surprised.

Why do I keep underestimating her? She's more educated than me, for God's sake.

"Simple deduction. No one here to meet you. No pipe-smoking tweedy men from the university. You're carrying no papers, no books. Your Comrade Bazakin is too smart to be employed in the civilian sector. And Peter . . . well, Peter looks like he'd be at home with a knife on your throat."

What the hell . . . Bear down, baby.

"Anna, they will—"

"Kill me if I talk? Sure, that's standard. So I'll just talk to you. Now, come on. You start work tomorrow morning, and I want you to see something of Moscow."

She pulled out a man's sable coat from a closet, and matching hat and mittens. "Come on, Alexander."

Nelsen pretty much hated sightseeing, at least of the conventional sort. His parents had dragged him and Matt through Scandinavia, their ancestral home, at an early age, and neither boy had been able to shake the memory of utter tedium that slow, measured walks through Viking boat museums had managed to instill. But tonight, with Anna on his arm, and with GRU waiting in the wings, there was no tedium. They traveled by foot, often running, and by Metro. The subway system, station after station, was as ornate and clean as a Newport mansion, inhabited by shrines, and statues, and goddesses. Moscow was swimming with military uniforms—frontier police, security troops and traffic policemen, soldiers and officers among the crowds on the streets, and frequent truckloads of young conscripts. War memorials seemed everywhere, with eternal flames guarded by young Pioneers and Komosomols carrying real rifles, showing no signs of being cold, despite thin attire. Music was omnipresent: a different classical tune was playing around every bend: Tchaikovsky, Balakirev, Borodin, Mussorgsky. There were poor people, there were even a good number of homeless people—things were not much different, in this regard, from an American city. Churches were everywhere, reaching by gold-plated spires into the heavens; Anna informed him that Moscow had been known as Holy Moscow for centuries. Alex got a sense of the Kremlin, of the entire complex, and he saw it as it had been intended: a fortress, one and one-half miles of red-brick battlemented walls as much as sixty-five feet high and ten to twenty feet thick, an inviolable fortress which only Napoleon, for a brief moment, had been able to hold.

In one hurricanelike night Professor Alexander Nelsen saw Moscow in its entirety, from Lenin Hills Tower to the Sports City, from the innermost ring to the outermost, up and down the grand and wide boulevards not present in any American city. And when it was over, when they returned to her apartment, they were too tired to make love, at least without resting for a while. They undressed and slipped into robes, left the lights off.

Anna opened a bottle of Georgian wine and they slouched down into one of her deeply cushioned couches, both of them looking out at the city through which they had been moving throughout the night.

"They gave you money?" she asked.

"Thirty-two million."

"You took it in dollars, I hope." She smiled; her eyes sparkled.

How could she be so at home discussing matters such as these? It doesn't fit.

"Yes, I took it in dollars."

"Such generosity. What are you giving them? The Holy Grail?"

"They do seem to expect miracles."

"Let me see. Computers. You're going to help them build computers."

"I don't know the first thing about hardware."

"Okay. You're going to *program* some computers."

"From what I can gather, that's essentially right."

"And these computers will . . . will what?"

"Anna, you're scaring me. I care for you. I don't want to find you with a bullet through your skull."

"Where's the danger if I keep my mouth closed?"

"If. That's the problem. I'm sure you already feel the temptation."

"To talk? Why? I'm a patriot. Whatever it is you're bringing us, I'm sure we need it."

Us?

After a few sips in silence, she placed her goblet on the glass table and said, "You know, Alex, you don't *seem* a mercenary."

A number of possible responses competed in his

head, but no victor emerged. Alex kept quiet, and Anna continued:

"You did it for the money, is that it?"

"You want to spend some of it?"

"No." She laughed, her head on his shoulder. "I'm just trying to figure you out. You're a professor in the States?"

"I told you that," Alex said.

"You did. That's the problem."

"Problem?"

"Yes. Isn't it true that American professors make little money?" she asked.

"Well, it's relative. Relative to investment bankers and star athletes: yes. I make a living, though."

"But now suddenly you're a mercenary."

"Isn't there a more charitable way to put it?"

"I don't know, is there? You didn't seem to mind 'traitor.' "

Alex pulled Rosenkrantz's analysis out of memory, said: "If *glasnost* is for real, if the Iron Curtain has truly been removed, there are no longer two opposing sides. Or at least there *shouldn't* be. Not in dance. And not in the world of science and technology."

"You sound like a GRU agent in the process of recruiting an illegal. Either that or you're awful at rationalizing."

"GRU?"

"Who do you think your employers are?"

"Well, the KGB."

"I doubt it. They're too young. You know, you're not very convincing."

"What do you mean?"

"Oh, the dissolution of East-West antipathy. Do you really believe that?"

"Yes."

"Well, then God help you. Espionage is espionage, Alexander. How many times have the Iraelis stolen from the United States? The CIA picks the pockets of MI6 all the time."

"This lingo comes rather easily to a dancer."

"I read the papers like everyone else."

"I don't know about that. I'd say you read between the lines. Can we move on? I don't see what the problem is. So I'm a traitor. And a spy. But I'm also with you."

"If the money is what got you here, your chosen field seems out of character."

"You're relentless. We're going around in circles."

"It's just that suddenly you're so materialistic."

"Climbing remote mountains has a tendency to burn holes in one's pockets mighty fast."

"Ah, so that's it," Anna said, obviously convinced of nothing.

Not being able to see her eyes was maddening: he couldn't tell if she was thrown off her track. She didn't speak for a few minutes. She was relaxed—utterly relaxed. Her hair rested on his chest, cascaded down his abdomen. A breast, covered only by the silk of her robe, touched his side. Alex fought to remain similarly loose. It wasn't easy. She had access now to his insides.

And I got myself into this on a lark. Jesus.

"And what about loyalty?" she asked.

She felt her lips moving on his skin.

"To my country?"

"Yes."

"It's thirty-two million dollars, Anna."

"But what does it cost your country?"

"Nothing."

"Why nothing? You're working on some kind of system that could potentially be used against America. Of that much I'm sure."

"Star Wars."

"So *that's* it. . . . Star Wars is a weapon."

"In a sense."

"In a sense?"

"Well, it's defensive. As you probably know, Star Wars is a system designed to stop an enemy's nuclear attack."

"Would your government see it that way?"

"No," Alex admitted.

"Would they kill you if that's what it took to stop you?"

"I suppose so."

"Your friends and family. They think you're here on a sort of vacation?"

"Yes."

She stopped talking for a while. Minutes passed. He wondered what was coming next. But then he realized she was asleep. And he realized his forehead was damp with perspiration. A few minutes later, when he returned from washing up, ready for sleep, she was awake again, and alive with desire. The conversation of but ten minutes back had disappeared as quickly as it had arrived. As they made love, he searched furtively for her eyes, but it was still too dark to see them.

Outside Anna's Apartment Building

Kasakov had violently and permanently squelched the questioning. Now, only silence.

"What is the point, Comrade Kasakov?" Bonderyenko had asked.

"Surely we have more efficient ways of spending our time," Bonderyenko had said.

"The man is here, safe and sound. He isn't going anywhere, comrade," Bonderyenko had opined.

And then Kasakov had seized Bonderyenko's jaw, tightening, tightening till teeth were in danger of snapping off his jawbone.

Thus the questioning stopped. In its place: silence, and a wait. For something.

Yuri Arkadeyevich Bonderyenko woke from his latest catnap to see that the claustrophobic situation hadn't changed: they were still in the Volga, its engine and heater running, and Kasakov was still looking up at her window. All in all, Bonderyenko would without hesitation have traded for a life-and-death situation in the field. They'd been keeping vigil in the car since Alex and Anna had returned from their whirlwind tour of Moscow. Four hours. No food or drink, no talk, no activity. Kasakov hadn't so much as stretched an elbow or a knee: he just sat there, looking up, motionless, silent. Bonderyenko knew something was wrong, but he hadn't a clue as to what it might be. An atmosphere of intense and unregulated emotion enveloped him in the car. And it was emanating from his superior beside him. Yuri couldn't put his finger on it. He cast a furtive glance over at Kasakov's face. And in the visage of the *Starik*'s master Yuri saw absolute unadulterated concentration. Earlier, when Yuri had reached toward the dash to turn on the radio, Kasakov had seized his wrist, had squeezed it like a vise, and had looked into Yuri's eyes with a cold unfeeling stare, clamping the wrist for a solid ever-tightening five seconds. The strength of the man, Yuri noted, was enormous; for a brief moment Bonderyenko was afraid his bones were going to be crushed. But Kasakov let go, and turned back calmly, sweat on his brow from the effort, turned back to look up at Anna's rooms. Now Bonderyenko's wrist throbbed with pain. He also had a pressing need to urinate, but he didn't dare get out to do so.

The strangest thing was that there wasn't anything to see. Only now and then, shadows. Kasakov finally dropped his upward gaze.

"I want a veritable army surrounding Dr. Nelsen at all times. Do you understand?"

"Yes, Colonel."

"And I want Anna debriefed daily."

"Yes, comrade."

"Now. Tomorrow is his first day of work. I want you here bright and early to pick him up. Bazakin will be waiting for Dr. Nelsen at headquarters."

"I will be here, comrade." *Even if I have to drive one-handed.*

Boston

Back in the States, while Alex and Anna slept, Lazery Malachev, former *spetznaz* officer, now GRU special agent, decided to rent at random, since he wasn't all that familiar with the current array of U.S. automobiles. At any rate, he thought to himself, *any* Avis car would blow the doors off the laughable Pobedas, Zhigulis, Moskviches, and even the Zaporozhets back home. Malachev asked Lauri, the pretty girl at the desk without a wedding band, to surprise him.

"Cost a factor, Mr. Barnes?"

"Nope."

"All right, let's see." She glanced over at him in the manner of a portrait artist sizing up a subject, was struck by the fact that she was looking at a muscular version of Omar Sharif, looked back to the file, picked through it for a few seconds, and then, smiling, pulled out a folder. "A Taurus SHOi. I think that fits."

Malachev returned the smile, thought for a second about taking her to dinner that night, but decided against it: she was wearing just a bit too much makeup for his taste, and when and if force was needed to consummate a night with penetration, as it often was on dates during these kinds of trips, Malachev preferred the feel of ravaging a perfect specimen. He had an awesome talent for bringing even prudish women willingly to the point of no return: half-naked, she still planning to refuse intercourse, he apparently under not-too-late-to-turn-back control, a few more kisses, a few more caresses, then he'd ask, softly; the refusal, another request, another refusal, and then he'd overpower.

Eight times out of ten the resistance lasted till his first thrust, after which Malachev returned to the unselfish mode, and was as tender as a rose.

The other two times, well, there was no way it could be construed as rape. Taking advantage, yes, but rape? No way. And besides, afterward he was profoundly apologetic, effusive, signing blank checks of every variety, and, above all, flattering.

Omar Sharif. With muscles. With lethal hands.

"You wouldn't by any chance have a map that could help me get down to Providence, would you, darling?"

Malachev knew Providence well, but he didn't know how to get there from Boston. He had flown directly into T. F. Green for his attempt at abducting Nelsen. This time Green had been fogged in. And so here he was. Going with the flow.

Lazery Malachev had the kind of utterly masculine and macho bearing that made subtly chauvinistic comments seem just fine to the opposite sex.

"I certainly would," Lauri replied cheerfully. She pulled out a map, put it on the counter, and showed him the route to Providence. He brushed her hand while she was highlighting the route down interstates 93 and 95; a hint of a smile appeared at the corners of her lips.

When he finally got clear of the congestion on 93 and began the clear straight run on 95, Malachev downshifted to third, hammered the accelerator, and, at 70 mph, took the car into fourth. When Ford's highest performance car reached 110, Malachev leveled off and said, "Thanks, Lauri."

* * *

When Malachev, flying at full throttle, got within ten miles of Providence, McNulty, already in the city, pulled up at a phone booth on Wickendon Street to look up Nelsen's address. He found 494 Benefit Street listed, checked the index on his street map, followed the code on the two axes, and found his destination. By the time Detective McNulty got back in his car, Malachev was only five miles from his exit, enjoying the handling capability of the Taurus through the S-turns 95 cuts through Pawtucket, Rhode Island.

Five minutes after finding Nelsen's street on his map, McNulty pulled over on a side street off Benefit, a few blocks short of Nelsen's house, and walked the rest of the way. Benefit was lined with replicas of Early American gas lamps; their soft light permitted enough darkness to appreciably reduce the odds of being spotted. In such situations hesitation is the cardinal error, and McNulty, cool, experienced, worked in rapid, clockwork fashion. The mechanics were relatively easy. When he reached Alexander's home he walked past as if the address had no special meaning for him, but in passing he quickly found the phone line above, and traced it to an accessible point on the side of the house. After passing three blocks beyond the house, he turned and walked back, and, without hesitation, walked off the sidewalk to the house, and cut the phone line with a pair of wire clippers. He then walked back to the sidewalk and strolled at a resident-of-the-area pace in the opposite direction. After he'd gone four blocks, he turned and walked back once again toward Nelsen's clapboard-sided, plaque-distinguished 1740 colonial house. Everything was quiet, so the Troy detective deduced that the phone line itself hadn't been alarmed. There was no sticker indicating the alarm company, if in fact there was an alarm, and so McNulty couldn't use his knowledge of the peculiarities of these companies to his advantage. He looked in through the sidelight to the right of the front door, aided by his flashlight: no sign of a keypad. He stepped back onto the brick sidewalk and surveyed the layout with a bit more care. He located the power line coming off the nearest telephone pole, traced it to its point of entry into the house, and made a mental note that that was where, on the inside, the electrical box would be located. The backyard was fenced in, and though it was visible from second-story windows in the two adjacent houses, it was clearly his best shot for a relatively unobtrusive forced entry. He walked around to the back, found himself in a garden with a clear view of the Providence skyline, and looked through a small window on the back door: again, no keypad. Either there wasn't one, or it was hidden; he assumed it was hidden, and thus that entry *would* trigger an alarm. He hoped, however, that this was a delay door, that upon entering, the owner was given the customary forty-five seconds to disarm the system. If communication to a central station or to the police was via phone, it of course wouldn't take place now that the line had been cut. So there were two remaining obstacles: the sound of a siren, which could alert neighbors; and, possibly, a rather expensive and rare radio backup message system aimed at a central station, something McNulty knew Sonitrol, and others, sometimes sold to wealthier customers. He lodged the flashlight between his teeth, made sure he remembered where the electrical box would be, and checked that no part of his right hand touched anything but the rubber on the handle of his designed-for-such-occasions hatchet. He kicked the door in, a siren sounded immediately, without the forty-five-second delay he had hoped for. He dashed for the box, found the main BX line, and severed it with one vicious blow of the hatchet; then he raced to the main control unit, ripped it open, and tore the backup battery out—siren killed, on for maybe ten seconds, not nearly enough to raise the suspicion of neighbors who, almost invariably, ignored sirens of this sort no matter *how* long they sounded. By flashlight he quickly checked for radio backup. There wasn't one; and so, taking a deep cleansing breath, Detective John McNulty knew that he was home-free.

Directorate Z had arranged things perfectly:

He went to the refrigerator first; it checked out: there was nothing perishable inside it.

Next, the closet in the master bedroom: it checked out too, because it looked like a good chunk of clothes was absent. Looking further, McNulty found little underwear present, not many shoes, indeed no winter footwear at all, and toiletries were gone.

Nelsen's computer room, which even in its owner's absence hummed and blinked, more forbidding than the cockpit of a fighter, was perhaps too tidy to have been manned recently.

No evidence, so far, in favor of abduction; and when McNulty found some travel books on the Soviet Union on the living-room coffee table, he ruled out kidnapping completely. Which left, he figured, coincidence and betrayal. Nelsen was either a traitor or a tourist with remarkably bad timing.

There was no point in staying any longer, and every reason to leave as soon as possible, but when McNulty started to depart, a car pulled up across the street. The detective didn't miss a beat: he knew that he would almost certainly be able to talk his way out of the mess, if it came to that. He was a cop, this guy would be a cop—they'd see eye to eye. It wouldn't be hard, even without a warrant. The man in the car across the street got out, but didn't walk toward Nelsen's house; he walked to the front door of the house *across* from Nelsen's house. At first it made perfectly good sense to McNulty: the cop was asking the neighbors if they'd heard or seen anything. But the *pace* was all wrong: the man appeared to be in no hurry at all. Under the entrance light of the opposite house, John could see that the man was asking questions, all right—he was even gesturing over toward Nelsen's house. But he was taking his sweet time. And then McNulty noticed that the *car* was all wrong: it was a Taurus, and no cop would be driving an unmarked car of this type; indeed, for a residential alarm the local force would have sent a uniformed officer in a marked cruiser. The driver of the car had finished his first interview, and now, McNulty saw, he walked over to an adjacent house, where he initiated a second.

A salesman? Coincidence? What the hell's going on?

McNulty hopped downstairs, exited into the garden, ran around to the front, and, making sure that the man didn't see him, slipped out onto the sidewalk. Then he walked across the street with the ease of someone slipping on an old familiar coat. The plate on the Taurus told him it was a rental; he lingered out of sight until the interviewer began making his way to the next house. And then McNulty walked straight ahead, so as to see the man's face. And he did. It was the hardened self-assured purposeful face of a secret soldier on a secret mission. McNulty passed with a friendly nod, turned the corner at the next intersection, got into his car, and nosed it up to the corner so as to keep the man in sight. Malachev was interviewing at yet another house, and for the first time McNulty noticed that he was scribbling notes in what appeared to be a small notebook. McNulty tried to force himself to think, despite the fact that his heart was pounding in such a way that he heard it in his ears. Malachev called on two more homes, then got into his car to leave. McNulty followed the Russian. Who, even to McNulty, looked strikingly like a hulking Omar Sharif.

22

More Underestimation

February 15—Moscow

The temperature had risen unseasonably and it was raining. Bleak. Gray. The snow was finally turning grimy. In accordance with Kasakov's instructions the night before, GRU, with Yuri Bonderyenko driving, sent a Volga for Alex; looking down from Anna's kitchen window, they saw it rumbling outside, sending up a trail of exhaust through the drizzle. They kissed; Anna wrapped her arms around him for a hug. Alex could find not a remnant of last night's interrogation. Her eyes did seem for the first time to be missing a bit of their usual fire, but Alex sensed it wasn't suspicion, only a tinge of worry, which was, he figured, perfectly normal under the circumstances. The vacation, after all, was over; work, dangerous work, was about to start. Nelsen ran out, holding the lapel of his coat over his head for a partial shield against the precipitation. Bonderyenko ran around and opened the rear passenger door for Alex, and the American got inside. As they pulled off he looked up at Annastasia's apartment and saw the outline of her face framed by the kitchen window. He waved, not knowing whether she saw the gesture. As they proceeded, Nelsen every so often caught Bonderyenko looking back inquisitively by mirror at his passenger, but their eye contact, each time, was fleeting.

Fifteen silent minutes later Nelsen was dropped off

outside GRU headquarters, into the hands of a waiting Bazakin. The two men shook. The Russian, sharing the cover of a large umbrella, escorted Nelsen inside. Alex gave his fingerprints, retina, and voice patterns to a computerized sentry that would, Bazakin said, hereafter grant him entry.

Alex then followed his guide to a large room filled with various kinds of Western desktop computers—IBM LT's, Mac III's and IV's, the latest Compaqs, and a good number of Sun and Apollo workstations. All from Uncle Sam. It was something for which Alex wasn't prepared, and Bazakin noticed.

"You are familiar with these machines?" the Russian asked.

Alex nodded.

"It surprises you?"

"Well," Alex said, "not the concept. It's the numbers. I figured you had some of our machines, but not in this quantity."

"This is just the testing room, Dr. Nelsen. In here we have technicians examining these machines, putting them through their paces. But we also have a warehouse devoted solely to storage."

"I see. Mind if I look at what some of your men are doing?"

"Not at all," Bazakin said.

Alex found that many of the technicians were simply running American end-user software: spreadsheets, graphics and CAD packages, even games and entertainment. As Alex looked around, he was compelled to chuckle. It was clear that many of the Soviet technicians were dumbfounded by the software, for which, to complicate matters, there was little or no documentation.

"Nothing like this software exists in the Soviet Union," Bazakin said to his guest. "You must realize that our need for your expertise is symptomatic of a general and pervasive problem. We have no tradition whatever in software creation. Some of the games on these machines are like magic to our best computer wizards."

Alex found someone running Falcon-5 on a Mac IV, and asked if he could make a few changes.

Bazakin nodded and the technician at the Mac gave up his seat immediately. Alex hooked the man's Mac up to another sitting beside it, restarted the "Special" menu, activated Falcon, and engaged parallel mode. Each Mac now represented the cockpit of an F-16, and the two machines could engage in electronic combat. Alex invited the technician to take the controls of the other machine; the invitation was accepted; and Nelsen and the technician enjoyed a simulated dogfight. After a few seconds the Russian's plane disintegrated.

The technician smiled from ear to ear. "You good," he said, calling on the little bit of English he knew.

"I hope so," Alex replied. "I wrote the code." Nelsen turned to Bazakin. "Running the two machines simultaneously," he explained, "involves a poor man's parallelism. Nice royalties."

Bazakin nodded.

Alex shook hands with his mock competitor and followed Bazakin on. They entered a maze of hallways. The decor reminded Alex of a "clean room": a scrubbed, clean, metallic, ultrasecure look. It felt more like Silicon Valley than Russia. They walked for a considerable distance, their shoes clicking rhythmically on the hard polished floor, before Bazakin spoke:

"You no doubt want to see your machines."

Before Nelsen had time to reply, Bazakin stopped at a door, pressed his hand on a sensor beside it, the door opened, and the two stepped inside. And there they were: six Neurocubes, shiny, undamaged, black as black. It was quite a bit like coming home: Alex felt the power of the machines, a familiar and always enjoyable feeling. He thought wistfully for a split second about his friend Renear, who had built the primogenitor.

Then Alex noticed that piled around a disassembled Neurocube were empty boxes from . . . from McDonald's?

Then Alex noticed that Jeff Renear was in the room, along with one of Renear's engineers, Fred Pattison. Alex established quickly, through eye contact, that he'd been kidnapped, not bought.

Wonder what they used on these guys? The same gun-in-the-crotch incentive?

And then Nelsen noticed that in addition to two of the Neurocube's creators, there were others in attendance: a bearded, disheveled, potbellied guy eating a McDonald's Big Mac, a good part of which, evidently, had nested in his whiskers; an amazonian woman who looked decidedly and indiscriminately mad; a tiny man with a long unruly beard and hair so greasy that it appeared to be plastered on his pallid skull. Viet Markov, hacker; Galya Matra, genius, bully, bodybuilder; and Ignatov, as small as a ten-year-old, but smart as a whip.

Alex had now set eyes upon the entire *Starik*. Looking upon the trio before him he felt the cohesiveness now, as he'd felt it in Manhattan when meeting Kasakov and Bazakin. But it was a visceral thing, and so as far as the deductive side of Alexander Nelsen's brain was concerned, his employer was simply GRU—GRU, a bureaucratic elephant, sluggish, with a complicated, unfocused agenda, in this regard quite a bit, he figured, like the rich, powerful, but often aimless National Science Foundation, or DARPA, the Defense Advanced Research Projects Agency.

Bazakin had lit a Prima, but the room didn't turn malodorous: the smoke was drawn up to the ceiling and immediately removed by filters effective down to .0001 microns.

No conversation. Guarded looks all around. The only sound came from Markov's munching. Presently Bazakin said, "Let me introduce you to your team, Dr. Nelsen. You are of course acquainted with our two newest members." Nelsen nodded to Renear and Pattison, and suppressed a smile and the urge to run over, reveal Dendrite, Buchanan's whole madcap plan, and suggest they grab a beer. "This is Viet Markov, formerly Vincent Markowitz of Brooklyn, New York." Bazakin gestured toward the overweight burger-eating man, who had now moved on to inhaling a McDonald's apple pie. "Comrade Markov used to do silly, unprofitable things like access restricted data bases for the thrill of it. He was once a nonprofit one-man team. Not anymore, I'm glad to report." Bazakin took a deep serene drag before continuing: "The Soviet Navy took out a tanker in the Strait of Hormuz not long ago, and a nearby U.S. Navy frigate, having detected the sub by sonar, suspected foul play. But when an attempt to relocate our sub was initiated, one of Comrade Markov's 'Trojan horses' was activated, killing their comm. Comrade Markov is currently trying to throw some wrenches into Technet, the new Cray-class network in New Mexico, linking Los Alamos and Sandia. And he takes road trips for us, mostly for the purpose of disassembling machines that could otherwise not be brought back undetected. B.S., computer science, MIT."

Markov nodded at Nelsen, then threw a french fry into a mouth the lips of which were hidden by his untamed, Big Mac-littered beard.

"Next, Dr. Galya Matra. Physicist. Lasers, in particular. And lasers for targeting, to be exact. Doctorate, Moscow State University. Only seven months ago, right, Comrade Matra?"

"Six." Uttered as if Bazakin's error was unpardonable.

Bazakin took in some nicotine, and, looking at

Alex, smiled with his eyes and said mentally: *No passes, now, Dr. Nelsen. She'll crumple you up like paper and throw you in the trash. And besides, some of us suspect that genitals are absent, or perhaps, if there, then of the male variety.*

"Forgive me, Comrade Matra. Six it is. At any rate, Galya Matra is consultant to the Antonov, Ilyushin, Mikoyan, and Mil Helicopter Design Bureaus. No sophisticated aircraft built in the Soviet Union flies without her contribution. GRU since the precocious age of five, at which time she was beating our brightest teenage boys at chess."

Matra moved her thick unappetizing lips into a petulant frown and greeted Nelsen with a grudging nod. Her head moved like a piece of heavy machinery.

"And finally, Dr. Nelsen, Captain Dimitry Ignatov, our practical-minded engineer. Expertise: propulsion." Ignatov wore large glasses: thick lenses, big black and bulky frames; looking out from behind them his eyes, magnified, looked the size of billiard balls. "Comrade Ignatov, along with Comrade Matra, has for the past two years been working on the interceptor project for which you are to write the software. He has made great progress in a short amount of time, and in a few minutes he'll give us an orientation. Before coming to GRU, Comrade Ignatov was at the TsIAM engine institute. He is the creator of the Tumansky RD-33 turbofan, which powers the MIG-29 fighter. Thrust in full afterburner, 8,300 kilograms. Thrust-to-weight ratio, 8.2, and bypass ratio, approximately four. He finished with the Tumansky before his twentieth birthday. Now, at twenty-three, he builds our demons."

Nelsen said, "Demons?" with his eyes.

"Our interceptors."

"Ah."

"There will be time later for you to get acquainted

with your team, Dr. Nelsen. Let us without further ado hear what Captain Ignatov has to share with us."

Ignatov brought the group over to an enormous color display and asked that they pull up chairs around it. Alex noticed that the monitor bore a Lucasfilm insignia. The major players in the American movie industry built their own monitors—with raw graphics capability that blew away anything on the market. At least the *legal* market. So sitting in front of Nelsen was a monitor that, by comparison, made what he used back in the States look like a royal piece of shit.

"All right," Ignatov began, "this is what we have so far. There's no AI whatsoever, no intelligent processing. Our demons, at this stage, merely send back a picture, and I manipulate the joystick. Markov here, who used to play video games in America, is remarkably adept at guiding these demons, but of course we need autonomy to do anything interesting. The picture is courtesy of a garden-variety low-light multispectral video camera, which Comrade Matra hot-rodded. She threw in a laser designator that emits a beam through the telescope for illumination. We can light up anything—even all the stealth shit the Americans have. So, a conventional macroscopic picture suitable for human sight. As you will now notice on the screen, an exam—"

"I'm sure we all get it," interrupted Markov, who had to this point been sucking noisily on a vanilla shake. "Why go on? You have a camera on the little beasts now, and that's it. So it sends you a picture, you *look* at the picture, and you try to find your target. If you see it, you maneuver the rocket accordingly. It's like working a high-tech tank, nothing more. What's the mystery? Our tasks are self-contained. If you've built the rocket well, we can do a significant part of our job in isolation. And of course it's painfully clear what we're to do. The present manual scheme obviously doesn't allow you to retarget fast enough. By the time your brain processes the picture and sets upon a course of action, the target will doubtless have moved appreciably. So what we need to do is automate a genuine vision system. You want these new machines to see, to retarget, to control thrust. The general concept isn't anything otherworldly."

Bazakin was smiling, Ignatov was manifestly deflated, and Alex was impressed. Matra spoke next, and initiated a rapid exchange of the sort Alex was accustomed to hearing at Brown:

"Too sanguine, Mark-o-weetz." Matra enjoyed masticating Viet's original Hebrew name.

"Why?"

"It's a toy world. It's what the American AI researchers have been specializing in for years. They write a program for painting simple cubes, and suddenly they're touting a solution to the Frame Problem. You're doing the same kind of thing, Mark-o-weetz. Americans love hype."

Markov was finishing everything off with an after-dinner drink: Pepsi. He guzzled half the can and burped thunderously. "I don't see it," he said with marked disrespect.

Matra grabbed the hacker by his shirt and with one arm lifted the rumpled genius clean off the floor.

"In a normal combat situation, Comrade Mark-o-weetz," she said, talking an inch from Markov's face, holding him aloft as if he were a feather, "you'd have literally *thousands* of targets. Shit, how many ICBM's do the Americans *have*? Then they've got an army of slicums, and those *fucking* cruise missiles. The vision system has to discriminate between all these objects."

"I don't see it," Markov whispered bravely, his voice box struggling to produce only a whisper. "They're all missiles, and hence they're all targets. We don't"—cough—"we don't need discrimination."

"Decoys," Matra snarled. "Remember that you're dealing with midcourse and terminal-phase targeting.

The missiles have MIRVed. One ICBM launched from American soil has become a hundred separate vehicles, some real, some fake. Each real one able to do damage that makes Hiroshima look like a fucking *paradise* in comparison."

For the first time in a minute there was silence—during which Viet Markov, airborne, thought, and awkwardly sipped a bit more of his soda.

Matra opened her enormous hand and dropped the hacker to the floor; some Pepsi went down his windpipe, and he coughed spasmodically by reflex.

Alex, incredulous, thought: *A circus of brilliance.*

After ineffectively wiping his beard with his sleeve and clearing his throat with the regal air of a king, Markov continued, undaunted. "I'm still not convinced," the Brooklyn-born software wizard said. "So, say there *are* decoys. So what? How many? Are there as many decoys as genuine vehicles? Let's assume so. Why not be profligate? Why can't we build a helluva lot of these bastards? Look at it this way: building another demon is cheaper than building a decoy."

"Perhaps," Ignatov said. "But perhaps not."

Markov said, "Okay, fine, have it your way. Let's face the problem. Why can't we discriminate?"

"We *can*," Matra said. "Shit, we're halfway there already. We're using laser scanning techniques here, and the accuracy should therefore be sufficient. We can send off a beam, hit a potential target, and take back a detailed image. If the image doesn't match the internal representation inside the machine, then let the thing go. What is it you say, Mark-o-weetz? Piece of cake?"

"But do we have the data to support the internal representation?" Ignatov asked. "We would need precise specs on genuine American vehicles."

"We have their rocket-plume wavelengths pegged down to the millimeter," Bazakin said, smiling through some of the smoke rising past his face. "Our little

Lear jet has provided us with plume characteristics of Canadian Black Brant sounding rockets, the space shuttle, Delta 2's, Titan 34D's, and even the brand-new Trident 2 D5's."

"So what's the problem?" Markov asked.

"Oh, there's a problem, all right," Alex interjected. "I begin to see why I'm here, and why the Neurocubes are too."

"I see it," Galya said.

The omniscient Bazakin saw it too, though he remained silent.

"Well, I confess I don't," Markov said.

"And neither do I," Ignatov confessed, pushing his glasses up the ridge of his nose with one hand and tugging at his beard with the other.

"Well, here's one way of looking at it," Alex began. "Suppose we talk about midcourse interception: the missiles have taken off, and have reached their zenith, in outer space. I don't know exactly how you plan to get the rocketry in place, but let me assume you carry your demons in orbit inside a large satellite, that you nurse them by way of large solar panels on the mother satellite, and that they are ejected when an attack is detected. Assume also that we've built the vision system; so each rocket sees many vehicles. But here's the rub, guys—I mean, comrades: which missile does a given demon *go* for? What's to stop ten demons from going after the *same* warhead? For that matter, what's to stop a *thousand* rockets from going after the same warhead?"

The coordination problem. Markov and Ignatov, catching up with the rest of the present *Starik*, had grasped the dilemma before Nelsen's explanation concluded.

Markov said: "Fuck."

Ignatov looked up at the hacker and nodded, which slid his glasses down the bridge of his nose. He pushed the lenses back up into place yet again.

"Agreement," Bazakin said. "Miraculous."

But not everyone in the room had expressed agreement: Pattison and Renear were still present, and hadn't said a word. The focus of the *Starik*'s cogitation shifted to the two kidnapped Americans. Their opinion was silently but unmistakably solicited by way of five pairs of eyes, directed now upon them.

"Hey," Renear said. "I build machines. Not rockets."

Pattison, beside Neuron Data's president, affirmed Renear's utterance with a nod.

"We're all thinking out loud," Bazakin said. "No harm in joining in."

Both engineers looked at Alex, who was looking at them. The trio traded searching looks.

"Well," Renear said, "I'm not sure I understand completely what you people are up to, but based on what I've seen, I'd have to say that you're being awfully optimistic." Pattison murmured assent.

A meditative interlude gave Bazakin the opportunity to offer everyone a seat around the large rectangular granite table that supported the Neurocubes. And everyone—Nelsen, Markov, Ignatov, Matra, and Bazakin, as well as Renear and Pattison—accepted.

Stretching as for a warm-up to an athletic contest. Cleansing breaths. Vodka was summoned. And some ice. And some Pepsi for Markov, who absorbed and metabolized caffeine as the rest of us do air.

Alex sank into one of the cushiony leather chairs and laughed to himself at the fact that the Neurocube in front of him, deep in the heart of communist Russia, was sitting inches from a McDonald's takeout bag. Matra overflowed her chair, gave the impression of being able to break off her armrests by simply taking a deep breath, hoisted her muscular forearms onto the table, cupped her vodka, and tossed down five ounces in one effortless gulp. Ignatov, on the other hand, was engulfed by the chair, and would have done well to find a New York phone book for a booster seat. Sitting was a position that ran violently against Vincent Markowitz's hyperactive nature: absent a keyboard, tools, food, something to manipulate, he twitched, fidgeted, gnawed on a pencil. Renear and Pattison, though captives, looked surprisingly calm and free of rancor. Bazakin, his brain ready for some exercise, was relaxed, his legs crossed, the Primas exhausted, but a Belomor now lit, dangling from his long thin fingers.

All in all a luminous group, the bulk of the light quite clearly concentrated in Nelsen and Bazakin. Everyone felt the imbalance.

"Well, my comrades," Ignatov said, "I share some of the skepticism Mr. Renear has expressed. I just don't see how it's tractable. You've got to take all the data about the vehicles in, vehicles traveling at . . . What? Mach 25?" Dimitry Ignatov shook his head and hissed, brushed a chunk of dark greasy hair from in front of his eyes, and continued: "So you take it all in to one of these new machines, and then you decide the schedule, the assignments: demon one goes here, demon two here, and so on *ad infinitum*. The complexity is enormous. My side, the propulsion, is no problem. But the software, that's another matter."

Ignatov nibbled at his vodka, swung his head to remove another out-of-place chunk of hair, and resumed: "And then, comrades, what about flight path? Even if you can make the assignments, you've got to have everybody in paths that don't cross at the wrong time. I just don't see it."

"I think it can be done," Galya declared in her best weight lifter's voice. "Let us hear from Alexander."

All present looked at Alex. Nelsen without hesitation opined: "It can indeed be done."

"How?" Ignatov said. "Certainly not on any ordinary digital machine, however fast."

Matra growled and looked ineffably annoyed. "But that's the point, you fucking mouse. Why do you think we went through all this trouble to get these Neurocubes? We're not talking ordinary machines here."

"No, we're not," Alex said.

"What exactly *are* we talking about?" Ignatov asked.

"Jeff?" Alex said.

Renear's reluctance surfaced once again.

"You're the expert, Jeff," Alex said, persisting.

Renear kept quiet.

"Perhaps you don't understand the situation, Mr. Renear," Bazakin said.

Renear was thinking: *They break, I'll fix 'em. I wouldn't have a choice. But play along here, conspiring against my homeland? Not if I can help it.*

He kept quiet, figuring perhaps he'd already said too much.

Bazakin laughed. "Prudence, Mr. Renear, would dictate cooperation. These Neurocubes of yours are indeed strange creatures, but do not be so foolish as to think that your understanding of them makes you irreplaceable. I would hazard to say that if I shared your defiance with Comrade Kasakov, the *Starik*'s leader, the bottom of the icy Volga would soon be your new abode. It would slow us down, of course, but eventually even the Neanderthals in the Soviet Union would come to understand every atom in your neural machines. And then we'd be back in business, wouldn't we? Prudence, Mr. Renear."

"Well," Renear began, looking at Alex, "the best way to think of them is as animate, as biological organisms. They of course aren't as complicated as real brains, but they do share some of the salient features of real flesh-and-blood neurology."

"How so?" Ignatov asked.

Renear said, "Well, we have inside these shiny black cubes an artificial equivalent to billions of interconnected neurons."

"Spare us the obfuscating fluff, Comrade Renear," Bazakin said. "You aren't talking to readers of *Popular Mechanics*. The unadulterated science would be most appreciated."

"Just trying to ease exposition, chief. All right," Renear conceded, "we don't *really* have neurons in these cubes, of course; what we have are mathematically well-behaved entities *isomorphic* to neurons; specifically, a descendant of adaptive Hopfield nets. As you probably know, it was long ago discovered that it's useful to treat neurons as either active or quiescent. But then it became known that atoms in a lattice can be in one of two states: in spins pointing up or down. And furthermore, just as neurons either excite or inhibit one another, so atoms exert on their neighbors forces that tend to set their spins in either the same or the opposite direction. So the properties of neurons in densely connected nets, the sort of thing inside our heads, are similar mathematically to atoms in a crystal lattice."

Renear's audience looked solidly at ease with what they'd heard so far.

"As you know," Renear continued, "in a digital machine, no matter how fast or slow, small or big, there is an invariant essence, a *discrete* essence: namely, a Turing machine which operates on a tape of indefinite length, upon which symbols are written. You can view a Turing machine as a single-man boxcar upon a railroad track of infinite length in one direction. There's a guy in the car, one guy, and he's singularly dim: he can only read very primitive instructions written on the track—move left, move right, erase, write a certain symbol, that sort of thing. Neural-net machines are nothing like this guy. They compute in accordance with natural, physical law. The general concept is nothing really new. The computing world is coming to see the aptness of treating even digital machines as artificially alive. The best way, for example, to understand a computer virus is *as* a virus, something that infects biological organisms. Work on cellular automata, large lattices of interconnected digital computers, has shown that giving such creatures just a few rules enables the creation of snowflakes, of designs that are infinitely complex. Analog machines like these Neurocubes simply take this direction further down the road."

"So," Galya said, "a computable function for you is a *natural* function."

"Precisely," Renear responded. "A function may be viewed as a kind of input-output device, right? In an ordinary machine a computable function is specified by discrete and definite instructions: you take some data in in a high-level language, say Pascal, and you translate it into machine code. And the machine code specifies the function, that is, how the input is to be treated. Then you can put your input onto the railroad track of the Turing machine. And then, in accordance with the machine code instructions, these data are manipulated by the guy in the boxcar. And then he simply outputs the result, in purely mechanical fashion. This input-output is calculated by a finite number of discrete steps. But what if such an input-output function parallels a natural phenomenon?"

"I begin to see," Ignatov said. "How about an example?"

"Of?"

"An actual computation?"

"Well," Renear said, "I'm telling you about the hardware. If you want this hardware to *do* something, then Nelsen here is your man."

Collective attention shifted to Alex.

Who reflected for a couple of minutes while the others sipped their drinks, all of them sitting in silence beside the shiny black Neurocubes, in a room with monitors from George Lucas' laboratories, a satellite hookup from here to the Tereshkovo complex on the Lena River in Siberia, wherein rockets with propulsion systems of unprecedented power were calmly sitting.

"Let's start with a homey example," Alexander said. "Get two small thin pieces of rigid plastic about six inches square, some nails, a hammer, and some soap."

Bazakin punched a button on a console built into the table and within seconds an attendant arrived to hear Nelsen's requirements. Within five minutes the team was beside a sink filled with soapy water. "Okay," Alex said, "I'm going to nail these two pieces of plastic together, but with a space between them where the nails are showing. Now, I don't know about the rest of you, but Comrade Vincent is no doubt familiar with the famous Steiner-tree problem. You have *n* points in the plane, represented by our nails, and you want to see how these points can be connected by a series of lines of minimal length. At ten points the latest Cray dies on this problem, which is, as some of you probably know, an *NP*-complete problem. But watch this."

Alex dipped his construction into the water and pulled it out. "Notice that the soap film connects our nails," he said, showing the soapy web between the nails to his colleagues. "This series of connecting lines is a solution to our problem: it's how to connect the points by lines of minimal overall length. And we got it in a flash."

The group was considerably impressed, but far from overwhelmed.

"I've heard of such analog tricks," Ignatov said. "But can you implement them on a machine? *That* is the question."

This guy doesn't have a theoretical bone in his body, Nelsen thought. *Engineers. It's always the same.*

Alex said, "Give me a minute," and began to think. The others relaxed, refreshed their drinks, and waited.

Thirty seconds later Dr. Alexander Nelsen said, "Chess."

The others stared.

"Isn't that something you Soviets are known for? Bazakin, you play, don't you?"

Bazakin nodded. "I have a rating of 2580."

"Great. How 'bout a match?"

A "dumb" chess-playing program, provided by Nelsen as shareware, was shipped with every Neurocube. The program was dumb in the sense of not employing any humanlike heuristics—it didn't value pieces, or position, or vulnerability: all it did was look ahead. *Way* ahead. It was a so-called "brute-force" approach. The Neurocube viewed seventeen billion possible board configurations per second. A "ply" is a move ahead by each player. The Neurocube was capable of looking ahead 160 plies. A typical game between human grand masters may go, from start to finish, forty or so plies. A human grand master will typically look only seven plies ahead.

After just ten moves the Neurocube declared that Bazakin could now not escape checkmate.

The Russian scientist raised his eyebrows. "I'd like to say that that is impossible."

Alex punched in a command to display the myriad branches which could be taken from the current board position. In one after another Bazakin was defeated.

"Games are fine," Galya Matra said, "but this is aerospace. Perhaps you could put together a more appropriate demo."

Nelsen nodded, and began thinking in silence yet again.

* * *

Five minutes later he said, "I've got it. Jeff, Fred, listen, I want this place to look like the TV section of a department store: I want everything hooked together, the six Neurocubes, and attached to each Neurocube, one of the Lucasfilm monitors."

Renear and Pattison, comfortable with some good honest mechanical work despite the fact that it was done in enemy territory, set to work.

And had the stuff rigged together in ten minutes.

"Ladies and gentlemen, I propose now to simulate what you might call a cosmic rifle, which will roughly model the interceptor system we are aiming at."

The others looked at each other.

Nelsen took a seat before one of the Neurocubes like a concert pianist.

"You see what I've conceived," Alex said, "is a more advanced form of our proposed SBI system, something I'm calling the cosmic rifle. You don't have these fancy rockets Ignatov has been building, you just have a gun—one big space-based mother of a gun. Now, I stipulate that it fires two-kilogram projectiles at twelve kilometers per second." Nelsen punched away at the keyboard for a few seconds. "Yup, there it is. One of the interesting things about this concept is that, according to my calculations, you could hook up fourteen thousand car batteries operating through a two-hundred-megajoule inductor, and get significant acceleration. Or you could use compressed helium, which would prevent barrel wear. The barrel could be, let's see . . . a tube of fiberglass, with epoxy injected at ten thousand psi, to help resist the rather formidable outward force that accrues when the gun is fired. At any rate, the first point is that the hardware seems pretty trivial; and so assume you've got one of these guns up there in space. Now, what I want to show in this simulation is that this gun would give you the ability, mathematically speaking, to handle, in real time, a nuclear attack involving up to eight thousand objects in space, at the same late-midcourse and terminal points that our SBI is supposed to spring into action. If you'll just give me a minute here."

Nelsen typed away. Quickly, smoothly, cleanly. For five minutes. After which, five of the six monitors, one by one, came to colorful life. Streaking across each were cylindrically shaped chunks of phosphorescent green. Sound effects were provided in the form of a threatening *whoosh*.

"You are now looking at eight thousand American ICBM's in action. What's that term of endearment I've heard some of you using? Roweena?"

"Motherland," Ignatov said.

"Okay. Then these ballistic missiles are bearing down on the Motherland, comrades. In a few minutes Moscow, Leningrad, and track for the Trans-Siberian will be rubble. But enter the cosmic rifle."

Nelsen tapped the keyboard and brought up on the sixth and final monitor a graphic representation of his imaginary rail gun. It was sleek and silvery and suitably menacing, something which, after a bit of polishing, could indeed have gone right into a Star Wars flick. Next, after turning back to smile at his colleagues, Alex, by hitting a certain key, began to fire. And the result was like a fireworks display on the Fourth of July: the simulated ICBM's bit the dust rapidly, one after another, each hit marked with a satisfying *ping*. The destruction continued until Moscow was safe.

The five screens representing five chunks of space were dark and peaceful.

The rifle shone placidly on the sixth screen.

"The visual display was of course excess baggage," Nelsen said. "The bottom line is that underlying my little show was computational reality. And so, my comrades, given that our interceptor system, while a good deal more primitive, is of the same ilk, the software problem is tractable. This was a genuine simulation—a little rough around the edges, but close enough to reality to make the point. The equations used presuppose twelve kilometers per second for the projectiles, and the standard parabola for incoming ICBM's—twenty-eight minutes start to finish, chaff and metallized plastic balloons for decoys, dispersed after boost phase, which I conservatively figured to be eighty seconds in duration."

All except Renear and Pattison nodded their heads, convinced.

Even Matra wore a smile of genuine joy, and her flaxen hair, short and spiked, suddenly looked somewhat becoming.

Bazakin offered everyone some of his foul Belomors, but everyone declined. More vodka, a special reserve from Krystall, was brought in and poured. The gargantuan and now chipper Matra threw down three glasses as if she were drinking water on a steamy day. Ignatov, possessed of a constitution that was saturated by a shot glass of vodka, began to teeter: more than once his female colleague caught him, preventing a fall. They toasted, the Russians saying "Cheers," Alexander saying "Skoal," and Renear and Pattison declining drink, and dour, saying nothing.

And there was much friendly, sparkling banter.

Ignatov—pushing up his glasses, blinking behind them, walking around in a lab coat that reached his little shoes, inebriated, swaying—pointed out that Alex's cosmic rifle would be powerful enough even to attack missiles in boost phase, and that, "just to offer some perspective, the twelve-kilometer-per-second rate would be approximately twelve times the muzzle energy of the forty-millimeter cannon on the MIG-X fighter currently under secret construction at the TsIAM Institute, where I still have friends who talk a bit too much."

Markov didn't say much: he popped open a voluminous can of Durkee potato sticks and a can of Pepsi, taken from the junk-food supply he'd carted over from the States, reran Nelsen's demo, and, absorbed, began to explore, by trial and error, the idiosyncrasies involved in programming a Neurocube.

Matra, who had not long ago described a "plasma rifle" for the skeptical earthbound Ignatov, saw Nelsen's demo as a vindication. And although she conceded that implementation of even the more primitive cosmic rifle was at least a decade off, she pointed out that "cryogenic aluminum, of course, would be the best way to carry electricity in such a system." No one knew what she was talking about; Ignatov muttered "Physicists," sounded a deprecatory grunt, took yet another sip of the vodka, and looked up at the others for corroboration.

Bazakin, never animated, never happy and never sad, sitting, thinking, smoking, said, "Now, my comrades, what about a division of labor?"

Renear and Pattison were ushered out by two cold, thuggish agents, summoned just for the purpose.

And the high-level planning began.

It took them all of ten minutes to hammer it out. Galya was the natural link between Ignatov, the engineer, and the software-oriented duo of Alex and Viet. As soon as possible Galya was to establish parameters for the data to be returned by laser scan to the neural machines. The three computer scientists were to begin using specs on American nuclear vehicles, supplied by Bazakin, to design an internal, machine representation of the targets. Writing the software in earnest was to begin as soon as Galya could provide some hard data; she and Ignatov were to fly back to the Tereshkovo complex in the morning.

"No," said Bazakin. "They leave now."

Smiles vanished, laughter ceased, a collective stare.

"Time is of the essence, my friends. Need I remind you about the summit our dear President has planned? If things go the way Gorbachev wants, which unfortunately is the way Secretary of State Simon wants, the *Starik* would be bankrupt overnight. Our fun costs money, my comrades. Quite a bit."

Sobriety descended. Ignatov struggled to stand as tall and rigid as an oak. Markov, minutes ago transported, pulled his face away from the Neurocube in which he was buried. Matra looked suddenly as if she wanted to drive an ax deep into the head of the Soviet leader.

Galya and Ignatov were jetting toward Yakutsk within the hour.

Nelsen gave Bazakin and Markov a complete, six-hour-long orientation to the Neurocube. The Brooklyn-born hacker was entranced with the power of the machines, and after this orientation told the other two that he would be sleeping in the lab tonight, after working on his own for a while longer.

Nelsen and Bazakin left Markowitz in the dark, the Lucasfilm monitor, the only light, glowing eerily on his face, and the two walked out together, down the scrubbed shiny floors of the facility, leaving as they'd come. On the way out, Alex noticed that innumerable Russians in clean white lab coats were still pondering innumerable programs running on innumerable pirated PC's.

"GRU never sleeps, my friend," Bazakin said, noticing the American's expression.

"And the *Starik*?"

"Ah. My apologies, Dr. Nelsen. We've kept you in the dark, haven't we? Well, you see, GRU, not long ago, was run by a fearless tanker, a Hero of the Soviet Union, General of the Army, Andreev Ivanovich Kasakov, who loved Great Russia. And he had a son, whom you met in New York. Now . . ."

Bazakin talked all during the drive back to

Anna's apartment. And for fifteen minutes while the Volga idled outside her flat. And when he finally finished, Nelsen, offering his own summary, said: "Renegades."

And Bazakin, incorporeal beside the American in the darkness, the orange glow of his cigarette hovering in midair, said: "Not yet. But we're working on it."

It was her preference, this night, to be submissive. She did not want to be on top, sliding over him, in control, his hips still. She wanted, rather, to be taken, fucked silly.

And he couldn't bring himself to even try.

Because it had hit Professor Alexander Nelsen that trashing the system was going to be one hell of a tall order. He thought of Everest, and, by comparison, it looked tiny.

Because Markov was a wizard, and would be constantly in sight of Nelsen's algorithm, and even his code. One day on the job, and the rumpled ingenious bastard no longer found Neurospeak, Nelsen's programming language for Neurocubes, the least bit inscrutable. He was *programming* the thing already, for God's sake!

Because the rest . . . well, shit, because the rest stacked up against the best minds Nelsen had worked with in the States.

Because the whole system was no doubt going to be test-driven many, many times. And it had to work on these occasions, or else there wouldn't be a system to sabotage.

Nelsen looked at Anna, open for him, and he was overtaken, not with extreme desire, but with apprehension: he thought that for the first time in his life he'd bitten off more than he could chew. It was too steep, too harsh, too frigid, too fast. The sinking feeling that sometimes comes with underestimation flooded Dr. Alexander Nelsen for the first time in his life.

"Allllex."

A slow-to-replicate virus? Possible. But timing. Shit. Too slow, and the system's operational. Too fast, and everybody'd set out to debug the blasted thing.

"Alexannnder." Brushing herself.

A software bomb? Either hooked up to the machine's internal clock or activated manually, perhaps from a distance over a network link. Maybe.

"Pleeeez."

Anyway, he had time. For now.

The wave of doubt vanished; the intrepid explorer returned.

And he was swollen, wanting her as much as ever, quite prepared, in fact, to fuck her silly.

Kasakov's Office, GRU Headquarters, Moscow

"Well?" Kasakov prodded.

"Like clockwork," Bazakin said. "Nelsen's genius is quite infectious. He gave a little demo that had even Galya Matra smiling."

"Now that, Comrade Bazakin, is *truly* remarkable."

Bazakin himself smiled now—a rarity.

"Well. What next?"

"It would be nice," Bazakin said, "if we could keep tabs on the Americans. Make sure they're still in the dark regarding our little group."

Kasakov nodded slowly, reflected, and presently said, "I'll put Vanderyenko on it."

"Does he have sources?"

"Does a bear shit in the woods? The *Macka* walks through fucking walls. People wave to him on the Hill; a good number of empty-headed dolts in the House and Senate know him variously as courier, reporter, janitor—to some he is even a first-year congressman. He is also in constant interaction with our Archives Directorate, and they have dirt on Mother Theresa. Don't you worry, if the Americans know, we'll *know* they know."

"Siberia, then?"

"Be my guest."

"Think I could borrow one of your coats, comrade?"

"Fox?"

"Well, I was hoping—"

"All right," Kasakov said, grinning, "take a sable."

Washington, D.C.

Theodore Liquori was a man's man, possessed of the kind of understated machismo the American military venerates. Annapolis, and then the Seals, a member of a special fraternity of warriors able to negotiate behind-the-lines penetration, assassinations, and underwater sabotage. "Ted" commanded the team that went into Grenada before conventional forces arrived, swimming eight miles to shore to set up commit posts to radio back information. The Navy brought him to the Pentagon as a special assistant to Navy Chief Conrad Glennie after Reagan's invasion. It seemed like the timing was right: Ted was forty, and despite the fact that he ran and lifted like a fiend so as to maintain a constitution which, in purely physiological terms, was that of a thirty-year-old, an inability to lead twenty-year-olds in taxing aquatic maneuvers was inevitable, and probably just around the corner. Ted accepted the new post, and greatly enjoyed it. At least until Vanderyenko left the tape.

It was there one evening, already in the VCR. He was going to play *Cinderella* for his daughter, but when he slid in the Disney tape he found resistance:

the deck was already loaded. He ejected the tape. It was alien to him: no title, no markings. He started to play it, and at first the naked bodies, though shocking, were meaningless. Then he saw the tattoo: the man was in the Seals. And then he saw the face: it was his own. His daughter watched Walt Disney while he wept in the adjacent room.

Nine months away from his wife, on the *Nimitz*, and one night of drunken idiocy. Liquori had had hundreds of women round the globe—kinky Filipinos, submissive Japanese, fiery Spaniards, even one or two Russians too husky to be KGB or GRU. Doreen, his wife, knew: but she also knew that her husband had energies that, when ashore and home, took her entire being to satiate. Sex in other ports, yes; release in other ports, yes; but *love* in other ports, no. Ted Liquori was a rabid monogamist. And, until one stupid impulsive drunken night, a rabid heterosexual.

Though utterly, staggeringly drunk, he remembered. He hadn't for a long time. But like a recovering amnesiac, it came back slowly—never completely, but, in flashes, it returned.

The guy had a beard.

He was burly.

God, it was in his mouth. Christ!

He saw his face pressed up against a spine running through rippling muscles.

And now the tape, which brought every repulsive detail back.

Five days later, each day a day of dread, wondering each morning if this was it, they called him. He had envisaged the drop-offs, and secret meetings late at night, and tiny cameras. But when the blackmail did come, the procedure was nothing so pedestrian as what takes place in movies. It was a subtly crafted E-mail note on his account on the IBM 3090 at the Pentagon. One day it was just there:

> Ted, hi. Tony, out at Virginia Beach. How's it hangin'? Charlene and I are taking a week off—the *Nimitz* is in for work. What do you say we bring the kids by and see y'all in D.C.? Charlene always did have the hots for you, Theodore. Water turns her on, you know; maybe she's had enough of this fly-boy. No, seriously, what do you say? We miss you, hell *I* miss you. How long's it been, anyway? Over a year? Remember that crazy night in Israel? You still throw 'em down like that, pal? Not me. How're the kids? How's Doreen? You can bring us up-to-date on what Uncle Sam is up to, seeing as how you're a big cheese and everything now, in the Pentagon. You got some of the inside scoop on Star Wars? Love the concept myself, only way to protect ourselves from Ivan, Gorbachev or no Gorbachev. Think Ivan's building one for himself? Anyway, you want to hook up, give me a holler over the net.

His first thought was suicide. But he had a family that, no matter what, he loved. And then he thought about confessing everything to his wife. Doreen loved him, and she was reasonable. Couldn't their marriage survive one night of what was essentially masturbation? Probably. But Doreen wasn't their target. His wife's forgiveness wasn't sufficient. What good would her forgiveness do if the rest of the country thought him gay? What good would her forgiveness do if he was unemployed, if his children were unsupported, if the story, accompanied by suggestive pictures, was plastered all over the papers, if the fucking tape was for sale under the table in video stores around the country?

They had him.

True to his nature and his training, Ted soon enough began to entertain thoughts of *licking* the dilemma. Besides, he figured, the request *was* rather benign, as these things go: his conscience was assuaged to some degree by the fact that he was not in any direct way threatening the country that had nurtured him. So he did it. And, given what Admiral Glennie was saying these days about Ivan's Star Wars, it wasn't hard to gather data sufficient, he figured, to keep the Russians off his back. His chief had dropped hints that the Soviets were very far ahead on their SDI. It was subtle, but it was there. And so upon receiving the note, Lieutenant Theodore Liquori mailed off an electronic letter which said, in sum, that apparently the Navy chief suspected that the Soviets were threateningly far ahead on SDI.

Within seconds the transmission, virtually untraceable, flashed into Vanderyenko's account; and Vanderyenko flashed it to one of the many accounts Kasakov oversaw from GRU headquarters.

A minute after its arrival, Kasakov read it. He found it vague, suggestive. Not, as it stood, anything to indicate that the *Starik* had been found out.

But it was enough to warrant pressing the source further. And that's what the *Macka* was told to do: squeeze.

23

Elite Force

February 15—Providence, Rhode Island

Malachev plodded along doggedly, with McNulty on his tail. To the Department of Computer Science at Brown University, where the *spetsnaz* agent asked questions of departmental secretaries, professors, and grad students. To various consultants on duty at various computer labs, including the one in which Malachev had accosted Nelsen. To a pay phone on Thayer Street, where the bear of a man placed a good number of calls. To five East Side houses McNulty assumed contained friends or colleagues of Alexander Nelsen, where Malachev conducted interviews. And finally to Providence's Biltmore Hotel.

And all along the way Malachev had written in the same notebook he'd been writing in back in the vicinity of Nelsen's house, earlier that day.

Dusk.

The Russian dropped his car off with the valet; McNulty parked on the street, and walked in on the heels of the GRU agent. Fitting the movie stereotype to a T, the detective purchased a newspaper, sat down, and surreptitiously watched the check-in. When Malachev left the desk, McNulty walked up, flashed his badge, and asked for the room number of the man who had just registered; the reception clerk, by reflex, told him: 413. McNulty climbed the stairs, found the room, and hid in the stairwell, waiting. Malachev emerged shortly thereafter, without his luggage, but well-dressed—presumably, McNulty reasoned, for dinner. McNulty took the opportunity to break into Ivan's room, and set about searching for the notebook, which he located in seconds. He opened it.

Russian.

So he briskly brought the notebook down to the main desk and, once again showing his badge, asked to have the pages within it photocopied. Though the clerk on duty had every right to refuse, he didn't. The Canon churned and flashed; within three minutes the Troy detective had a complete copy. McNulty went back upstairs, returned the notebook, and raced his Subaru up to Brown University. He asked the first person he saw where the library was.

"Which one?"

"The biggest."

"Oh, okay, that's the Rock. Right behind you."

"Thanks."

He parked illegally and ran in. The reference librarian was off duty, so he asked at the book checkout counter where he could find a Russian-English dictionary. The girl on duty walked him to the reference shelves, pulled out the dictionary, and he began to attempt the translation. But it was hopeless. Transliteration of the Cyrillic alphabet into the familiar Latin letters of English is, as is well-known, irregular, and the Russian alphabet has letters that are utterly mysterious to someone new to the Cyrillic—someone like McNulty. The script was for the most part indecipherable. He managed a couple of the words in the first sentence, but realized that at this pace, by the time he finished a meaningful chunk, Ivan was liable to be back in the Soviet Union, or wherever it was he was planning to go next. McNulty went back to the girl at the counter.

"Do you know if Russian is taught at Brown?"

The girl studied him for a second. "No, I don't. Sorry."

"How 'bout a course guide? Do you have one around?"

The girl turned back toward the office behind her and called, "Bill, we got a course guide around here?" Nothing. Louder: "Bill, we got a course guide?"

No verbal response, but Bill emerged with one.

"Thanks," McNulty said. He looked for a Russian course, and, after a minute or two, found one, and copied down the instructor's name.

"Can I use your phone?" McNulty asked.

The girl, by now, thought something downright evil was going on.

"There's a pay phone up the street."

McNulty pulled his wallet and showed his badge; it seemed to him he'd done this a hundred times tonight. "Look, I need to use a phone."

"Okay, in there," she said, pointing to the office wherein Bill evidently lurked. McNulty walked around the counter and into the office. Bill was there, at a desk, reading a textbook, his face buried.

"Nine to get out?"

"Huh?"

"Nine to get an outside line?"

"Uh, yeah, nine."

McNulty dialed information and asked for the number of "Syzmanski." He was told that there was no one by that name in Providence. He hung up.

"Hey Bill, listen, you got an undergraduate catalog in here?"

"What?"

"Undergrad catalog?"

"Uh, sure, right there."

McNulty pulled it off the nearby shelf, turned to those pages devoted to the Department of Languages, and found the chairman's name: Benedict. He called information back, asked for the number of "Benedict," and this time information had the number; he dialed it.

"Professor Benedict? . . . This is an emergency. I need to get hold of Syzmanski, the person who teaches Russian in your department. There's been an accident involving some of his family. Do you have his number? . . . All right, all right, do you know where he or she lives? . . . Rehoboth? Okay, thank you."

McNulty hung up.

"Bill?"

"Jesus, man, what is it now?"

"Rehoboth in Rhode Island or Mass?"

"Mass. You know, I got a test on this tomorrow."

"How far?"

"You know, you come in here and—"

"How *far*?"

Something clicked in Bill's brain, telling him he'd better cooperate. "Just across the border. Five minutes."

McNulty dialed 617-555-1212 and asked for Syzmanski's number, got it, and dialed it.

"Hi, Syzmanski?"

"Yes?"

"This is Detective John McNulty." Bill, for the first time, looked up from his textbook of his own initiative. "I need to ask you to do me a favor. I'm in the middle of an investigation, it's life-and-death, and I need somebody who can translate Russian. Could I ask you to come over to Brown's library right away? I'm in the main office."

"Which library?"

"The biggest."

"The Rock?"

"Uh, yeah, the Rock."

"Okay. Thirty minutes."

"Start from the beginning."

Syzmanski flipped through the notebook, spotting at least five pages of writing.

"You don't expect me to translate all of it, I hope."

"Yes, I do."

"Impossible. It's a slow process. This is Russian, not Spanish."

Syzmanski studied the pages for a minute or two, and then looked up at McNulty. "What's the matter?" the detective asked.

"What are you involved in here?" Syzmanski asked, a tough-looking, husky Pole whose appearance did violence to the thin-and-tweedy professorial stereotype.

"What the hell kind of a question is that? All I want you to do is give me the translation."

"You expecting anything in particular?"

Syzmanski's truculence was the last thing McNulty needed. The detective's efforts tonight seemed to be moving along like molasses; Ivan might already be in another state.

"Look, buddy, you did me a favor in coming over here, but I'll be damned if you're gonna jerk me around like this. I've showed you my ID; I'm legit. Now, just give me the fucking translation."

Syzmanski considered a brawl right on the spot; McNulty could see it in the professor's eyes. But the square-jawed Pole decided against it. Though McNulty refused to use the Nautilus machines at his health club, he still stood six-foot-three and had the air of a man who had weathered his share of fistfights.

"Suit yourself," the translator said. And then he began to dictate without a hitch:

" 'First house nothing ditto on second and nothing at third except owner said he saw subject throwing luggage into a cab not long ago. Guy stated that subject flies down to New York City quite often and that that was probably where he was heading. Started to call colleagues not residing in . . . the area. First, Eugene Baudet, said subject vacationing in Soviet

Union, probably up on some mountain. Second colleague, Marsha Anderson, said . . .' "

A potential shortcut struck McNulty: *Would he have come to the Biltmore if he hadn't found something?*

"Stop. Go to the last page."

"You said you wanted me—"

"Go to the last fucking page. Now."

"Suit yourself," Syzmanski said and then read: " 'Graduate student of subject, Mohammed Ashri, stated that his adviser was in Russia and that this sort of thing was normal and he then pointed out that it had in fact interfered with the defense of his dissertation and that Nelsen had given him advance notice so that the other members on Ashri's committee could find a replacement to sit in. I asked when the defense was to take place. He said February 22. I asked when subject had called him. He said February 13. I asked whether morning, afternoon, or what. He said morning. I said are you sure. He said definitely.' "

Syzmanski paused. "Uh . . ."

"What is it?" McNulty said.

"An Americanism. Let's see . . . bingo. Yes, bingo. And then he writes: 'Subject propositioned on evening of February 13, didn't leave Kennedy until early morning, next day.' "

Syzmanski looked at McNulty, just in time to see the detective's eyes light up.

"Traitor, tourist, or bloody secret agent!" McNulty exclaimed.

"What?"

"Here." McNulty threw down two twenties, grabbed the photocopy, and ran out, heading for the Biltmore.

It was really plain as day, and the deductions necessary to shed light on the whole situation were not half as tortuous as those carried out by Sherlock Holmes. For McNulty, a man who, in the course of building

Sherlock, had, with the help of the knowledge engineers from RPI, extracted and structured into the system the nearly thirty thousand rules generally used unconsciously by human missing-persons experts, it was transparent: Ivan was here to find out if Nelsen was legit, and that meant Nelsen wasn't a tourist. He was either what he was selling himself off as, or not: he was either a traitor or bloody double agent working for Uncle Sam. And the next step in the deduction was trivial. "Bingo," Syzmanski had read. So he had found a discrepancy. Nelsen had called Ashri on the morning of the thirteenth, but hadn't been propositioned till the evening of the same day. Which meant Nelsen had been *planning* to leave. Which implied double agent. McNulty figured the Russians weren't gullible enough to discount the possibility that Nelsen was a double agent. But he also figured it would sure as hell be better if they were kept guessing. If this stuff got back to Ivan's boss, Nelsen would, at the very least, be in hotter water.

Oh, sweet Jesus, how the hell did I ever stumble into this mess?

McNulty parked, pulled his 3-inch .38 and set it, reholstered it, got out, and ran for the Biltmore's front entrance. It was eleven P.M. when the clerk on duty, joining the multitude who had seen McNulty's badge on this night, assured the Troy detective that no international call had been placed from room 413, and that the occupant had not yet checked out. McNulty thanked the clerk evenly, turned, and walked back out the front entrance. He circled around to the back, and within five minutes was inside the hotel, climbing in the stairwell.

McNulty figured that if he knocked, Ivan was likely, within an instant, to be in command of a friggin' Uzi, or whatever it was that Russian secret agents packed. His only chance was surprise. He looked underneath the door: dark. He pulled out his locksmith kit and worked as quietly as humanly possible. It was slower than last time, but he got it within fifteen seconds. He took a deep breath, raised his gun, and slowly eased the door open. He achieved a three-inch crack, which brought the chain to its maximum length.

Shit.

McNulty slowly and soundlessly pulled the door closed. He went out the back of the hotel, ran to his car and retrieved his tire iron, and returned to the door of 413. He rested for a minute, and caught his breath—and thought perhaps, if given another chance, he would listen to the instructors at his health club.

When his respiration began to approach normal, he turned the knob and slid the door slowly to the stopping point. He raised the crowbar with two hands and slammed it down with all his might on the chain. The mechanism flew apart.

He dashed in, slid his fingers along the wall, found the switch he had located during his first intrusion earlier in the night, flipped it, the lights came on, and McNulty aimed at Malachev, who had sprung up to a sitting position in bed, wide-awake in a nanosecond. His torso was solid, defined.

"Hello, Ivan."

"Who the fuck are you?"

"The Sandman. You're under arrest."

"Yeah? For what? Sleeping?"

"For participating in the theft of four computers from the campus of MIT." McNulty figured the best thing was to lock Malachev up, keep him from calling his superiors, and thus keep Nelsen living. Then he could get the CIA or the FBI. He had a feeling that this time they'd show up at his door, and in a flash.

"You got a warrant?"

"I have this." McNulty waved his gun slightly. "And I have this." He waved the stapled photocopy of the notebook. "Which contains Russian. Now, that's odd, wouldn't you say? I understand you hit the jack-pot tonight on Benefit Street. Bingo, huh?"

Malachev suddenly remembered McNulty's face from passing the detective on the sidewalk earlier; the Russian's eyes flared.

McNulty searched the room slowly, keeping Malachev in line with the solid ribbed barrel of his gun. Within seconds he found Ivan's wallet. "Oh, it's Mr. Barnes now, huh? Think this license number is going to be in New York State's motor-vehicle computer system? How 'bout if we go find out, what do you say? Or should we just call Moscow?"

Malachev's expression darkened; he cursed in Russian. Then he started to move toward one side of his bed.

"Freeze! I'll blow your communist head off!"

Malachev stopped.

I don't have the guy's piece yet. Shit.

McNulty resumed the search.

Malachev said, "You're blind as a fucking bat. It's right here."

The gun? His gun is on that chair?

It was. In plain view of both of them. And it was a monstrous .44, McNulty pegged it immediately as an SSK handcannon, a gun that made his own .38 seem a toy.

"Now, you listen, you little mouse. I'm going to reach for my gun in ten seconds, which gives you just enough time to get your little amateur ass out of here, and then you can forget you ever got involved with the big boys. If you don't leave, it's you or me, but one of us is going to be carried out of this hotel. Eight seconds."

As nervous as he naturally was, the reasoning was quick and cogent: *I leave, Nelsen might die. He's a phone call away from Moscow, if he hasn't already made it from a pay phone. He gets that gun, and* I'm *likely to die, and if I'm going to shoot, there's no point in shooting after the bastard has his piece.*

"Six seconds, pal."

McNulty feigned the lowering of his gun, Malachev lurched toward the chair, McNulty raised and fired, and a .38 caliber bullet blasted into the Russian's right temple. Lazery Malachev, paralyzed, fell onto the floor beside the bed. His pulse stopped as McNulty was checking it for the fourth time, almost one hour after the shot.

McNulty sipped Malachev's vodka and began to think with the utterly focused concentration of a chess master about how the hell to get rid of the body. If the authorities found out, the Russians would; and if the Russians found out Malachev had been shot, they'd assume foul play, and Nelsen might very well be fried.

Wait a minute. Isn't this the Ocean State?

McNulty secured the room, and set out to get maps, hopeful that before too long some bit of local water would be at least partly Russian.

The maps raised McNulty's spirits: after but a momentary glance at them he saw that Providence abounded with water. He vaguely remembered that at one time the city had been headquarters to the New England mob, and he thought for a second that perhaps all this water, much of it presumably suitable for cement-boot swimming, was at least part of the reason why. Two rivers, the Providence and the Seekonk, ran within city limits, and flowed into Narragansett Bay, which in turn flowed into the Atlantic; this geography provided encouragement: there seemed to be many promising sites for a watery grave. The detective roped Ivan's body, wrapped it in blankets, stuffed it in a closet, and put a "PLEASE DO NOT DISTURB" sign on room 413's door. Then, with his maps beside him, he drove around in his Subaru for two solid hours, surveying all the possibilities. The Providence River ran through the heart of the city, and consequently too many people were always near it, which was a pity, because the bridges over this river would have made splendid diving boards for Ivan. The bay was also unpalatable, because he couldn't find a place where the body could be thrown out in water of sufficient depth. But then, starting from Brown University's boathouse at the meeting of the Seekonk and the bay, he made his way north along the bank of the river—and shortly after passing the Narragansett Boat Club, he found the perfect spot: a secluded portion of the Seekonk's bank, beneath Blackstone Boulevard, one of the wealthiest streets in the city. There was a jogger here now, at daybreak, but at three in the morning, he figured the site would be vacant. There were no houses with a view, no cars on distant roads close enough to allow their occupants to see, and there was a way to get the corpse far enough out into the river: an old, craggy, deteriorating dock stumbled out nearly to the center of the Seekonk—a river which, he had read, had been at one point navigated by oil tankers, and so was doubtless more than deep enough to forever conceal his devious purpose.

McNulty got out and strolled by the Naragansett Boat Club and satisfied himself that the building would be deserted at the hour of his deed.

Then he began shopping.

Using the Yellow Pages and his street maps, he bought some black nylon cord, a short length of heavy chain, ten cans of ready-mix hydraulic cement, and a good deal of cardboard, along with a pair of scissors for cutting it—all purchased in small chunks at ten different local hardware stores, and all stored in the trunk of his car.

McNulty returned to the Biltmore's 413 and waited, somehow half-expecting Ivan to pop out of the closet, alive.

He turned away two maids, saying he wanted no cleaning till the next day. He slept in catnaps totaling no more than two hours.

At 2:45 A.M., using a fireman's lift and a healthy dose of adrenaline, he lugged Ivan down the stairwell to the back entrance of the Biltmore, near which he had parked his car. He was taking a chance here, even at this hour: someone could easily spot him. But McNulty knew, as a cop, that the odds were overwhelmingly in his favor. No one seeing him would recognize him, and neither would an observer call the police merely on the basis of seeing a man carrying some sort of bundle. And if someone *did* call the police, the cops would have no clue where to look. *Perhaps* they'd send an officer to inquire over at the Biltmore, but even this measure would be viewed by a gung-ho cop as supererogatory. At any rate, there was absolutely no way they'd alert patrol cars to be on watch for a Subaru, given just a vague call-in. McNulty had no intention of returning to the hotel: after dumping, he planned to get right on Route 146 North, aiming for the Mass Pike. And so inquiries at the hotel wouldn't be a problem. If the cops happened to go over at the right time, and hit a clerk with whom McNulty had dealt, they might hear something about a cop who'd been flashing his badge. But McNulty had never given his name, and he'd flashed his ID fast enough to prevent the clerks from reading it. For all practical purposes, McNulty was a drifter; and the *real* beauty of the situation was that Malachev was too.

McNulty had left the Russian's room in spotless shape; there wasn't a hint of the blood that had spurted from the victim's head. McNulty had even left a cash tip for the maid, and a note, printed with his left hand, apologizing for the fact that he had had to leave without checking out at the front desk, and requesting that the charge be placed upon his credit card. The fact that Ivan had a rental car told McNulty that the Russian agent traveled with plastic; and if, per chance, Ivan hadn't used it for the hotel bill, nothing of consequence would ensue. The key for room 413 was on the note.

The bottom line was that once he buried the body, the ripples caused by a fluke call-in tonight would soon dissipate: Ivan had no family or friends in the States to push for a continuing investigation, and so though the GRU agent's car rental would eventually be located, giving rise to a mystery, no repercussion would ever find its way back to McNulty.

But all this, of course, was predicated on the assumption that he *could* get rid of the body without being spotted.

He drove the route down from Richmond Technology Square, along the water, to the relevant spot, without headlights, and rolled to a quiet stop alongside the vacant boat club. Once again, working without the slightest hesitation was the key. He stepped out of the car, looked around, and was satisfied to see that the location was as desolate as he had thought it would be.

He examined the locks on the club: they were flimsy.

An alarm?

Doubtful: the odds of someone wanting to steal a glorified rowboat were small enough to make the expense of an alarm prohibitive.

He hoped. As he picked the lock, turned the knob, pushed in the door.

Yup: nothing: silence.

Now, quickly, he opened his trunk, pulled Ivan out, flung the Russian over his shoulders, and conveyed the body inside. The same for his supplies.

Boats. More boats. Oars and more oars. Everywhere. No apparent organization. Cluttered. Some pictures of rowing teams on the wall. The smell of marine paint in the air.

Using the custom-designed cardboard for forms, he poured the hydraulic cement around Ivan's legs, right up to the Russian's knees. The cement was dry within fifteen minutes. McNulty peered out, saw nothing and no one, hefted the now-heavier *spetsnaz* officer and, without hesitation, walked over and then out to the end of the old decaying pier. He placed Ivan on the weathered and warped two-by-six boards, and, as a precaution, dropped the nylon cord, with the small bundle of chain at the end, into the water, and lowered it till it hit bottom. At least thirty feet deep. He stripped the blankets off Ivan, leaving him naked. McNulty pulled out his jackknife and tore a hole in the Russian's belly so as to eliminate buoyancy, and then without hesitation flipped the Russian into the water. The body sank immediately, and after collecting the blanket, McNulty walked briskly back to his car and started back for Troy.

Detective McNulty reached the department at five-thirty that morning, just as the sun was rising over the patina-coated copper roofs of RPI's massive old brick buildings, casting a shimmer over the Hudson's wavelets. Seeing the river fired off a mental picture of Malachev, blue and bloated and cement-shoed, standing on the bottom of the Seekonk River. McNulty shook his head sharply.

He was in his office, alone, dragging on a Camel, bone weary. He had nearly nodded clean off a number of times on Interstate 90; he mused now that his drive back home had been more treacherous than his escapades in Providence. McNulty laughed, which caused him to cough, first softly, then hackingly. Sherlock, like an old friend, was up and running on his humming SUN workstation. And the pictures of those he and the machine had saved were still hanging on the walls—smiling four-year-olds in the embrace of a parent with a new lease on life, the letters of gratitude

. . . and directly above his computer: Malachev and Vanderyenko, the latter in the guise of both a suited corrupt captain of industry and Billy Joe Dupree, dispatcher for Jet Express.

He felt no guilt. None at all. He had done what was necessary. He just hoped that Nelsen could pull off whatever the hell it was he was up to in the Soviet Union. He ignited the little picture of Malachev: it shriveled into ashes. McNulty swept them into his hand and then brushed them into his ashtray.

Should he tell? Perhaps the FBI or the CIA?

No. Because maybe *they'd* tell—and then maybe someone would prosecute. And McNulty wasn't about to go to jail for possibly saving Uncle Sam's ass.

No, it was over. Let it die. He stubbed out his Camel, leaned back, closed his eyes, and hoped to God that some ordinary, threadbare, utterly unchallenging missing-person case would soon arrive.

24

Tereshkovo

February 16—Moscow

They woke, still in each other's arms from their recent lovemaking, limbs entwined. She kissed him, slid her fingers into his hair, and, aiming for the slow-and-easy pace she preferred the second time around, moved her pelvis almost imperceptibly against his thigh.

But he said, "I have to leave," and she froze, looked into his eyes.

"Galya and Ignatov are ready for us out at Tereshkovo. Viet and I fly out in"—he consulted his watch—"one hour."

"It's the middle of the night."

"I know."

"They've only been working out there for two days," she pointed out.

"Yeah, I'm a bit skeptical myself. But they're supposed to be geniuses, Anna. That was one of the fundamental premises behind the *Starik*."

She laughed softly; he felt the exhalation against his neck. But it was a sigh as much as a laugh, and there was no smile: Anna was clearly saddened. Her head felt heavier upon his chest, and there was suddenly a good deal less life in her body. Their time in Moscow, despite the fact that most of it had been consumed by Alex working with Markov on building into the Neurocubes an internal model of the American missiles, had been magical. Anna began to weep. She thought of all they'd managed to cram into a little more than seventy-two hours: Alex trying ski-jumping for the first time in his life in Lenin Hills, crashing like a wild windmill; riding horses through powdery snow at Bitsa Forest Park; Alex scaring her to death by bringing an ice sailboat up to dangerous speed, outside the city on the frozen, polished Volga. Making love in Gorky Park, under the stars, up a path off one of the four main rinks, on an arctic blanket, Tchaikovsky in the air, faintly, floating over from the distant loudspeakers, the Ferris wheel turning, a luminous semicircle against the dark and starry sky, and coming together beneath the fur of their great coats. And at Yaroslavl Station they had seen the Moscow–Peking Express, huffing like an animate leviathan, and the return of the Trans-Siberian, which reminded both that Alexander would soon be off to Siberia.

Now it had happened. Sooner than expected. The fact was, Anna was in love.

"Can I come with you to the plane?"

"I'd like that."

She rose to take a shower, her face streaked.

And on this morning he could not possibly have let her shower alone, unseen.

It was painful, but he waited—through an infinity, each moment of which, naked, he could have taken her, without resistance. He waited until her hair was filled with lather, her eyes closed. And then he slipped in and stepped up behind her in the shower, and wrapped his arms around her waist, and, bending a bit at the knees, came up, already hard, between her legs. He felt a shudder, slight and brief, and then, though she didn't look, a complete flowing-out of tension, and a change of posture to accommodate his cock.

* * *

On the way to the airport they talked.

The little region of duplicity that each retained, that region in which both were agents for competing powers, had shrunk, by now, to the vanishing point. Riding in the early-morning darkness, their secret war ended.

"You know, Alex, I haven't heard you once talk about the money."

"Back on that again?"

She didn't respond.

"Not once," Anna continued, "have you even *intimated* what you would do with the money. You've talked about going on an expedition in the Pamirs, and you seem to be greatly enjoying the project on which you're working. But there isn't a shred of evidence to confirm the fact that you are what you say you are: a mercenary with hedonistic tastes."

There was a full moon, and the intense starlight one never sees in or around any American metropolis: this time he could see her eyes clearly. And what he saw when he looked into those emerald eyes was much more a beckoning than an accusation.

"You're persistent."

"Relentless," she said, kissing him, and growling.

He pulled back, said solemnly, "They took my niece."

She pulled back too, and there was a pause.

"Why didn't you tell me?"

"Just more baggage. For a while we had a very simple life together."

"They threatened to kill her?"

"What else?"

"But the money. How—?"

"I asked for a fringe benefit."

"And you asked for me too."

"It's not the same, is it?" he asked. "They didn't have the power to give you to me. I asked only for an introduction."

"They have the power," she said in a tone that spoke of a connection, firm and black, between Anna and the *Starik*.

"They?" he prodded.

She said nothing. He saw no ulterior motive flickering in her eyes. They were open, limpid. But there was something. Hate?

Alex said, "Lisa would have died, but I can't help regarding my work here as betrayal. I'm just not sure how to . . . how to stop them."

Nelsen saw something flicker now behind her eyes. And suddenly he had a vision of Buchanan with his head buried in his hands.

Anna had not responded beyond the involuntary lurch deep inside her mind. But he had crossed the bridge; there was no turning back. So, looking at her flawless face, her small symmetrical button nose, her full lips, her green sparkling eyes, he said it:

"Marry me, Annastasia. Defect."

She hesitated still.

He said her name again: "Anna."

She breathed as if for the first time in a long while and said: "They'd kill me if I did."

"We'd give you a new identity," Nelsen said without hesitation.

She looked at him. *We*, she thought. It was out of the bag now. Man or country. It was time to choose. And she chose the man. In not pulling her gun and turning him in, she chose the man.

"It would be a step down, Alexander. Dancing is my life, and the Bolshoi is dancing. It is dancing like no other company, if I do say so myself."

He loved ballet, but loved it viscerally, and simply didn't know enough to even hazard the contention that the New York City Ballet would be a suitable home. And though Alex had been here for only three days, he had come to appreciate completely what Anna had told him on their first night in Moscow: in

Russia, Art is Religion, and artists are high priests. Anna was in the ranks of Tolstoy and Dostoyevsky, venerated by the masses who, unlike their Western counterparts, understood dance as only the cognoscenti do in America.

"You'll never leave, then," he said.

"I suppose not," she said.

"But it's more than the dancing. You do obey."

"What do you mean?" she asked.

"You do what they tell you. You've been telling them about me, no doubt."

Her hesitation confirmed it.

"Yes," she admitted, fully in his arms, her lovely body his.

"But there isn't much to tell, is there?"

"Nothing, really."

"They do suspect, though, don't they?" he said.

"No. Not at all. You're their savior."

"Come on, Anna. They're probably operating under the assumption that I'm sponsored by Langley. Markov eyes everything I do."

"Perhaps."

"Perhaps? Face it, Anna. And what about you? What do *you* think?"

She looked at him boldly, but she tightened her arms around him as she said: "You're here to sabotage the system. I know it in my bones, Alexander."

The taxi motored on toward Domodedovo.

"And what will you tell them now?" he asked presently.

"Nothing, of course."

She closed her eyes and brought her lips nearer his: they kissed. And so she had turned.

He was skeptical, but she insisted. And she was right: it was possible. Not only that, but wondrous—to hold her in the fur, inside the car, and she him, and at the same time he inside her, no skin exposed, both dressed too bulkily for even the slightest thrusting, coming solely on the strength of her tightening, loosening, tightening around his shaft.

Within the hour Alex, asleep with Markov at his side, was aloft, on the way to the *Starik*'s Tereshkovo complex, via Yakutsk.

Tereshkovo Complex

The flight from Domodedovo Airport in Moscow to Yakutsk was uneventful. It was by Aeroflot jet, and though the service was at a lower standard than that of international flights, it was decent. The cabin was sparsely populated; passengers consisted of a few arguably insane tourists, a couple of party officials, and the scientific duo.

At Yakutsk they changed to the plane for Tereshkovo: yet another de Havilland Twin Otter, the workhorse of the arctic, East and West. The Otter had been waiting for Markov and Nelsen for quite a while, wood fires burning beneath her engines to prevent them from freezing solid. In passing from the jet to the smaller plane, a wind of unbelievable cold stung the two men.

"This is scary," said Viet. "This is only Yakutsk. They say the climate here, relative to our destination, is like Yalta."

Nelsen was a bit weak on Soviet geography, as evidenced by his expression.

"Think of Yalta as our . . . your . . . their Florida," Markov said, overwhelmed by the allegiances, past and present, that the two circumscribed.

Within thirty minutes they were over a desert of pallid ice, their eyes searching in vain for a contrasting piece of topography, or even just a shadow. But the frozen monochrome landscape below merged into cerulean sky. When they had been in the air for fifty minutes the pilot informed them that he would soon know whether they would be able to land or whether they would have to turn back. Nelsen and Markov looked at each other. The pilot explained that the runway at Tereshkovo could clog with snow so quickly, and unnavigable crosswinds could stir up so suddenly, that a pilot had to get within twenty minutes before making a decision. The two scientists looked at each other again; Viet took two large and determined swigs from a flask of vodka he pulled out of his down coat; they laughed, but Viet laughed nervously. As it turned out, however, the pilot received word that landing was a go. And it turned out, in fact, to be a smooth one despite the enveloping grayness of clouds and windblown snow severe enough to prevent a view of the Urals. Upon deplaning they shook hands with a bundled-up Captain Ignatov and a sable-shrouded Bazakin, both piloting arctic snowmobiles, which, if shut down, would be, because of the minus-forty weather, instantly out of commission. After a few noisy minutes, during which a semblance of landscape came in and out of focus evanescently, they saw what had to be their destination: an enormous domed structure. They all hopped off, struggled against a terrific wind, and managed to pass through a doorframe almost completely occluded with hoarfrost. Once inside, they pulled off their hoods, and saw that everything was reassuringly high-tech and warm. It reminded Alex of mission control at NASA.

Galya greeted them; she looked like an amazonian warrior back from a bloody but triumphant battle. Nelsen was once again stupefied by her sheer bulk.

"You've made progress, I take it," Alex said.

"You might say that," Galya replied. "The ball is in your court now. Ignatov and I bring you the data in the form of an uninterpreted stream; it's up to you to get from there to an image."

"You're finished?" Markov asked.

"Don't patronize me, Mark-o-weetz," Galya spat.

"There's no need for surprise. We tackled the heat problem first. Remember, in the terminal phase of flight these demons are traveling at velocities that exceed those of tactical missiles, and the nose shroud has been long discarded. These are the fastest rockets known. Well, what we did was simply set up a flow of cooling gaseous nitrogen over the exterior of a sapphire window through which infrared energy is received. It works like a charm. In fact, we're going to recommend a large-scale model of this system for the orbiters. Maybe we can get rid of those damn tiles that always keep falling off during liftoff and reentry, and then maybe we can sell the technology to the Americans."

Matra struck Nelsen as an unlikely entrepreneur. But he had a not-unpleasing vision of her flattening Walter Reitman.

"And the rest?" Viet asked.

"Piece of cake," Galya said. "You've got to remember that Bazakin simplified things a bit: he pointed out that we only had to do limited decoy discrimination, because the decoy reentry vehicles are lighter than the genuine article, and will thus tend to burn up as they enter the atmosphere. So what we have is a design with fifty rows of two hundred and sixty separate infrared-sensitive elements. A readout chip receives output data from the focal plane array and converts it to a serial stream—which is where you high-level boys come in. The seeker is finished, and gift-wrapped for you. It shares an optical return path with a laser ranging unit. We settled on a neodynium-doped aluminum garnet laser transmitter. The infrared seeker points the laser rangers; they shoot; and reflected laser energy is then received through the sensing array, which gives you the serial stream. That's all there is to it. I might say, incidentally, that you have your work cut out for you, and that Dr. Nelsen's machines had better be as powerful as he says. Because you're going to have to process four hundred by four hundred arrays of data elements. And you're going to have to refresh every half-second to have any hope of maintaining a bead in terminal phase. That adds up to a demand for three Cray 4S supercomputers *per* rocket."

Though they'd expected excellence from Galya, Markov and Nelsen were stunned. She and Ignatov had accomplished three months' work in two days.

"Would you guys like to see the seeker? I have one over here. It's no bigger than a breadbox."

The men nodded, and broad-shouldered Galya Matra led.

Washington, D.C.

Whether because genuine insanity was coming to his rescue or because it was in fact the case, it was nonetheless true the Ted Liquori soon came to perceive his employers as supernatural agents. He communicated with them over the computer networks effortlessly and in an attenuated, disembodied way. They seemed to be everywhere, though he saw them nowhere. It was maddening.

One day he found a small gift-wrapped box on the passenger seat of his Nissan Maxima when, having waved to Doreen, he entered the car for his commute to the Pentagon. In it was a small note that said: "One for the Chief's office, one for the Chief, and one for sociable you. Manage it and you're free." Along with the note were three small objects Ted knew immediately to be listening devices. Forty-five minutes later Conrad Glennie's office was bugged, and by the end of the day the small plastic cylinder that sealed the end of the shoelace on Glennie's right wing tip had ears.

The third bug stayed on Liquori, who decided to play a little squash with the Chief.

February 17—Tereshkovo Complex

Nelsen and Markov announced they were ready for Ignatov to run a test. Which the midget gladly did.

Ignatov slapped the fidgety potato-chip-munching Markov on the small of the back, which was as far up as he could reach. "Don't be nervous, Comrade Markov. If it happens to lock onto you, we'll activate the safety abort system."

Markov didn't look particularly reassured. The idea of having one of the demons take a short-duration flight inside the Tereshkovo dome rubbed him the wrong way.

"Okay, boys," Ignatov said with a wave of his tiny hand.

With only a slight lag the demon took off. Markov had expected a roar, but the noise was minimal. The kinetic rocket hovered above them, its 335-pound-thrust liquid engine pulsing, hissing like a giant snake.

Markov was perspiring. Alex himself was not completely comfortable with the situation, despite his confidence in the software he had himself designed. The protective nets enclosing the flight-test area looked to him rather flimsy, like trying to pen in a shark with mosquito netting.

"All right," Ignatov said, "let's see how the software works." He gave a thumbs-up signal to the operators at the controlling computer. A flare ignited in the test area. And then, instantly, the target scene was laser-processed, the vision system liked what it saw, the kinetic-kill rocket was guided home by exploding pitch-and-yaw-control thrusters, and the dummy target was demolished. The force of the collision shook the entire building.

Flare to obliteration in under two seconds.

"Flawless!" Ignatov exclaimed. Alex was smiling by his side. Markov was wiping his forehead with a handkerchief, immeasurably relieved, drawing on a can of sweating Pepsi.

The next day saw a reunion of the entire *Starik*. Vanderyenko and Kasakov flew in from Moscow, witnessed another successful flare test, nodded politely, but all in all looked profoundly unimpressed. Then Kasakov, turning positively grim-faced, called a more formal, sit-down meeting, which he opened by saying:

"The demons are without a doubt impressive, comrades. But we have some problems."

"Explain." Matra scowled defensively, wanting very much to have her work on the demons count for everything.

Vanderyenko pulled out a microcassette. "The Americans," the *Macka* said.

"What *about* the Americans?"

"They evidently know."

"How can they?" Matra asked.

"Let me remind you, Galya Ivanova," Kasakov said, "that our friend Ignatov, before the *Starik* took form, engineered Lockerbie. And *after* we got together, collectively we took down a MIG and a shuttle. Uncle Sam has very good eyesight."

"No, it's impossible," Bazakin said softly.

Vanderyenko waved the tape.

"I don't care about the fucking tape," Bazakin said in his measured, quiet voice. "They know but they don't know. They know the Soviet Union has an SBI capability. But they don't know about *us*."

"Perhaps," Kasakov admitted.

"Let's hear it," Markov suggested. Cradling a bowl of popcorn, he looked for all the world to be settling down for the watching of a movie.

Vanderyenko slid the tape into a Sony recorder, clicked it on.

Smack. Squeak. Squeak. Smack. Smack. Smack. Fuck. Fourteen nine? Uh, huh, uh, yeah, right. Deep breathing. *Smack! Smack. Squeak. Smack. Smack. Aaagh! Shit!*

Good game, son.

Another, Admiral?

No way, Ted. Next *time we'll do best out of three. Shit, it wasn't long ago you were swimming between fucking Caribbean islands. I'm lucky if I can get it up for one dip every few days.*

Laughter.

Lockers and locks clanging. The hiss of water in the background. The hiss got louder. They were in the shower. Naked.

Naked?

Markov said, "How the . . . ?"

Vanderyenko shrugged.

So what's new these days, Connie?

Oh, Ivan, I suppose. He's pulled one over on us.

Really?

Yup. SBI.

Sir? SBI?

Smart rocks, Ted. The Sovs have been throwin' 'em.

At?

You remember Lockerbie?

The jet crash?

You got it, son. Then they lost a MIG and a shuttle.

They?

Yeah, that's the odd part. But of course Ivan always does end up skull-fucking his own.

Just the hiss of descending water for half a minute.

And us, sir?

Aaah, we're not doin' shit. The President retains

dreams of disarmament. So does Simon. You'd think Gorbachev was a fucking saint in the Holy Catholic Church.

What do you want to do, sir?

You know me, Ted. I'd like to preempt the fuckers.

Nuke?

Just one, son. Maybe the middle of Siberia. Nobody fries. Ivan just wakes up. Puts his toys away.

The hissing of the flowing water again.

How's Doreen these days, Theodore? She still have that tight little—

Click.

Kasakov and the *Macka*, having heard it before, remained impassive.

Viet Markov said, "Jesus."

Bazakin looked up into the dome overhead, smiling, calm as could be.

Ignatov's face bore a sheen; he pushed his glasses up, they slid down, he pushed them up again. And then he tugged at his beard with unusual vigor.

Nelsen, his body loosening, muscle tone flooding in, the involuntary response that overtook him before a descent, hoped to hell that Admiral James Buchanan was in control.

And Galya Matra slammed her fist down on their conference table with the force of a sledgehammer. "Bastards!" she shouted in a voice that boomed like thunder in the cavernous dome.

Troy, New York

For more than twenty-four hours now he had felt someone's gaze upon him. He raised his lids and looked again at the two pictures of Vanderyenko, the *Macka*'s eyes the same in both, and knew it *wasn't* over.

McNulty suddenly resolved: I'll find you, you bastard.

But then, suitably humbled by the task, he asked himself: How?

Nothing in McNulty's possession could be construed as a lead. Malachev had been carrying fake identification: no one by the name of Barnes lived at the address on the Russian agent's fabricated Massachusetts driver's license. Malachev's rented Taurus had been clean as a whistle. There had been prints in the Biltmore hotel room, of course, but Malachev sure as hell didn't have a record, and besides, McNulty had already decided to keep the feds out of the game.

So what did he have?

The notebook. Malachev's notebook. That was it.

McNulty leaned forward, took his chair out of the reclining position, took up the notebook, and flipped through it. Russian. Fucking Russian. I suppose I ought to get the whole thing translated, word for word, he thought. Hell, it *is* my only lead, if you can call it that.

And that's when he saw the "at" symbol. It leapt out at him because it was the only symbol in the entire spiral book that wasn't indecipherable Cyrillic. The symbol @ appeared on McNulty's keyboard: it was not a Russian symbol; it was a universal one, like numerals. And there it was, in Malachev's hand, flanked by a series of Cyrillic letters: @.

Holy shit.

McNulty realized that this string had the canonical form of a computer address on Bitnet. The userid, then the @, and then the Bitnet node, the last digits of which specified the computer in question. McNulty himself had an account on RPI's 3090: CTKW@RPITSMTS

Ten letters. Ten Cyrillic letters. Context-free. All he had to do was translate ten bloody Russian letters. Looking at the address, he could himself come up with some educated guesses. But he needed to know for sure. And then he would have a start.

McNulty gave his eyes a dose of Murine, lit another Camel, picked up some god-awful but caffeine-loaded coffee that had been made last night by the secretaries, and set off for RPI's Folsum Library, in search of a Russian-English dictionary. It wasn't until he was halfway there that he realized how empty the streets were. And then it hit him that it was six in the morning and that the library would be closed.

Fuck it, he said to himself, I'm not waiting.

McNulty headed straight for RPI's security office.

PART IV

25

Demon Dance

February 20—Lake Baikal

Knowing that Navy Chief Conrad Glennie's threat of an American preemptive strike could prove infectious, the *Starik* worked three days straight, Nelsen and Markov thriving on the feverish, sleepless pace, the rest dragging; but after seventy-two sleepless hours the demons stood ready for a genuine test, which Bazakin set about arranging. All, save for the still-scheming Bazakin, were given a one-day respite. Alex spent his on a rendezvous with Anna, hopping 750 miles southwest in one of the Otters.

Irkutsk's Central Hotel had packed a picnic with *omul* (white salmon), pilaf, and just-baked bread, and Anna and Alex had taken the basket and a large blanket and set out on the hydrofoil. Now they were reclining amid snowdrop crocus, which here and there popped through remnants of melting snow, on the vast banks of the deepest, coldest, bluest lake in the world: Baikal. Anna had scooped their beverage from the freezing mist-kissed waters themselves. Sitting on the banks of the sacred sea of many a tribe, snow-capped mountains in the background in every direction, Nelsen was reminded of Tibet—and of a mirage: it was nearly too beautiful to be true. One-sixth of the world's fresh water; the world's first lake. Three hundred and thirty-six rivers feeding it, but its only outlet the mighty Angara. A hand-held mirror tossed in could be seen glimmering one hundred feet down in the crystal-clear water.

"What the hell is that?" he asked.

Anna laughed. "A cow."

"A what?"

"A sea cow. Relax, Alexander."

But his eyes wouldn't let him. "What? What the hell is *that*?"

"That's a seal. Playing."

"This is a land-locked fresh-water lake."

Anna shrugged, smiled. "Not even the baikalogists, the wizards who study only Lake Baikal and its environs, understand. But they're here. Along with twelve hundred other creatures found only in this mysterious body of water." Nelsen shook his head, amazed. Russia was incredible. Anna said, "They were trapped, perhaps." And then she added, "Like you."

He looked at her: she wasn't smiling.

"What are you getting at?"

"Your plan is to have us return to America, correct?"

"Mmm," he said.

"Astonishing naiveté," she said. "You've seen the insides of a system that spells deep trouble for the West, and you think Peter and his friends are going to let you waltz away and spend your money back in America."

She had a point, of course. One he hadn't failed to anticipate, but a point. She noticed the complete absence of tension in his body.

"So you foresaw the problem."

"Of course," he said.

"And?"

"It's obvious." Nelsen looked out across the snow-capped mountains to the west.

"Escape?"

Alex formed an expression of "Perhaps" upon his face.

"And me?"

"You, I love," he said, reclining, taking another sip of the wonderful icy water and a bite of the salmon that swam only in the lake beneath them.

She laughed. His serenity was infectious.

"So we're going to leave together."

"If you're up to it," he said. "And if you want to."

Her eyes bespoke a come-what-may commitment to their union. Alex had been put before the Bolshoi.

"May I make a suggestion?" she asked.

"Shoot."

"Don't sabotage the system. Build it so that it works. Then they'll let us take a vacation. And then, maybe, just maybe, we'll have a chance."

He seemed to be considering her plan as he chewed; the corners of his mouth turned up in a slight grin. He nodded, swallowed, took another sip of the water. Then reclined, looking up at a sky whose cerulean clarity rivaled the waters of the ancient lake.

"Are you listening to me?"

"Mm hmm." He shifted his gaze from the sky to her. Her hair should be down, he thought.

"May I ask how you plan to do it?" she asked.

He just looked into her concerned green eyes. She was beautiful. Truly, utterly beautiful.

"Alex?"

"Haven't decided," he said. "Unfortunately, anything of the software variety isn't likely to work. There isn't a member of the *Starik* I could get a virus, worm, or bomb—to use the lingo—past. They are, as you say over here, wizards. I've been in the intellectual fast lane for ten years, at America's best universities, and I've never seen a group as clever. Any of them, now, could hop over to America and give a very constructive jolt to the AI community."

"I see." She took a sip of the water, looked down at his head, resting on the blanket. "But if you succeed, you'll be killed. Once the system blows up, they will come for you. And they never stop coming. The *Starik* is founded on a tradition a thousand times firmer than today's free-market Russia. Spying is . . . as old as this lake. Retribution can pass across generations in their world."

"Hmm." Nelsen seemed to be considering Anna's speech as a food critic might an entrée. Sometimes she hated his calm.

"Alex. Listen to me. When they see the system working, they will still keep you prisoner—if nothing else, to maintain it and refine it, and to teach others how to do so. But they will drop their guard, and we will at least have a fighting chance of getting out. We could, as I say, take a vacation."

Alex didn't respond.

"Look," she continued, "they are going to build the system sooner or later, with or without you. Maybe it will take another two years without your expertise, but it will be built. And the system is a *defensive* system. How much direct harm can they do with it? You yourself have said that it can only be slightly effective against incoming missiles."

The Bolshoi's ballerina was speaking sensibly.

"And you?" he asked.

"I'll come."

"Yes, you've said that. But you're a dancer."

"I can dance in America."

"If you make it."

"If *we* make it."

"*You're* the dancer."

"What is that supposed to mean?"

"If we leave, it won't be in the back of your Chaika, Annastasia."

"Let's see *you* dance ballet for four solid hours."

He looked over at her forearms, the start of her biceps: feminine lines, but underneath, yes, tone that perhaps only a few athletes on the globe possessed. Then he looked at her hair: luxuriant, black, highlights ignited by the Siberian sun above. He wanted it down. He thought about how far down it would come: to her waist. At which he now looked.

She let down her hair and reclined, and having followed his eyes, placed his hand where he wanted it to be placed. There were only seals and sea cows within sight, bobbing in the limpid frigid waters of Baikal. And a small fishing boat, in the distance, floating on the lake, but too far, surely, to see a pair of lovers loving on the bank.

February 21—Tereshkovo Complex

Markov and Matra, relieved of late from their work on the demons, had been working feverishly to give the Tereshkovo complex a bird's-eye view of the world's nuclear battlefields. Due to their efforts the *Starik* now presided over an unfinished but already glittering war room, one that promised to eventually rival the conception for such a suite in the mind of an imaginative American moviemaker. The center of it all was to be an enormous high-density TV monitor, twenty feet across, eight feet high, which, though now in place, was as yet illuminated only by a fraction of the data that would be needed. Markov, with information supplied by Bazakin, had created a data base for American counterforce targets, and he had just finished a graphic representation of this data: up on the screen, in variegated glory, shone a state-by-state view of ICBM fields, bomber/tanker bases, naval nuclear bases, interceptor bases, and nuclear production sites. All the software was to be mouse-driven; at present, clicking for example on the fields adjacent to Warren Air Force Base in Wyoming instantly brought up another window, in which MX and Minuteman silos glowed. In addition to this data, the monitor was already hooked into some of Ignatov's primitive cameras, visible light-spectrum devices operating outside the dome, planted at the *Starik*'s nearby launch site, and atop the nearest mountain in the adjacent Verkhoyansk range. The previous night had been clear and fogless; and the *Starik* had sat inside their war room looking up at the massive screen—upon which they saw horizons both in the far east and west, as well as the frigid Laptev Sea to the north, and finally, four hundred miles to the south, the nighttime glow of Yakutsk.

The war room had quite a ways to go, but it was sufficient for the final test.

Which was to take place now.

Bazakin looked at his watch. "This is it, comrades."

It was to be Bazakin's surprise. Two demons waited upon the iced-over poured-concrete surface of the Tereshkovo launch site. They were visible now, on the movie-theater-size Japanese monitor.

Markov glowed with pride. Ignatov looked up through his big black-framed glasses. Nelsen looked, guessing. And Matra was petulant.

"You will tell us nothing," she said.

"Nothing," Bazakin repeated, emotionless.

"Something will arrive?"

"Of course," Bazakin said. Matra looked up at the screen, and in so doing, with the help of the cameras, scanned the horizon in all directions. Quiet. Nothing. Siberia looked utterly lifeless.

"When?" Matra asked.

"Very soon, my dear," Bazakin replied. "Are you confident, Alex?"

"Absolutely. I believe in simulation."

"Our seismologists are forever simulating earthquakes," Bazakin said. "We still can neither control nor anticipate them. Go visit Armenia."

"The planner works. It's *going* to work. Trust me."

Bazakin looked at his watch yet again. It occurred to Alex that looking twice at his watch in such a small period of time was the closest the robotic Bazakin had ever come to showing any emotion.

"And the essence of your planner?" Bazakin inquired.

"You're one of two people who understand it," Nelsen said.

"For the benefit our other illustrious colleagues. Or if you wish, we can sit in silence." Bazakin pulled mightily and contentedly on a Prima.

"Well," Nelsen began, "think of it this way. Inside this Neurocube is a set of points in Euclidean three-space. Each point represents either a demon or an incoming vehicle or missile."

"An analog representation," Bazakin said absently, exhaling smoke through his nose, eyes upon the screen.

"That's right. Of course that's a platitudinous way of putting it; here's how to visualize the situation. Suppose that the U.S. does launch an attack; and suppose that our demons are installed. And now suppose that from some superhuman point of view you can take a snapshot of the situation. You get back a picture of what's going on: each rocket or missile, let's pretend, shows up as a plume of some sort; and each demon shows up as a plume of a smaller sort. What you have is a picture of a bunch of points—points of light against a black background. But the picture is of course two-dimensional. So suppose somehow the picture becomes *three*-dimensional—think of it as a hologram, if that helps. And now, with this three-dimensional picture in your mind, begin to shrink it. Shrink it and shrink it until it's small enough to fit into this machine."

Bazakin nodded, and it hit Nelsen that the man was savoring. Like a man counting money even though he knows the total. Caressing the bills. In this case caressing the interceptor system. It suddenly hit Nelsen that Bazakin evidently had no wife, no kids, no girlfriends, not even any friends outside the *Starik*.

"Continue, Dr. Nelsen."

"The planner assigns incoming missiles to demons, one to one, under a straightforward algorithm. At the first moment of processing, the initial assignments are simply made on the basis of who's closer to whom: a given demon goes after a missile if that missile is the closest one to that demon. And then, after a moment, a *very* brief moment, a new configuration is given by the movement of the missiles, and a trend can be computed for the missile paths. Once this trend is—"

Bazakin looked at his watch, held up his hand, and said, "That's it. They're in flight." The scientist's face bore the subdued mania of a demon-possessed man.

"What's in flight?" Matra asked impatiently.

Bazakin sighed. "You'll see."

All eyes turned to the high-density monitor. But there was nothing. The horizons were vividly outlined against an arctic sky of intense blue. The demons were motionless.

Above Kubinka Air Base

With his hand wrapped around the lollipop grasp of one of the Blackjack's four throttles, Colonel Alexy Korolkov pronounced his career move a success. If he had stayed with fighters, the powers that be in the Soviet Air Force would have seen to it that he was forever stuck in the cockpit of the antiquated MIG-23; and the MIG-23, as the U.S. Navy had demonstrated in Iraq was a piece of shit. F-14's aren't exactly shitkickers, as any Soviet pilot could tell you, but Navy F-14s had managed to ram a Sidewinder up the ass of a MIG-23 without breaking a sweat. Had he stayed, he might have had a shot at a MIG-29 Fulcrum, but the probability had been exceedingly low. And besides, thought Korolkov to himself as he held the Blackjack's four turbofan engines in the palm of his hand, even the MIG-29, relative to the American F/A-18, was a dog, no better, really, in terms of cockpit design, than the American F-4 of the 1950's. But the Blackjack—the Blackjack was another story. Arguably, Alexy Korolkov was in command of a plane that was the best of its kind, East or West.

Especially today. Because for some reason the General-Colonel who had set the flight plan had taken Korolkov aside and told him to go to afterburner, indeed he'd told the pilot to go for it, period: Mach 2.3, and slightly beyond "if your bird can handle it." For Korolkov it was a dream, but it was also a mystery, since full throttle wouldn't contribute one iota to the main point of the mission, which was to release, in the first test of its kind, the new AS-X-19 supersonic cruise missile.

But mystery or no mystery, Korolkov did it. His 590,000-pound baby hit Mach 2.45, and part of the thrill, while there, was knowing that the American B-1B, when it wasn't busy crashing, had a top speed of only Mach 1.25.

Then he slowed down, activated his variable-sweep wings, and gave the command to empty his two internal weapons bays, letting the cruise missiles fly toward Siberia.

NORAD, Cheyenne Mountain, Colorado

As Bazakin and Kasakov had planned, the 12-foot, 6000 infrared-detector telescope on the Defense Support Program's Block 14 spacecraft picked up the heat from the Blackjack's afterburners. Ground-based computers compared the spacecraft's laser-transmitted real-time data on the Blackjack's plume with stored launcher and rocket-plume wavelength information on all known Soviet and Chinese missiles. Within 120 seconds the DSP ground controllers were confident of their information, and sent it on to NORAD. And within another thirty seconds NORAD was equally confident—that no threat existed. Best hypothesis: just a MIG-29 Fulcrum. American SAC bombers sat serenely on their runways. The information was sent electronically to NSA, where it was archived.

Tereshkovo

The supersonic AS-X-19 cruise missiles, past Omsk now, screamed over treetops like streaks of light, hurtling toward Tereshkovo. Bazakin, closing his eyes, drawing down the nicotine, envisaged them perfectly in his mind. But the war-room screen still showed Siberia in all its desolate calm.

"I guess this'll violate the ABM treaty, huh?" Nelsen said.

Bazakin said, "Yes."

"Will the Americans know?"

"I hope so," Bazakin answered.

That's a twist. I thought they wanted to keep this a secret.

Bazakin checked his watch yet again. "All right, Ignatov, launch them."

"Roger." Ignatov punched a command into the keyboard and the two exoatmospheric interceptors that had been sitting patiently outside on the launch pad, in the Siberian air, churned up a cloud of airborne ice, and lifted, propelled by their liquid rocket engines. They rose to an altitude of two thousand feet, and then hovered in place with the help of quartz tuning gyros that guided their thrusters. Their ascent was captured by Ignatov's cameras, and sent back flawlessly to the war-room monitor.

Bazakin lit another Prima.

"Come to mommy," Alex said.

Bazakin smiled at the American.

And then there they were. The visible light cameras brought back merely two streaks of light, on the western horizon. The missile plumes had been picked up by the laser seekers on the two hovering demons, and Matra's laser ranging system kicked into action. The demons exploded horizontally so fast they seemed to have vaporized.

And seconds later: an inner-ear-rattling boom that dwarfed the sound of a jet breaking the sound barrier. The vibrations rippled through the *Starik*.

NSA Headquarters, Fort Meade

"H-o-l-y s-h-i-t."

"Herb?"

"Listen, you got me. The world is beginning to look like one big fireworks display from where we sit."

"When's Lacrosse due for a pass?"

"Now."

"Right now?"

Light checked his watch. "That's right."

The two men waited for a few minutes, and then looked at the real-time visual feedback. Herbert Light knew the signature of the Soviet AS-15 subsonic cruise missile like the back of his hand, even after it had been disemboweled. He didn't realize that he was looking at the remains of the supersonic descendant of the AS-15, but it didn't really matter. He punched the level above Top Secret on his STU-4 phone, tapped in his name and identity, an NSA computer approved the transmission, and the call was patched through to Admiral James Buchanan.

"What did they destroy?" Matra asked.

"Supersonic ALCM's," Bazakin said, smiling. "It's time to call our friends at Plesetsk."

"Cruise missiles?" Ignatov said. "That's the final test?"

"Yes. Don't look so worried, Dimitry. Your wind tunnel alone gave us tests at sufficiently high Mach numbers. Taking down the Buran shuttle confirmed that our demons can function at severe aerodynamic pressures. Thanks to Pan Am, Air India, and the Mikoyan Design Bureau, we passed base-line agility. And now, my comrades, we know that our demons can dance. Pitch angle capture, limiter turn, loaded roll, straight acceleration—I don't care what maneuver you're talking about. These demons make even our hypersonic space plane look like a Sopwith Camel."

The rest of the *Starik* looked decidedly happy.

"Now, how and when will you base them?" Alex asked.

Bazakin had extinguished his Prima with the slow precision of man savoring success. "When? Now. As for how, that's easy. The exoatmospheric interceptors, like our recently sacrificed friends, who reach impact near earth, will be placed along our borders. The endoatmospheric demons, those to achieve impact in outer space, will be placed in orbit, beginning"—Bazakin looked at his watch—"now."

"Orbit? Where's the power source?" Matra asked.

"Come now, Galya Matra, you yourself entertained the possibility of housing clusters of demons inside solar- and nuclear-powered mothering satellites."

"But are you prepared for that?"

Bazakin smiled. "We even have Glavcosmos, the civilian agency, helping us."

"Unwittingly?"

"Of course."

"But the numbers. Can you bring that many up?" Alex asked.

"Our boosters fly as regularly as commercial planes in your country, Dr. Nelsen. We can launch the SL14, 16, and 17 almost daily; we already nearly do. The Energia alone, in one mission, can carry a payload of one hundred thousand kilograms. And in terms of the needed spacecraft, we have the Progress 38 tanker to carry our demons, and the Cosmos 1966 and 1974, and other similar satellites, for early warning of ballistic-missile attack."

"I see."

Russian vodka, top-of-the-line Priviat, in bottles that plagiarized, *perestroika* style, those of a Swedish competitor, was brought out for a little celebration. Matra inhaled three glasses in quick succession. Ignatov's tiny frame was permeated from head to toe by his first few gulps, swallowed in such a way that the tumbler pressed against his gigantic glasses. Markov accompanied his drink with some potato chips. Nelson took his drink on ice. And hoped he wouldn't have to ask.

He didn't:

Bazakin announced that the technical quartet were free to take a short vacation, and that he and Kasakov would tackle the problem of deciding what the *Starik* should *do* with the interceptor system.

And dreams, accordingly, were voiced.

First, sleep was on everyone's agenda. And after that?

Matra announced her plan to get some decent power lifting in, and sternly rebuked the other three for not exercising, though, she pointed out, "In your case, Ignatov, it would be pointless. And in your case, Mark-o-weetz, it would take two marathons a day to purge your body of the poisons with which you continuously pollute it." Both men smiled up at the amazonian Matra.

Ignatov planned to rest for a while in Tallinn, his hometown in Estonia, on the coast of the Gulf of Finland, simply watching the boats slide in and out of dock. And then he thought maybe he'd stop by to visit his old friends who were working on jet-engine propulsion at TsIAM, the Central Institute for Aviation Motors, where, he said, "I have an idea to use Dr. Nelsen's parallelism to simulate the use of directionally solidified monocrystal blades in the RD-33 engine I designed for the MIG-29. Perhaps I'll be able to break the seventeen-hundred-degree Kelvin limit on heat for metal blades." No one knew what the hell he was talking about. But glasses were nonetheless clinked against each other in a toast to his aspirations.

Markov said he hoped to be able to do a road trip to America, to replenish his supply of junk food, to hit a few American fast-food chains, and to take apart, for theft by GRU, more American computer equipment. "Wonder what's inside Seymour Cray's new machine?" Markov snapped off part of a Cape Cod chip in his mouth, lost in reverie.

And Alex—Alex said, "Any suggestions, my comrades?"

"Yalta," Ignatov replied instantly. "You have the money to do it. That's the place. Palm trees. Beaches. Sun like you never see in Moscow."

Matra snickered at the thought of Ignatov in a bathing suit.

Markov remarked that he didn't know much about "Yaltan" cuisine.

But Bazakin said the Crimean coast was indeed the best the Motherland had to offer.

"Well, then," Alex said with a smile, "it's settled."

The five shook hands. Bazakin and Markov stayed on to continue working in the war room. Nelsen expressed good-natured skepticism about Markov ever taking a true vacation. Then Alex, Matra, and Ignatov took the Otter to Yakutsk, toasting once again as, rising into a hyperborean sky, they looked back at the Tereshkovo dome, then, above it, at the rugged, sharp- and snow-peaked Verkhoyank Mountains, and, in the distance, the still-burning rubble left by the final test.

In Moscow they separated. But before they did, Matra, in an uncharacteristic show of affection, hugged Ignatov, lifting him off the floor as if he were a feather. She knocked his glasses off in the process, but reinstalled them, and sent the tiny engineer on his way to Tallinn as a mother might send a child to school.

Nelsen flagged a cab and headed to Anna's flat, in search of an embrace of a rather different sort.

While Nelsen's cab rolled toward his lover's flat, Bazakin and Kasakov spoke by phone.

"He's on vacation?" Kasakov asked.

"Yes. As I said before, they all need it. I've given even Renear and Pattison a breather. They're in Yakutsk, touring our Supercomputing Research Institute."

"That's not my idea of a vacation."

"It's what they wanted," Bazakin said.

"Fine. But what about Nelsen? I assume he's dragging a team of spies with him."

"As ordered, Peter Andreevich. *Spetsnaz*. And as backup, Yankolov has given us the entire KGB Border Guard."

"Very well."

Troy, New York

An RPI security officer let McNulty into the library and stood by as the Troy detective first found the dictionary and then made the simple, letter-by-letter translation from the Cyrillic. Which resulted in:

"MASK@PRINCEVM." Which meant an account owned by a user with ID "Mask," on, McNulty was willing to bet, one of Princeton's IBM mainframes.

Back to the office. Where he logged onto his account on the Michigan Terminal Emulation System at RPI, and sifted through a data base of Bitnet nodes, looking for Princeton. In seconds he found the university. Which had four nodes. Once of which was, indeed, PRINCEVM.

On a lark McNulty punched in a request to see who was logged at the moment. "Mask" wasn't. McNulty knew that would be too easy. And besides, he thought to himself, a remote log-on by modem and phone line was likely. From, presuming the kind of circumspection that would doubtless be used here, a portable phone. Applied for incognito, with fake identification. Hypotheses which were, of course, correct.

So call Princeton, of course, said McNulty to himself.

Within ten minutes, via a series of on-line messages to the VM operator on duty, some of which contained convincing facts about McNulty's professional identity, the missing-persons expert had convinced Computer Information Services at Princeton to E-mail him the archived history of the account in question.

Within fifteen minutes he had uploaded the data into a UNIX file on his workstation.

And within sixteen minutes his laser printer was churning out the hard-copy history of the account.

26

Quartet

February 22—Zagorsk

The two black Volgas sped out of Moscow, one behind the other, leaving in their wake a breeze that left still-barren branches waving like arthritic hands. Vasputin and Yankolov, from the Politburo, sitting behind tinted glass, were ensconced in one; Kasakov and Bazakin rode in the other. Dusk. Soon after leaving the city, the enormous monastery of St. Sergius, Zagorsk's great landmark, became visible in the distance; its blue and gold onion domes, high enough to remain lit by a sun falling in the west, rose from the eastern horizon like the turrets of a fairy-tale castle.

The two cars rolled regally past gray-clad slow-moving pilgrims, some feeding pigeons, some streaming into the monastery for genuflection and prayer, some in line, waiting to drink holy water offered in the small open-air chapel. Out of the ecclesiastical town of Zagorsk and into the surrounding wilderness. Past birch, and pine, and oak, their boughs soon to bud. Slowly over rough unpaved puddled roads. And finally to a stop outside the late Andreev Kasakov's handmade teahouse.

They built a fire, and assembled around it, drinks in hand. The scent of the pine beams filled the air—as powerfully now as when Andreev had hoisted them into place.

Vasputin said, "Not the same without the old tanker here to tell the stories that bring these pictures to life."

Yankolov nodded wistfully, looking up at Andreev's victorious 1st Armoured Army, and now, beside it, his medal for Hero of the Soviet Union. Peter Kasakov looked up also, but briefly, and sighed, more out of impatience than piety.

"He was a prophet," Yankolov said. "Things are not only falling apart as he predicted; they're falling apart exactly in the *manner* he predicted. Gorbachev completely underestimated the fervor of nationalism, and now that these ingrates have tasted freedom, there appears to be no turning back—at least not without force. The trend appears to me to be rolling along like a steamroller."

"Nationalism?" Vasputin said. "In the context of the conflagration sweeping across the Motherland, the problem of nationalism strikes me as but a spark. The fools who have thus far left Great Russia will soon come back begging to return. Even the economies of the Baltic republics are like dust compared to those of the other European nations. No, nationalism is but a thorn in our side. Our problem, our *real* problem, is the economy. Russia makes America during the Great Depression look like a garden spot. They didn't like what he did the first time around, but they called for his return. And now that Gorbachev is back, we have returned to a course set straight for complete insolvency. Half of the Soviet Union is on strike. The other half couldn't work even if they wanted to. Inflation is . . ."

It was true. It seemed every miner in Russia had turned militant. From the Ukraine, to the Arctic, to Central Asia. Marching in hard hats, with fierce chants. Related industries had followed suit: the iron mines, the steel factories, the oil refineries—all as quiet and deserted as ghost towns. Strident calls for fresh meat, sewing machines, hospitals with at least *some* hygiene, retail stores with something on their shelves.

"The situation is dire, comrades," Kasakov said. "That's why the *Starik* was formed in the first place. But let us not whine; let us act."

"The SBI system is complete?" Yankolov asked.

"Even as we speak, General Yankolov," Bazakin said, "the system is being lifted into orbit and stationed at key points along our borders for terminal defense."

"And what do you propose to use it for?" Yankolov asked.

Bazakin smiled wryly, smoked, shrugged. "Why the fuck do you think we're here, General?"

White House War Room

Buchanan, upon hearing of the *Starik*'s latest test, called an emergency meeting. Beepers beeped, portable phones rang, wives summoned husbands, and in some cases young marines showed up in person. And as a result, family dinners were abandoned, lovemaking was interrupted, and vacations were canceled. Buchanan himself, the President and Vice-President, the Secretaries of State and Defense, the Joint Chiefs (save Marine Corps Commandant General Wally Green, who was on the west coast, and tied into the discussion electronically, via the new 9.6-kilobit-per-second conference-capable SelTel 1500 voice terminal), the scientist Arnold Bramsen, and Herbert Light—all, within thirty minutes of getting the call, were sitting in the war room. Clothes had been shed. Showers had been taken. A sensor had scanned skin and hair for bugs. Special attire, stored for such occasions, had been donned. And so the eleven men, but thirty minutes after the DCI's call, found themselves scrubbed clean, sitting around a table in a submarinelike room approximately thirty feet by twenty feet, with seven-foot ceilings, constructed of two-foot-thick galvanized steel. A digitized map of the world, the position of the Soviet Navy indicated by red dots, the position of Soviet silos indicated by blue ones, looked down upon the leaders. Cipher machines clicked away with incoming information. A computer screen for each seat, tapped into NORAD and the NSA, glowed. A bank of ultrasecure phones, one of which ran directly to the Kremlin, blinked vigilantly.

Buchanan rose, took his light-based pointer in hand, nodded to Light, who was manning the computer on which their data were stored, and was about to start his presentation—when Navy Chief Glennie preempted. "Listen, save the movies for another night, I just want the motherfucking coordinates," he growled, his voice like gravel. Glennie was a walking stereotype: crew cut, a bull's physique, square jaw, a beard that needed to be shaved twice a day, and a conception of East-West relations diametrically opposed to the New World Order. But men like Glennie won wars, freed lands, repelled invaders, and, when stepping down, returned to the academies to help mold men prepared to die for America.

"That's dumb," Bramsen responded, boyish, brash, tousled black hair, not a strand of which he'd lost. "There's no evidence the Soviets have made it to first base." The Nobel laureate, as usual, had the demeanor of a man who has divined the meaning of life. Before hitting thirty-five.

"Hell," Glennie responded, "I'd say their shuttle was a home run."

"Hardly," the scientist retorted. "In probably no more than six months, using similar methods, we could take out *our* shuttle. They're just not that far ahead on the smart-rock approach. And now that we know where they are, we can catch up. I view this as just a ripple in overall parity."

"Bullshit," Glennie said. "You live in a fucking whitewashed laboratory, with spotless computers and spotless minions to run around like ants at your beck and call. A glass house. You're not thinking deviously enough. This is Ivan we're talking about, son. Kapish? Ivan—the guy who took Afghan rebels and hung them on trees. The guy who still sends people off to the Arctic on permanent vacation. They get this fucker operational *during* your six months, and they might *use* it. Where's *that* in your equation?"

Bramsen hesitated.

"Arnold," Allen Newell said, "Conrad has a point. It is indeed far from self-evident that the Soviets would refrain from using SDI superiority, were they to have it. After all, that's the main reason why *we're* building SDI."

Buchanan saw an opening, pointed to the first slide, and started to speak—but was cut off again by Glennie. No frustration showed on the Admiral's face, only a world-weary patience for the folly of men more impulsive and less thoughtful than himself.

"Mr. President," the Navy Chief said, throwing protocol to the wind, "Newell's right. You can't just *assume* they won't capitalize on their superiority. Shit, Ivan blew up a multibillion-dollar laser facility to lull us into a false sense of security. He trashed the Buran and took down a MIG and its pilot. Not to mention Lockerbie and who knows how many other civil air disasters. This shows commitment, it shows offense. To hell with Dr. Bramsen's rosy view of things."

The President pushed out his lower lip, thinking.

Bramsen, by now, had regrouped, and reentered the fray: "This is idle chatter. The fact is, we're simply going to differ on the basic question of whether they'd use the system if they had one and we didn't. And this is no time to trade heartfelt feelings about the Soviet Union. The fact remains that they don't *have* the system. Unless there's a breakthrough on the software side, I'm of the opinion that we can sweat this one out and get our two nations back on track after parity is reestablished."

"But we heard last time, Dr. Bramsen, that they had acquired computers of the appropriate sort." This time the objection came from Secretary of Defense Newell.

"True," Bramsen admitted. "But machines don't program themselves, Allen."

Glennie slammed his fist down on the table; the sound of the blow was muffled by the sealed steel enclosure, but each man felt the vibration. "This is preposterous! They have the rockets, they have the computers. Bramsen here is betting the house on the hope that they can't write the programs. They have six bloody fucking months to write the software! If this project is backed from on high, that's an eternity." Glennie looked again to the President for support.

"What kind of strike are you thinking about, Conrad?" Randolph Atwood asked.

"We've got a lot of options. Special-forces mission. Conventional explosives. Treetop bomber mission. Nonnuclear cruise missile. Hell, maybe Harold over here can get us one of those stealth missiles we've all been hearing so—"

"Gentlemen," the soft-spoken Buchanan said, breaking in, "please. We are putting the cart before the horse. I called this meeting, and I called it for a purpose. I'm sure Chairman Singletree here"—Buchanan smiled at Air Force Chief Harold Singletree, Chairman of the Joint Chiefs—"has some interesting weapons, but I'm afraid it would be quite premature to put them to use. Now, if we may."

Buchanan and Light, using slides projected directly from a Mac V, proceeded to describe the death of the Soviet supersonic cruise missiles over Siberia, and the Blackjack bomber that had dropped them.

"Well, that's it. They just fucked the ABM," the

Secretary of State said, his plan for superpower disarmament coming to strike him more and more as a bitter joke.

"Waking up a little late, aren't you, Orville?" Glennie said. "You and Bramsen ought to get together, write a book on positive thinking or something. You've got your heads so far up your asses, everything looks fucking rosy. You know why that Blackjack went to afterburner? They did that to laugh in our faces. To show off. Any of these Russkies would cut your balls off in a second, Orville."

"If I may finish, gentlemen," Buchanan interrupted softly. "If you'll bear with me for a minute, I'm sure you'll all agree that a preemptive strike is premature."

Buchanan proceeded to reveal Dendrite to the others.

When he was done, Newell said, "Who are you, the Lone Ranger? A civilian scientist on the inside, working to sabotage their smart-rock SDI? I thought the days of private wars waged by the CIA and NSC were over. This was your own little secret, huh?"

"Yes. Only my DDO knew. But it's hardly a war. And I would point out that Nelsen is still alive. And not known to the entire staff of the New York *Times*."

"It would have been canned," Simon said. "The Hill would have pissed all over it."

"Perhaps."

"I would have been the first to *try* to can it," Simon said.

"That's okay," Buchanan said, "because the Sovs have canned *you*."

Anger crept into the face of the Secretary of State. Anger and embarrassment.

"Jesus. It's Nelsen," Bramsen said in a spate of apprehension.

Buchanan nodded unabashedly.

"Well, there goes my hypothesis," the young scientist said. "Software isn't a problem now. They have maybe the one guy who could pull it off. Wonderful."

"*Have* him?" General Singletree said.

"Well, what the hell has he sabotaged?" Bramsen responded. "Taking out these cruise missiles—that's not the sort of thing that can be effected manually. He's given them the software."

Singletree said, "You're saying he's turned?"

"I'm just giving you the facts. He's built some pretty damn good software."

"It's *supposed* to work during testing," Buchanan said. He now had his pipe out and was busy tamping it at a leisurely pace. "Otherwise they'd know it was sabotaged, wouldn't they, now, Dr. Bramsen?"

It was a solid, unassailable point.

The group seemed to have arrived at a natural resting place; there was a minute of silence during which everyone reflected.

"We'd kill him," Glennie said, the first to speak.

"There's a good chance," Buchanan agreed.

"Maybe we *want* to kill him," Simon said. "Maybe he *is* a double agent."

Buchanan had lit up, and released a stream of fragrant smoke. "Now, Orville, why would Nelsen turn? He's already got money, they don't have any dirt on him, and he's just not—"

"The type?" Orville Simon finished. "Oh, and I suppose you've known him for years, James? Come on, stranger things have happened. What if . . . what if he's fallen for a woman?"

"Fallen for a woman?"

"Yeah," said Simon. "He's not gay, is he?"

"No."

"Well."

"Implausible. The man's not about to screw the free world because he's screwing some Natasha."

"Well," Simon said, "I don't care *what* you say. It *is* possible."

"It's possible that a meteor will kill you the moment you step out on Pennsylvania Avenue," Buchanan said. "This is real life. We play the probabilities, Orville."

"Speaking of probabilities," Newell said, "what about Nelsen's chances?"

"On paper," Buchanan replied, "good. If anyone can do it, he can. In reality? Hard to say. There's no contact. We know he's alive because he sends innocuous E-mail back to the States. But beyond that, nothing."

"But surely he has a way to send signals," Newell said.

"He can send one electronic message to me in an emergency, over the phone lines. But it's a one-shot deal: if transmitted from inside, they'd doubtless see it. Otherwise he's on his own. No transmitters, no receivers, nothing. Such machinery would only be one more thing to go wrong. No matter how good your cover, Ivan is always watching. He's paranoid. In Nelsen's case there's nothing to see. It's about the tightest cover we've ever managed in this short a time, in large part because we have him out there hanging, flying solo, in strict silence."

"Then how will we know?" the President asked.

"It's up to him. He'll find his own way. Moscow Station has been told to keep their ears open for messages from the inside."

"Jesus," Glennie said, "this guy must have ice for blood."

"He does," Buchanan said, thinking about his recruit's favorite pastimes. "And I'd like to make sure we don't spill any of it. Needless to say, none of us should mention a syllable about this to anyone. Congress leaks no less now than it did under Reagan and Bush."

Everyone nodded sardonically.

"How long do we give him?" Glennie asked.

"As long as it takes," Bramsen volunteered.

"No," Buchanan said, "I'm afraid not. Dr. Nelsen and I agreed that if he fails to send a success signal before March 15, it should be assumed that he has failed, and a rescue should be attempted."

"Too long," the President said. "Get him out now. We need to face the music: the Russians are becoming dangerously overconfident. I'm inclined to favor a surgical preemptive strike, designed to humble them, and thus preclude any cockiness. Nelsen is an unknown element; he may fail or turn. At any rate, he's been out there long enough. I suggest that you, Conrad, together with Allen and Harold, and colleagues of the both of you, sit down and map out, as precisely as possible, options for surgical preemptive strikes against the Soviet Union."

Everyone nodded. Within fifteen minutes the group was back out in the sunny world, dressed in normal attire, walking among people who consigned such meetings as the one that had just taken place to the realm of movies and make-believe.

In three hours, courtesy of Theodore Liquori's bug in Glennie's clothes, the *Macka* had a tape of the Navy Chief's plans for a preemptive strike.

27

Unblinking

February 23—The Kremlin

On Yankolov's command, the black Zil limousines spread rapidly throughout Moscow to retrieve all members of the ruling Council, whether with mistress or wife, awake or asleep. Within fifteen minutes of the KGB chief's order, they were heading in. At full speed. Through lights, stop signs, dangerous intersections.

They were not all cut from the cloth of a Gorbachev, but it was a seasoned group, and, to a man, the red-brick ramparts of the Kremlin, standing proudly and solidly against the moonlit sky, were structures the fall of which, even the *threatened* fall of which, was quite unthinkable to the proud men who worked therein. It was unscheduled, it was early morning, nothing but a serious emergency could justify such a hasty meeting, but each voting member looked calmly and confidently out the window of his Zil, speeding down the center lane reserved for the *vlasti.* The cars rushed through Red Square, passed Lenin's corpse, whisked through the Kremlin gates, were checked by KGB guards, and screeched up in front of the Arsenal, depositing men who walked steadily and evenly up to the conference room. It had taken thirty years for Russia to cultivate and bring to power men who would never again blink, as Khrushchev had when staring into the eyes of John F. Kennedy. Even those outside the power-holding quartet of Gorbachev, Polyanov, Yankolov, and Vasputin, the middle-of-the-road men, the followers who were fundamentally self-interested rather than visionary—even these men were fearless.

On this still-dark morning the Council had two young visitors: Kasakov and Bazakin. And it was Bazakin who, when everyone was sitting, announced, with no flourish, and with supreme serenity, that the Americans were considering a preemptive attack on the Motherland.

"What?" Polyanov exclaimed.

"I believe my colleague spoke clearly, Comrade Polyanov," Kasakov said. "We anticipate that they will strike somewhere in Siberia."

"We?"

"Ah, well, you see, Nicholas, Bazakin and I, as well as Comrades Yankolov and Vasputin, are members of an unassuming little group called the *Starik*."

"*Starik*. That was what they called Berzin," Polyanov said.

"Commendable. Especially for someone who finds espionage anathema."

Gorbachev had not spoken. It had come to him immediately: a coup was under way. His second one within the year. This time it looked to be rather more quiet and surgical. The President, at this point, merely shook his head and smiled philosophically. Polyanov, however, was frantic.

"What is this facility?" he asked.

"It's where we've built our primitive Star Wars," Bazakin said. "And Star Wars makes the Americans very nervous. They would like to destroy Tereshkovo."

Energy Minister Velstin said, "Tereshkovo is a hydroelectric facility."

"Was." Bazakin now had one of his ever-burning Primas lit.

"But why?" Polyanov asked. "The Americans would never launch unprovoked."

"Very true, comrade," Bazakin said. "We have provoked them."

"What are you saying?"

Bazakin said, "We were hoping to avoid all the histrionics, Comrade Polyanov. It's really very simple. We've built an interceptor system. The Americans know about it, and they're scared—they're scared we think very highly of our system, and will thus do something rash. So they want to make a point of getting through our shield."

Polyanov looked at Gorbachev. "We must tell them we will destroy the system, then. Initiate diplomacy. Stall them. Negotiate."

Gorbachev looked at his right-hand man and laughed. "You don't understand, do you?"

Polyanov looked back at his mentor blankly.

"It's too late," Gorbachev said. "Isn't it, Peter Andreevich?"

Peter nodded.

Polyanov was beside himself. "This is madness! We must call the Americans immediately."

Bazakin was smiling. "By the time they try to strike, Comrade Polyanov, they will have good reason to."

Polyanov buried his face in his hands.

"What exactly are they considering?" Gorbachev asked with a grin, in an exceedingly polite voice.

"A conventional strike," Bazakin replied. "We are getting direct transmission from listening devices planted on the American Navy Chief. However, they will of course soon shift to a nuclear strike."

"Of course," Gorbachev said, nodding. "And how reliable is your SBI?"

"Very," Bazakin said. "Our perimeter terminal defense is almost completely ready, and more space-based interceptors are being carried up by booster even as we speak."

"And may I ask when?" Gorbachev said.

"Oh, maybe an hour or so," Kasakov said, as if he were telling his wife how much longer he'd be at the office. "The American strike immediately thereafter, of course."

"I see," Gorbachev said.

Silence. Polyanov in tears. Gorbachev resigned to what he had long ago regarded inevitable. A good many men stunned speechless. A good many now waiting patiently for the coup to begin outright.

Which it did.

Kasakov, following the script, took the floor:

"Now, comrades, what I would like to suggest is that the General Secretary and I share a vision of what ends are desired. For years now Comrade Gorbachev has been telling us that various reforms will secure the ends all of us seek: a higher standard of living for our people, independence from nations which currently supply us with unrefined resources, and international competitiveness. My feelings about these reforms are well known, but what I fear *isn't* well-known is that I share with Mikhail Gorbachev his conception of *where* we should go, and his utilitarian conception of *how* we should get there. Our differences center around what *means* should be employed: I think that, being a *military* superpower, we should not shy away from using force to achieve our ends. Our leader has pulled us out of Cuba, Central America, Kampuchea, Poland, and Afghanistan. He has cut the Red Army by a million men. And he tells us that we need only a 'reasonable sufficiency' in nuclear forces, not parity with the West and the Chinese.

"But I, and all the members of the *Starik*, would rather use the military than sacrifice our people for the ends we both want.

"We have before us a historic opportunity. We shall fracture NATO without shedding a single drop of blood. And it is all astonishingly simple, and painless.

We tell the Americans to remove their troops from Europe or else we drop our next warhead on, say, Kansas City. If they don't give in, we launch. One such missile will have tractable environmental consequences. If they launch one of their own, our SBI immobilizes it. If they understand the situation, they will not consider launching larger numbers of ICBM's, for fear that the exchange would escalate into all-out nuclear war. The rational thing would be to blink, and to remove their troops. I believe they would do precisely that."

"This is absolute madness!" Foreign Affairs Chief Polyanov screamed. "We are achieving reductions in Vienna even as we speak. Relations between the Soviet Union and the United States are better than they have been since World War II. Should we throw all this away for some idiotic blackmail attempt? We can't even be sure that the system will work. It has never been tested in a realistic situation. This is insanity!"

"It is extreme," Bazakin said calmly, "but hardly insane. You mention, Nicholas Lazevich, arms reductions. But where are you taking us? Are you aiming at a point at which neither side has any nuclear weapons? I trust not, for that is geopolitical suicide. The awful truth is that even multilateral disarmament, thought by many to be the best of all possible worlds, would be hell. If everyone threw away their nuclear arms, then every conventional conflict would be unimaginably scary. There would always be the possibility that the other side was secretly building just one nuclear missile—and just one missile, in an otherwise nonnuclear world, would be enough to ensure victory. I can think of no more unstable scenario than the elimination of nuclear weapons combined with the ability to build them discreetly, and this ability, ever since the Manhattan Project, is part of the very nature of human existence. If, on the other hand," Bazakin continued, "you are simply bringing us down a road of *partial* reduction, then what is the point? As long as NATO has enough to massively retaliate, what do we gain by playing these word games in Vienna?"

"And furthermore," Kasakov said, "let us keep in mind how little our SBI system will have to *do* here. Their response to our threat will undoubtedly be right out of the textbook: it'll be tit for tat: *they'll* threaten to launch one ICBM if *we* launch one. But our interceptor system can without question take out one missile; it already took out two supersonic cruise missiles. The SL-16 and 17 have already brought up *thousands* of these kinetic-kill rockets. One incoming missile will be a piece of cake."

"Perhaps it won't *be* just one missile," Polyanov objected. What if they send five, or fifty, or a hundred? What then?"

"Be serious, comrade," Kasakov responded. "There's nothing to be gained by being intellectually dishonest. They would never launch a large strike upon hearing our terms. Either they wait it out to call our bluff, or they don't. If they don't, then they'd have to preempt in a way proportional to our threat, and suddenly launching a massive strike is out of all proportion. If, however, they *do* call our bluff, they will simply absorb the one missile, and then begin a tactical response—of, surely, *one* return missile. And one lone missile, again, is something our new system can certainly handle."

Gorbachev stood, and spoke in earnest for the first time:

"Comrades, it is said that they would respond with one missile, and that the *Starik*'s SBI would protect us. Assume for the sake of argument that this is true. The problem is that the Americans would then launch *two* missiles, hoping that at least one would get through for retaliation. If neither did, they would launch *three*. And then it stares you in the face: the process loops, it iterates until they *do* manage to get a retaliatory missile through our strategic defense. And surely we must all agree that these smart rocks, these interceptors, for *some* number of incoming warheads, will fail."

Silence.

Broken, presently, by Bazakin. "Mikhail Sergeevich," he began, "let me share with you a little parable. Sam and Ivan were boxing. Ivan had started off the bout by landing a strong, solid blow, not a winning blow, just one that woke Sam up to the reality of his foe's power. So Sam began to counterpunch. But his first flurry failed. So he tried again. Only to fail again. But Sam was nothing if not tenacious, so he tried yet again to hit back. And, unfortunately, failed yet again to penetrate Ivan's guard. Now, while Sam had been punching away at thin air, Ivan had been retraining himself, quite amused by his opponent's impotence. But finally, realizing that all fights end, that time was growing short, Ivan told Sam: Look, stop trying to punch back at me and I'll end this discreetly, without breaking your neck. But if you attempt to counterpunch once more, I will land another single solid blow. Indeed, Ivan said, every time you attempt to counterpunch, I will land one crushing blow. Sam, I'm glad to report, had the brains to bow out gracefully; though not the victor, he still had his face, and it was still intact."

The transition was smooth and easy. Impossible in the States, but in Russia? Unproblematic, as many an American analyst had through the years warned.

Gorbachev retained his title as President—even, superficially, retained control of the Defense Council.

The Marshal of the Soviet Union, a quiet sycophantic follower of the General Secretary to begin with, became, along with his mentor, a puppet.

The same for Polyanov.

The *Starik*, along with Yankolov, and the KGB

under his control, ruled. The part of the GRU not under the *Starik*'s control flapped innocuously in the breeze of *glasnost*, toiling under what they thought to be the status quo.

Vasputin was the figurehead. Which, as planned, pleased a large chunk of the public.

And thus, Sam and Ivan, the latter reconfigured, approached the ring.

St. George Hall, Kremlin Palace

In most men it would have been the reverse: talkative when drunk, tight-lipped when not. But Nicholas Polyanov, drunk on the job for the first time in his life, an hour after the coup, was quiet amid the pomp of the lunch reception. Though he had succeeded the icy Gromyko, and was thus inevitably regarded a friendlier person, the fact was that Polyanov was by nature warm, gregarious, even witty. He had taken the Western diplomatic corps by storm, charming them all. But now he was turning inward. How silly the American portrayals were, he thought to himself. Russians who betrayed the Motherland because of the loss of a wife, or a son, sometimes even in battle. The psychology was all wrong, filled with false notes. He smiled to himself—wasn't there some American novel about a man who defects by bringing a submarine to the United States, all because his wife died in the Soviet Union? Preposterous. The idea of holding a *nation*, thousands of people tied together in a gigantic web that diffused responsibility—the idea of holding such an amorphous entity accountable for the unfortunate but freak loss of a loved one struck Polyanov as absurd. It was *love* of the Motherland, not irrational *hatred* of it, that would cause a true Russian to pass on information of the sort he was about to pass on. And Nicholas Polyanov loved the Motherland too much to sit back and let madmen talk seriously about nuclear blackmail. It was precisely this sort of harebrained scheme that Khrushchev had specialized in. Asinine. He had known and, some would say, worshiped Mikhail Gorbachev since the communist youth organization Komsomol, and he was not about to stand by as the great man was reduced to a puppet. The Americans had to know immediately what was being contemplated. And the sooner they knew, the better.

It was easily accomplished. A parting handshake, and the note was deposited in the palm of an "embassy official" Polyanov knew to be CIA. The American didn't miss a beat, though his eyes, Polyanov noticed, widened just a bit upon feeling the pass.

For an amateur, a marvelous little piece of tradecraft. Which nonetheless failed.

Yuri Illyevich Zulisk, the *Starik*'s watcher, had seen. Polyanov was thus met at the door as he was leaving, and was stuffed into a GRU Volga like a piece of meat; within the hour he was being treated for schizophrenia with a multitude of mind-bending drugs.

The American, watched by hidden camera from the time of the pass, was discreetly confronted before he had a chance to read the message. After handing over Polyanov's note, his liberty was returned, and no interrogation followed.

Washington, D.C.

Liquori got into his Maxima for the drive over to the Pentagon, and there it was: another box on the dash. And inside, another bug. But of a radically new design: it was flesh-colored, larger than the previous ones, and . . . shit, it felt like flesh, Liquori noted.

Bio chips or something?
The note was once again short and sweet:

Push this against the skin inside Glennie's ear. You play squash, don't you? Have a collision.

28

Escape

February 23—Simferopol, Crimean Peninsula

"Aeroflot," Alex said.

A stewardess with gold teeth and broad muscular shoulders handed them two trays: pickles, black bread, and vodka thrashing precariously in plastic cups, the ride bumpy despite a cloudless sky.

"No car," Nelsen said.

"It would make it harder for them."

"Them."

"I've told you. You're priceless. They watch every move."

"A pleasant vacation this'll be," he said.

After landing, they took a twenty-minute helicopter ride over to Yalta, flying low enough to take in tropical scenery as beautiful as anything Nelsen had seen. Anna pointed out "Bear Mountain," which did indeed look like a bear bending over the sea.

"A greedy group of bruins once tried to drink the sea, and a fairy turned the greediest of them to stone," she said.

"Ah."

They flew down into the valley of the Vodopodnaya and Bystraya rivers; and there was Yalta, gloriously situated, like a jewel, in the horseshoe formed by the spurs of the Crimean Mountains.

They were taken by taxi to their hotel, the Oreanda, a drive which took them past acacia, laurel, magnolia, and palm trees, and also past orchards and vineyards. Lush, redolent, peaceful. Nothing here seemed gray and communist, just, very simply, beautiful. Within a few minutes they were unpacking.

Their suitcases were but half-empty when he pulled her to him.

She shook her head and smiled.

"Anna."

She put her forefinger in front of her mouth. Pointed around the room, nowhere in particular. Then whispered in his ear: "Bugs. Maybe even cameras."

He whispered back, "So?" And slid the straps of her sundress over her shoulders, revealing her breasts.

Thirty minutes later they dressed and departed to sightsee and sample local wines.

Seventy-five perfect degrees and the air was perfumed with magnolia. A breeze rustled leaves in the palm trees. They walked down to the Old City by way of Roosevelt Avenue, and reached Lenin Street, Yalta's main thoroughfare. Then, arm in arm, they strolled to the seaside promenade, which offered a wonderful view of the sea. From the promenade they meandered onto Litkins Street, a shady route leading up the mountainside, and sampled some Massandra and Livadia wines. And then they stepped down to the harbor, from which they saw a good many yachts, blindingly white in the sun, on the deep blue sea. From the harbor they wandered over the Vodopodnaya bridge into the enormous Gagarin park, wherein Chekhov stood, and from the park they ventured down to the city beach, where they rented chairs, stripped down to bathing suits, and reclined at the edge of the Black Sea, their feet in the water, the strange salt-water swans of Yalta dancing before them.

"Have you done it yet?" she asked.

"No."

"When?"

"There'll be a reunion. Then."

"How?"

"Good question. As a last resort I can use a hammer."

"Subtle."

"Hey, whatever works."

She said, "But they're not supposed to know."

"True. I'll think of something."

Thought. The water lapped at their feet.

Anna said, "Don't do it. We could go on another vacation, this time to a strategic location. And—"

"And make a run?" he broke in.

"Yes," she said. Her green eyes were lit with fear for the one she loved.

"Can't we enjoy *this* vacation?"

"It's the only way out, Alexander. Let them have it. Then we'll have a chance."

"How 'bout a swim?"

"Alexander, please."

"Come on. Swim with me."

He pulled her up.

Within five minutes they were locked in an embrace, bobbing in water up to his navel, he inside her, Anna's hair falling down into the water.

"I love you, Alexander. Let them have the system. Then at least we'll have each other."

He cupped her buttocks and pulled her in roughly but playfully, trying once again to change the subject.

She smiled.

"Have you ever read Ecclesiastes?" he asked.

She shook her head; then, smiling deviously, said, "Song of Solomon, though."

He smiled too; but, ignoring her amorous allusion, said, "According to Ecclesiastes there's a time for everything, Anna. And this is a time for vacation."

She nodded. But he was not at all sure she was convinced.

Moscow

Yuri Zulisk was paid handsomely by his own GRU to be paranoid—every day, twenty-four hours a day, week after week and month after month. He was to be skeptical, distrustful, and vigilant. He was to suspect model members of the party of treason, and to anticipate scenarios in which sons and daughters of the Motherland sold out to Uncle Sam. America had SIG-I, their own counterintelligence, or CI, unit, but compared to Yuri Zulisk and those under his command, SIG-I looked to be composed of empathetic grandmothers congenitally unable to conceive of turpitude in their wonderful children.

On the Communications Programs Unit, ninth floor of Moscow Station, business was slow. During the height of the cold war the Moscow-Washington line had been buzzing, but now, with Gorby back in power, the line was more often than not taken up with undiplomatic diplomatic gossip and arms-control argot: "They've come down on the number of aviation systems, but shit, they're on Soviet soil. They take some out of Europe and we'll pat their asses a bit." "He's a fucking movie star. Goes down to Bonn and the Germans fall in collective love, swooning for the bastard." "And this reluctance on the SS-23's? Bullshit. It's in the INF. They have no choice." "Simon's blueprint is for complete denuclearization of Europe. And that's what Gorbachev wants too. But I don't know, Paul, they can pull a fucking nightmare down from the Urals in a couple of hours. We, on the other hand, face the Atlantic."

Buchanan's message didn't fit the pattern.

Transmitted by commercial satellite at 9,600 characters a second, it came through one of the cipher machines and was decoded. A brief bio for Nelsen and Annastasia, and a succinct, direct imperative to bring Nelsen home. No mention of Dendrite. Nothing about just who exactly this Nelsen chap was. The technician on duty, refreshed by the arrival of what he correctly guessed to be genuine espionage, cheerfully carried Buchanan's communiqué to the station chief, who, frowning at Buchanan's use of "immediately," proceeded to order agent Spencer Olsen out to try to bring the scientist in. There was no time for planning; the operation had to be extemporaneous. "Time is of the essence, gentlemen." Olsen's orders were simply to try to get Dr. Nelsen into the American embassy; his only lead was the ballerina, Annastasia Marianov, and he set out for her apartment.

Olsen drove, tailed, to Anna's flat. As he pulled up at the curb, Yuri Zulisk pulled up behind him and flashed the lights on his Volga. Olsen remained in his vehicle. Zulisk walked over to the agent's window and looked inside.

"What's the problem?"

"Seat belt," Zulisk said. "You're not wearing your seat belt. And the speed limit in populated areas is sixty kilometers per hour."

Olsen noticed that the man detaining him wasn't police.

"Have you jurisdiction?" the American asked.

Zulisk hesitated.

"Are you authorized to write me a ticket, sir?"

The GRU agent saw that Olsen was no dummy. They were moving toward confrontation.

"Let me see your papers," Zulisk barked.

Olsen, in a split second, thought back to the urgent look on his chief's face. He knew none of the details, but he knew that his mission was an important one to the boys at Langley. And so he made a decision to go for it. In reaching in ostensibly for his license, he wrapped his hand around his revolver. Before he could pull it out, however, he felt the cold hard end of a barrel on his temple.

* * *

"Nothing from Olsen yet, sir."

"Can we get hold of someone on the outside?" asked the station chief.

"Sir?"

"This came from the DDO himself. I don't know what this guy Nelsen has been up to, but the very top wants to try to get him out, and they don't care if covers are blown. Can we get hold of an operative who could poke around without stirring up suspicion?"

"Ambassador," Rungren paused to think. "We have Professor Clark, visiting lecturer at Moscow State University."

"Hire him. In person"

Rungren exited on foot directly onto Tchaikovsky Street and noticed the tail immediately. But he also shook it immediately. He walked nonchalantly to the corner, but once around it he bolted down into the Metro, into the capacious underground world of Moscow's subway system. He crisscrossed the city a few times and then, satisfied that he wasn't being followed, surfaced at October Square and walked down Lenin Prospekt toward the Academy of Sciences. The ambassador found Stasovoy Prospekt, Koller's street, and then found the apartment building.

"Professor Clark?"

"Yes?"

"Are you busy?"

Clark had been hoping for this sort of thing for a good many years. He surfaced at the Sverelova Metro stop on Marx Prospekt, two blocks from Anna's apartment building. He found it without any problem, and rang her room: the lobby door unlocked. Upstairs, he found her door ajar. He pushed it open, peeked inside, and saw the smile first, and then the gun.

"Have a seat, Professor. Anna is out of town," said

the GRU CI agent, smiling, visions of Yuri Zulisk's praise dancing in his head.

Zulisk hadn't heard anything back from Malachev, but it hadn't been all that long.

He called to see how his men were doing in the Crimea. The last he had heard, they were sunning on the beach, close enough to Anna to send back a detailed and lustful report of the ballerina's body.

Kasakov had his secretary call out to Tereshkovo.

"Comrade."

"This is it, Bazakin. Reunite the entire *Starik* immediately."

Bazakin hummed his acceptance of the task into the receiver.

"You seem happy," Kasakov commented.

"I am. Markov and I have been working like fiends. We have a war room now, Peter Andreevich. State-of-the-art."

"Good. We'll need it."

"The ship is on the way?"

"Yes."

"You seem happy," Bazakin commented.

"I am."

February 24—Oreanda Hotel, Yalta

They were tired as could be. After aquatic maneuvers, and more sun, and more aquatic maneuvers, they took dinner at Swallow's Nest, a castle perched atop a cliff rising three hundred vertical feet from the Black Sea, and watched a golden sun dip into a sapphire sea. Then after-dinner drinks back at the Oreanda. Then lovemaking—slow, gradual, soft. Now they were on the bed. Resting, in the dark. Naked. Through the open windows blew a breeze perfumed by magnolias and salt-laden air wafting off the Black Sea. The only sound was the hissing of the breeze passing through the screens. It was one in the morning. A half-moon hung in the sky, and provided sufficient illumination for the two of them to make out the contents of their room.

"Well," he whispered in her ear, "shall we leave?"

She rolled her head, looked at his profile.

"Leave?"

"Well, I *was* hoping to see the room wherein Stalin, Churchill, and Roosevelt carved up the world, but I'm afraid it's now or never, Annastasia."

"You mean you—"

"Follow my lead," he whispered. Then, loudly, he said, "Anna! There's blood! Jesus, it's coming out of your mouth!"

He nudged her with his elbow.

"Oh, God, I don't know what's wrong with me," she moaned. "I'm sick. And dizzy. The room is spinning. Oh, God, Alex, help me!"

He said softly in her ear, "It's a damn good thing you're a dancer and not an actress."

Anna punched him in the stomach and then resumed her attempt at looking and sounding deathly ill. She felt moisture on her face, reached up with her hand and touched her chin, looked at the red stuff on her fingers, and, without missing a beat, continued to suck down her last breaths.

"Enough," he said.

"Was the catsup necessary?"

"A camera was a possibility," he replied. "At any rate, now we know. They can't hear, they can't see."

"Which means they're relying on watchers."

"Yep. Outside our door, the lobby, et cetera."

She looked at the window. "And we're on the fifth floor."

"Mmm. Let's see just what kind of physical condition a ballerina is in. Get dressed."

"Wait a minute, you can't mean—"

"We have four hours of darkness left. This is hardly the time for debate."

Anna began to pull on her clothes. As did Alex.

"What are you doing?"

"You'll see," Nelsen said as he ripped out a light fixture from their bathroom and pulled out a strand of electrical wire, sliding the cord in his pocket. He next ripped a leg off the queen-size bed and lodged the makeshift club inside his belt, partway into his pocket. And then he walked over to the window and looked out. Five stories down and thirty yards away, the sea. The cafés were quiet; the small landing stage was shut down; tethered boats bobbed; no pedestrians on the Lenin Embankment below. He pulled out the screen and then, sticking his head out, got a better look: yup, deserted, as far as he could tell.

"Alex, we're five stories up. That's about seventy feet."

"You're right. You don't use your wrists and hands much when you dance, do you?"

She frowned. "Look, this is insane. What will you hold on to? When I said escape I didn't—"

"Wrap your arms around my waist. Put your chin against the small of my back. Keep your feet bent back toward your own back. Lock your wrists together. Like this."

He wrapped her arms around him, joined her wrists below his navel.

"What about a rope? What about *making* a rope? Don't people trapped in a fire take sheets and tie—"

"Slide your legs out. Don't think, just do. Like dance. Go on instinct."

"Shit," she said, but listened nonetheless.

He followed suit. His first hold was on the window frame. All in all he gauged the weight to be not appreciably more than a heavy pack. He slipped one hand out, grabbed a protruding brick, slid the other hand down, latched it onto a brick too, and they were out, hanging. The sea spoke rhythmically. Still no pedestrians. Quiet.

Nelsen thought maybe he heard her praying under her breath; he smiled to himself.

Hand over hand, down, smoothly, unwaveringly. All in all, it wasn't bad at all: no ice, no cold, no water.

They were on the street.

Anna was unutterably pale.

"How are your wrists?"

"Fine," she said, rubbing them.

They crept around the corner, peeked into the lobby. A crowd of men was seated therein, some reading, some sharing a bottle of vodka, some playing cards.

"GRU," Anna said.

"Yep. Competent suckers, ain't they?"

"What now?"

"What else? Transportation, my dear."

He directed her to a parked car.

"You'd be comfortable with this." It was a big black Chaika, a double for Anna's own auto.

"How will—?"

He tried the driver's-side door: open. "In you go."

He removed the bed leg and, with the doors and windows closed, began to ram the keyhole. Viciously. Finally it popped. She watched while he cleared away the debris, brought the short length of electrical wire out of his pocket, found the three wires, one hot, one for ignition, one for starting, and joined them. The Chaika's big engine rumbled to life.

"Could we have used these instead?" she asked, holding the keys she'd taken off the dash.

Alexander shrugged; Annastasia laughed.

"You drive," he said.

"Where to?"

"Feodosia."

"I'm from Moscow."

"East, along the coast, about sixty-five miles."

"Do you have a map?" she asked.

He tapped his head.

"What's in Feodosia?"

"A stepping-stone."

"You evasive bastard," she said, smiling.

He looked at his watch. "Nearly two. Three hours of darkness left. I suggest you drive."

The moon cast a sheen over the hood of the speeding black Chaika. Within twenty minutes they hit Planerskoye, perched on the five-mile-long Kara-Dag mountain, which rose directly out of the sea. The sun, though still hidden, sent enough light around the earth for them to see the Gate of the Kara-Dag, out on the sea, an arch of rock large enough for sizable yachts to pass through. By the time they reached Sudak, still hugging the coast, there was enough light to see the Sudak Valley, its vineyards and little white houses. They began to climb the Feodosia hills as the first sliver of a yellow-orange sun emerged in the east, igniting the sea.

Tereshkovo Complex

Kasakov deplaned at daybreak, rode over in the Landcruiser, and entered the dome.

He noticed immediately. It was on the faces of Bazakin, Markov, Matra, and Ignatov. Plain as day.

"Nelsen?"

They all nodded.

"Fuck. How?"

"You wouldn't believe it if I told you," Bazakin commented.

"And Renear and Pattison?"

"Firmly within our grasp in Yakutsk," Bazakin said. "We're in the process of bringing them back."

"The system?" Kasakov inquired.

"We've been over it from top to bottom. It looks fine."

"Though we can't be sure," Kasakov said.

"True," Bazakin conceded. "Life is a matter of probabilities."

"The war room?"

"Finished," Markov said.

"Before we use it for war, let's use it for catching our American," Kasakov said.

"And a Russian," Matra interjected.

"Anna?"

Bazakin nodded. Kasakov kicked himself internally for not simply snapping her neck on the many occasions he had been tempted to do precisely that.

They were in the war room. Kasakov had assumed control of the chase, the start of which was represented on the large HD screen: Yalta glowed; a semicircle defined the distance Alex and Anna could conceivably have covered; nearby borders were illuminated. Kasakov had Zulisk on the videophone, back in Moscow.

"Now," Kasakov said, "I want the entire region monitored continuously for covert transmission. Bazakin, do we have a way of checking for such a thing?"

"Comrade Zulisk," Bazakin said to the Moscow-based GRU agent, "we have a portable control for a Collins 515R-1 miniature COMINT receiver that covers the frequency band of 2–1,200 megahertz. It's based on an off-the-shelf IBM 386 laptop and is hooked up to the receiver for control and display of signals. Any attempt to contact CIA will be picked up. Go to the Sixth Directorate and demand some in my name, and distribute them to your men."

Zulisk nodded.

"Stay with us for a minute, Comrade Zulisk. There

are three attractive routes out of the country from Yalta, my comrades: across the Black Sea, further south across the Caucasus Mountains into Turkey or Iran, or further north across the weakly patrolled borders into our former satellites."

All eyes assimilated the relevant geography by looking up at the screen.

"Now, Comrade Zulisk. I want KGB informed of Nelsen's escape, and, though it seems impossible that he ever get this far, I want them to triple patrols on the aforementioned borders. And I want the same for all Black Sea ports receiving ships of any size—Odessa, Sevastopol, Sochi, and so on. Understood?"

"Yes, sir."

"Yankolov himself is in our camp, so you will have no trouble motivating our KGB friends, even those outside the Border Guard. Very well. Now, I also want you to prepare for more drastic measures, should it ever come to this: you must be ready to halt the Great Siberian at the drop of a hat, including the new BAM line. The same readiness must be achieved for all domestic flights; it must be possible to lock down Domodeddovo, Vnukovo-1 and 2, and Bykovo, all in an instant. I want you also to prepare to pounce on internal shipping—the Moskva and its canal, the Dnieper, and the Volga. In addition I want other conceivable water escape routes under watch immediately, with special emphasis on the vulnerable Baltic, which means, of course, that Baltiysk, Klaipeda, Riga, and Tallinn are to be swarming with KGB. For more manpower, instruct the Border Patrol to pull men out of other KGB directorates."

Zulisk nodded yet again.

"That should take care of the perimeter. Now for the most likely scenario. They have probably wrangled a car somehow, and are heading for the border of their choice. Nelsen retains his legitimate papers, and consequently motor travel is easy for them. The Intourist motor routes are of course readily handled."

Kasakov fiddled ineffectively with the mouse, popped up a few unwanted menus.

"Markov. Help."

Markov clicked the mouse; a map of all Intourist routes burst onto the screen, in its own window.

"Okay," Kasakov said. "They've been on the road for as long as four hours now; therefore they could be as far away from Yalta as"—Kasakov traced out an arc with the mouse—"just short of Dzhankoi in the north, and Feodosia in the east. Set up blocks at these two locations. And then march down—"

"Comrade Kasakov," Bazakin interrupted, "if I may. Why not exploit the natural choke points around the Crimean peninsula? Render Kerch impenetrable in the east. And do the same for the two northern routes, one along the Karkinitskiy Bay, one over the Sea of Azov. Simple." Bazakin pointed electronically at the choke points. "They'll never make it to the perimeter."

"Did you hear that, Comrade Zulisk?" Kasakov asked.

"Yes."

"Once you seal off at the choke points," Bazakin said, "you can bring in men by helicopter, and march over every inch of land."

Kasakov nodded.

"And as far as the Black Sea itself," Bazakin said, "the same strategy can be employed. Call the commander of the Black Sea fleet and tell him to seal off the Bosporus and the Dardanelles. And tell him to use the Navy's RORSAT spacecraft to flash every ship. I believe a Cosmos 1967 is in nearly perfect position. With the help of this craft and others, it won't take long to get close-up photos of every freighter in the area."

"Comrade Zulisk?"

"I have heard, comrades."

Zulisk's face disappeared.

Kasakov looked at his watch. "Now, Markov, show me how to use this war room. You have fifteen minutes."

"After which?" Matra prodded.

"After which we cross the Rubicon," Kasakov replied.

First there were the tentacles. The *Starik* was hooked into two over-the-horizon radars, ten Hen House, Hen Roost, and Hen Egg phased-array radars situated around the perimeter of the Soviet Union, and also the controversial ABM-violating thirty-story early-warning receiver at Krasnoyarsk. They were also recipients of every drip of data from the Soviet battery of early-warning satellites. No American missile could possibly escape the *Starik*'s notice, and hence no U.S. missile could escape at least an attempted demon attack.

Then the war room, which was a wonder.

Data—all relevant data—was available at the click of a mouse, and each seat around the war-room table had a keyboard and mouse. Markov provided Kasakov with a glimpse of the data base. First, the world. Naval choke points, the position of American and Soviet naval fleets, points of current conflict, American command regions—all highlighted in various luminous shades of green, red, blue, orange. Then, the United States—from every relevant angle. First and foremost an indication of "high-value" counterforce targets in the American mainland: silo-dense areas glowed in green, as did SAC bases, and cities with numerous nuclear facilities (Seattle, San Francisco, Oahu). Markov shifted to a more fine-grained view of U.S. nuclear assets, and invited Kasakov to click on an area of his choice. He clicked on an ICBM field near Warren Air Force Base. Up popped a detailed view of the field, each MX and Minuteman represented by a digital dot, and each dot placed precisely within the sites of a latitude/longitude grid. Then he clicked on some state names. He found out that New York State contained nineteen hundred warheads and twenty-seven nuclear facilities, and he saw the location of these assets pinpointed in a magnified view of the state. Kasakov learned that Vermont, a state he had always liked, had zero warheads, but eight nuclear facilities worth targeting in an all-out counterforce strike. He turned to look at the American Pacific, of concern to him at the moment. The Americans, according to what he saw, could deliver approximately five hundred ASW, antisubmarine-warfare, nuclear warheads from carriers, subs, and planes. Kasakov clicked on Adak, in the Aleutians, and saw that it, in particular, was filled to the brim with ASW warheads. He saw the VLF transmitting facilities, from Northwest Cape, Australia, to Wahiawa, Hawaii. Australia intrigued him. So Kasakov clicked on the U.S. Defense Support Program's base in Nurrungar, in the heart of Australia. He was rewarded with information that told him Nurrungar was a key early-warning processing station and a "must" in any preemptive counterforce strike. Finally, Kasakov took a look at Nevada. He clicked on the icon for Camp Mercury, and was told that this was the headquarters for the Nevada test site, and that Nellis AFB was adjacent.

"Impressive, Comrade Markov."

Markov bowed.

"Of course in five minutes we'll know just *how* impressive."

Feodosia

They reached the top of the Feodosia hills. A seemingly infinite expanse of green grass to the north; the sea, now shimmering from the sun, to the south; and the hilly Kerch Peninsula to the east.

He said, "It's a beautiful country."

She said, "Alex."

"What?"

She pointed to the sky. An enormous swarm of locusts appeared to be moving east. Helicopters.

"Shit," Nelsen said.

"There are only three ways off the Crimea. You realize that, don't you?"

He nodded absently. The number of helicopters was incomprehensible. The two escapees began to feel the rumble of the rotors. The ground itself shook.

"Boat over the sea, and we're not in a boat. North past the Azov, and we're not heading north. And east through Kerch. Which is where we *are* heading. Along with what looks like the entire Soviet Air Force."

"Look on the bright side," he said. "They aren't trying to kill us."

"No, but they're not going to welcome us with open arms, either."

"Have faith."

They were driving directly underneath a squadron of copters now, heading down Bald Mountain.

"Have faith," she echoed. "What kind of hollow unhelpful shit is that?"

He laughed. She did too.

"Where to?" she asked.

"The station."

"Station?"

"*Train* station."

"Which way?"

Nelsen closed his eyes for a moment; then said, "Continue down the hill, pass into the old quarter." But then, after opening his eyes, he looked left, past Anna, and said, "Cancel that. Stop here. Stop here and *run*."

He was out of the Chaika and tearing toward a

lumbering freight train from Simferopol before she came to a complete stop. He turned and waved; and, looking at her, decided that it was fun to watch a ballerina run through an uneven meadow as fast as she could. When she caught up, panting, she slapped him in the face, and hand in hand they ran alongside the train. He tossed her in an open door. She pretended to shut it, said "Good-bye"—then burst out laughing, gave him her hand, and pulled him in.

They sat, and leaned back to rest against boxes Anna said were marked "Sochi."

"That's what we want," Nelsen said. "The rail ferry to the Caucasian side does present a problem, though."

Through the open sliding door they saw the sea, dotted with boats of all shapes and sizes.

Alex closed his eyes for a minute, meditated. "Kerch is seventy miles away," he announced.

She spied something in his back pocket, pulled it out. A map: Crimea, the Caucasus.

"Have it all in your head, do you?"

He smiled and cocked his head. She studied the map.

"Kerch is *fifty* miles away. That's where the helicopters were headed. It's the only way out."

He snatched the map back. "Then we better find a damn good hiding place."

"We have time," she said, her voice deeper, softer, and her lips drawing toward his.

29

Poetry

February 24—Tereshkovo

The *Starik* looked not the least bit sinister. Vodka was out, and had been generously distributed; each nursed a tumbler, save for Markov, who sipped a Pepsi and munched on popcorn as if he were at the cinema. Galya Matra, fresh from her vacation of pumping iron, looked especially massive and indestructible in a bicep-revealing T-shirt. Ignatov, who could barely see over the top of the war room's polished granite table, looked up at the others and smiled his elfish smile for each, brushed recalcitrant bangs back from his eyes, cleaned the lenses of his gogglelike glasses, and otherwise occupied himself with a thousand other jittery gestures—which were all, for him, normal, and not due to the occasion. Bazakin displayed the serenity of a Buddhist monk with a nicotine vice. Kasakov had his eyes closed; his face was smooth, relaxed, worry-free.

The American mainland was displayed brightly and unflickeringly above them on Markov's enormous screen, the outline of each state emblazoned in sharp, glowing green. Two spots glowed most prominently, one yellow, one red, one off the coast of California, one in Nevada, one in water, one in desert, one a Soviet fishing trawler, one the 1,350-square-mile Nevada test site.

"I consider it rather poetic," Bazakin said, a Prima

dangling from his long, thin fingers. "The Journey of Death desert would have been perfect. Hit them where the atomic age dawned, where Fuchs did his spying for us; that would have been very nice. But I'll take Desert Sands."

Kasakov quoted, " 'If the radiance of a thousand suns/ Were to burst at once into the sky/ That would be like the splendor/ Of the Mighty One . . ./ I am become Death,/ The shatterer of worlds.' "

Matra frowned. "The Americans," she said, "put a theological twist on everything. Let's not follow suit. This is business. Nothing more, nothing less."

Ignatov and Markov nodded.

Bazakin squinted at Matra, pulled deeply on the last eighth-inch of his Prima, nothing more than an ember; then the tobaccophile killed the butt, exhaled through his nostrils, and said, "Business? That's got to be the understatement of the century, Comrade Matra. You think Uncle Sam's going to call us up and say, 'Okay. What do you want?' We're fucking around with history here. Nothing less, nothing more."

Matra frowned. "Truman?" she pointed out.

"He hardly set a precedent for what we're doing," Bazakin replied. "He gave the Nipponese an ultimatum before *Enola Gay* dropped it. They had seventy-five hours."

Matra shrugged. "So ours will come a little later. Insignificant."

"Our missile is a million times more powerful, my dear. And don't think that if our demons fail we'll be living in a rose garden. Our BMD system, even that around Moscow, couldn't stop an American cruise missile in a million years. Ditto for our upgraded SAM's."

"The demons will work," Matra proclaimed.

"On paper, yes," Ignatov said in his quick, high-pitched voice. "But who knows? The man that designed the fucking system is gallivanting around the

Crimea. Maybe he fucked up the software. Who knows?"

"We've checked it," Matra said.

"As best we can," Markov interjected.

"Top to bottom, you said. Inside and out."

Markov smothered a fistful of popcorn. "Yeah," he mumbled. "But the proof is in the pudding."

"Five minutes," Kasakov said. "And the Lord said, 'Let there be light.' "

"Oh, shit," Matra said.

Markov toned the lights down. America, glowing above them, shed a multicolored incandescence over each face.

Troy, New York

McNulty studied the hard copy of the Princeton computer account.

The only files on record were letters in the account's electronic mailbox, and all the letters were from the same person, certainly not, judging by their colloquial tone, from Malachev. McNulty began to read them, and thought that he had stumbled upon some thoroughly innocuous gossip, and nothing else.

> Hey, Tony. Theo. How's the surf? Remember that night we were crocked out on the Chesapeake bridge-tunnel? I still can't believe you dived off, you bastard. I'm the Seal, remember? I thought that was one bet I had a lock on. Anyway, good to hear from ya, old buddy. I hear you're going up for full commander. Not bad for a guy who couldn't do a fucking chin-up at the Academy. So Charlene always had the hots for me, huh? Bullshit. She's one monogamous fox, Tony, you know that. And she'd never do diddily with anyone but a fly-boy. At any rate, it

ain't hangin' bad at all; the old lady's still got it. By all means, when the *Nimitz* is in the shop, stop by—we'd love to have ya. Doreen and Charlene'd talk up a storm; we could hit the links. No, I don't have any dirt on Uncle Sam. I'm still just a grunt in a lot of ways. You care about Star Wars? I don't. The sucker's never gonna work, if you ask me. But I'll tell you this, Sam thinks Ivan's ahead. Sputnik all over again, as far as the brass is concerned. They're sweatin' bullets here in the Pent: Glennie walks around with a hard-on, man, thinkin' about how he's gonna fuck Ivan. So, anyway, you give me a holler to set up a date. Doreen says we've got the next three weekends free. When they hauling that shit-bucket boat you fly off of in? I'll set up a few for ya, Tone. C.U.

Innocuous military gossip.

Whoa, hold on.

It hit him that Star Wars, in one way or another, turned up in every message. No details. No specs. Nothing automatically incriminating. But it was always there. And so was this guy Glennie, and his hawkish attitude toward the Russian Strategic Defense Initiative.

Is Tony one of theirs?

Is there really *a Tony?*

McNulty confronted, reluctantly, the need to answer these questions. Which meant some messy, strenuous digging. Well, not that messy: he had the ship, he had the rank, he had the name. One quick road trip to Virginia Beach coming up.

Wait a minute. Wait one fucking minute! I'll *be Tony.*

McNulty composed and sent the following shot in the dark, and *then* packed his bags.

Ted, hi. Tony again. I ain't kiddin' about Charlene. I've heard her murmuring your name in her sleep! I'd like to get together, just you and me—no kids, no wives, just the two of us. We could hoist a few. I'll be in D.C. tomorrow, 2/25; meet me at nine A.M., Washington Monument. Haven't seen it since I was a kid. Don't let me down, old buddy. I'll be wearing the old Yankee hat you so despise. C.U.

Nevada Test Site

Nine seismographic technicians were vaporized in the blinking of an eye. Despite the lightning speed at which their flesh turned to gas, there was a moment, an evanescent moment before impact, when each man, hearing the whine of the incoming cruise missile, turned his head.

The resultant fireball was so bright that someone standing on Mars could have seen it with the naked eye, and the heat at its core was one hundred thousand times greater than that found on the surface of the sun. A deep, indescribable roar, one like the voice of God himself, built up and rolled out over a fifty-mile radius. The wind and thunder rattled the desert floor for a ten full minutes after detonation. And the billowing mushroom cloud rose up in exact conformation to the innumerable pictures of such an event floating around in the American psyche. The active cloud, however, died out long before it reached past the desolate desert portion of southeastern Nevada, and therefore the fallout was minimal.

There were a few sightings of the cruise missile at treetop level in California, but those that saw it thought they saw a plane.

All in all, no one had tracked the missile, and now, no one knew.

Except the military.
And thus the administration.
Which was the surgery the *Starik* had sought.

PART V

30

Retaliation

February 24—White House War Room

The same pattern: forks dropped, marines, solemn and stiff, knocking on doors, kisses blown to open-mouthed wives, sprints to car doors held open by ramrod soldiers, limos racing. Then the briefing. Followed by the incredulity. The cursing. The fluttering in the stomach. And in some, the nausea.

The war room. The Soviet Union, and her military assets, glowing above them on the computerized screen. The Nevada strike point throbbed. The sea and skies were filled with digital blips: B-52's, B-1's, B-2's, scrambled; not a single able-bodied American nuclear sub was in port. The world was dotted by ten thousand points of nuclear-armed light; it looked as if fireflies were taking over the earth.

The group of those willing and able to make calm, logical contributions had been whittled down to Secretary of Defense Newell, Navy Chief Glennie, the President, and Buchanan. The remaining men were thinking about loved ones, possessions, the afterlife, the earth itself; the last place they wanted to be was locked inside a war room fifty feet below the surface of the earth, the fate of the human race staring them in the face.

"Thank God it's small," Newell said. "Here's the data brought back by NDS." The Secretary of Defense brought up a window of data on the situation screen, near the glowing point at the southeastern tip of Nevada. "Looks like two kilotons. It's all based on how fast the electrons from the ionized fireball travel up to outer space. And the GPS clocks say small, maybe *less* than two kilotons."

The President asked, "How?"

Newell cleared his throat, wiped perspiration off his forehead with a handkerchief, and said, "We don't know for sure, but by elimination I would say a slicum. These cruise missiles are launchable in many ways. We can send them out of standard twenty-one inch torpedo tubes, for example. My guess is that they had an armored box launcher on the deck of a trawler off California. Painfully easy, I'm afraid."

Atwood said, "Christ Almighty! Do you realize what we've spent on tactical warning systems, Allen? Do *any* of you realize? All right, look, I can see the Distant Early Warning system fucking up; the bastard's antiquated. But after that we're supposed to have state-of—"

"No, it's not," Buchanan interjected calmly.

"What's not?" the President said.

"Distant Early Warning," Buchanan responded. "DEW. We overhauled it, to the tune of three billion dollars. Right, Allen?" Newell nodded stiffly; he seemed to be wiping his forehead continuously. "We have thirteen giant minimally attended radars interspersed with, oh, I believe, forty short-range 'gap fillers'; they all swing mechanically in azimuth."

"And they saw nothing?" Atwood steamed.

Newell nodded. "However, I would point out, Mr. President, that the upgraded DEW line is much more cost-effective than a line of AWACS aircraft, which your predecessor prudently nixed."

"Oh, that's wonderful news," Atwood said. "What about our other systems? Tactical warning is supposed to be superredundant."

"Well, it is," Newell said. "We have over-the-horizon backscatter radars, which are backed up by the satellite early-warning system, which is bolstered by our Pave Paws for detection of SLBM's, which is—"

"Jesus H. Christ," Atwood broke in. "I'm not taking a fucking inventory. Just tell me how the hell the Sovs fucked us up the ass. Succinctly."

"Mr. President," Buchanan said, puffing on his pipe in the manner of a grandfather fishing on a calm, mountain lake. "If I may. They used what was no doubt a very low observable cruise missile; in this regard Secretary Newell is certainly right. I would bet, however, that the plume on this missile was nonexistent. Satellite detection is passive; it relies on the fact that certain solid-state material can be used to convert electromagnetic energy, in the form of photons, to electrons, which is something computers can readily measure. The problem is that if the spectral radiation is low enough, even highly sensitive detectors like mercury-doped germanium are blind as bats. In my opinion the Sovs strapped a propeller engine onto a cruise-missile warhead with a standard terrain-tracking radar system. It puttered along slowly at low altitude, reached Desert Sands, and bingo."

The President shook his head.

Orville Simon said, "Tell me something, James. How the hell is it that you're as cool as you are, given the simple but overwhelming fact that Dendrite, your brainchild, has apparently brought the West to a position of abject servility?"

Buchanan exhaled some Captain Black tobacco smoke. "I considered the worst case, Mr. Simon. If Nelsen hadn't gone, we still would have arrived at the very same nightmare. It simply would have taken the Sovs a bit longer. And besides, I'm still not convinced that Dendrite *has* failed."

"James," Atwood said, "no matter how you slice it, your man sure did us one helluva favor."

The DCI tilted his head in a vague, philosophical admission.

"The rescue attempts?" Glennie asked.

Buchanan shook his head.

"Think the bastard turned?" Glennie said.

"Perhaps," Buchanan replied.

"Maybe he's dead," Simon interjected.

"Buchanan or Nelsen?" Glennie quipped.

"Oh, yes, that would be marvelously convenient," Simon said. "Yeah, maybe he cut himself shaving and bled to death. Maybe Nelsen never made it to first base. Maybe they built these interceptors without him. Wonderfully convenient. Maybe Langley didn't cut our throats. Maybe, maybe, maybe. No, I'll tell you what happened. Nelsen built it, took the money, and is catching some rays on the Black Sea." Simon glowered at the impassive Buchanan.

"Gentlemen," the President said.

"What's most distressing," Newell said, "is that we have no model for this. Our software isn't going to be of any help. All the standard nuclear war games—AEM, AMM, Harlot, etc.—fail to apply. We have one strike here. Not against a value target and not against a military target. One strike in the place least likely to do any damage. And no ultimatum, no request. Our new SIOP, gentlemen, is silent."

"What about the rationale for our *own* strategic defense system?" Glennie said. "One of the reasons we continued SDI was to erect a partial shield—one effective against fifty percent of an all-out preemptive SS-18 attack. Didn't you yourself, Allen, say that our interceptors could be used to help assure the survivability of our offensive missiles?"

As Newell nodded, Glennie said, "Well, we did a lot of thinking about SDI. Didn't we render any of this in the form of games?"

Newell was wiping the lenses on his small horn-rimmed glasses. Evenly, smoothly. Not a muscle in his body was outside of his conscious control. He slid his eyeglasses back on.

"No, Mr. Glennie. These were half-baked rhetorical arguments delivered to Congress. They haven't been codified, formalized. There are no computer programs covering what we're involved in here."

"Which is?"

"It's obvious," Newell responded. "To speak as you often do, Mr. Glennie, they've already *built* the fuckers, and they evidently have a good number of them in place. Otherwise such a strike would be patently irrational."

"There's no sign of an orthodox defense?" Randolph Atwood asked.

"None," Newell replied. "Look." The Secretary of Defense punched at his keyboard; data on Soviet preparedness appeared on the screen. "For example, here's Kalingrad, Baltic Fleet submarine base. It's completely quiet. Dead. Nearly every Gold II is in port. And"—Newell typed at the keyboard again—"here's Irkutsk. Their Air Army is sleeping like a log. Their Backfires, Badgers, Bears, and Bison long-range bombers are sleeping on the runways like curled-up, purring cats. And look at this. Here's Vladivostok, Pacific Fleet. Both of their VTOL carriers floating in port like indolent sunbathers. Nearby, at the Backfire base at Alekseyevka they think we don't know about, you'll see more of the same."

"Well," the President said. "I suppose it's academic. If we can show them their SBI has holes, they'll talk. If we do nothing, I suspect it'll be master-slave before you can count to three. Ergo, my friends, we try. Tit for tat."

"Uh, Mr. President?" Buchanan said softly. "Before we proceed, I'd like to share some of my thoughts. If I may."

Atwood nodded.

"Well," Buchanan said, "I believe that we are no longer dealing with Ivan here. I don't think our friend Gorbachev had anything to do with this."

Everybody present looked at Buchanan with renewed concentration.

"Another coup?" Atwood said.

Buchanan nodded slowly. Relit his pipe.

"You have evidence?" the President prodded.

"Oh, we all have evidence," Buchanan said. "It stares us in the face. If I didn't know he was dead, I'd say Andreev Kasakov was the mastermind."

"Who's he?" Atwood asked.

"Former GRU chief. General of the Army. Arguably the most brilliant military mind the Soviet Union ever produced. He had a passion for surprise. He was on the front lines battling the Nazi Wehrmacht when they swept four hundred miles into Russia in only four weeks, despite the fact that they were overwhelmingly outnumbered in aircraft and tanks. Hitler understood the value of surprise; Stalin didn't. Kasakov went to school on Hitler."

The Joint Chiefs looked at each other, seemed to be coming to life a bit. Buchanan looked at the four of them and smiled; the Chiefs nodded.

"Kasakov reportedly told an aide, 'You will never learn what I am thinking. And those who boast most loudly that they know my thoughts, to such people I lie even more.' "

"That's Hitler," Atwood said.

"Precisely," Buchanan said. "It was Kasakov who engineered the 1968 invasion of Czechoslovakia. And, though apocryphal, it was Kasakov, and Kasakov alone, who supposedly urged consideration of bolt-from-the-blue nuclear attacks against the United States. In 1956 General of the Army Omar Bradley testified before Congress that the Soviet Union would probably not start World War III in Europe without surprise nuclear strike against the continental United States. Bradley had met Kasakov, and reported later that he'd met Lucifer himself."

Much food for thought. Silence.

"I don't know, James," the President said. "You don't have any hard evidence."

"You're right," Buchanan admitted. "It's still just a hunch. But I suspect we'll soon see it either verified or falsified."

"Well," Atwood said, "to the dastardly task at hand."

"Mr. President," Glennie said, "I believe our best option may be to go with the new D-5 on the Trident 2. She's fast, has a depressed trajectory, and a star-tracking guidance system that makes her impervious to ASAT attack. Let's see." Glennie attacked his keyboard for a minute, then nodded toward the situation screen. "Yup. There we go. We have a Two in the vicinity."

Atwood said, "Harold? Wally? The rest of you?"

"Why not use a cruise missile?" Marine Commandant Wally Green asked. "Poetic justice."

"No, no," Glennie said, "we already know their system can handle cruise missiles. They ran a test on two of their own, remember? And besides," Glennie said, "if their SBI is good enough to take down a D-5 launched from just off the coast, we had better find that out pronto. We billed the bloody D-5 as the ultimate first-strike weapon."

"Set it up, Conrad," Atwood said.

Glennie nodded.

Glennie did indeed set it up. The bug heard him doing so. And consequently so did Vanderyenko. Who sent an E-mail note to Tereshkovo about the planned strike, from where Bazakin issued the enabling code; Twenty-five demons on the coast of the Sea of Okhotsk hummed to a state of readiness, left the ground, and hovered at five hundred feet, eyes open, looking across the Pacific.

Back in the White House war room, Glennie informed the President that the Navy was ready.

"All right," Atwood said, "let's go."

Glennie said, "Do it, boys," into a receiver.

All eyes focused on the relevant portion of the situation screen.

Atwood picked up the hot line, aiming to have a few words with Gorbachev about *glasnost.*

The Sea of Okhotsk, Russian Waters

The drill ended, and Fitzie fired up a game with his opponent, a digital grand master playing at 2500. He'd found today's target inane: not Baikunor, not Kirovsk, no base at all. Just plum fuck in the middle of the Siberian wilderness, seven hundred miles due north of Irkutsk, near the Angara River. Bloody limbo. Permafrost. No ICBM silo within a thousand miles. He had time-saving macros for all the usual destinations, but this one wasn't usual, and so he'd had to program in the target himself. Shit, Fitzie thought, even if one of these birds had flown, only a few pariahs would have been vaporized, Russkies exiled to count trees and chop wood for some trivial crime against the party. The whole charade left him feeling pretty good. Relaxed. *Supremely* relaxed. Away from Laura for nine long months, most of the time a thousand feet underwater—these drills, the thrill of them, and then the mellowness afterward: it was the closest he came to making love. And now he was spent, his limbs nearly floating. Time for a game.

Lieutenant Commander Steven Fitzgerald enjoyed chess immensely, and he enjoyed it all the more knowing that the Trident sub upon which he was playing was deep into Ivan's waters. He'd been there before; it was no big deal to be there again. Chess encapsulated what he did, what they *all* did, which was to play rather cerebral cat and mouse with Ivan—to slither in utter silence into the other's home, to frolic there a bit, and to return unscathed. It was a game that never failed to thrill. And the magic was working once again: they were in the Sea of Okhotsk, in as deep as they could go without beaching, and he felt the addictive pleasure only daredevils know. The silence was so complete that Fitzie could hear his heart beating in his ears; but for the modulating of sonar and the gentle clicking of buttons, the crew was motionless; an unwarranted whisper at this stage could qualify a man for subsequent court-martial. At the moment the match was even; neither side had the initiative. It was all going to boil down to the endgame. Fitzgerald was happy with is pawn structure, somewhat displeased because of his *opponent's* pawn structure, with the fact that his only bishop was black. But overall he was utterly content. The happiness of a military man controlling a workstation as beautiful as this baby, while inside a vessel as gigantic but fast as a Trident 2, deep in enemy territory, without the slightest quiver of fear, is hard to beat, Fitzgerald thought.

But the chessboard vanished, and Death replaced it. His target from the drill was back on the monitor. Siberia. *No way. Just no fucking way.* But then he cursed his incredulity: *You're an idiot. After all, why the* fuck *do you think they send you in here? It's always been rehearsal. This is it. Live. Onstage.*

The closest Fitzgerald usually got to the violence of war was a kingside attack. It was always the sonar jocks that felt the heat—with ears schooled by years of quiet searching for another sub, they hunted in the silence. And if they missed something in Ivan's backyard, that could be all she wrote. But after the drills—after the usual playacting, the alarms and lights, the selection of a target, which to Fitzgerald and his machine was nothing more than an exciting video game—after the drills, he played chess, snacked, relaxed. There was just him and his parallelized DEC 3100, and the unthinkable cylinders that housed a hundred Hiroshimas—cylinders he had assumed would never be emptied. The closest he came to conflict was practice targeting on an unreal series of grids of the Soviet Union, mostly military bases and silos. But now sonar was on vacation, and Fitzgerald was at the vortex of an ungodly storm.

The new system mocked him. He stared at the screen—the screen of a 1,280-by-1,024 resolution, whisper-quiet water-cooled raster display, the resolution high enough for full 3-D modeling; the transputer-boosted 24 MIPS speed—how nice is it now? he asked himself. Fitzie couldn't dispute the icons—the images were sharp as could be, the import clear. The techies back at Groton had just hot-rodded the entire system to include a state-of-the-art graphics and voice interface. There was no arguing with the pretty little pictures on the monitor: there was the *Henry M. Jackson*, there was Lieutenant Commander Steven Fitzgerald, there was the Go button, there was the selected grid representing that by now familiar point in Siberia, and there was his missile, blinking. The icons made the scenario perfectly clear; the miniaturization made it nauseatingly cute. And a soft, ludicrously amorous voice whispered: "L-DEFCON." The commander, whose blood usually passed for ice, was, beneath his uniform, suffused with sweat; soon enough he had to wipe his eyelids dry to see. L-DEFCON, Fitzgerald knew, was total preemption: this wasn't a retaliatory strike. *Check the code, baby, and be cool. This is why you swallowed all that shit at Annapolis, why you sucked up to torturers with more stripes, why you beat your body into shape. Code, code.*

Pages refused to obey his trembling hands. It was hard for him to read. Hard to focus.

Here it is: simple: L-DEFCON. Fuck. That's it. It's gone. This pretty little sphere's gonna vanish. Wait, verify the chain. "Give me chain verification." *That's not even your voice. Get it together. Breathe. That's it, breathe.*

The response was quick: an iconic representation of four hands appeared on the screen, right up to the President's. Fitzie's handprint was the only one missing; the blinking outline of a hand beckoned coolly for his touch.

He saw Laura—in flashes: naked, embracing him, smiling deviously, throwing back her hair. Then his daughter: tiny Karen, impish, mischievous, in his lap, then a glimpse of her sleeping angelically. And then the long-forgotten chants of Annapolis, sung in unison with other jogging mids, rose up in him involuntarily: *I'm a soldier and I can do, whatever I am called to do.*

Feeling the pain of a thirty-mile run on the coast of Maryland thirteen years ago, Fitzgerald, by an act of sheer willpower, put his hand on the screen. His prints were read, right through all the perspiration.

White House War Room

"This is the President of the United States. I would like to speak to President Gorbachev."

"Now, why would you want to speak with him?" Kasakov asked.

"Who's this?"

"Colonel Peter Andreevich Kasakov, GRU."

Atwood looked as pale as a black man can look.

"What happened to the President?"

"You need to ask?"

"Mr. Kasakov, this is the President of the United States. In order to demonstrate to you and your people that your SBI will not protect you, we have launched a D-5 nuclear missile from one of our Trident 2 submarines. The target is a desolate part of Siberia, and consequently there should be little or no loss of life. We hope that this will put a quick end to the exchange you have initiated. Do you understand?"

"Oh, yes, I do," Kasakov replied. "Let's talk again in a little while, shall we?"

Atwood placed the receiver back in its red cradle slowly, softly.

"James," the President said, "Did this General Kasakov you've told us about have a son?"

Fort Meade, NSA Headquarters

"What the hell is that?"

"What?"

"That." Herbert Light pointed at the screen.

"Some sort of heat source."

"Jesus."

"What is it, Herb?"

"I know *exactly* what it is. That's a fucking missile, in boost phrase."

"A missile? Launched from what? There aren't any ships in those waters."

"A sub," Light said.

"A sub? A missile launched from a sub? Wait a minute. The only sort of missiles on that sort on a submarine are—"

"SLBM's," Light said.

"Christ, no."

"I'm afraid so."

"Hold on. It's gone."

"It's gone?"

"That's right, Herb. Vanished."

"What the hell is going on here?"

DSP and NORAD were not similarly perplexed;

they were simply depressed. They sent the news to the White House over the Ground Wave Emergency Network, in a test of the communication network built to withstand even a massive nuclear attack. The men waiting in the war room had seen the D-5 evaporate from their situation screen before the message came through.

"You got any bigger guns, Allen?" the President asked.

31

Ultimatum

February 24—Ten Miles West of Kerch, the Crimean Peninsula

They were sitting, legs outstretched across the sandy floorboards, backs against the Sochi-headed crates. Looking out together at the sea. Every now and then they heard the passing roar of a helicopter.

Anna said, "I'm not sure I'll like it."

The train lumbered on, to a rhythmic, clacking beat.

"You will," Nelsen said.

"I'm an artist."

He shrugged. "I'm a scientist."

She frowned. Her black hair was, for the first time, wild, though still bundled up. To have made love with it up, even love of the rapid type they'd just enjoyed, was unusual. Smudges of dirt dotted her face. The smell of her was still in the air. "Art is a business in the States," she said.

"Isn't everything, ultimately, business?"

"In Russia, no. Russians make films for an audience of twenty."

"Films?"

"After dance I was thinking of film. My father runs Gosinko.

"Go-what?"

"State film bureau."

"Ah."

It occurred to him that despite his earlier teasing,

Annastasia would surely be as good an actress as a ballerina. He looked at her face, the smallest quiver in which could mean everything. The start of a smile upon her perfect lips was something men would kill for. Certainly they'd spend seven dollars to see it on the silver screen.

"Can I get hired for the love scenes?" he said.

"I'm serious."

He looked at her and thought of hazy, cerebral, elegant Bergman-like movies.

"Hollywood turns out a work of art every now and then, Anna."

"When? Americans find *Dark Eyes* a thing of beauty. Russians see a masticated Chekhov."

Nelsen looked at her blankly.

"See, you don't even *know Dark Eyes*."

"Yours, I do."

"I have green eyes," she said.

"True. Look, you're a film aficionado. I'm not. But I don't see how you can prefer Soviet filmmaking to American. Didn't you tell me that . . . oh, what was it? . . . uh . . ."

"Gosinko?"

"No, uh . . ."

"Mosfilm?"

"Yeah. Didn't you tell me that Mosfilm makes propaganda, that the party tells them what to do?"

"That was before *glasnost*," she said.

"Oh, *glasnost*. Well, I have bad vibes about your *glasnost*."

She arched her eyebrows.

"I don't think the *Starik* is particularly impressed with *glasnost*," he said.

"I agree. So what?"

"So I don't think the *Starik*, not even GRU or KGB, usually controls the Soviet Air Force."

"What are you saying?"

He let it sink in. The train rolled on to a metronomic pulse. Copters passed overhead, rumbling.

"You wanted me to leave. To give the *Starik* SBI. Well, I listened, but I don't think Gorby much cares for SBI."

"So why would he be chasing you down?"

"You're catching on."

"You mean the *Starik* is . . . is in control?"

He nodded.

She looked out, across the sea, to the sky. It was cobalt blue, and now, as far as she could tell, copter-free. But she had seen and heard them. That was why, after all, she was riding as a stowaway in a freight train.

"A coup?" she said.

"I would say, my dear, that the evidence points in that direction. Hollywood, Anna. Think about it."

She shook her head. "The system works?"

"It works."

"God."

"See, you'll like America. Over there, he lives."

She smiled.

"Now," Nelsen said, "let's see about *getting* to America." He attempted to peel back some boards on the floor of the car. No luck. "Nope," he said. "The planks are solid as a rock. We'll have to get underneath."

"Underneath what?" Anna asked.

"What else? The car. Now, hold my feet."

Alex, on his belly, slid partway out the door of the rocking car, curled his upper body around the edge, and, upside down, looked underneath. It was not a paradise, but there were some brackets and bolts and girders. It was possible, and what was the alternative?

"Come on," he said, "follow me," and then, flipping over, Nelsen disappeared.

Annastasia rolled out on her stomach and inched her head over the edge, half-expecting to see splattered blood. Instead she saw him, whole, holding on below, his feet inches from the passing ties beneath. His knees were braced against two steel girders; his hands were free, and though outstretched, Anna found them utterly uninviting.

"Like the hotel wall. Don't think. Just do it."

She did. Her toe hit the track, bounced up violently, some skin was ripped off the flesh around her Achilles tendon.

He had her.

"Good," he said.

"Maybe we should reconsider," she panted. "*Starik* or no *Starik*."

White House War Room

Where there had been a streaking ray of green there now was nothing. The Sea of Okhotsk, the Far East, Siberia—calm as could be.

"Jesus," Glennie said. "The D-5's the best we have, gentlemen. They took it out without breaking a sweat."

Newell added, "Data from the DSP's geosynchronous satellites indicates that our missile didn't even make it to midcourse."

"Kasakov," Buchanan said.

"Not alone, surely," Atwood said.

"No, not alone. GRU and KGB. Or a subgroup therein. They stole our Neurocubes, built the interceptors, and now they're turning the screw."

"How could it be so fucking easy?" the President asked.

"With all due respect, sir," Buchanan said, "we spooks have been warning of such a coup. The first one was sponsored by hardline troglodytes; this one is for real. Gorby was a genius, but Gorby had enemies—men willing to die a thousand painful deaths for Great Russia."

Atwood shook his head. "The command and control, though. The logistics."

"No big deal," Buchanan said, smiling, "when you look soberly at Soviet nuclear operations. "KGB has always run their own self-contained strategic warning systems—base watchers, 'diplomats,' moles, the standard stuff. And the Chief Intelligence Directorate of the General Staff, GRU, sharpened into a razor-sharp army of techno-spies by the late senior Kasakov . . . well, GRU has for years presided over an array of technical early-warning systems and, sometimes, elite, high-technology weapon systems. Interceptors would by no means be outside their purview. Nor would low observable ground- or sea-launched cruise missiles. Evidently the junior Kasakov and his men have supplemented their SIGINT by tapping into the nine-member Molniya early-warning constellation. They've evidently gained control of the troops of the Anti-Air Defenses."

"But the politics of it all," Atwood commented.

Buchanan shrugged. "No big deal, really. Not when you consider that the President is like a feudal lord in the Soviet system. He goes, anything goes. Recall 1982: Brezhnev died. And there was a full four-day vacuum. Anyone could have filled it. The Sovs don't have well-oiled power transitions like us, Mr. President. And the thing is, the President chairs the Defense Council, which is composed of—"

"The Minister of Defense, the Minister of Foreign Affairs, and the Chief of the Committee for State Security, which is KGB."

Buchanan nodded. "So you railroad the General Secretary, you leave the helm vacant. And then you seize it for yourself."

"Yankolov runs KGB. So we're talking Kasakov and Yankolov here."

"It would seem so."

"All right, look," Glennie broke in, "enough analysis. Let's get the show back on the road. We launch again. This time two D-5's."

"Perhaps there is a more promising line of attack," Atwood said.

"What?" Glennie said.

"Harold?" the President prodded.

Harold Singletree, Air Force Chief, said, "I'd love to pull a rabbit out of my hat, gentlemen. Unfortunately, the nastiest thing I have is a supersonic ALCM, and as Conrad pointed out earlier, that's exactly what they ran their final test on."

Atwood nodded, then said, " 'Course, maybe that was staged. To prevent us from going to a cruise missile."

"Possible," Singletree said.

"But probable?" Glennie said.

"Who knows?" Atwood said."Who knows anything anymore?"

"I say we stick with the D-5," Glennie said.

"This has got to be gradual," Atwood said. "I assume you all realize that. They haven't harmed a hair on our heads. We move to all-out retaliation, we'll no doubt get through. But that would be the end. Of them. Of us. They see it coming, *they* go all-out. And even if they don't, I'd be the nigger who fucked humankind. No, thank you."

"Well," Glennie said, "two D-5's."

"Objections, gentlemen," Randolph Atwood said. "James?"

Buchanan nodded. "I'm a spook, Mr. President. Ask Allen."

"Allen?" the President said.

The Secretary of Defense was as motionless as a wax figure. Were it not for the sheen on his forehead and the blinking of his eyes, he could have passed himself off as a rather homely, bald-headed mannequin. Newell spoke, deliberately, his hands folded in front of him, frozen. "Try the D-5's. If that fails, I have some unconventional ideas perhaps worth toying with."

* * *

So they tried. Again. Glennie picked up one receiver out of fifty on the war-room table and issued the command to the *Jackson*, by way of the AFSAT COM satellite transponder system. Within thirty seconds Fitzie slid two D-5's into position. Atwood called Kasakov and let him know. And Kasakov said:

"Tell Buchanan I said hi."

They saw the green dots, two of them, moving toward the Russian mainland. Over the sea. And . . . over land, this time.

But then: gone.

"Holy shit," Glennie said.

Kerch, Easternmost tip of the Crimean Peninsula

"Remember," Alex whispered, "they only want me to come back and maintain the system. They don't want us dead. Keep cool."

The train was halted. Shouts. Voices. Boots. *Military* boots: black, shiny. Close enough to either of them, at times, to reach down and touch.

The search was on. Car after car, front to back.

"Take it easy," Alex whispered to the trembling dancer.

It lasted forever. Their car was searched: they heard footfalls above them.

Then the searchers were through. The train rolled off the ferry, onto the Taman Peninsula, heading down the Caucasus coast.

At Anapa the train stopped, and they dropped down, hobbled out into a brilliant sun, and tried to stretch out the kinks. She hugged him.

And then they climbed back in, the inside luxurious compared with the underside.

"How far to Sochi?" she asked.
"Look on the map."
"All right, give it to me."
"You have it."
"No I don't. You have it."
"Ohhh, shit."

It had been found by a brown-nosing, not-too-swift sergeant in the Border Guards Directorate of the KGB—a man who, wanting maximum glory, held the map until he could get direct access to a lieutenant liable, he figured, to send praise directly up to the gods in Moscow.

"Comrade Lieutenant, I found this on the train," he announced. "Not conclusive, but surely promising. They must have jumped off short of Kerch."

The lieutenant studied the map. No route was penned in, but finding a map of the region *was* too much of a coincidence.

"Perhaps even earlier," the lieutenant said. "You checked the car well which held this map?"

"Thoroughly, Comrade Lieutenant."

"Hmm. Did you look underneath?"

"Underneath?"

"Underneath the fucking train."

"Uh . . ."

"Where was the train headed?"

The sergeant began to reflect. And reflect. And was grabbed ferociously by the lieutenant.

"So-So-Sochi," stammered the sergeant, kissing praise good-bye.

Washington, D.C.

Japanese tourists walked here and there, burdened with video equipment. The Hill stood majestic in the distance, its dome tinged with the light of an early sun. The White House, from the outside, looked utterly serene, giving not a hint of the battle being fought fifty feet below her first floor. Abraham Lincoln looked out from his memorial toward the monument beneath which McNulty waited.

America, all in all, looked like an empire destined for imperishable glory.

Detective Lou McNulty was standing beside the Washington Monument. He was wearing a Yankee baseball cap.

Come on, Theodore. Come on, baby.

Someone slapped him hard, *very* hard, on the back.

"Tony! Great to see you."

McNulty turned and looked up at a clean-cut man more solid than an oak tree, and nearly as tall. A man in uniform. Navy.

Jesus. The fucking Seals?

"Likewise, Theo."

"So what's up? Face-to-face a little out of the ordinary, isn't it?"

"Well, we've run into some trouble," McNulty extemporized. "Extraordinary trouble."

"Really?"

"Really. What have you managed so far?"

"What the hell kind of question is that?"

"Well, we're a little short on results."

"You're not getting the transmissions?"

"No."

"Well, that's awful news, Tony."

"You've fucked with us."

"No, I dropped them. All of them. Even had Glennie laid out on the squash court for your second gift."

"Liar."

"Nope. It's poetic justice. And now I'm afraid you won't *ever* get results."

Liquori pulled out a revolver.

"Rather messy, don't you think?" McNulty said.

"Very bad odds, too. There are three cars filled with sharpshooters. We like to travel in packs."

Liquori was distracted just enough. He glanced at a nearby car. McNulty grabbed Liquori's wrist, smashed it down against his knee; the gun dropped to the ground.

McNulty felt a hammer fall against the right side of his face: Liquori's left fist. The detective went down. Grabbed for the gun. But too late. Liquori had it.

"You know how long it took me to get a policy that would cover my family in this event?" Liquori said.

"What?" McNulty said, trying desperately to focus on the figure looming above him.

Tereshkovo Complex

Bazakin said, "As you can see, our friend Buchanan has quite a mind. We enjoy the luxury of listening in; he doesn't. Yet still the American DCI deduced who is running Great Russia. None of Peter Andreevich's praise regarding this American, I now realize, was hyperbolic."

Bazakin's face was shrouded in smoke. The others nodded.

"Now to business," Bazakin said. "The engineers Renear and Pattison should soon be here. There is no way Nelsen and his girlfriend can escape. We'll have them back soon enough. Comrade Kasakov is personally seeing to their capture. In the meantime, Markov, you must pick up whatever slack their absence creates."

Markov nodded.

"And to the heart of the matter: our ultimatum." Without further ado Bazakin picked up the receiver on the DCL hot line. But then, suddenly, before he placed the call, a transmission from Vanderyenko came in.

White House War Room

"Well," President Atwood said, "that's that. Zero for three. Let's hear your ideas, Allen."

The Secretary of Defense removed his glasses, wiped his face dry, replaced his pince-nez, and began: "All right. Suppose we take a conventional torpedo and somehow reconfigure it with a nuclear warhead. We then sneak a sub in near a military port; perhaps Vladivostok. And we let it go toward shore. It skims just beneath the surface, and when it hits, boom, tit for tat, ours a good deal less elegant, makeshift even, but still quite a bang. The only other option, as far as I can see, it to walk a thermonuclear device across a Soviet border, fire a timer, and run like hell."

"Hmm," the President murmured.

And then the phone rang. The hot line.

"This is the President of the United States."

"Ah, good, you're in. This is Bazakin."

"Bazakin?"

"A friend of Kasakov's."

"I see."

"It would be most prudent to let the others hear. Can you manage that, Comrade Atwood?"

"Yes." The President clicked the DCL line to conference mode.

"All set?"

"Yes."

"Excellent," Bazakin said. "Now. Your Comrade Newell is most inventive. Unfortunately it will take a bit too much time to nuclearize a torpedo and worm a submarine in under our noses. And smuggling in an

A-bomb? On foot? That would take a while too, I'm afraid."

Randolph Atwood's brain, for the first time in his life, refused to work. He said nothing.

"Our delivery system, on the other hand, as you have seen, is most efficient. At the moment, I believe we have eleven coastal cities within our sites. All we ask for is cooperation. We want NATO out of Europe. Yesterday. But more importantly, we want some food, free, at some point down the road. Same thing for fossil fuels. And we want you to ensure similar cooperation on the part of the Germans and Japanese."

"I see."

"Of course you do. It's really very simple. Should we detect you and your gang pointing even a handgun in our direction, we will launch again. One warhead, same size, but on a medium-size countervalue target. Is this clear?"

"Yes."

"Excellent. You know, I could have let Admiral Buchanan describe the situation."

All present looked at Buchanan. He was smoking his pipe. And the Admiral said wearily, "The late General Kasakov took so-called self-deterrence very seriously. He dreamed of a situation in which a surprise Soviet counterforce attack could restrain Washington from retaliation, by reserving escalation dominance and holding American cities hostage."

"Most impressive, Comrade Buchanan," Bazakin said. "Now, let's discuss your compliance signal. Here's what you do. Within five minutes after our chat, using the SCARS-III link, have SACEUR begin to conspicuously pack his bags—tanks, planes, artillery, everything. We'll be watching. You have five minutes. Oh, by the way, we call ourselves the *Starik*."

Click.

"*Starik*?" said Glennie. "What the fuck is that?"
"History," Buchanan said.

Beside the Washington Monument

The world came back into focus for McNulty. The first thing he saw was the barrel of Liquori's gun.

"One night. One fucking night. I was drunk off my ass. Well, that's life."

A woman screamed. Peripherally, McNulty saw people scattering.

"Finding out that the bugs malfunctioned. I can't tell you how happy that makes me. I won't be around for a second try, my Russian friend."

Liquori put the barrel into his mouth and very literally blew his head off.

McNulty felt pieces of brain fall in a mist on his face; medical ministrations were superfluous; he rose and ran for a phone. For once, he very much wanted to talk to the feds.

32

On the Run

February 24—Sochi, the Caucasus, on the Black Sea

"We're here," Alex said. "Let's go."

They jumped out of the still slightly moving freight car.

"Why don't we just grab a passenger train on the same line?" she asked. "We'd head straight into Turkey."

"Yeah, and straight into our pursuers. They've no doubt sealed off all the obvious exits ahead of us. And I don't think ducking under the train's going to work twice."

"So what do you propose?" she asked.

Nelsen closed his eyes and lost himself in thought; Anna rolled her eyes.

"A bus," he said.

"A bus?"

"Yup. Come on."

They walked into Sochi. Now and then a helicopter, sometimes two or three, overflew the town. And the pair had to change their direction a number of times to avoid uniformed members of the Border Guard.

"They know we made it past Kerch," she said.

"Looks that way, doesn't it?"

They entered the harbor area.

Countless ships—sailboats and steamers, motorboats and hovercraft—some of them surprisingly large, slid in and out of the harbor. They came from other ports on the Black Sea, and even, by the Volga-Don canal, from Moscow and Leningrad. Horns sounded off and on, from near and far. Tourists waved from decks. Everyone seemed to be smiling. Cypress, laurel, camphor; yew and box trees—all healthy and well-maintained. It was a beautiful, lively city.

"We need supplies," Nelsen announced.

They entered a camping/climbing shop on Voikov Street and, at his urging, Anna bought ten sweaters, none of them particularly thick. And also blankets and canteens. And backpacks. And boots. And wool hats and gloves.

"Why?" she asked.

Alex lifted his head and looked off to the east. She followed his eyes—to the snow-covered peaks of the Caucasus Mountains.

"Oh, no," she said.

"Oh, yes," he replied. "But don't worry. We're taking a bus."

Which they did—at least for the initial segment of their hike. A bus to Lake Ritsa, in the mountains of Abkhazia. They rolled along the Black Sea as far as Gagra, and then turned inland, into the Bzipi Valley, winding along rivers and ravines and ancient forests, and despite being on the run, there was something irresistible about the ride—the beauty without, the rickety bus, the jabbering tourists within, and then, farther on, the dizzying Yupsara Gorge, pine trees as big as sequoias, caves, and waterfalls like luminous lines in the ascending rock.

"I don't know, Alexander. A cabin in the wilderness here would be sufficient. Perhaps America can get on without us."

"You like camping?"

"I've never been."

"That's gonna change."

The bus stopped: Lake Ritsa. Clear blue water in

the hold of snow-capped mountains; it was as if a giant's icy fingers cupped a bright and shining sapphire.

"It's beautiful," she said.

"You'd like Tibet," Alex said. "Come on. For us, the bus ride is one-way."

Fifteen minutes later they were alone, away from the group, on the shore of Lake Ritsa, towering pines above, a meadow not far off—a sunlit meadow running up and up to the glistening peak of Mount Atsetuko.

"The cleaner your skin, the warmer it'll be."

"You mean . . ."

He nodded.

They bathed. The water, cold at first, was so clear and still that, submerged, her breasts were clearly seen, as were their genitals. She floated on her back, her eyes looking up at the branches of the great pines, her hair falling toward the bottom, and her legs wrapped around his head. With his nose above water, and his tongue beneath, he kissed her until she came, shuddering, struggling to remain still on the surface of the water as a lovely warmth overtook her. Then he lowered Anna's legs over his shoulders, down his chest, around his thighs, and entered her. And they came, he for the first time, she for the second, together.

Then they filled all the canteens.

And dried off.

And started through the meadow, aiming toward the mountains.

Two helicopters flew by in the distance.

White House War Room

"They're listening," Atwood said.

"Impossible," Glennie snorted.

"They knew the details of Allen's proposal."

Heads shook. Silence. Pervading the room was the sickening feeling that the enemy was utterly superior.

One of Buchanan's secure phones lit in front of him; he picked it up. It was McNulty. Talking so loud that everyone in the room could hear the sound of his voice in the receiver.

"Oh, I can imagine," Buchanan said. "Wanting to be patched through to the DCI—that's not a request they get every day at Langley. . . . Glennie? Yes, there's a Glennie here. A bug? Where? In his ear? A bug made of . . . of *flesh*?"

Buchanan put the receiver down. "I need a magnifying glass and tweezers," Buchanan said.

Glennie bent his head over the table, feeling silly; Buchanan searched first the left, then the right, looking, with his white hair and calm demeanor, like a country doctor.

"Aha."

"What the hell is it?" Glennie asked, quite repulsed by the feeling that he was some sort of cyborg.

"DNA-based transmitter," Buchanan said. "Instead of moving electrons around, it moves DNA molecules. There are a number of experimental computers based on this idea already running, at CMU and Stanford. At any rate, the scanners can't pick this beasty up."

Buchanan smashed his fist down on the bug. "Now, gentlemen, shall we talk?"

"I don't know what difference talk'll make. We have a grand total of four minutes, gentlemen."

"It's automatic," Buchanan said. "Right out of Kasakov's twisted textbook. We have no choice. It's not outright domination. If it were, if they were going to march in and rape and pillage, then it would be worth trying to torpedo their coast, and risk our population in the process. They of course realize that. And so they're after what might be called *quasi*-domination. You heard what this Bazakin said: a shortcut to the goals of *perestroika*. They want handouts in the future: food, oil, technology, and so on. And they want their border cleared of NATO troops. Given the situation, I'm afraid these are eminently reasonable requests."

"Compliance will buy us time," Newell said. "They can't watch our every move. Six months, a year—eventually we'll figure a way to penetrate their SBI with a proportionate retaliatory strike."

Randolph Atwood buried his face in his large hands.

"A year?" Glennie exclaimed. "Out of the question! I say we start right now to try to get a torpedo in."

"Could you do it in two minutes?" Newell asked.

"Not in two minutes, but I could—"

"Well," Newell followed up, "in two minutes we may emerge to a flattened city. Rubble, Admiral Glennie."

"All right," Glennie said, sweating now for the first time during the entire nightmare, "we call SACEUR and CINCEUR, tell 'em to pull out. That buys us time. We start right in on the attempt to get an A-bomb in Ivan's backyard. When we—"

"Mr. Glennie," Newell interrupted, "don't you think it would be prudent to first find out how good the *Starik*'s intelligence is? If they detect us working on either the nuclearized torpedo or the smuggling, they will strike again before we get to first base. Five minutes ago they were listening to us, for God's sake. That's more than enough reason to think they'll see us, the Navy, whoever, working on reengineering a torpedo or smuggling in a thermonuclear device."

Glennie's forehead beaded with sweat; he slammed his fist down on the table: sheets of paper, pencils, pens, phones—everything bounced into the air.

Within minutes Lances, GLBM's, and conventional tanks and artillery, not to mention the men themselves, were leaving Western Europe.

Caucasus Mountains

"I'll take Afghanistan, Nicki."

"Me too," replied the gunner. "Rebels are rebels, a known quantity. But what the fuck is this about? Two civilians? And where?"

"Who knows? We have our region, though."

"Hmm. Half the fucking Caucasus range."

Scarat Coniski, pilot, and Nicki Rukov, gunner, were bonded by near-death. They'd flown experimental Mi-28's together in Afghanistan; and one night an American-made Stinger blew up in their copter's composite armor-plated face. Scarat reached for the pyrotechnic charges that would blow the cockpit doors out and inflate bladders over which they were supposed to roll before opening their chutes. But Nicki screamed, "No! Insufficient altitude!" And then he manually activated the explosive charges that locked their restraint systems into place, and the two Soviet airmen dropped like rocks into a twenty-meter-per-second vertical descent, g forces tugging their flesh toward the heavens. The restraint system, though a prototype, worked as hoped: it snapped the two of them into erect positions upon impact, preventing their heads from smashing to pieces on the instrument panel.

Nicki, a broken femur; Scarat, two mutilated ankles.

But they healed.

And now they were back, in a glass-fiber five-blade main rotor Mi-29 attack helicopter, a prototype, the nastiest motherfucking attack copter Ivan had: turn rate, 180 degrees per second; top speed, nearly 250 knots; a 30-millimeter cannon, and an array of radar-guided missiles and rockets. The Mi-29's two Isotov TV4 turboshaft engines were shielded by infrared suppressors, shielding the copter from overhead enemy sensors; the 29 was designed to fly nap-of-the earth missions, skimming up and down over the roughest terrain like a supersonic flea.

"What do you think, comrade? Should we test the Flir system?"

"Why not?" Nicki responded. "We have nothing better to do."

The Mi-29 was equipped with a Flir—forward-looking infrared—sensing system. The Flir sensor was a seven-inch ball mounted on the exterior of the craft; the sensor slewed in azimuth, which allowed it to transmit horizon-stabilized images back to the pilot and gunner even when the copter was rocking and rolling.

Coniski and Rukov strapped on their Flir helmets: a computer graphics image of the outside world was presented in each eyepiece.

"Oh, shit," Scarat said, "this is beautiful."

Nicki just smiled. "Can you adjust it for low radiance?" he asked.

"No problem. Boresighting is a matter of pushing a few buttons. There."

They moved their heads, and the Flir sensor outside moved in parallel. Everything radiating heat above room temperature lit up like a Christmas tree: they saw the glow of animals, at 307 degrees Kelvin, just seven degrees above the threshold of discernibility.

"*We* built this?"

"I'm sure the Americans cooked up the initial designs."

"It's gorgeous."

"The system or the scenery?"

"Both."

They skimmed between two snow-capped peaks. Altitude, eight thousand feet. Then down. To a plateau.

"What's that?" Scarat said.

"It's fucking *them*," Nicki said. "They're glowing like lightbulbs.'

Scarat grabbed his stick and threw the Mi-29 into a steep dive. Nicki armed one of his infrared missiles.

"Anna! Run!"

He grabbed her hand, and they ran together—into the start of a ravine.

Then: light. Brilliant as a thousand suns. And pebbles everywhere.

"You okay?"

"Yes," she coughed. "I thought you said they wanted you back alive."

"They don't seem to anymore."

"Really?"

"How does it work?" Nicki inquired of his pilot. "We don't see an image. So they're dead?"

"Well, a corpse *is* cool, comrade. But I'm afraid they made it into the gorge. We're not supposed to kill them, anyway."

"Ahh, bullshit. Some pencil-pushing bureaucrat's just being anal-retentive. I'll take the heat."

"I was hoping you'd say that, comrade."

Scarat Coniski flung his copter into a spiraling vertical climb, and then shot her forward over the top of the narrow ravine.

Anna and Alex had reached the other end of the ravine. When they peered out, they saw the Mi-29 hovering, black as black and baleful as the devil himself.

"Shit," Alex said.

"You catch that, Nicki?" Scarat said.

"A head?" the gunner said.

"Mm hmm," the pilot responded.

"This system is a work of art, comrade. You know how many rebels we could have toasted if we'd had this in Afghanistan?"

Both men kept activated their helmet-mounted display, which projected Flir imagery on two combiner glasses situated directly in front of their eyes. With regard to living beings, those falling into the selected portion of the electromagnetic spectrum, the two Russians had superhuman eyesight.

"Let's return to the other side," Anna said.

"They can't be that dumb," Alex said.

"What do you mean?"

"Well, either the copter stays here or it goes to the other side. But either way, a Russian gets out."

Anna eased an eye around the edge of the gorge.

"See you, Nicki. Stay in contact."

The gunner saluted and smiled and then jumped out, holding an assault rifle. He pressed himself to the ground as the Mi-29 shot upward, screaming. Then he stood erect, took a potshot at the entrance to the gorge, and laughed loudly.

Anna pulled her head back just in time. Dust from the bullet flew.

"Alex!"

He was looking up the walls of the ravine. Which were worse than vertical. And smooth as glass. He shook his head. "Ever been spelunking?" he asked.

"What?"

"Caving."

"No, is there a cave?"

"Possibly. Come on."

"Nicki?"

"Here."

"I'm down, and standing at the mouth of the gorge."

"Me too."

"Let's do it," Scarat said.

"What do the Americans say?"

"Roge."

"Right. Roge, baby, let's do it."

At each end, they entered.

"That crack?" she said.

"Hopefully. Come on."

She squeezed in, he followed, scraping his back and chest. He lit and threw a match—which illuminated a small but bona fide cavern.

"The world is filled with caves," he whispered. "You have to know where to look. There's a cave in Central Park, you know. In the upper reaches."

"Manhattan?"

"You know how much money they saved when the subway system was built?"

They heard the cackle of a radio outside.

"Here, light a match."

She did.

"Now, let me have one of the sweaters," he said. "And keep lighting the matches."

"What are you doing?"

"Making a ball of yarn," he said as he unknit the sweater.

Scarat almost shot his gunner, and Nicki almost shot his pilot.

"Fuck!" Scarat said.

Nicki shook his head. "This thing is four feet wide. The sides go fucking straight up."

"There's a side entrance," Scarat said. "Has to be. You go back to that end, I'll go back to the other. You take this side," the pilot said, slapping against one rock face, "I'll take the other. We check every inch."

"Roge."

"Think we could fly the copter?" he asked.

"I couldn't."

"All the insane shit I've done in my thirty-two years, and I've never flown. Always wanted to."

"Procrastination," Anna said.

"Mmm."

"We probably could jump them. They'll find the crack sooner or later. And they'll have to slide in. One rock bashed against a head in the dark. Even if they have lights of some sort, we'd have a very good shot."

"Well, I'm a dancer, remember? I can't fly that helicopter, Alexander."

"Wonder how hard it would be to teach myself."

"Why not use it as a backup."

"What do you mean?"

"Well, first we see if this comes out someplace. If it does, great. If it doesn't, we come back and try to take the copter. Logical?"

"Very. 'Course, by the time we come back, there may be *fifty* copters out there."

"The alternative?"

They heard a hand groping at the entrance. Then excited talk into a radio.

"All right," Alex whispered. "In we go."

He lit and threw a match, glimpsed the receding tunnel, and they started walking in, hand in hand, slowly in the black, every once in a while throwing another match, letting out the yarn.

The yarn proved prudent: there were many forks. It was like crawling through a mass of underground spaghetti. But then they ran out.

"That's it on the yarn," Alex said. "Give me another."

Anna dropped off her pack, pulled out another sweater.

"Light."

He unknit another, tied the two ends together.

"Okay."

They walked, crawled, squeezed. His watch held a compass, and glowed, and by it they stayed in a southern course.

Dead end.

Back to the last choice point. A different tunnel. Dead end.

Back to the choice point again. A different route. Another dead end.

Tracing back the yarn to . . .

"Oh, shit," he said. "Light." Alex was holding the yarn. "Feel this."

Anna wrapped her fingers around the yarn. Which was moving of its own accord.

"The bastards found it," Alex said. "They're following us."

A light in the distance, north, was now unmistakable.

"Pocket it," he directed.

She squeezed the yarn into the pocket of her jeans.

"Let's go, Anna. No more matches."

They moved like molasses, feeling their way along.

"It ends," Nicki said.

"Ends?"

"Mmm."

"Well, back to the copter," Scarat said. "They could be anywhere. This is a fucking maze."

"Damn!" Nicki said.

Ten feet away, hiding, not breathing, Anna jumped beside Nelsen.

He knew before he told her. It was the temperature. He had charted by it many times before. Dead ends were slightly warmer. That was one thing about caves: inside, the temperature was a constant. Except when outside and inside air mingled.

"On what basis are you choosing?"

"Trust me."

It still took a long time, given their pace. But presently: a frigid breeze. Then light. And then, the heavens: a full moon, limpid, sparkling stars.

"I was ready to die in there, you know."

"You know how many times I've been ready to die, Anna?"

She snuggled up against him; it was frigid at the mouth of the cave. A helicopter flew across the moon, distant, the hum of its rotors like a whisper.

"When you're ready to die, Death runs. That's my theory. When you vow not to go; when you think about cancer, and clogging of the arteries, and driving defensively—when you think like that, Death, laughing, comes."

"Such a cheerful theory."

"It's been fun accumulating the empirical evidence in support of it."

"How far is Turkey?" she asked.

"From where these mountains end, Turkey is a stone's throw."

There was no end in sight. Just peak after snow-covered peak.

"I don't know if I can do it."

"Someone once told me that ballet dancers are the most highly conditioned athletes in the world."

"A ballet dancer told you this?" she asked.

"Yes."

She nodded. "Mmm."

"Come on. Our two friends may well have called for backup by now. The sooner the better. When you walk, move your toes inside your boots; keep your fingers moving too. If we move, we'll live."

"If we stop?"

"Up here? Well, then we'll . . . On the other hand, maybe Death doesn't like it here. Noah defied her, after all."

"Noah?"

"The Ark, Anna. You can see Mount Agri in the

distance. There." He pointed to a moon-ignited peak on the horizon, southeast. "It's called Ararat in the Bible."

"You've been there."

"Twice. I've seen it."

"Are you serious?"

"Completely."

"Where *haven't* you climbed?"

"The Pamirs."

"In Russia?"

"Yup."

"Where haven't you caved?"

"You're not going to believe this. Kentucky. I've never been in the world's largest cave: Mammoth. It's an American state park. Only about a third of it has been charted."

"What's your favorite cave?"

"Howe."

"Howe?"

"Upstate New York. There are underground lakes no one else knows of. I go there when . . ."

"Akiko?"

"Are you telepathic?" he asked.

"Have you forgotten her?"

Nelsen kissed her and said, "Completely."

They set off. South. Toward the border.

Now and then the stars blinked from helicopters passing in front of them. Inside one of the distant copters, Nicki and Scarat, heads covered by their black Flir helmets, looked down, seeing nothing.

Turkey

Minutes after NATO's 39th Tactical Group removed their thirty-six nuclear-capable F-4's and F-16's from the Incirlik Air Base in Turkey, leaving the city-unto-itself looking like a ghost town, Kasakov screamed in on a now-*Starik*-controlled Backfire bomber. An Mi-28 attack copter was waiting for him. He knew exactly where he was going.

Sunrise. They'd taken cover only twice during the night, squeezing into crevices to avoid infrared sensors. In the west, the Black Sea. In the east, bending toward the south, the majestic edge of the Caucasus Mountains, at the edge of which glistened the Caspian.

And to the south? Beneath them?

Turkey. NATO.

They began the descent.

"Going down seems harder on the knees," she commented.

"For some it is."

The foothills. The warmth of the sun at the lower elevation was wonderful. They passed over the border uneventfully.

They descended, finally, to the edge of a vast open plain dotted with flocks of nomadic sheep, and shepherds with canes and turbans, and, rising in the distance, the golden dome of a mosque.

"Ani," he said. "We've made it."

They ran, holding hands; they ran through a gate in the tall, massive basalt walls surrounding the city of Ani. Churches. Mosques. Dusty windblown streets. But no people. Rubble. Ruins. Stones strewn randomly about.

"What is this place?" she asked. "It's a ghost town."

"Good old Ghenghis Khan," Alex said. "He razed it. No one returned."

"We could become nomads," she said, seeing a shepherd in the distance, wandering past a jewel-laden mosque, guiding his sheep.

Then, over the tan, dusty, monochromatic plain, Nelsen saw it. On a copter not far off. A red star.

"Jesus."

"What is it?"

"Turkey's in NATO, for God's sake."

"So?"

"That's a Soviet helicopter."

She looked up and toward the sun, too much glare to see much of anything. "Are you sure?"

Exercises? A NATO craft dressed up to look like Ivan?

Then he saw another. Closer. And another red star.

"Something's very wrong, Annastasia. Very."

He pulled her into a long-abandoned mosque, and, looking out through the vast doors, a limitless tiled dome above them, he spotted the vehicle. They dashed out, holding hands, Alex leading.

"We need camouflage. Get in."

"What is this?" Anna asked, her face pressed up against the black, scraping stubble of a goat farmer's face.

"This, my dear, is a *dolmus*. And it's about the only way we're going to be able to travel without being spotted."

A goat nibbled at Anna's neck. A bale of cotton was pressed up against her thigh. The men and women who were packed onto the mini-bus like sardines looked uniformly fierce. They all seemed to be staring at her.

"Where is this thing headed?" she whispered.

"Didn't you read the sign?"

A horde of copters overflew the bus, their rotors drowning out Anna's whispered reply.

"What?" he said.

"No. I said no. I didn't read it."

"Van," he said as the bus rolled on, Mount Ararat in the distance, the castle of Tushpa approaching.

They jumped off in Van, beneath giant carved friezes of Jonah and the Whale, Adam and Eve, and

St. George and the Dragon. Anna's rubles had thrown the *dolmus'* fare-taker into a murderous fit, and to pacify him Alex had ripped off her necklace and handed it over.

"Do you have any idea how much that was worth?"

"We don't need any more enemies, Anna."

They walked.

When the station came into view, she said, "Another train?"

"You got any better ideas?"

"Where does it go?"

"You know, I've been thinking, Columbia must be damn short on geography."

"Indulge me, Professor."

"West, Iran; east, a long haul, is Istanbul."

"Which destination is ours?"

"I don't know. I'm leaning toward Iran. Peter and his pals might've nailed NATO, but I doubt they have the Iranians in their pocket. Then again, if we lie low, we may be able to cruise to Istanbul."

"Do you have any money left?" he asked.

"Yes. But very little."

"You can take a train from Van to Istanbul for thirty thousand liras, Anna."

She squinted; thirty thousand seemed a large number.

"That's about thirty American dollars," he said. "You have that in rubles?"

She nodded.

The ticket agent, bearded and surly and silent, pushed her money back without speaking.

"Give me your watch." The agent's eyes lit up upon fingering the gold Rolex. "Two for Istanbul," Alexander said.

When the train chugged up, they emerged from the domed mosquelike station through decorated glass into the hot sun—and there he was. Kasakov. With a gun.

"I banked on your predictability, Dr. Nelsen."

The train was now still, behind the *Starik*'s leader. The platform was almost completely deserted. Two Turks saw Peter and his gun; they scampered off. A conductor at the other end of the platform detrained. He was too far off to be of help, and had he been closer he would only have promptly stepped back on board for cover. The three were alone.

"This time, you'll have to kill me, Pete."

"You know I can't do that. You really are the only one who truly understands the system. Our credibility is based on our ability to maintain it, indeed to enhance it."

"So we're back to this wound-him stuff? Shoot his balls off and then cart him back to Mother Russia?"

Peter cocked his weapon. "No. You're right. That might be messy. Maybe minus your virility, which Anna here seems to think so much of, you wouldn't be yourself."

Peter took one quick step forward, placed the barrel against Anna's temple, and wrapped his other arm harshly around her neck.

"Now. We're going to walk calmly to my copter."

"So I'm supposed to love her, is that it, Pete?"

Nelsen saw Anna's eyes flare.

"Why do you and I have to be so fundamentally different? I don't see any jealousy in *your* eyes. Maybe I'll just walk, and let the lady die. Maybe you were right. Maybe she dances better than she fucks."

Anna squirmed. Her eyes were wide. Kasakov pressed the barrel into her temple, depressing her skin. He looked a bit flustered for the first time.

"You're bluffing."

"And let me tell you something else, Petey. Right about now your system is fucked up real bad. Why don't you call home?"

"I don't believe you on either count. I'm counting to five. Then one of the most perfectly shaped heads on the face of the earth will have a big gaping hole it. Do you understand?"

"Suit yourself, Pete." Nelsen shrugged and without delay boarded. The train was already moving as he walked up the stairs, waving with a smile at the two Russians.

Anna shouted, "Alex! Alex!!"

"In love, my dear, you really are cursed. If I don't kill you, my word won't mean much in the future, and I couldn't have that. By the way, I have a thousand men flanking this rail line. Half at Tatvan to the west. Half at the border to Iran. Coming alone would have been just plain stu—"

It was funny, but Anna sensed the blow before Peter did: one second she was in a vise, the next she was free. The toe of Nelsen's shoe had rammed into the base of Peter's skull at approximately ninety miles per hour. The American, upon boarding, had raced to the rear of the train, and as it pulled up behind the Russian, he had struck. Perfectly.

The gun clattered to the concrete. Anna dashed to the wall of the station and leaned against it for support, panting, holding her throat.

Nelsen jumped down.

Kasakov, still dazed, glimpsed the gun, half in focus, half out, and lunged for it. But just as his hand reached it, Nelsen pinned the Russian's wrist with his shoe.

Peter, the world still a blur, operating on instinct and adrenaline, drove his head up into the American's crotch, which freed up his wrist. He had the gun now.

He rolled and took aim at Nelsen's leg, but the scientist kicked the weapon out of the Russian's hand before he could fire.

Anna found the gun at her feet. She picked it up.

Kasakov unsheathed the hunting knife from his leg;

stood; smiled. And that's when the top half of his skull disappeared.

"Did he say anything about a backup?"

"Yes. Soldiers to the west and east."

"Something's wrong here. I need a fucking phone."

He dragged her into the station's tiled, ill-lit bar. A row of uncooperative black eyes atop chiseled cheekbones turned from their drinks.

"A phone. Do you have a phone?"

The bartender was wiping a glass dry with a filthy towel. He looked like an ax murderer. A dead man was lying on the concrete outside, half his brains blown away, but in here the *raki* was flowing.

Nelsen played charades, holding an invisible receiver up to his ear. "A phone," he repeated.

The bartender moved his head half a centimeter in the direction of a phone that looked to have come straight from Alexander Graham Bell's laboratory.

The operator spoke enough English to understand "America." Nelsen gave his number. And then:

"Buchanan! What the hell's going on here? I'm in Turkey. Van. Over the border. The bloody Russkies *own* the place." Nelsen looked at his watch. "The system's trashed, Admiral. It's gone. Everything. All the software. There shouldn't be a piece of code left by now. Do you understand? Trashed."

He hung up.

His system in Providence converted the incoming voice message to text, and then, following the preprogrammed procedure Nelsen had left humming in his office, sent it on to Buchanan.

"You sabotaged it?"

"Yep. Delayed reaction. Enough to follow *part* of your advice."

Anna shook her head, kissed him on the cheek, pulled back, and smiled her magic smile: her green eyes connected with the edges of her mouth somehow, and something happened: you felt the warmth of her alight upon your spirit. Despite the trek, no sleep, dirt smudged on her face; despite uncombed hair and baggy tattered clothes; despite the fact that she'd killed a man—despite all this, Annastasia was, Nelsen noted, as beautiful as could be.

D.C. Suburbs

Buchanan, in a night robe and slippers, was padding up from the kitchen to the master bedroom, bearing a midnight snack of Ben & Jerry's Chunky Monkey. On a whim, he decided to look in on his computer. And there it was.

"Trashed?"

Buchanan dropped his bowl.

His wife, in the adjacent room, screamed, "James?"

33

Again

February 25—Oval Office

"James, have you any idea what you're asking me to do?"

"He's done it, Mr. President," Buchanan said.

"How can you be sure? Some half-baked message in the middle of the night? You want me to risk losing New York City because you get a paragraph-long computer note? I've already fucked up. I've fucked up like no one else, with the possible exception of Stalin himself, when he treated Hitler like an angel up until right before Barbarossa broke. Stalin had a breakdown. I'm not so far away. When this gets out, you think a black man's gonna hold an office in this country again? The black man's gonna be lucky if he runs a local PTA, Admiral."

"He's done it. I know it."

"How do you know it was Nelsen that sent it?"

"It sounded like him."

"It was text."

"The *text* sounded like him."

"Oh, Christ."

"He said he was in Van, across the border. Light at NSA says he's been watching copters buzz the Caucasus Mountains for the past twenty-four hours. This would explain things."

"Couldn't the Russians have tortured him? Learned about Dendrite? They could have sent it."

"But why *would* they, Mr. Atwood? They already have what they want. The *Starik* doesn't want to kill for the hell of it."

"Don't be so sure."

"I know them," Buchanan said. "I knew Kasakov."

"You know them."

"Yes, I do. Its Berzin's GRU all over again. Techno-spies who believe, with all their hearts, not in Marx, but in Great Russia."

"So you want me to try again."

"Yes," Buchanan said. "One more time. If it gets through, this is all over."

"And if it doesn't?"

"Well, like you said, New York."

"Or Boston, or Philly, or Miami. Dear God in heaven."

"Look, Nelsen says it's trashed. He *says* it's trashed."

"What if it was and they fixed it?" Atwood asked. "If you're right, he's been wandering in the mountains for hours."

"If it's not fixed now, Mr. President, eventually it *will* be. And then you'll be the nigger who *really* fucked up."

Atwood paused; then said: "This is recorded, you know. Nixon had it right, in principle. I've got *everything* recorded. This missile doesn't make it, history's gonna hate your ass too, Mr. DCI."

Buchanan nodded.

Atwood punched a button.

"Get Glennie in the war room. Now."

Atwood made good and sure Glennie understood completely. The conversation was recorded for posterity. And then the three of them sat there, in the war room, the world glowing above them.

"All right. Fuck the D-5. We'll cruise the bastards."

Atwood picked up a receiver. "Bill, do it." That was it; Glennie hung up.

"Hell you doing?" Atwood said. "You didn't tell your man what to do?"

"What do you think, Randy, while you've been frettin' in the Oval Office, me and my boys have been picking our noses? We've been ready to go on this since yesterday afternoon. I've got another Trident. North. In the Laptev Sea. Under the ice. She'll bust out from underneath and launch a slicum. Right where we figure it is."

"Where what is?" Atwood inquired.

"Their SBI, of course. Your boy was sloppy there, James. He could have told you. We've been watchin' planes fly in and out of a low-priority hydro plant on the Lena River for weeks. Only it ain't a hydro plant. It's the nerve center. Trust me." Glennie nodded up to the situation screen. A green dot glowed in the water north of Siberia. "There she is."

A red dot appeared next to the green, smaller; and the red began moving south.

Glennie cracked his knuckles.

Tereshkovo

"Look," Ignatov said, pointing. "They're trying again. Must be a slicum."

The *Starik* saw the missile, lit on their own situation screen, a luminescent green dot.

"Most illogical," Ignatov said.

"*Too* illogical," Bazakin said, drawing calmly on a Prima. "What's the demon defense like on the northern perimeter?"

"Very crowded," Ignatov said with a smile.

"Pearl Harbor all over again," Bazakin said.

"Pearl Harbor?" Matra said.

"The Nipponese believed their surprise attack

would be so swift, so devastating, that America would surrender on the spot. Instead America risked everything and fought. Well, they're sure as hell risking everything now. I didn't want to hit a countervalue target. I really didn't want to. Miami, Ignatov?"

Ignatov nodded.

"Wait a minute," Markov said. "It's through."

"No, just hold on," Bazakin said. "It hasn't come inland far enough."

"No, comrade. It's through," Markov repeated.

"What!" Matra exclaimed.

"The system's dead," Markov said. "The Neurocubes are dead."

"Explain," Bazakin said.

"I don't know. They're just dead. Blank."

"Go to manual," Bazakin instructed.

No one moved. The green dot had moved well in over land. And was speeding south.

"They're aiming for us!" Matra exclaimed.

"Go to manual," Bazakin shouted again. "Fuck the Neurocubes. And fuck this view. Get us local."

Markov clicked to local video, turned everything on the northern horizon, and threw himself down beside the joystick. He was on his own now. He had a shot: Nelsen hadn't defused this part of the system.

"Launch a demon off our airstrip," Bazakin said with a voice of iron.

A demon lifted into the sky; they saw it hovering. The horizon was clear.

"According to over-the-horizon data, it's almost here," Bazakin said.

And then they saw it. A blur. A streak.

"Markov!"

"Markov, steer!"

The demon took off toward the incoming missile. Sweat popped out of Markov's pores, drenching him. He held the stick, moved it in utter concentration.

"Steady, Markov."

Two blurs. Markov guided the demon. The *Starik* watched intently. They saw the demon rise over the horizon, and they saw two plumes form an X. But no explosion.

"You missed!" Matra screamed. Performing the most useless act of violence since the dawn of man, she clubbed Markov on the head.

Why Matra, Ignatov, and Markov ducked is hard to say. Instinct, probably. But instinct based on what? Bazakin asked internally, looking at them during the last few seconds. There would be no pain, he knew. And sure as hell no point in ducking.

34

Home, Sweet Home

February 25—Eastern Turkey

The helicopters in their path had flown off like frightened birds, a flock from the east, a flock from the west. Alex knew Buchanan had received the call.

"How did you manage the sabotage?" Anna asked.

"Ah. Well. In digital circuitry, a single transistor performs the most elementary operations of Boolean logic. And as a result it takes dozens of transistors to accomplish even simple addition. I told you once that Neurocubes are analog devices. Well, the analog approach uses circuitry voltages to represent numerical values directly. You gain tremendous speed this way—a few transistors, for example, can extract logarithms—but you lose accuracy in the storage of information. Analog information degrades and drifts with time. So what happens in these Neurocubes is that information is *stored* digitally, but converted to analog form when *computation* begins. I made one little change when no one was looking: I made each of the Neurocubes work in thoroughgoing analog fashion, so that data is stored analogically. And hence all the code we assembled was bound to decay, irretrievably, over time."

Anna looked at him.

"Got that, Annastasia?"

"Oh, all of it," she said as their train chugged up

in front of them. There was only a red stain where Kasakov had died. "What about your friends?"

"One whisper."

"Sorry?"

"I told them to get lost during their vacation in Yakutsk. With any luck, they should be flying home right about now."

In Istanbul, when they detrained, Anna said to the ticket agent, a severe-looking dark-skinned fellow, "We want a sleeper."

"No problem. The *Istanbul Express* leaves in about . . . uh, ninety minutes. You can pick up a sleeper in Belgrade for the rest of the trip through Yugoslavia and Bulgaria."

"Hold on," Alex said. "Isn't there another alternative?"

The agent looked at the pair before him. They were in rags. Students traveling on a wing and a prayer. He saw them every day. Although these were *older* students. Graduate school, the Turk surmised.

"No, the *Istanbul Express*. That's it," he said.

"Come now, sir," Alex said. "There's no other train to Vienna?"

"Well," the agent huffed, "there's the *Orient Express*, but you two are in no—"

"We'll take two seats. You let me borrow a phone to make a collect call and you'll be able to retire in fifteen minutes, my friend."

Alex to Matt; Matt back; the Turk was rich; they had their tickets. Departure: five minutes.

They walked down into Sirkeci Station, where, glimmering, stood the *Orient Express*.

"This isn't quite your style, is it, Alexander?"

Anna was disrobing. Slowly. Seductively.

"Trips you find worth taking, after all, invariably involve potential loss of life and limb. Correct?"

She slid her finger up a thigh. Undid her blouse.

"But you have a partner now. And your partner thrives in a bit of luxury. You've dragged me through tunnels, over mountains, under trains, in freight cars. That's your element. This is mine," she said, exposing her breasts. "Where you go, I'll go. But sometimes we'll reverse it, okay?"

Her nipples were erect. She brushed them.

"I'm a dancer. With the Bolshoi. I like a little warmth. I'd be fun on something like the unsybaritic *Istanbul Express*, of course, but here I'm more than fun. Here I'm hot."

She was stroking herself now.

Mahogany paneling, brass highlights; cream-colored muraled ceiling; a small window framed by curtains held in place by tasseled cords; a spotless, gleamingly white marble lavatory; dark green rug, with a hint of red flora; brass doorknobs and headboards. Their bed was palatial.

She sat upon it.

"These are the kind of accommodations I take to. We've done it in lakes, on planes, in trains. All over God's creation. But we haven't done it in such a place as this, Alexander."

She spread her legs. Coral pink. He could see the moisture. She was fingering herself.

"Now, I want you to take me. Completely. Thoroughly. A little violently if you want. And then I want to dress for dinner. In a gown. And I want you in a tux. And if we play *under* the table, okay, but *on* the table I want silver flatware and bone china, and on my china I want food, real food. Can you accommodate me, Alexander?" she said, her clit swollen and visible from five feet away, her legs as far apart as they could go.

Epilogue

Soft Wars

March 17—Palm Springs

They were a most formidable trio. Donald Rizzi ran IBM. Walter Reitman ran what was left over. And James Buchanan ran the CIA. They were golfing. Thunderbird. Buchanan and Reitman shared a cart; the enormous Rizzi had his own, and needed every inch of it. It was amazing how a slick, handsome billionaire like Reitman could look like a certifiable fool on the links. With a short, choppy swing, he duck-hooked every bloody thing he hit. Rizzi, on the other hand, carried thirty clubs in his bag.

"Donald," Reitman said, "aren't you allowed only fourteen or so?"

"On any given shot," Rizzi replied, "I'm only choosing from among fourteen clubs."

Buchanan was relaxed, smoked his pipe between shots, but was awful nonetheless. Four out of five shots—shanked violently.

But they weren't really in town to play golf. They were in Palm Springs to pay a visit.

After their round they drove over to the multimillion-dollar Spanish-style house that was their destination. Buchanan knocked. An elderly woman with diamond earrings answered.

"Hello. Mrs. Rosenkrantz?" Buchanan said.

"Yes?"

"Could we have a word with your husband?"

"Mr. Reitman, is that you?" she asked, looking back to the rearmost visitor.

Reitman nodded solemnly. "We'd like to see Josiah, Margaret."

"Of course. Come in."

They found him huddled in his office. Computers. Optical disks. Scanners. Pictures of the brain. Oversize monitors.

Professor Rosenkrantz recognized his employer, Reitman.

And Reitman said, "Josiah, these are two friends of mine. Donald Rizzi." Reitman nodded in Rizzi's direction; the IBM CEO nodded. "Donald heads IBM. And James Buchanan," Reitman said, nodding toward the DCI. "James runs the Central Intelligence Agency."

Rosenkrantz looked ill already.

"James?" Reitman invited.

"Why don't we sit down, gentlemen?" They did. Buchanan filled, tamped, and lit his pipe, calmly puffed out a few sweet-smelling clouds of Captain Black. "Now, Mr. Rosenkrantz, let's be forthright, shall we? Walt tells me you've been exporting some of his products to some pretty unsavory chaps. And Donald tells me you've been tinkering with software on some of his parallel machines. Oh, what a tangled web we weave, Professor."

If Rosenkrantz had looked any older, any more helpless and brittle, he would have disintegrated on the spot.

"I'm afraid, Josiah, that your Soviet employers have suffered a setback. Quite a *big* setback, in fact. I don't think Directorate Z will be sending you any new business anytime soon. So we'd like you to come work for us. Be a double agent, as we say. Maybe feed people stuff that blows up in their faces, you know? Throw some of your viruses in the direction of our enemies. See what I mean?"

Rosenkrantz didn't respond at first. He swallowed. Twice. And it was funny, indeed Buchanan wasn't sure it made any sense at all, but the DCI suddenly saw Rosenkrantz, sitting here in his mansion, as Liberace grown old, wrinkled amid glitter, shriveled underneath a cloak of gems.

"Enemies," the scientist echoed. "We don't have any en—"

"The Sovs, no, not with your lovely little clique vaporized. And our terrorist friends don't use computers much. But you never know about the future, Professor."

Rosenkrantz looked at Buchanan, then at the other two men.

"Of course," Buchanan said, drawing on his pipe and releasing a series of tobacco rings, "you could politely refuse. In which case Walt and Donald here won't like you much. Walt and Donald have a lot of, shall we say, *pull*—with the authorities. They file charges, Josiah, and, well, this quaint little Spanish villa, your wife's earrings . . . *poof*, gone. Do we understand each other?"

Rosenkrantz nodded.

"Excellent," Buchanan said. "As a sign of your cooperation, we'd like you to jump right into things. Walt here's building what he calls a . . . Walt?"

"An Encephalocube."

"Right," Buchanan resumed. "Now, we'd like you to work with this computer, Josiah. See what you can do to its software. We want it to be real contagious. Then you give it back to us, and when we find an enemy, we export it for you." Buchanan laughed, looked at the IBM CEO and the venture capitalist, and said, "At any rate, Josiah, we export your products and someone has a little epidemic on their hands. You see, we in the Agency, we don't like cold wars, Lord knows we don't like Star Wars. We like Soft Wars. We think that's the future."

GLOSSARY, TECHNICAL TERMS

ABM Treaty—The 1972 treaty between the U.S. and USSR restricting the deployment and possibly the testing and research of antiballistic-missile technologies.

AI—Artificial Intelligence. The branch of computer science whose ultimate goal is the building of a robot that behaves like people.

ALCM—Air-Launched Cruise Missile, which is a cruise missile carried by and launched from aircraft. See also *Cruise Missile.*

ASAT—Antisatellite systems, weapons designed to destroy an opponent's space-based aircraft. Given that the featured technology in *Soft Wars* is SBI, it is interesting to note that the first "modern" ASAT weapon, pursued by President Carter, was a small air-launched ASAT designed to be carried by an F-15 jet and to destroy its target by high-speed collision (as is the case with the "demons" of *Soft Wars*).

ASW—Antisubmarine Warfare. Measures designed to identify and track an adversary's submarine fleet.

Ballistic Missile—Any missile designed to propel a payload up and through the atmosphere and then release it to travel to its target by gravity and various aerodynamic forces.

Bitnet—A low-speed computer network used extensively for communication between machines of various types around the globe. Other networks mentioned in *Soft Wars* are Ethernet, a higher-speed network, and Technet, a small specialized network proposed for an area of New Mexico.

BMD—Ballistic Missile Defense. Star Wars, or SDI, or even for that matter SBI—these are all types of BMD systems. These systems were being actively researched even well before 1960. The U.S. Army had two programs going in the 1950's and early 1960's (the Zeus and Nike-X), which were designed to defend American cities against nuclear attack. In 1967 President Johnson decided to build the Sentinel ABM missile. (BMD and ABM can be used interchangeably.)

BMEWS—Ballistic Missile Early Warning System. A system of radars located at Clear, Alaska, Thule, Greenland, and Fylingdales Moor, U.K., providing warning and tracking of Soviet ICBM launches.

Boost Phase—The flight of a land-based ICBM usually begins with the silo cover popping open. The missile is usually ejected by hot gases, and its flight starts for real when the first-stage booster fires. Then, later, the first stage falls away and the second-stage engine takes over. (In the MX, this process iterates.) The portion of flight from the earth's surface to the point at which the last stage stops burning is called boost phase. In *Soft Wars*, "boost-phase interception" refers to the interception of a ballistic missile while it is in boost phase. The "demons" in *Soft Wars* are unable to achieve boost-phase interception; they attack warheads in mid-course and reentry phases.

Cellular Automata—A mathematical computing device equal in power to a Turing machine (see below), but especially useful for modeling parallel machines. (Described to an appreciable degree in the book.)

CI—Counterintelligence.

CIA—Central Intelligence Agency. The chief intelligence agency of the United States. Founded in 1947. The CIA was the successor to the Office of Strategic Services (OSS) of WWII fame. Headquartered in Langley, Virginia, which is a suburb of Washington, D.C.

C^3—Command, Control, Communications, and Intelligence. The web of equipment, people, and procedures used by the leadership and commanders at all levels of a given country to monitor and direct the operation of military forces in times of both war and peace.

Connectionism—The approach to AI which takes the flesh-and-blood composition of the human brain seriously, and tries to map this composition into a computing device. Connectionists generally oppose those (*e.g.*, logicists; see *Logicism*) who don't think the actual structure and constitution of the brain are important for AI. Connectionism's strength, so far, has been in getting a machine to learn.

Counterforce—The use of strategic forces against the weaponry and command and control centers of an opponent, rather than against, say, population centers.

Countervalue—The use of strategic forces against the population centers of an adversary.

Cruise Missile—An air-breathing missile that is essentially a pilotless airplane. Most cruise missiles fly at subsonic speeds (*super*sonic ones turn up in *Soft Wars*). They are difficult to detect by radar, can carry nuclear, conventional, or chemical warheads, and can be launched from a great variety of platforms.

Decoy—BM's designed to thwart BMD's carry decoys—objects intended to confuse defense systems. The "bus" that carries warheads can also carry a vast number of very light metallic objects, called chaff, which reflect radar and confuse the image seen by a defensive system.

DEFCON—A rating system for ranking the readiness status of U.S. nuclear forces. DEFCON 2, the level just before wartime conditions, was reached during the Cuban missile crisis in October 1962, at which time President Kennedy is said to have gauged the chances of nuclear war at between one in three and fifty-fifty. Kennedy stated that if a missile from Cuba was launched against a country in the Western Hemisphere, a full U.S. retaliatory strike would rain down on the USSR.

DEW Line—The Distant Early Warning. A string of thirty-one conventional radars running along the arctic shore from western Alaska to Iceland. Used for the detection of aircraft and cruise missiles.

DIA—Defense Intelligence Agency. Established in 1961 in order to coordinate intelligence activities of the military services. DIA is also the intelligence agency for the Joint Chiefs of Staff.

ES—Expert System. The branch of computer science in which programs that replicate human expertise in restricted domains are created. For example, there are at present expert systems for diagnosing illness, locating mineral deposits, and configuring computer systems.

FBI—Federal Bureau of Investigation. A U.S. agency under the power of the Attorney General. Responsible for domestic counterespionage, counterintelligence, etc. Established in 1908 (then named Bureau of Intelligence) within the Department of Justice. In 1924 the FBI was formed and J. Edgar Hoover was named director.

First-Strike Capability—The ability to launch a paralyzing first strike against one's adversary.

Flexible Response—The doctrine of being able to respond to invasion with various levels of force, including nuclear force.

GRU—Glavnoye Razvedyvatelnoye Upravlenie. The chief intelligence directorate of the General Staff, i.e., the Soviet military intelligence directorate. It is also referred to as the Fourth Bureau of the Soviet General Staff. Established in 1920 by Leon Trotsky.

GSI— Gigascale integration. The stage in computer chip design in which each chip contains at least a billion transistors.

Hot Line—The colloquial expression for the direct communication link between Washington and Moscow. First installed in the wake of the Cuban missile crisis.

ICBM—Intercontinental Ballistic Missile. A land-based ballistic missile able to deliver a warhead to a range of about 3,500 miles.

IJCAI— International Joint Conference on Artificial Intelligence. The most comprehensive and prestigious conference for presented papers in the world of Artificial Intelligence research.

Illegal—An espionage agent who comes into a country under the guise of a fabricated identity.

INF—Intermediate-Range Nuclear Forces. These forces are theater nuclear forces, that is, weapon systems based in the areas in which they would be used. The U.S. and USSR recently signed a treaty eliminating some INF weapons.

KGB—Komitet Gosudarstvenny Bezopasnosti. The Committee for State Security. Since 1954 responsible for state security and internal security during the years 1960–66. (Internal security now handled by MVD—Minister of Internal Affairs.) KGB is the successor to several Soviet intelligence organs that evolved from Cheka, which was established by Lenin in 1917.

Laser and Particle-Beam Versions of SDI—The lasers and particle beams mentioned in *Soft Wars* are all mentioned in connection with SDI. Though, in *Soft Wars*, the technology underlying SDI is the more realistic soon-to-be-achievable "smart-rock" approach, some characters in *Soft Wars* sometimes refer to laser-based directed energy approaches to SDI, and it seems appropriate, then, to describe these approaches briefly here.

The highest velocity attainable is the speed of light (300,000 km/sec), and lasers approach this velocity. Beams of atoms or electrons are nearly as fast as lasers. The speed of either of these weapons, *if* such weapons could be perfected, would apparently make boost-phase interception of ballistic missiles possible.

Several types of lasers appear to show *some* promise of *eventually* giving rise to real-world SDI systems: chemical lasers emitting infrared light (= 2.7 micron wavelength); excimer lasers emitting ultraviolet light (= .3 micron wavelength); lasers pumped by a nuclear explosion that emits X rays (= 0.001 to 0.0001 micron); and free-electron lasers which emit visible light. Let me provide a few details on chemical and X-ray lasers. In the chemical laser the infrared beam is produced by the reaction of two gases, such as hydrogen and fluoride (the beam is then focused and aimed by a system of mirrors). The X-ray laser consists of a nuclear warhead surrounded by a bundle of very thin metallic fibers. When the warhead is detonated, the fibers emit a burst of X-ray pulses during the fraction of a second before the entire device is obliterated by the explosion. X-ray lasers, because they capitalize on the enormous power of a nuclear explosion, can be very light, but on the other hand X rays cannot be reflected by mirrors, and, at least into the foreseeable future, because they are not as parallel as the rays of conventional lasers, X-ray lasers would have to be placed on (say) a low-orbit satellite.

For the record: a comment on laser-based versions of SDI: I have no doubt, personally, that with adequate funding, a 120-megawatt chemical laser will *someday* be buildable. If such a laser were built, and suitably deployed in space, even superhardened ballistic missiles could be incapacitated in boost phase after the beam dwells on the same spot for just an extremely short time. On the other hand, *Soft Wars* is a *near-future* book (events within it occur during 1992 and 1993). A 120-megawatt chemical laser, indeed a 120-megawatt laser of *any* sort, must be consigned to the next decade, at the very least, and beyond that if funding for SDI continues to decrease. What about directed-energy versions of SDI? Well, this type of weapon essentially exploits "atom-smashing" technology; and the basic idea is to have (*e.g.*) protons fired at ballistic and cruise missiles in such a way as to disable these missiles by (among other things) penetration of protons into the semiconductors in the electronic circuits that govern the missile in question. There are a number of problems with particle beams (*e.g.*, it is exceedingly difficult to aim charged particles, like electrons and protons; some circuitry appears to be relatively immune, etc.), but as far as I am concerned there is one problem which will of necessity force deployment of particle-beam SDI weapons into at least the next decade, *viz.* weight. At present, it appears that a particle-beam device able to destroy distant targets would need to weigh many tons.

Logicism—The approach to AI which assumes that there is an underlying formal "language of thought" that is instantiated in the human brain, but could in principle be instantiated in hardware radically different from that composing the brain.

LOW/LOTW—Launch on Warning/Launch on Tactical Warning. A doctrine according to which a nation launches its strategic forces after it receives warning from sensors that an adversary has initiated a nuclear strike.

LUA—Launch Under Attack. A doctrine in which a country's strategic forces are launched *during* an attack, but only after confirmation that enemy weapons have detonated on its homeland.

MAD—Mutual Assured Destruction. A situation in which two or more players could absorb a nuclear first strike but still be able to cause an unacceptable level of damage to the attacker.

Massive Retaliation—A policy adopted by the U.S. in the 1950's that threatened the USSR and China with massive nuclear attack should they encroach upon vital American interests.

MIRV—Multiple Independently Targetable Reentry Vehicle. Two or more reentry vehicles (a reentry vehicle is the shell around each warhead on a ballistic missile, which protects the warhead during its reentry through the atmosphere) carried by a ballistic missile, each of which can be individually directed toward a separate target.

NATO— North Atlantic Treaty Organization. The defensive alliance of North American and Western European states founded in 1949. Currently composed of: Belgium, Canada, Denmark, Germany, Great Britain, Greece, Iceland, Italy, Luxembourg, the Netherlands, Norway, Portugal, Spain, Turkey, and the United States.

Neural Networks—Webs of interconnected cells that appear to have a capacity for storing information derived from experience. A neural network's knowledge is acquired through training rather than conventional programming. The human brain exhibits behavior that serves to classify it as a neural network.

NORAD—North American Air Defense Command. The combined U.S./Canadian command responsible for the detection and monitoring of any missile or bomber attack on North America.

NSA—National Security Agency. Department of Defense (DOD) agency formed in 1952 to direct all U.S. cryptographic and signals-intercept activity. Located at Fort Meade, Maryland, north of Washington, D.C.

OCR—Optical Character Recognition. A branch of scanning technology in which text is scanned, and letters are detected and disambiguated, so that the text ends up "inside" the machine.

Satellite Orbits—There are three types of orbit followed by military satellites: (i) geosynchronous (36,000 km, remaining at a fixed point about the equator, and moving with the rotation of the earth); (ii) highly elliptical (max. 40,000 km and perhaps beyond above northern hemisphere, dipping to less than 1,000 km near southern hemisphere; (iii) low-earth (150 to 2,000 km).

SBI—Space-based Interceptors. A specific incarnation of SDI in which defense against nuclear attack is secured by destroying incoming missiles with ultrahigh-velocity but conventionally propelled rockets which employ technology already existing as of 1990. This realistic incarnation of SDI is to be distinguished from laser and particle-beam incarnations, which are cited and discussed above.

SDI—Strategic Defense Initiative. A program inaugurated by Ronald Reagan which has as its goal the defense of the U.S. and its allies against nuclear attack.

SDIO—Strategic Defense Initiative Organization. The group of scientists and officers responsible for monitoring and promoting and reporting on the SDI program.

SIGINT—Signals Intelligence. A general term for the interception, processing, and analysis of data obtained from electronic communications and other signals. Subdivided into three subsets: Communications Intelligence (COMINT), Electronics Intelligence (ELINT), and Telemetry Intelligence (TELINT).

SIOP—Sing Integrated Operational Plan. A highly classified plan for employment of U.S. nuclear weapons in the event of war.

SLBM—Submarine-Launched Ballistic Missile.

SLCM—Sea-Launched Cruise Missile, or, colloquially, a "slicum." A cruise missile launched from a surface ship or submarine.

Smersh—A brutal counterespionage and internal security organization formed under the ruthless master spy Beria (who, though long dead, plays a role in this book), designed to purge the Motherlands of spies. Smersh is an abbreviation of the Russian words *Smert Shpionan*, which means "death to spies."

Stealth—A combination of cutting-edge technologies designed to make advanced aircraft and cruise missiles invisible to enemy radar.

Strategic Warning—Detection of actions that indicate that a nuclear attack is forthcoming.

Terminal Defense—Defense against nuclear missiles when they are in reentry, *i.e.*, at the stage just before impact on targets, such as silos and cities. As warheads and decoys approach their targets, atmospheric drag burns up the lighter objects, and a fiery plasma sheath forms around heavier objects. Deceleration takes place. U.S. vehicles typically smash to the surface of the earth at a velocity of about 3 km/sec. In terminal defense, nuclear warheads are attacked in this luminous reentry phase. In *Soft Wars*, "demons" (of lesser velocity than their space-based brothers) are deployed on the surface of the earth for such defense.

Trajectory—The flight path of a ballistic missile can have either a lofted, normal, or depressed trajectory, the latter being the "flattest," *i.e.*, closest to the surface of the earth, the first reaching a point in outer space. The Trident 2, in *Soft Wars*, launches missiles (the D-5, to be specific) which have a depressed trajectory, giving a decreased overall flight time.

Transistor—A number of transistors are mentioned in the book in connection with Neurocubes: MOSFET (metal-oxide-silicon field effect transistors), MESFET (metal semiconductor field effect transistors), and the transistor technology which underlies the Neurocube, *viz.*MODFETs (modulation doped field effect transistors). Though it's horribly idealized, perhaps the best way to view a transistor is as a simple discrete input-output device—a certain permutation of zeroes and ones coming in determines a certain output of zeroes and ones going out.

Turing Machine—A simple, mathematically defined, idealized computing device, composed of a tape for holding input and output, and a scanning/writing head that operates on this tape in accordance with simple instructions, such as "if you see an *x*, then erase this symbol, write a *y*, and move one square to the right." It is a well-known fact that whatever a high-speed digital computer can do, a Turing machine can eventually do. It is less known, but nonetheless apparently true, that a neural net is not only capable of doing whatever a Turing machine can do, but also that a neural net is no more powerful than a Turing machine (or other idealized computers of equivalent power, such as a Register Machine, a Probabilistic Turing Machine, Cellular Automata, etc.). The lesser-known fact is what enables *Soft Wars'* main character to treat neural nets as if they are ordinary general-purpose automata.

Warsaw Pact—A now defunct alliance that was formed in 1955 as the Eastern European counterpart of NATO. Used to be composed of: Bulgaria, Czechoslovakia, E. Germany, Hungary, Poland, Rumania, and the U.S.S.R.

ABOUT THE AUTHOR

Selmer Bringsjord was born in White Plains, New York, in 1958. After obtaining a B.A. from the University of Pennsylvania and a Ph.D. in philosophy from Brown University, he joined Rensselaer Polytechnic Institute's faculty in Troy, New York, where he teaches philosophy of mind, artificial intelligence, and mathematical logic. Selmer, whose principal research interests are the mathematical foundations of artificial intelligence and computer-generated fiction, now makes his home in Brunswick, New York, with his wife, Elizabeth, his daughter, Katherine, and his son, Alexander. *Soft Wars* is his first novel.